Witness to the Revolution

The Enlightened Series, Book One

KIERSTEN MARCIL

CHAMPAGNE BOOK GROUP

Witness to the Revolution

This is a work of fiction. The characters, incidents, and dialogue in this book are of the author's imagination and are not to be construed as real. Any resemblance to actual events or persons, living or dead, is completely coincidental.

Published by Champagne Book Group
712 SE Winchell Avenue, Depoe Bay OR 97341 U.S.A.

First Edition 2022

pISBN: 978-1-957228-80-8

Copyright © 2022 Kiersten Marcil All rights reserved.

Cover Art by Melody Pond

Champagne Book Group supports copyright which encourages creativity and diverse voices, creates a rich culture, and promotes free speech. Thank you for complying by not distributing this book via any means without the permission of the publisher. Your purchase or use of an authorized edition supports the author's rights and hard work and allows Champagne Book Group to continue to bring readers fiction at its finest.

www.champagnebooks.com

Version_1

To my wonderful family—for all of the many, many hours that I disappeared into another world and you let me, knowing I would one day find my way back home.

Historically yours,

Kingston

Dear Reader:

One of the joys of writing historical works is delving into the lives of those who came before us. All of the political opinions in this book are entirely those of the men and women who lived through the American Revolutionary War. They are recreated here so we may come to understand a little better the worries and challenges faced by the people who helped secure the freedoms we hold so dear.

Please visit my website to learn more about their stories, beliefs, and world. Plus, you will discover extras such as a map of the Highlands of New York and a glossary of the eighteenth-century slang and the Dutch and Scottish phrases used in this book. Come explore at: https://www.kierstenmarcil.com.

Kiersten

Chapter One

Time hates me. A five-week blur of parading witnesses ranging from law enforcement to "Eff you. I'm not talkin' to no D.A.," blended with fielding press calls, a mislaid shell casing, possible witness tampering, and other courtroom drama. It culminated in this one moment: the jury had come back with a verdict. Less than two days of deliberation and few notes with questions, other than a mind-numbing request to rewatch hours-worth of surveillance video, my first murder trial flying solo was being undermined because the weekend was staring us down, and the jurors were clearly over it.

Tick.

Officer Wilson rapped the prosecutor's table twice with his knuckles as he sauntered to his station by the judge. The jury shuffled between the rows to take their designated seats. I couldn't catch his eye. Juror Six was on the edge of his seat, twitchy like he couldn't wait to bolt out the door to freedom. Number Three was grimacing again. She'd spent the entire five weeks with her ultra-raspberry painted mouth squeezed shut, arms crossed. Seemed jury duty wasn't her cup of tea. Her lips weren't even visible when she slumped into her seat. The others were solemn.

Tick... tick. Tick.

Figures the damn clock—a tourist-worthy feature of the original courthouse, built eons and eons ago—felt the need to put in some effort. Each random clack of the second hand was like someone pinging pennies off the back of my neck. Any other day, I wouldn't have cared. I snuck a peek at the thing. The D.A. was sitting in the gallery. A brisk nod, then I resumed jury-watching.

Tick.

I hate history.

Smiley Nine raised his fist to hip-level, thumbs up. He flashed his infamous grin before turning his attention to the judge.

The foreperson announced the verdict, her voice filling the courtroom, though a nervous laugh broke through when the defendant interrupted her to swear at his attorney. She'd been a good choice. The jury was polled. Unanimous guilty votes to every charge except one count of endangering. Livable. Definitely livable.

"Bullshit, lady." The defendant aimed his ire at the foreperson, who flinched. "Ya know that's bullshit." Wilson retrieved the verdict sheet from the floor when it fluttered from her hands. The other court officers closed in on the expletive-laden diatribe launched at the public defender.

Another day at the office.

I remember little else from the trial. An hour, maybe more, of phone calls and locking up evidence and congratulations from co-workers. Drinks some other night. Java James tried to snag me for a quote as I raced downstairs. I tossed a promise of a press release by close of business over my shoulder. AJ owed me one.

"Taking the rest of the day off?" Sergeant Miller asked from his station by the front door. His eyes remained glued on the security feed.

"Going home to celebrate," I confirmed.

"Nice work. The guy was scum. Go hug that kid of yours, Savvy."

"You know it."

Of course, nothing was ever simple. My free afternoon was wasted. A ten-minute errand deteriorated into a headache-inducing debacle. Slamming the car door closed with my foot, I flew through the mudroom of my house, glancing at the clock while I dumped groceries on the floor, frustrated. The store had been crowded. A shipping cart overwhelmed with boxes filled one half of the baking aisle. A lady pouring over the ingredients of a fluorescent-orange frosting container blocked the other. It's just fat, I'd grumbled when she didn't move.

Sock. I snatched the wayward bit and tossed it at the laundry basket. It missed.

"Goldie!"

Dog saliva caught my attention on the second attempt. It also carried a noticeable aroma of past playground adventures.

Evan didn't wear Captain Jack this week... or last. Gross.

I rinsed my hands after dumping the sock on top of the washer.

Stripping off my suit, I grabbed the first long-sleeve tee and pants I could find. Music blared from the depths of my jacket pocket. Justin. I slipped my ring off and tossed it onto the pile. Nothing was going to spoil my afternoon with Evan. I let the phone wail away.

"Let's go, Goldie." I shook my head at my other baby lolling her tongue at me.

Another check of the clock. Fifteen minutes until school let out, add in a half-hour bus ride... I figured there was time to take the dog for a walk. Leaving the surprise treat of ice cream softening on the counter, I'd planned to unload the army of sprinkles, candy pieces, and whipped cream later. And of course, Evan's favorite—caramel sauce—along with a new Hot Wheels car I'd spotted in the check-out line. Plenty of make-up snuggling on the agenda, too.

Snapping the leash onto Goldie's collar, I noticed the front window was empty. No Moosey Moose at his post. Running late meant no time to search for the stuffed bestie amid the tangle of blankets and other toys in Evan's bed before we left.

When I get back.

I would've looked if I'd known it was my last chance.

Chapter Two

A grave was cradled within weeping willows. It was gigantic, like something meant for a museum rather than lingering beyond the tightly shorn backyard of a suburban church. Moisture darkened the marble woman's cheek as it seeped from a patch of moss. Goldie snuffled through the border of shrubs underneath and found a rabbit hole to paw at. My second reprimand inspired her to decorate a tree. I unwound a Doggie Doody bag from the canvas pouch clipped to her leash and waited.

As I admired the drip of nature's tears onto the man lying dead and broken in her arms, something rushed me. Almost as if a gust of wind had raged from the depths of the statue and hammered into me. There was no sound. The long strands of the weeping willows remained still even as the unseen force struck and blurred my vision. Goldie spooked, her leash jerking my arm behind me.

An ocean wave broke in my head, spinning my perception of the world around me. The ambient growl of traffic receded into the distance, and the stink of funerary lilies wilting in the breeze faded with it. A wash of seasickness came in its wake.

Silence.

My hands were empty. I never felt the leash rip away. Never heard Goldie run off. Twisted twigs and the skeletons of countless bushes littered the miles surrounding me, hushed and lifeless. A thin carpet of powdery snow stretched beneath them. No paw prints of any kind. Goldie was gone.

Frosty puffs swelled in front of my face.

When did it get cold?

A filthy layer of clouds, like grimy clumps of lint from the dryer's trap stretched thin, shadowed the once-clear skies.

I'd lost some time.

Just as I noticed the towering oaks surrounding me weren't the willows from the churchyard—in fact, there no longer was a church—I was jerked backward; my body mashing against the one enveloping me. A blade pressed to my throat. I gasped and tore at my attacker's wrist, trying to pull the knife away, as I begged, "No, don't!"

Flailing when I was first thrown off-balance, my palm landed onto the thigh behind me. The unmistakable shape of a gun was there. A hand clapped over mine before I could steal it and eased my grip from the weapon's holster.

A man's faced loomed into my periphery, lips hovering near my ear. He inhaled, as if breathing me in. The tang of spice floated across my skin, blowing loose hair along my cheek. *"Ipse revelat profunda et abscondita."*

Something stirred deep within me. A spark of heat, flickering to life.

I couldn't make sense of what was happening. Wool fibers from his coat crushed under my fingers as they tightened. The rational part of my mind shouted through the void, urging me to react. An odd thought surfaced through the panic, a tiny something warning: Don't let him know you recognize Latin.

Instead, I cried with honest fear, "I speak English. Please, don't hurt me! I speak English."

The man's grip slackened. After a pause, the hand clasping mine slid, bit by bit, to my upper arm, as if waiting to see how I'd react, before steering me part way around to face him while the blade lifted from my throat. Taking advantage of the reprieve, I grabbed onto the fear, letting it power me, and drove my fist into his groin. I swung my arm between us to prevent the knife from finding purchase when he reacted to the blow. It fell with a heavy thump, disappearing into the weeds, then I dropped my weight to break free.

Hoping help was nearby to hear my screams, I scrambled from underneath him before he could recover, and ran. Wet leaves shuffled beneath my feet, catching me up as they glued themselves to my legs. I didn't get far before there was an incline erupting from the once flat expanse where the grave had been.

What the…?

A cock of a gun as the hammer was drawn back.

"Hold!"

I ignored him and bolted uphill. Court officers always warned,

"Guy pulls a gun, you run. Get shot from behind, better your chances of survival because the vital organs are more vulnerable from the front."

Miller would be proud.

Funny, the things you think of.

Grace goeth before the fall. I slipped on the tangled mess clutching at my feet, bellyflopping uphill, though my hip took the brunt of the impact. Forest debris carried me downhill, back toward the man who was approaching, arm extended. His shot was perfectly aligned, the length of his arm serving as a guide, gun trained on my torso.

"Please," I repeated. Lacking options, other than to confront the man, I raised my hands, open-palmed, staring into the darkness of the gun's barrel. "I don't have any money."

"You are a woman," he said.

"Yeah...?"

His brow furrowed. He paused to study my pants and hair. "Lay down your arms," he demanded. The crease between his brows deepened when I lowered my hands. "Your *weapons*. Lay down your weapons."

"I don't carry."

His aim faltered. He didn't get to entertain whatever misgivings for long. Shouts echoed around us. A man in a red coat and… tricorn hat rushed toward us, yelling as he charged, unlike my silent attacker, who whirled to meet the assault. A flash as he fired, and the redcoat dropped, a burst of blood shooting back at us through the smoke as the bullet found its mark.

A shriek caught in my throat.

The air cracked. Another shot whizzed by the man's head. Drawing a sword from his side, he pivoted toward a second soldier emerging from the trees, slashing in a wide arc to force some distance between them.

More than enough violence for one day, thank you. I bolted to my feet and ducked behind a nearby evergreen, which—I realized too late—was much too small to protect me. The left portion flew into pieces as a bullet tore through the outer edge, wood filling the air in a cloud of splinters. The end of a long gun followed.

I didn't think. I just grabbed the barrel and yanked as hard as I could. It released into my grip when my foot slammed into the guy's stomach. He stumbled backward with a pronounced "Oof!"

"Freeze," I yelled. I struggled with the weight of the gun but managed to swing it around. I guess I'd hoped the threat of having it pointed at him would be enough. My finger never found the trigger. Didn't matter. The weapon jostled, and he came to an abrupt stop. Surprise filled his face, then pain.

He was young. Cheeks full. Sunburnt. Spotty with freckles. A zit he'd picked near his nose was crusted over. He was just a kid. That was what struck me: how young he was and the look of sheer surprise.

Our focus dropped to the muzzle of the gun. Steel extended forward several inches before penetrating his uniform coat. Fluid oozed onto the metal, drips tumbling faster as the weapon grew heavy. The man's stance softened. Musket. It was a musket in my hands, bayonet in place. The man—no, boy—raised his gaze to mine before the color drained from his face. He slid off the blade's end to the ground.

What just happened?

I threw the thing as far from me as I could.

The boy didn't get up again. His cheek relaxed onto a pillow of browned weeds. Fingers clutching his stomach released, palms slick with red.

Coldness wormed from my guts to my chest.

My eyes connected with the man who'd taken me into his arms. Splatter darkened his face. A strand of hair hung loose from its tie. It drifted along his jawline. His coat was blue. He wasn't wearing red.

The tip of his sword angled off to the side, blood running along its edge. A little breathless, he eyed the boy I'd impaled—who'd impaled himself—then regarded me. "Madam?"

But I was transfixed, tracking the blood collecting on the fallen leaves.

I retreated several steps until two more soldiers came charging from behind the bluecoat. He heard in time to engage this new enemy. Another wide swing of his sword sent one of them off to his right. He yelled, "Stay within sight!" the steel of his blade singing when it met a downward slice.

The other redcoat must've pegged me as an easy target because he charged me instead of attacking the man in blue. He guessed wrong.

Again, with no time to think, I allowed myself to react, windmilling my left arm to knock aside his right. His blade sliced the air to land inches from my thigh. Without hesitation, I drove my fist into his throat. The jolt slammed up the line of my arm. He clutched his neck, sword forgotten. Helpless to catch his breath, he doubled over with the effort. I made a sledgehammer with my fists, driving them onto the base of his skull. His face met earth, and down he stayed.

There was a pistol on his hip. I snatched it and swung toward the sound of footfalls struggling to keep their balance. The bluecoat had his back to me as he drew a path across the final redcoat's chest, pink flesh tearing beneath ruined fabric. His latest kill crumpled.

A trail of bile rose in my throat. The man's features tensed, his brows crowding together, when I didn't lower my aim. Even though my hand shook, he let his sword sink to the ground, palms raising.

"Get down!" I shouted.

There was a moment's pause before my words registered, and he ducked. I fired, and a charging redcoat—saber ready to thrust into the bluecoat's back—was jerked in the opposite direction as his face imploded with the passing bullet. The body collapsed, revealing—*how many guys are there?*—a bulkier redcoat lumbering right behind him. I was horrified, both at the gore showering the forest floor and in seeing yet another sword raised and coming straight for me.

What the hell?

The bluecoat tackled me as the redcoat's sword drove through the space where my body had been, plunging into the dirt. The bluecoat, full on top of me, his fingers digging into my arms, yelled, "Hold on to me!"

I mimicked my captor and gripped his arms. He flung us toward the redcoat, his body rolling against the implanted blade, forcing the sword to wrench loose from the redcoat's grip and fall flat to the ground. Before I could even think of trying to break free, the bluecoat swung me off him, taking us back the other way as the redcoat lunged. The bluecoat killed him, flying a knife once meant for me across the man's throat.

I only felt the spray because I tilted my head toward the sounds of danger charging us. As I lay crushed under the weight of the bluecoat straddling me, I patted along his waistband, desperate for a weapon. He leaned forward, pressing his chest to mine, smooshing me further into the dirt. His right arm flew past my temple, and an explosion sounded. The charging redcoat fell.

The world was ringing.

Wild with fear, I swung my head to the side, searching for the next onslaught, then back again. The bluecoat checked the other direction without lifting his torso or releasing me.

Nothing. No one.

Something was clutched in my hand. The wool flank of the man's coat. No matter what I did, I couldn't get my fingers to open. My breath caught in my throat; the taste of bile was still fresh. The bluecoat's arm relaxed, the crook of his elbow cradling my cheek. I thought about grabbing the gun. Acrid smoke drifted from near the flint. But the thought drifted away too.

Another strand of hickory-colored hair had come loose, framing the other side of his face. Blood and filth smeared his skin, bits of dirt peppered throughout his beard. A gray halo encircled the brilliant blue of his eyes.

“You are injured,” he said, studying the area beneath my chin.

I lifted my head to see what he meant, and the first sting bit into my neck. My fingers shook as they made their way to the source and jerked away as the sting bit again, stronger. I couldn’t catch my breath. My fingertips were wet. Bright red. Blood. Fresh blood. He’d cut my throat after all. I couldn’t breathe. I stared back at the man lying on top of me. His eyes were so blue, like cobalt. Then darkness took me.

Chapter Three

Pain woke me. My body jerked upright with the sudden sensation. The fire across my neck forced me into reverse. I reached for the cut and lay there, light-headed. A man's voice brought me full awake.

The man in blue was sitting on the bed, thigh pressed against me to avoid falling off the edge, his coat buttoned to the neck. He'd cleaned his face. The rest of him wasn't. The stench of blood, mixed with sweat and dirt, added a wave of nausea to the mix. He was too close. The bed was too small. I shot backward.

"I will not harm you," he told me.

"You tried to kill me!"

My head collided with a fabric enclosure. It wasn't a bed I was on but a cot, pushed into a corner. I was trapped with the man who'd cut my throat.

"I beg your pardon. It was done in error." He reached for me, but I flinched. "I swear, I will not harm you."

"Who are you?"

"My name is Captain Jonathan Wythe." After a noticeable moment of consideration, he said, "At your service."

"Captain?"

"Aye."

"Captain of what?"

He faltered and considered the bloodied cloth he'd been pressing to my neck when I woke. His mouth fluttered, not finding actual words as he passed it to me. The possibility of not accepting occurred to me, but his humble apology seemed sincere enough, and I wasn't sure resisting such a simple offer was the right move. He rose once I did take it, leaving me alone on the cot.

We were in a tent which, at one time, had been white. Captain Wythe stood lost in the middle, boots shuffling on the plank floor as he shifted his weight. Their condition, I imagined, were unhelpful in inspiring conversation because he glanced up from his study of his toes, mute, then shied away.

Behind him was a pine desk, simple and small. Another cot was stationed to its right, perpendicular to the desk and the one I occupied. Sunlight reached in tiny bursts through the tent's fluttering entrance to Wythe's right. He caught me looking while I was weighing how far I might get.

"What is your name, madam?"

I questioned whether it was smart but answered anyway, "Savannah. Savannah Moore."

"Moore. You are English."

"Uh…?"

"But Savannah. Is your name not Spanish?"

"I think my parents just liked the name."

"Ah." Another moment or two of broken conversation crawled by. "I am sorry that I could not leave you to the surgeon's care. He was treating a wounded man and said there was not room. He suggested I tend to you myself. The cut. Tend to the cut on your neck. There was nowhere else…"

I decided to save him. "Where are we?"

He hesitated before saying, "It was not right to leave you," and flashing a nervous smile.

"Thanks." My returning smile was more fleeting. "Where are we?"

"You are safe. You need not worry."

"You're not going to tell me?"

The tent's entrance seemed miles away.

Wythe was flustered until, apparently finding some solid argument in his mind, he straightened to demand, "Why are you wearing those clothes?"

"What do you mean? What's wrong with my clothes?"

"In truth? You wear men's attire!"

I breathed a laugh of surprise at him. "Excuse you."

"I, ah…" He stared for a moment. "I thought you were a regular."

"A regular… man?"

Wythe's expression grew incredulous, his eyes and mouth matching in their impression of an expanding sinkhole. His hand gestured up and down, following the length of my body. I shook my head, frustrated, not sure what his problem was. I was about to give him the same treatment of pantomimed bodily critique when—

Stockings…?

Stockings. He was wearing some sort of reenactment costume complete with slate-colored stockings. The solid blue coat extended past his thighs and, at a passing glance, looked like any other winter dress coat, except for the long lines of dull, silver buttons lining the facings and encircling the wide cuffs of his sleeves. A knife was stationed on his hip in a leather sheath. His hand rested on the hilt, the way our precincts' police officers kept a hand on their service weapons. Black boots, rising to knee height, hid the hem of his tan pants brushing against the boots' tops when he wasn't moving. Only an occasional flash of his unexpected hosiery was visible underneath.

Figured the random snag from the laundry basket would bless me with a brilliant red shirt, which was flapping around my hips and khaki jeans.

He thought I was a redcoat?

An uneasiness roiled the pit of my stomach. I ignored it.

"I was moving quickly," he explained when I glanced up at him. "You were the only obstacle in my way."

"So, you cut my throat?"

"From behind you looked like a—"

I scoffed at him.

"I meant…"

Oh jeez.

His verbal stumbling had returned. "Hurried as I was, there were regulars on every side, your back was toward me, and I saw what appeared to be a slight, femininely-shaped soldier." A desperate hand finished whirling by his hip, as if he could stir an excuse from thin air.

"Makes perfect sense."

"I did not have time to analyze the situation. Now that I have such luxury—clearly, a man, you are not." He concluded his version of our encounter with a modicum of defensive heat in his voice, then embarked on a thorough examination of the desktop, planting his hands in front of him to lean on it. A moment passed before Wythe peered across his shoulder, evidently not sure what to make of me, then retreated to his study of the rough pine surface.

Trapped between the contemplative Wythe and his desk was a bow-back chair. A cherrywood box lay next to his hand on the desk. The second cot was tidy, since it lacked any blankets or pillows. A pale, leather trunk huddled at its end within immediate reach of the cot I occupied. Reddened water in a basin sat on top—my best option for a weapon. The only other item visible was a mustard-colored trunk at the foot of my own cot.

The bus. Evan!

"Would you take me back?" I broke the silence.

"You want to return to where I found you?"

"Actually, I want to go home." I scooted to sitting on the edge of the cot.

"Where, pray tell, is your home?"

There was something niggling at me beyond not wanting to tell a stranger how to find me again. It sidled alongside of me. Questions about what I'd witnessed and done were itching to be heard. I wasn't willing to listen. "I can find my own way from there."

The suspicion in his eyes returned. "You are from one of the neighboring farms?"

"No…"

It was at least twenty minutes to the nearest farm from the church.

"It would not be possible, anyhow." He filled the empty air before the latest thought could formulate and demand my attention.

"Well, if you won't take me there yourself, how about you point me in the right direction?"

Wythe didn't answer and dropped his gaze.

"Are you kidnapping me?" I jerked toward the washbasin but stopped myself.

"Indeed, I am not. The entire region is overrun with enemy soldiers." His glance passed over my outstretched hand. "It would be foolish to return there."

"Look, I'm not a part of your… camp. If you don't want to go, fine." Having made it to my feet, I had to lift my chin, since my head only reached the top of his shoulders—a chore that hurt way too much—to snap, "I have to get home."

I bolted from the tent before Wythe could stop me. Not that he needed to worry because the scene bursting through the initial shock of sunlight dazed me. The captain clasped my arm. I yanked it away before returning to staring, unable to take it all in as my stomach sank. Somewhere it registered how he stayed within arm's reach as I stumbled around, the hilt of his blade inches from his fingertips.

When I was little, my father—a history professor—took a month's vacation every July. Instead of going to the Cape like my friends' families, my parents tortured us with endless museums and historical sites. Many a hot and boring hour dragged on, with my father chattering away with fellow authors of dusty tomes about people long dead. Costumed reenactors with their bad accents and replicated artifacts from roughly the time period they were discussing, give or take a decade, were his greatest delight. Much to the chagrin of the historians, it was my father's favorite game—Find the Anachronisms.

Oh, if only.

Multiple tents, soiled from the elements, occupied the wooded area around us, many with clothes strewn on top to dry in the chilly sunlight. Men and women in garb similar to Wythe's non-Continental uniform focused on some task or another: repairing items, sewing, tending horses, sharpening or cleaning weapons. No one was idle. No one lingered in front of their station, telling rehearsed stories to tourists. There was no audience gathered for a demonstration.

Close by, the evidence of cooking struggled to overcome the stench of horses, forest decay, campfires, and unwashed bodies. It was difficult to breathe through it all. Listening hard brought only the ambient noise of the camp and a little birdsong. The sky overhead was clear. Nothing to tie us to the modern world.

"What the…?"

"What say you?" Wythe asked from my shoulder.

"Is this a joke?" I whirled around and grasped the front of his coat, examining the hand stitching, the imperfectly stamped buttons, searching for something, anything, to save me from the growing dread.

Why is the air so thin?

Wythe pulled my hands from their clutch of his coat's collar. "Madam."

"It's not possible. It's… not…" I fought to take a breath. His brows drew together as my knees betrayed me. I was gone, again, into his arms and the darkness.

Chapter Four

"Dad?" The door to my father's study was cracked. A dim rose-colored glow bled into the hall. Some vague tune chanted by a woman's voice drifted with it. The rest of the house was silent, dead to the world. I pushed into the room. "Dad?"

The bronze floor lamp guarding his split-leather chair was off. An old clay mug sat by a bulky text spread on a side table, the spine broken with age. A mature brew wicking over the lip of the mug stained the string from the teabag. Floor-to-ceiling bookshelves cowered in the distant recesses of my father's study behind dusty oak trees. Their roots emerged and dipped, then disappeared through the painted floorcloth carpeting the room.

Midnight obscured the yard outside the partially shuttered windows. Stars were absent from the sky. Thunder rolled, muted as if from a distance. The floorboards beneath my feet trembled anyway. Papers shifted in the stillness, an unknown breeze trifling with the scattered documents on the antique desk. The rosy glow dawned brighter from its surface. Flowing wisps sprouted from the light, swirling and dancing. An ethereal vineyard bloomed before my eyes, full of life.

But as it stretched toward me, thunder rumbled from within. The color shivered in fits and bursts and became muddied. The life wilted like blossoms starved for water. Cracks broke along the strands of decaying rose, a single slit at first, then gathering in strength, fracturing in multiple rifts, coursing down the tendrils. Flecks of ash peeled off, tumbling from the dying light. Only the light didn't extinguish. It continued to sicken. Deeper and blacker. And it grew.

I backed away. The decay trailed farther from its source,

swelling into a dismal pall shrouding the room, the trees, the air with its emptiness. I whirled around, desperate to escape, but no matter how far into the forest of bookshelves I ran, the door was miles out of reach. Towering oaks blocked my view as it receded into the distance. Ash blew in a gust of wind to glue itself to my skin, stinging where it struck. I glanced back. The Darkness was shadowing me. It would tear into me if it caught me. Like it did every time.

I collided with a tree, the bark scratching my palms as I flung them forward to protect me. I darted behind the trunk, terrified. A soldier in red was waiting there. He was young. Just a kid, really. Surprise filled his face, then pain. Our focus dropped to the muzzle of a gun. A musket, bayonet in place. Inky sludge burbled from the wound in his belly, falling from his body, glop by glop. Black eyes stared, empty.

But it wasn't the boy standing there. It was me the bayonet had pierced. Then the Darkness consumed me.

Chapter Five

A billowing cavern, frigid and echoing with the snapping of its linen walls, surrounded me when I gasped awake. A tent. The glow of sunset stained the canvas, creating a second horizon along the surface of the desk. It gave the wooden box on top a halo. Men's voices carried from outside, their silhouettes shifting against the light. On the nearby trunk was a bowl of something. Stew, maybe. Swollen beans had sunk into the depths of a greasy, thin broth. It looked cold.

Everything rushed at me—the onslaught of soldiers, the fighting, the spray of gore, the sights and reek of the camp—I barely made it to the basin before the contents of my stomach splattered its empty bottom. Captain Wythe hurried in, scoring a front row seat to a second round of vomiting. Another man held open the tent flap but didn't enter.

When there was nothing left, I sat back to wipe at a moist chunk clinging to my lips with an unsteady hand. Wythe retrieved an item from his pocket. My mind registered only a mass, floppy and perhaps flaxen-colored, without being able to identify what he was holding out to me. I gave up and stared at the floor. A colorful turn of phrase preceded the other man questioning the captain's sanity before storming off.

Wythe sighed. The weight of his gaze as he towered over me didn't help. I pulled my knees close to my chest and sat there shaking. Rather than walk away, as he started to, he crouched next to me and placed the unknown item in my hand. Linen collapsed into my fist.

"You are not a spy, then." It wasn't a question.

"No," I whispered.

He scanned my clothes again. "But you have received training for combat."

"Just… self-defense classes. Nothing, like…"

Real. It was real. Every bit of it. Those men, the kid… I killed a kid.

This can't be happening. This can't be real. This can't be happening.

Wythe's hands enclosed my upper arms, stopping the rocking motion I couldn't seem to slow on my own. "Those men would have killed us both if you had not acted as you did," he said.

His eyes were impossibly blue. Their steady, sympathetic gaze tempted me to believe him. Only I was far from capable of making peace with myself or my situation. None of it made sense. How could it have been real? And if it was real, where was I? And when?

"I don't understand how this is possible," I managed, the words tumbling from my mouth before I could weigh the wisdom of sharing them. "If you won't tell me exactly where we are, please, please, give me a general idea?"

He hesitated, then answered, "We are in the southern part of the Independent State of New York. Less than a two-day ride into the city of Manhattan."

Not Saratoga. If he was telling the truth.

"How far are we from the place where you found me?"

"An hour's walk, at most."

I took in each bite of information before venturing to the next. "What's the date?"

"April 8th."

The year. He didn't tell me the year.

How would I survive? At any moment, the whole thing would end as a cruel charade, right? But no. That ship had sailed, and I was stranded on a foreign shore.

I began again, trying to formulate what I could tell the captain to get the answers I needed without raising additional alarm. "I'm in the American Colonies, right?"

"America *States*, now."

War of 1812?

"This shouldn't be possible." I swallowed hard. "Did you see anything, hear anything unusual when you first saw me?"

"What is it you think I should have seen?"

Asking about a magic portal wouldn't be a good idea. I needed something down to earth. "I was walking my dog. Some… one rushed me. Someone, not you."

"There was no one, other than the regulars. I never saw a dog. I am sorry."

Little surprise there. I was pretty sure Goldie had bolted before I was sucked into the captain's world. Still, it was a small reassurance to know she was safe.

"I seem to be missing some time." Not so much a lie as an artful truth. "I think I was kidnapped and dumped here because the last thing I remember, I was walking my dog. Then, you…" I fought to push away the memories of what happened next.

Wythe appeared to be accepting my story. The suspicion hadn't returned to his face, and there was sympathy in his voice when he asked, "Where is your home?"

"I… I'm not sure. I could describe it to you," I rushed to tell him and prevent the look of suspicion from returning. "But… my memories are kinda fuzzy, I guess. I don't remember leaving my own country, or who took me, or any sort of journey here. Just what I told you. One moment, I was in the woods back home. The next, I was here."

"Indeed. And your family? Husband?"

"I was born in Connecticut. I remember—Well, I don't remember being born, of course, but I remember that about my life. Near Trumbull."

You're rambling.

"You are an acquaintance of General Trumbull?" His eyebrows shot upward, impressed.

"Uh, no. I…"

Oh hell.

"But you are from Connecticut?" he asked, a hint of frustration seeping through the tone of confusion.

It felt wrong to deceive Captain Wythe. He'd saved me from the soldiers' attack and brought me to safety instead of leaving me with a pile of corpses. So, my words were somewhat true, even if out of context they were misleading. I didn't dare tell Wythe everything. He might think I was crazy. Or worse, what if he thought I was bewitched? Things never went well for the accused or their supposed victims.

Come on, Savvy. Think!

"M-my father moved us when my brother and I were little. He traveled a lot. I saw some of Europe when I was younger. It's probably very different now. I mean, I don't consider myself from the Colonies."

My father took a sabbatical between changed positions from one university to another and dragged us across Europe. I love my dad, but as a kid, freezing on a barren wasteland in autumn, it was hard to care about which clans died during the battle.

Still, I had to tell the captain something. It was the best story I could shovel on the fly to explain why I seemed foreign. I hoped having a connection to the Colonies might garner me some sympathy, even though I was claiming to come from somewhere else. Besides, if I outright lied to him, I risked losing track of those lies and getting caught.

Wythe and I studied one another.

Yeah, this is going great.

But I needed answers. "I don't know how much time I'm missing. Please." I took the final step. "What year is it?"

"You do not know what year it is?" At least he looked concerned rather than suspicious. Kindness filled the deep pool of his eyes.

"I did, but… No. I don't think I do."

"It is 1778."

The world melted into a blur.

It shouldn't have been a shock. The evidence was clear and convincing. Still, to hear him say it was terrifying.

The Revolutionary War. How the hell did I get to 1778? More importantly, how was I going to get back? Anything I did could change history. And if I changed history, what would happen to my life in the future?

My father was merciless in his endless recitation of Revolutionary War stories during my childhood. A random act of kindness started a chain of events, culminating in the prevention of a catastrophic disaster—the possible capture of George Washington due to Benedict Arnold's betrayal. A discovery brought about by sheer serendipity.

How many casual moments were the moving parts of greater devices in the War? What if by one word, one action, that one crucial, casual moment never happened? If the dominos shifted because of me, would the whole thing collapse along a different path? The wrong path?

But it was already too late. I'd killed. Hundreds, maybe thousands of lives would never exist because I bayonetted the freckled boy with his oversized redcoat and spotty face. What of those other men? Would they have died if Wythe hadn't been stopped by his encounter with me in the woods? What if other men were meant to die elsewhere but didn't? Did this mean descendants would be born, who were never meant to exist? Because of me. Or would the universe somehow correct the whole cluster?

I hadn't asked for any of this. I hadn't chosen to be catapulted into history. Someone or something chose for me. Didn't I deserve a chance to live? To defend myself?

But what if, because of my presence here—my interference—the War was lost and America never won its freedom? What was my culpability? And what did it mean for the life I left behind? Ahead, I corrected myself.

"Madam!" My attention snapped back to my inconceivable present. Wythe had been trying to get through to me. He pressed a wooden object into my hands. "Drink. It may help."

My mind was slow to recognize the canteen for what it was. When I did, I gulped what he'd offered, then gagged. "Ugh. What is that?" There was something unpleasant flavoring the contents.

"Water." He sounded like a parent trying to explain the obvious to a child.

"What's in the water?"

"Vinegar."

"Why would you do that!" I shoved the canteen at him.

"To cleanse the water." His expression mirrored my thoughts—he was fricking nuts. "To make it potable," he explained.

"Po—?"

This is crazy! I don't belong here. This is crazy.

I think the rocking resumed.

Wythe sighed. "You should eat." He attempted to hand me the stew, but I couldn't move. I didn't dare say anything. Do anything.

Would I even be able to get back now things have changed?

Chapter Six

The sun had advanced—or perhaps rewound? I wasn't thinking clearly—to a far different position in the sky when I noticed that Captain Wythe was missing. Panic attacks hadn't plagued me since I was a teen. I'd learned to control them, finding solace in the orderliness the pursuit of law can bring. But without warning or any discernible reason, life wasn't playing by the rules, and I couldn't expect to find solace during a war, long before America's laws were even written.

No wonder women fainted and men drank to oblivion. It had nothing to do with corsets tied too tight. Never mind trying to avoid filthy water. It was the sheer audacity of the world. Men drank to forget. Women were smarter. They saved their livers and just checked out for a brief respite while the men floated away on a river of beer.

My mind was on a complete tear. I began laughing. The whole ordeal was ludicrous anyway. Soon, I was hysterical, which invited a prolonged round of hiccups. Tears flowed down my cheeks. With them came their companions, Fear and Regret.

I pictured Evan, waiting at the end of our driveway when I wasn't there to meet the bus. I loved the seclusion of our house, nestled in the woods away from the street and other houses, but the occasional cries of coyotes scared him. He worried they'd come to get him if he walked its winding path by himself. He was only five.

Time escaped me. First centuries, now hours. I was dizzy and nauseated from lack of food, my throat raw from sobbing, but I didn't dare leave the tent. Here, I was alone. History was safe from me and whatever damage I could inflict by the simple act of breathing in and out in the company of others already destined to do and speak and act in ways the future once knew and had forgotten.

Wythe eased his way through the tent's flaps, a wooden bucket in his hand tapping against his knee. Seeing the state of me, he grimaced. "Please make yourself presentable. I must introduce you to the major." He took a wide path around me to his trunk and refilled the clean basin waiting on top with water.

"You don't need to," I whispered.

Frustration crossed his face, his mouth tight like his cramped brows, though he'd skirted a look toward the tent's exit rather than direct it at me. "Unfortunately, I do."

I stood, a bit unsteady on my feet. "Could I use the bathroom first?"

"Aye," he answered, his voice sounding unsure. "The water, there, is for you to wash."

"No, I mean…" I struggled to think of the phrase they'd use. "I need to relieve myself…?"

Color flooded Wythe's cheeks. His embarrassment might be cute if it didn't make things so damned difficult. It was tempting to ask him whether he knew women farted. Knowing my luck, female flatulence would be the comment to change the world. A butterfly flaps its wings on foul air, etc. Not to mention, it would've been mean, though the idea of having to explain myself to a complete stranger who held more authority than the man who *had* taken pity on me didn't inspire a whole lot of generosity.

"I can escort you to the women's latrine," he managed.

An actual bathroom! Sort of.

Wythe deposited the bucket outside and held the tent flap open for me. Once I passed his outstretched arm, his gaze hesitant to meet mine, he led me along the row of tents to the edge of camp.

Everyone was already deep into their day, with red embers burning hot beneath campfires and a steady pace to their respective chores. My stomach gave an audible growl as we neared a cooking mound, the aroma of roasting meat rich in the air. Several horses later, my appetite abandoned me again to nausea. Fortunately, Wythe's tent wasn't far from the end of the row and the endless woods beyond.

He pointed to a small, wooden enclosure tucked between the trees. "I will be watching." Despite my rush, the captain's comment stopped me. "It is for your protection," he assured me. "Only please do not force me to chase after you. Things shall not go well for you."

"Um, and where would I run to? I need your help to find my way home again, remember?"

He cleared his throat, then gestured to the latrine.

Wythe's troop had been there for a while. Or else they believed in avoiding the chore of burying and digging new latrines often because, the cold April air notwithstanding, the smell was overwhelming. Squatting over the trench was an experience I hoped to avoid having to repeat. It was the pile of dried corn cobs instead of toilet paper that convinced me it was past time to go home.

He was grimacing at the ground when I returned. A parade of unspoken thoughts marched across his shifting expression.

"I've got a great idea. You're going to love it," I started right in on him. "Return me to where you found me. I go home. You go back to your war. There'll be no reports to write or questions to answer. Everyone's happy. No bother."

"What if I have misjudged you? You may be here to report to the enemy where we are encamped, how many we are, our supplies."

"Follow me. Watch where I go, who I talk to." If I was lucky, I'd disappear in front of the jolly ole' captain as neatly as when I'd first arrived in the Colonies. He'd be too damned shocked to say anything to anyone. The history books would never know me.

"You forget," he frowned, "it was nearly an hour's journey to bring you this far."

"But—"

"Even if it was safe to make the attempt," he said, hand raised, "there is not the time. Major DeForest knows you are here. He expects an introduction to be made."

"How?"

"Alexander informed him."

"Who's Alexander?" My vision blurred. Pressing the bridge of my nose between two fingers didn't help.

"Captain Alexander Brott. He is… a friend of mine."

"Oh. Which is why he tattled on you to the major about me, I guess."

"Someone had to make my excuses for missing training!" The crevice plunging into the slim space between his brows deepened. Unlike before, the sheer aggravation on Wythe's face was intended for me.

"Sorry." I meant it too. "Could it at least wait until after I've had some breakfast?"

"You have missed breakfast. It is midday."

No great secret I was stalling, no sir.

Memories of my father's beloved reenactments and endless summertime lectures on limited supplies flashed across my mind. My stomach protested hard. Wythe's expression softened when I drove a fist into my belly, embarrassed. He reached into a linen satchel at his hip to hand me a small lump bundled in another handkerchief. "I have only a trencher."

"But it's yours." I hesitated at accepting the portion of dense bread tucked in the fabric's folds.

"Take it. You appear to have the greater need."

Chances were the bread was intended to be eaten with something saucy poured on top, but dry bread was a zillion times better than nothing. I hoped for Wythe's sake the cooking smells from earlier meant there was more than aged carbs on a regular basis. A chunk I'd wolfed down latched to the side of my throat, sending me into a coughing spasm.

"Here now." His brows shot together, concerned. "There is little reason to hurry."

I choked out my thanks when he passed me his canteen. Flat water with a splash of vinegar, just as disgusting as the first time. Still…

Wythe returned his well-drained canteen to his side and led the way back to his tent. He shoved the flap aside, holding it open for me—*okay, he's a gentleman*—and gestured to the trunk and its contents. The original handkerchief was tucked under the rim, waiting. It was cleaner than before, if you ignored the stains from his attempted version of first aid. At least, I hoped I was the source of the color.

While I was critiquing my bath linen—such as it was—Wythe busied himself by retrieving a letter from an inside coat pocket, though never showing his back to me. A couple notes of a jolly tune, reminiscent of something I'd heard at reenactments, murmured from the direction of the captain. He cleared his throat, having caught me staring while admiring his musical skills, and quieted as if he'd never started. The page was read aloft, keeping my progress at the washbasin within his easy view. I submerged the cloth and waited to see if it would bleed.

The captain's coat billowed around him, unbuttoned. A black neckcloth cinched a white shirt shut, both secreted under a deep blue vest encasing his entire torso like body armor. His clothes were costume-party formal. It was odd to think he'd killed enemy soldiers in them. They looked more appropriate for a fireside afternoon pondering the merits of federalism versus states' rights.

My gaze must've lingered too long because, without missing a beat in his reading, Wythe chastised me, "It does not do to keep one's superior officer waiting, and he has been waiting for an introduction since yesterday."

"He isn't my superior officer," I grumbled.

"Yet he is mine." The captain gave me his full attention to glare, exasperated. "Mark me. Woman or no, you are bound by the same regulations as am I."

"I could just leave," I whispered.

"Your punishment for insubordination would be no less harsh." His sharp tone, coupled with my dread of what was said, silenced me.

The first sign of trouble showed itself as a black splotch soiling the handkerchief. Several tries to clean my eyelids revealed the telltale signs of make-up adhering to the cloth. I cursed the new waterproof mascara I'd been excited to try. I should've stuck with the grocery-store variety, infamous for tie-dyeing my pillowcase when I was too exhausted to wash my face before bed.

"God's teeth, woman. What have you done?" Wythe had noticed my dilemma.

"I can't get it off," I explained.

"I have been more than patient with you."

"I'm not doing it on purpose."

"Where did you get this?"

"It's my mascara. It smeared when I washed my face."

The totality of my circumstances—being kidnapped, the War, being yelled at for something in every respect out of my control by a man who, let's be honest, tried to kill me along with a bunch of other guys—was too much. My hand shook when I wet the handkerchief again, splashing water from the basin and dampening the trunk.

He gave an exasperated sigh as he slapped his letter onto the desk and wrenched the handkerchief from my hands. He searched the inside folds, perhaps for the source of my mascara, as if I'd hidden some small piece of charcoal or equally devious thing in there to sabotage his day.

Satisfied, and appearing a little mystified nothing was in there, he scrutinized me, then threw the handkerchief on his desk. Retrieving a fresh one from his pocket—I hoped it was fresh—he demanded I hold on to it. Wythe seized the basin and dumped the water outside. I was grateful it didn't crack under such rough treatment, considering how hard he plunked it down upon his return. The next round trip brought the bucket to refill the basin.

After snatching the clean handkerchief from my hands, he swirled it once through the water, seized my chin with his grasp, and made his own efforts at cleaning my eyes. I was shocked stiff.

"What is this on your face?" he demanded, glaring at my lower lashes.

"It's mascara," I reminded him.

"What, pray tell, is mascara?"

"It's eye make-up. So, my eyelashes appear… longer, darker, thicker." I kept offering adjectives, hoping one might cease the intensity of the captain scrubbing the area under my eyes. "You're hurting me."

He had the decency to look mortified and released my chin, placing as much distance between us as the cramped tent allowed. It took him a moment to extend his arm and return the cloth to me. I accepted it and rubbed at the sore remnants of his grip on my jaw. "I'm not trying to make your life difficult."

"Though you are certainly succeeding," he exclaimed with a mix of self-deprecating horror and complete exasperation. His body drifted, as if uncertain of a direction to face.

"It requires eye-makeup remover to come off."

"Something, I am quite certain, of which we have none."

"I know. I… I just want to go home."

Silence settled between us.

"I would accommodate you were it possible," he mumbled.

"I know."

We met each other's eyes, aware—or as close to it as we could be—of the other's predicament.

"Do you have any soap?" I asked.

"Soap?" He paused, confused. "There is not time to launder your garments."

The sight of my torn and bloody clothes that, from what I gathered, I'd slept in for days, didn't instill me with confidence. It did explain the funk catching my attention every now and then. The shirt was plastered to my chest. Grass stains and mud streaked my pants in multiple directions. Rust-colored splatter festered in clusters across my front. I didn't think any of it would ever come clean, even if I did make it back home. When. I meant when.

"Not my clothes. Soap for my face?"

An eyebrow raised when he asked, "Your family can afford soap to bathe?"

There were any number of conclusions for this man to draw, ones I couldn't foresee. I didn't begin to know how to answer him.

Noting my muteness with a lift of his chin, he cleared his throat and continued, "Regardless, the supplies are overdue. There are limited items with which to trade with the local farmers. Soap is a luxury I have had to do without of late."

I'd never felt like such a spoiled child as I did right then, filthy and embarrassed and forced to beg for help from a complete stranger, whose depleted supplies outnumbered my own.

"There is nothing for it," he said. "I shall have to present you as you are."

"What are you going to tell him? The major?"

"I do not know."

I told myself the subsequent churn of my stomach was due to the lack of a real meal rather than the dread of meeting the major and what he might do to me. "They say the truth is always best," I offered, the words lame even to my own ears.

"I hardly know what *is* the truth. Are you being truthful with me?"

"Yeah. As much as I can be."

Liar.

"Madam, I dare say you have left a great many things unspoken." Wythe sighed and flapped a hand as if to brush away the accusation. "Only time will tell if you are what you claim to be."

I wanted to laugh and cry at the sheer irony of his remark. "Captain, if we are stuck with one another, I'm sure there will be plenty of time to learn about each other and what we claim to be."

"God forbid," he said before he exited the tent.

That stung a little. I didn't ask to be here. I wanted to go home! He was the one who was forcing me stay because he was too scared to take me back and too selfish to tell me how to do it myself. The idea of me making it through the woods without him probably goaded his eighteenth-century, misogynistic ego. After all, I held my own in the woods. I…

The memory of the redcoat's baby-fat cheeks, the eyes that widened then dulled as the life emptied out of him, ended my internal diatribe. I followed Captain Wythe.

Chapter Seven

The captain was already deep in conversation with another man, their heads lowered close to keep their words to themselves. I vaguely remembered him from when I'd decorated the washbasin with the contents of my stomach. Also not in uniform, he looked severe in a similar coat, buttoned the traditional way. Well, traditional by my modern stance, whereas the uniform coats my father wore to reenactments only buttoned at the top with the bottom portion flaring out to the sides. Nor did the pair wear shoulder epaulets or an officer's sash around their waist.

Like Wythe's, the man's hair traveled to mid-shoulder blade, though his was pale and light enough to make me examine his hairline for the telltale signs of a wig. It was his own hair. The powder covering it was what made it appear bleached from a distance.

The men ceased speaking as I approached, the newcomer's expression one of appalled shock. "What have the Heavens wrought upon us?"

"Nice to meet you too." I couldn't help it. It was a cruddy enough morning. I didn't need the guy's attitude. I held my head high, Cover Girl be damned.

"Madam." Wythe was none too pleased. "This is Captain Alexander Brott. Alexander, meet Mistress Savannah Moore."

"Miz is fine," I shared and offered to shake hands.

"Indeed. The stray." With that, Brott dismissed me.

I dropped my ignored offer. "Charmed, I'm sure."

Asshole.

Brott focused on Wythe, saying, "DeForest has been whining

since sunrise. He is going to report you for dereliction of duty."

Dereliction was a serious charge with serious consequences. Wythe shrugged it off with equal disdain. "In truth, he will be writing to the general any day now."

Brott huffed a laugh in response. A common refrain, it seemed, holding little water for the two captains.

"Let us go," Wythe ordered without looking at me. He bolted toward the center of camp, leaving the friend behind and me to obey or be abandoned.

Curious eyes trailed after us, not to mention delicious smells streaming from more than one campfire. One was too tempting to pass by—cutlets roasting on small, iron grill with a lone carrot crisping to the side. My lingering drew the attention of the man stirring the flames within the small, box-like contraption. His expression shifted to a grimace after squinting at my face, then clothes, then returning to my face. Guess I didn't pass inspection.

It took me a moment to find Wythe again. He was tall and moved with purpose. I had to jog to catch up. My bruised, starved muscles were not appreciative.

We neared a tent which, judging by its magnitude, was where we'd be treated to an encounter with the major. Two teenagers pretending to be soldiers loitered near the entrance.

Wythe swung around to face me. "Do not speak unless questioned, for both our sakes. Is that understood?"

Despite my anxiety, not to mention desperate need for his help, I didn't appreciate the tone. "Sir, yes, sir." I saluted.

"This is no game, Miss Moore."

"No kidding."

Wythe seemed to sense my inner turmoil as I stared at the entrance, trying to rebuild my depleted courage. He sighed in lieu of further comment, then set his shoulders and faced the tent's guards to announce himself. Or rather, he made the expected salutations to the major waiting, unseen, inside. The teens in green uniform were for show. I wondered what they did to deserve such a painful assignment, or else, which wealthy families paid for their safer if minimal duty.

The captain swallowed his frustration at the silence, though he couldn't hide the annoyed shift of his jaw at the resulting delay. A ringing endorsement for the man keeping us in suspense, if ever there was one. I half expected we'd have to genuflect once admitted, judging by Wythe's demeanor.

The teens straightened their stance under the captain's glare and nodded. The major was at home. Wythe began to re-announce his arrival when a gravelly bark interrupted him. "Do you think that because I am a major I cannot hear you, *Captain* Wythe?"

"Of course. Sir," Wythe answered.

The major didn't deign to respond, and Wythe and I were left in limbo outside. When the weight of his answer registered, I glanced at my unlikely companion. The corner of his mouth twitched upward as he acknowledged my surprised look. Then, the weight of his insubordination must've caught up with him because he cleared his throat and returned to Ready, Front.

Several minutes passed before we were commanded to enter. Wythe marched into the tent. The heavy canvas slapped closed in my face. What I assumed to be the major's voice chastised Wythe for his arrogance in making the major wait, then expecting to be admitted whenever it suited him.

One of the teens snickered as I gawked at the flaps waving inches from my nose. I glared at him, affecting my best impression of a commanding officer. "Something funny, *Private*?"

"Nay… ah." He smacked his lips, not sure how to address me, and came to attention as Wythe flung the canvas aside.

Pronounced silence augmented the awkwardness of me being ushered in under Wythe's arm and deep scowl. A flustered glance and returned shrug of shoulders between the teens didn't escape my notice.

The major stood at the opposite end of the tent behind a desk not much larger than Wythe's, despite *Major* DeForest outranking *Captain* Wythe. Two empty chairs faced him. We weren't invited to sit in them.

A panoply of papers huddled on the desk's surface, stacked to mountainous heights. It threatened to topple onto an enticing tin plate of hard cheese and apple slices. A large, silver knife with a horn—or maybe wooden—hilt was suspended above a map, where a couple drops of juice had dripped from its blade to the document underneath. The borderline of some inked territory blurred as the liquid seeped along the paper's fibers.

The major wasn't as tall as Wythe, though more solidly built than my trim companion. Double gold epaulets topped the shoulders of his pine-green uniform coat, and a row of stamped, golden buttons traversed two red bands past the waistline. He wore a gray wig with the hair secured behind his head and a stern, intelligent look on his face.

DeForest had been leaning over the table and its contents. Upon my entrance, he rose to full height—maybe five foot nine—with arms crossed as he scrutinized me from top to bottom and back again. For the first time, I thought about my hair.

Having been distracted up to this point with insignificant matters like death, mayhem, and mascara, it never occurred to me that my shoulder-length waves might be snarled and had, no doubt, gathered souvenirs from the forest floor during my unfortunate brush with the redcoats. The urge to fuss with it was overwhelming.

"You broke the line?" the major questioned Wythe while he continued to take in my disheveled state.

"Aye," Wythe replied.

"You should keep me informed of such things."

"General's orders."

DeForest grimaced. "Naturally."

The tension was concerning. There was a power-struggle going on between Wythe and the man I'd assumed was his commanding officer. Superior officer not being the same thing, it seemed. A balancing of military hierarchy, good manners, and warring orders was at work. It was also a fair guess my presence played a role, however small, in the limited sharing of information and, most assuredly, choice words.

"How many were there?" the major asked.

"They were scattered through the forest. Scouts, I should imagine. We encountered a half dozen or thereabouts." The last part was said with an inclination of Wythe's head toward me.

DeForest didn't react to my inclusion. "Getting closer?"

The captain nodded. "Less than an hour's walk from here."

"Damnation." The major's stormy expression zeroed in on me. I kept quiet and my face neutral. "Does this one have a name?"

"Major," Wythe answered, "allow me to introduce Miss Savannah Moore."

"Do you speak for yourself?" the major asked me.

"I do." There was a subtle intake of breath from my left. I wondered how, with only two words, I could've said something wrong. "Nice to meet you, Major."

"You came from the general?"

"With all due respect, I'm not at liberty to say." I figured mimicking Wythe's tactics was the safest bet. A quiet exhale told me it was the correct choice.

"The general flogged the last woman posing as a soldier."

Awesome.

"The lady is here under my protection." Wythe didn't meet my eyes. He kept them locked with the other officer, so I returned my attention to the major, as well.

"Your men have been good hosts, Major," I told him. "I appreciate the hospitality I've been shown so far." Not fueling the testosterone fire was probably not a bad idea, either.

The major leaned forward with both hands on his desk when he said, "You have seen poor samplings if you come in here, dressed in a sad trim, and think you have been paid any sort of hospitality."

Wythe's fist tightened at his side. I swallowed my nerves and plastered a smile on my face. "There hasn't been time yet for things like cleaning up."

A cluster of women's complaints about the results of the latest attempt to dye a skein of wool passed along the outer wall of the tent. One exhaled in surprise. The sounds of several items flopping to the ground tumbled after. Remarks on her own clumsiness accompanied her laughing while one of the guards recovered her lost items. Women's chattering receded into the distance.

The guard's voice broke with a youthful squeak as he bade the other, who was snorting at him, to, "*Haud yer wheesht.*"

Ambient noise from the camp's inhabitants ensued. At length.

The major was keeping silent, no doubt using the manufactured discomfort to encourage me to fill the void with chatter and revealing information. Not a lot of work required to achieve the uncomfortable part, but I refused to play into it. It was a game I'd led the charge on many times as an attorney. Nevertheless, I was more than ready to hand the verbal reins back to Wythe.

Thankfully, the captain complied with my unspoken wish. "I shall need to take leave. I must cross once more through the line to escort Miss Moore to our rendezvous point."

"I have no love of spies, Captain Wythe." DeForest's glower turned on him. "You had best remember it."

Another common refrain, I gathered, when the tension returned between the two men.

"Major." Wythe's nod of recognition was polite on the surface, but the use of DeForest's rank came off like a reminder. Wythe reported to someone of higher authority. Watching their intense and wordless study of each other, it became clear there was more to Wythe's admonition to remain silent than simple male dominance.

"Well, it shall all have to wait." The major searched through one of the tall stacks and retrieved a letter.

They eyed one another as the message was delivered to the captain. Wythe noted the wax seal before returning to his mute exchange with DeForest. When the major seemed resigned to the fact that Wythe wasn't going to open the letter in his presence, he returned to the terrain of documents, further discussion apparently being absent from the daily itinerary.

Chapter Eight

Captain Wythe held the tent flap open for me, allowing me to exit before him, though he rushed toward the camp's boundaries once freed from the major's lair, his gaze burning a hole through the letter as if trying to read its contents without opening it. He paused, tapping the edge of the folded paper against his fingers.

I cut him off before he could say anything. "Thank you. For what you did back there."

I couldn't imagine what possessed him to help me. It was a considerable risk on his part, claiming responsibility for me and promising to cross enemy lines for my sake. Yeah, I'd demanded it. Didn't mean he was under any real obligation to give in.

"You saved my life," he said. "It would be wrong of me not to acknowledge the debt."

"Not that I want you changing your mind or anything, but you also saved mine."

Wythe appraised me with a small grin warming his expression. He seemed appreciative of the reciprocated acknowledgment. He didn't owe me anything more than I owed him. After a silent moment of contemplation, he cleared his throat and bent forward at the waist, in a mere fraction of a bow, so he was leaning closer to my ear. "This letter is of vital importance. I must read it at once. Might you occupy yourself and avoid trouble?"

I returned the smile. "Odds are good."

"Hmm. You have my thanks. Later, we shall seek better accommodations for you."

I scanned my mostly masculine surroundings before saying,

"Uh, the tent's fine."

"I-it would not be possible."

"Why? Who uses the other cot?"

"It… he…" Scarlet burst through the dark patch of his beard and spread to his cheekbones. "It is beside the point."

"Excellent. Everything's settled. Now, how about you direct me to a pond, river, brook, stream? Something with water, where I can wash the rest of me? I stink, and this shirt's disgusting. You can read your letter in private. And then, maybe lunch?" I hoped ramrodding the whole enchilada at him would do the job.

"Nay, it is not settled." Nope, it hadn't. "It would hardly be appropriate for a woman to share a tent with a gentleman."

"It's *because* you're a gentleman I trust you enough to share a tent with you. Besides, how else are you going to protect me?"

His mouth parted, and he hesitated. "Why should you be certain that I will not harm you?"

I sighed and hoped I was right before explaining, "If you intended to rape me, you would've done it already. You've had plenty of chances."

"Madam!" Wythe blanched.

"How about Savannah?"

But Wythe was in such a rush with his apology, he spoke over me without stopping. "Please forgive my response and allow me to reaffirm my vow. I have not, nor will I, harm you."

"I know."

"I was in earnest when speaking with Major DeForest. You shall have my protection whilst you are here. Whilst I assist you in finding the answers you need to return to your home."

"Thanks."

"All said, to remain in my tent is…" He was losing the battle. Recognition hung heavy in his shoulders. He just wasn't ready to surrender yet.

"Be honest. If I had my own tent, would I be safe? Could you promise me the other zillion men here would be as honorable as you?" Tight-lipped silence. "Trust me," I told him. "I'm not happy about my life—not to mention, unconscious body—having been in the arms of a perfect stranger." He shifted his weight away from me at the reminder, so I asked with a little less insistence, "Please, if we have to wait a few days before you take me to the hillside where you found me, would you try to tolerate sharing a tent with me? I'll do my best to stay out of your way. I'll even help with whatever chores you have, though you may need to teach me. Life here's kinda different from back home."

"Indeed, it must be." He shook his head. "I have never met your equal, Miss Moore."

"Almost sounds like a compliment. And hey, in return, I'll promise not to seduce *you*."

"Madam!"

"Savannah." I chuckled.

His shoulders relaxed as he caught on. "You jest."

"Yeah, well. I'm nervous," I confessed. "It's a habit of mine."

He offered a sympathetic smile. "You bear it well."

Our eyes met.

I broke the silence before it became awkward. "Look, if we're going to be stuck with each other for a bit, we could at least be friends, right?"

"I… would not be so unkind as to deny you the hand of friendship in your hour of need; however, I will not be calling you by your given name."

"All right, Savvy, then."

"Savvy?"

"My friends call me Savvy."

He smiled when he said with his own dry humor, "How quaint."

"Are you making fun of me?"

"I am certain it was considered an apt endearment by someone."

"Wow. You *are* making fun of me. Don't you have a very important letter to read?"

Wythe turned serious. "Aye, I do."

"And I get water where?" He hesitated at my question. "You don't trust me to bathe on my own. You aren't planning on watching me, are you?"

"Of course not! Watching you, that is."

"Good." Since we were going endure some unknown quantity of time camping together—Shh! Don't tell the local gossips—I decided to test the waters of dropping a few more formalities. "Jon…"

"Ah, now. Jonathan, if you must, though Captain Wythe would be most appropriate."

I smirked. "Captain Jonathan?"

"Heavens, but you are bold."

I breathed a laugh. An amused hum from him accompanied me. "Jonathan…?" He sighed but nodded for me to proceed. "Can I trouble you for some clean clothes?"

Leary as I was about putting too much pressure on the delicate nature of our compromise, I had real needs, not the least of which was some semblance of sanitary conditions of the non-enemy-inspired fashion. Nothing fancy. Eighteenth-century catwalk edition being both unlikely and wholly unwanted.

"I do not keep women's attire," he said.

"Oh, well. It's just… the major—"

"Take no heed of his threat. Insubordination. Thievery, for certain. Never have I heard tell of a woman being flogged for… being as you are now." A simple nod was exchanged for my relieved sigh. "Miss Moore, I… do not have the means to… Rather, I am not acquainted with any—"

"A clean top would be fine. This one's seen better days."

Goodness knows, I wasn't any more comfortable than he was asking the women in camp to donate a spare gown. With the exception of the officers and their staff, soldiers and camp followers were expected to carry their own baggage—a point my father's historical vacation spots loved to drive home, often with actual oxen and wagon trains to demonstrate. Given how bulky women's gowns were in the Eighteenth, little chance any of them had more than one extra outfit with them.

A potential protest died after a review of my destroyed His-Majesty's-Best red shirt. Even Captain Jonathan Wythe had to admit I couldn't stay in what I was wearing. He led the way to his tent and disappeared inside, resigned. Figuring it was best to give him space, I waited outside on Forest Thoroughfare. Most camp inhabitants passed by without a second glance. Those who noted my general appearance and relative location to Jonathan's tent gave me a decided wide berth.

The closing of a trunk preceded his return with several articles. "I cannot vouch for the fit," he apologized. "You shall have to make do with these. I do not think it best to supply you with my own garments."

"Whose are these?" I hesitated in accepting the pile.

The seriousness returned to his face. Instead of answering, he indicated the way to a nearby stream, then excused himself to retreat back into the tent. Since I probably didn't want to know, I didn't pursue it.

I risked a quick whiff of the clothes and was relieved. Karma had overlooked me. They didn't smell like fabric softener, but they also didn't smell like an unwashed someone else. I took the collection and—what the heck?—the bucket to search for a place to bathe.

Chapter Nine

Sunlight burst unhindered through a break in the foliage, telling me I'd reached the stream. I dropped the bucket and lowered myself along the water's edge, gratefully though not gracefully. My body was screaming from abuse. An exasperated voice followed my hands dipping into the water.

Startled, I scurried to my feet to discover a cluster of women to my left. Figuring they were camp followers—the wives, daughters, and other women trying to scrape a living by doing chores for the soldiers—I surveyed the area, chastising myself for not checking first to make sure it was safe before entering the clearing.

An armed soldier—local militia, maybe, judging from his clothes—guarded the women and mountains of laundry they were laughing over. He wasn't in uniform but a wannabe white, fringed shirt and short pants. Gaiters, similar in style—meant to keep his legs warm and stockings clean from splatter—were strapped to his calves.

The man advanced, his grip tight on his musket. Remaining motionless, I hoped I didn't look like a threat despite my disgusting appearance and red shirt. The militiaman surveyed first me, then the bucket and pile of clothes on the ground. "Lobster mounter." He shook his head before returning to his watch of the woods.

The women also studied me while they laughed and scrubbed, continuing their chatter about a bold conquest of stolen beef from the regulars. The celebrated brunette chuckled as she recalled marching there and back again with "nary a hallo, 'cepting when I feared myself clean done in 'cause I dropped a shank. But would not you know, one of the regulars, an officer no less, retrieved it and placed it in my arms with a tip of his cap and a smile on his lips. I might have burst to laughing would it not have meant being found out and his leading me to dance the hangman's jig."

I longed to borrow the lump of soap being shared.

Oh crap.

The water was flowing downstream from where I'd dunked my hands, sending blood and filth to invade where they were rinsing their laundry. No wonder the women had been exasperated. Having committed a huge social faux pas—one of many, many more to come, I had no doubt—I apologized and moved to the other side of the group. Hushed voices followed my passage. I didn't hear most of what was said, but "Captain Wythe" was thrown in.

The iciness biting my skin notwithstanding, the idea of getting clean made the water heavenly. I began with my face, then rolled up my sleeves to douse away the splatter crusted along my arms. My sore muscles wailed at the chilliness, and I swear my senses decided to step it up a notch. Stretching forward to scoop water had me wrinkling my nose in disgust at the *odeur naturelle* wafting from my underarms.

The Laundry Klatch was still present, my actions feeding the gossip. I shook my hands dry and gathered my change of clothes to move farther downstream, which curved behind a tangle of bushes, making for a convenient hideaway.

"Eh! Where are you goin'?" the militiaman asked. His musket lingered in the purgatory realm of neither at attention nor at rest.

"Just over here." I pointed out my chosen spot.

"Return to the others."

"I need to wash my shirt, not to mention myself."

The women didn't hide their interest, whispering and giggling at the excitement unfolding.

"There are enemy soldiers a'lurking."

With a telegraphed show of observing my stained front, then returning my stare at him, I responded, "I hadn't noticed."

The women hooted with laughter, their voices even louder after I disappeared into the vegetation. Depositing my stuff on the grass, I began stripping off the ruined shirt. It gave an audible lament as the mix of dried blood and sweat tore from my skin, pulling the tiny hairs as it peeled off. I cringed and threw the thing away, then hesitated.

Part of me wanted to leave the red shirt—a wadded, detestable souvenir from my gory entrée into the Revolutionary War—to rot. The other part clung to wanting to protect those few connections I had to my own century.

A man's sputtering interrupted my quandary. The militiaman

hadn't gotten the message and had followed to my side of the bush. The sight of my bra and nothing else above the waistline captivated him. His mouth was working out notions spawned less and less from his brain in favor of someplace lower.

"Don't even think about it," I warned as he stepped closer. "Hey!" My yell caught his attention; his gaze leapt back up to where it belonged. I added the commanding officer tone for emphasis. "Do your duty and protect those women. I don't want your help."

Unlike the major's teens, the militiaman wasn't cowed and took umbrage at my impersonation. Red splotches multiplied across his face. His grip on his musket tightened, and he stalked toward me again.

"Back off," I insisted, taking a fighting stance and fisting my hands.

A wicked smile erupted. This was going to be fun. For him.

His attention darted to the undergrowth behind me, and there was the largest man I'd ever seen.

Sensei often says size doesn't matter. Focus on leverage, the structure of your opponent, the positioning of their body, so you can knock them off-balance. Yeah, right. Try finding your courage in those words when you're no longer in the safety of class and facing a human version of the Great Wall.

My hands faltered, and I may've squeaked a little.

The bear of a man said nothing. Took in the scene of me squaring off empty-handed and half-naked against armed militia. Regaining a defensive stance, I pivoted, enabling me to monitor the militiaman's position without losing sight of the newest addition to the party. The wicked smile returned, and my opponent advanced. I shuffled backward, though any more would have me wading.

The Wall settled his hand on the hilt of a blade strapped to his side. The damn thing was huge. It probably suffered from an existential crisis about whether it was a dagger on steroids or a juvenile broadsword.

The man's steady gaze, however, wasn't on me. A blank expression crossed the militiaman's face, no doubt consistent with the contents of his brain. The Wall shook his head at the next step. Letting loose a lengthy expletive, the militiaman stalked off in the direction of the camp followers and their laundry.

Which left me at the mercy of The Wall. He surveyed me again, all of me, a little too appreciatively. The upper curve of his mouth reached its pinnacle around the time his gaze devoured the valley of my stomach rising toward the height of my breasts. My courage wavered. The visual expedition was eternal. But I held my ground. The subtle opening and closing of my fingers notwithstanding.

"Captain Wythe?" was the extent of what the man asked when his gaze completed its exploration.

"Yeah." It sounded more like a question than an answer.

The Wall returned to the forest as abruptly as he'd exited it. His silence, irrespective of his size, was disconcerting as he moved through the vegetation.

I clutched my arms to my chest, releasing a shaky breath.

You've been in enough volatile situations with defendants losing it in court, I reminded myself. It's fine.

Then again, I'd never been to war before. Never witnessed first-hand the slaying of another person. Felt the spray of blood as it rushes into the air. Watched the life drain from someone's eyes. I'd never had to take a life to save my own. And if I wasn't more careful, it would be my life taken without a second thought from my killer.

Chapter Ten

No one came to give me sympathy or make efforts at sending me to my maker. I was on my own. I picked up the pace in case there were other unwanted distractions lurking in the woods, careful to keep tabs on the nearby symphony of splashing and laughing and women's chatter.

There was a salt-colored shirt in the pile Jonathan had given me. The length extended partway down my quads. I leaned forward to prevent the linen from touching my skin as I shucked off my bra from underneath. It was unstained except for a spot or two at the upper edge.

Since it was my blood—or so I told myself—I wasn't tempted to throw it out like the offensive red shirt. That thing was a death wish in 100% cotton while I was trapped in the Colonies. Or an improvised washcloth. I found the cleanest spot there was to scour my stomach and sides.

There was too much fabric to tuck the white shirt in. Skip the pants, maybe? Captain Jonathan was putting up with a lot, but I doubted my parading around in a substitute minidress was going to win his approval. Dollars to doughnuts Mr. Militiaman would've had opinions of the unpleasant-for-me variety. There was the question of my khakis. With a hatching of grass stains and a stippling of dirt, they'd become a literal study of earth tones.

Further review of the clothing options turned up a brown vest. A resounding hell no!

And… a pair of linen pants. Unlike Jonathan's short pants, these extended to my feet. Well, almost to my feet. Another half-inch of fabric would've looked better, but given the choices... A single button in the center joined the front, and yay for me, the waistline was adjustable thanks to two fabric ties in the back. A little snug around the middle. Figured the man who last owned them was typical, eighteenth-century sized instead of sporting some height like Jonathan or extra-extra-large, athletic bulk like The Wall.

Two other buttons guarded my hips, one on either side. Undone, they allowed a front panel to drop forward. Good for a man needing to take a leak in the woods. Not good for a woman trying to hide lace panties. I knew I should've worn the granny panties. After a check, they held the front closed, for the most part, without exposing Victoria's Secret.

By the sheer factor of them being the first pair in reach, I'd changed into slip-ons instead of sneakers before taking Goldie for a walk. Hiking, apple-picking, shoveling, even daytrips to the city—those boots could handle anything. Mocha, lay-it-on-me-weather leather. Also, non-descript, meaning less likely to advertise yet another way I didn't belong in the Eighteenth. At least, not without close inspection.

Cinching my leather belt over the shirt kept the fabric from hanging loose. I didn't want it catching on something if I ended up running for my life again. Rue the thought.

Evan would've loved the get-up. A pirate hat and a sword to go with it, I'd be set for Halloween.

A wash of longing for my son had me clutching my arms to my chest… except my nipples were visible through the white fabric. I groaned, questioning the skies, why? Another moment's indulgence in self-pity, a deep breath, then I pulled myself together.

Brown vest? It would've been warmer, but it was too much a reminder of how displaced I was. I was going to do things on my terms, damn it. Instead, I underwent the process of undoing the belt and ducking my arms out of the sleeves, so I could slip my bra back on before redoing the whole thing all over again. The bra would have to get washed some other time. Jonathan hadn't supplied me with a coat. Another topic to spawn more awkward banter. I smiled, thinking of his earlier reaction.

I took a brief stab at cleaning my clothes. My hands were shaking from the cold before long. A nice change from shaking with fear, I guessed. The final straw to my how-not-to-remove-stains efforts was the unexpected and pronounced allegretto of the Laundry Klatch's gossiping and shuffling before the entire Camp Follower Orchestra faded into the distance. I hoped the militiaman had followed the women and wasn't waiting to pounce from somewhere in the woods.

Maybe, along with a coat, I thought, I'll talk to Jonathan about getting me a gun.

If only I'd let the guys back home teach me how to shoot. The court officers had clucked their tongues when they first learned I didn't carry.

I gathered the litter of fabrics, even the red shirt. As I suspected, there was no one there when I rounded the bushes.

Nothing looked familiar in the area surrounding the stream. Of course, why would it? Jonathan said he'd carried me for about an hour back to his camp. He might've lied to me, an unknown entity, about the distance. I doubted he would've told such a lie to Major DeForest.

Better report to Captain Jonathan, Private Reliance.

Chapter Eleven

Woodsmoke seasoned with stewed meat slapped me in the face when I reentered the camp. It was time, with none to spare, to address the need for lunch. Movement caught my eye—The Wall emerging from the undergrowth to reenter the camp, as well. He didn't acknowledge my existence, but continued with his own purpose, disappearing into a canvas alleyway. Probably the presence I'd sensed haunting my footsteps on the way to camp, though… A churning of my stomach, followed by a wave of dizziness, told me to think later. Get lunch first.

Yeah, Jonathan's tent was in the last row with the woods at its rear, but I was lost. They all looked the same! Grubby-white soldiers lined up for revelry. Right around the time I questioned my cognitive abilities—how hard can it be to find a man who was tall and had a voice like classic movie star?—Jonathan and his friend materialized farther down Forest Thoroughfare. I hurried over to them, trying to make a mental note about his tent's place in formation.

"Ah, Miss Moore. Oh!" A lift of his brows, then a pleased look accompanied him as he eyed the refilled bucket. He reclaimed it from me and set it next to the tent's entrance. "I am glad you have returned. You have saved me the time of writing a message." Jonathan tensed at a snort from Friend Alexander, who looked anywhere except at me. The argument had already been had about me, I could tell, and would be had again.

"I must leave," Jonathan said.

"Oh?"

"We shall return soon," he replied, tipping his head toward Alexander.

"Wait, I'll come with you."

"On Saint Geoffrey's Day," Alexander snapped at him.

"Wha—?"

"Miss Moore, Captain Brott is right to insist," Jonathan said. "The nature of our mission is… delicate. Few are privy to its purpose. You had best remain here."

"Jonathan—"

"You dare?" Alexander pointed a finger at me. "This is a distraction we do not need. You should turn the creature over to Major DeForest. Let him deal with her."

"The *creature* has a name." Jonathan growled a sigh before addressing me again. "I apologize for Captain Brott's rudeness. Please try to understand, *Miss Moore*." I dipped my chin to acknowledge the unspoken request. "What we do… I fear you would be a distraction." At my wind-up to object, he sort of tut-tutted me. I forewent the inclination and allowed him to finish. "I have sworn to protect you. As such, my attention would not be focused on my task but divided by attempting to see you safe."

Like it or not, I had to admit Jonathan had a point, though he said it a lot nicer than his alleged friend. There were countless ways things could go wrong if I went with them.

"Okay. Captain Wythe," I said, though I couldn't keep the trepidation to myself.

"Perhaps her skills *can* be put to use." Alexander's tone had an unpleasant snide quality to it, the kind that warned Smug Comment Ahead. "She can guard your possessions."

Jonathan's jaw shifted. "Thank you, Miss Moore." His tense response was tempered with forced patience. For a moment, Jonathan's gaze roved my face. He spoke next with sincere kindness to only me. "I will honor your request to lodge with me. In my absence, the arrangement should grant you some protection."

Some, I noticed. Not complete protection.

"Now, we must make haste," he announced, "else we might not return before nightfall."

"Sure," I whispered.

What else could I do? I had no right to stop him, and who knew what would happen if he didn't go and do the things history had in store for him? I had to keep my interference in his life to a minimum. But damn it, I hated it.

A compassionate smile was his only goodbye. He turned to leave with Alexander at his side, snapping at some snide comment—the specifics of what was said, too garbled for me to hear—which earned me

a dirty look from Captain Asshole. They disappeared into the depths of camp. What the hell was I going to do now?

Chapter Twelve

Lunch. Lunch had to be the next thing I did, though I worried if I wandered off, I'd have problems remembering which tent was Jonathan's again. Especially because I was finding it hard to concentrate while my blood sugar was plummeting. As luck would have it—I wasn't too far gone yet—a solution came to me. I tore the bottom hem off my red shirt with a satisfying *riiip*. It was dead to me, anyway. Might as well put it to good use after the stupid thing got my throat cut. I double-knotted the strip around one of the ropes securing the tent. A truce signal in red, flapping from our shared tent of white.

Interior decorators of the twenty-first century would've rejoiced at the breathtaking minimalist effect within Jonathan's tent. Only the furniture was visible. Everything else was locked away in the trunks, including—presumably—his wooden box. Washbasin, as well.

Guard his possessions, my ass.

I dumped my clothes onto the trunk nearest what had become my cot, then wandered outside. It took a moment to gain my bearings.

Following the aroma of something edible smelling led to an opening in Tent City, where a large cooking mound was established. It looked like a tiered wedding cake of the dirt variety. Stacks of chopped wood filled a trench surrounding it to feed the fires burning in the bottom tier. The first tier stood about knee-height and housed random ingredients stored in baskets along its surface. Vents were carved over the fires, and pots placed on top like a frying pan on a modern stove burner.

A decent-ish line gathered by the cook, waiting to be served. Only a few customers brought dishware, I was relieved to discover. Most were empty-handed. Something similar to rice pudding, but chunkier and more yellow, was the entrée being ladled onto trenchers. It looked like the same bread Jonathan had given me earlier.

Joining the line earned me more curious looks.

The cook palmed the bread, fingering drips back onto the trencher with his bare hands, which he smacked against his grimy pants from time to time. Thoughts of the festival of germs he was giving a free ride to sent a shiver up my spine. Thank goodness my mother wasn't there. Evidence of poor hygiene inevitably led to a lecture, even if I wasn't the culprit violating her surgeon's sensibilities.

I shook it off and tried to engage the woman in front of me in conversation. At first, she seemed shocked to see me, her eyes widening, but then she shied away, refusing to respond. Nice. All I'd commented on was how good the fire felt.

She perked up, though, when a handsome young man emerged from a sizeable tent. Not only didn't she mind him cutting the line when she was next, she seemed glad of the timing. Like a switch turned on, her demeanor sparked to the animated setting as she prattled away at him with coy compliments about some suggestion he'd made to her once and did he see how improved her condition was, and blah, blah, blah, ha ha.

The interloper offered a simple apology to go along with his negative response. She rallied well and carried on with her twittering. His appearance didn't slow her in the slightest, not even when she devoured his front side with her eyes. His *lower* front side.

We could've been twins, this man and I, had we met upon my disembarking from the twenty-first century, right down to the matching sun-kissed hair and blood. At one point, he must've been wearing a triangular-shaped apron, pinned to his shirt in the vicinity of his collarbone, because there was splatter around obvious demarcation lines. His stockings, stretched beneath his tan short pants, would've been white, like his shirt, had they not been decorated with more than a little of the same telltale signs of previous violence. How was he not cold without a jacket?

When he noticed me, he stared. Then he kept on staring. "Sarah?"

Lunch Lady peered at me from the corner of her eyes, as if anxious for the answer to his question too.

"Uh, no." I shook my head at them.

The cook slapped a serving into his bowl, returning the man's attention to his chosen mission. He mumbled an apology to me and excused himself, tucking his somewhat-clean hands underneath the bowl, embarrassed. After ducking inside the large tent again—the cold having become apparent, and perhaps a coat might be in order—he settled into a lonely chair near the entrance. The first time in a long time since he'd last sat, judging by his collapse into the chair.

He risked another glance in my direction, then his gaze drifted to an empty stare into his bowl without his actually touching its contents. Peace and quiet weren't in his future. Lunch Lady followed as soon as she was served, all lowered chin and feigned humility.

"Who are you?" the cook asked.

"Savannah Moore. Pleased to meet you." The food smelled so damn good, I was willing to brown nose anyone right then. Even Typhoid Martin.

He squinted at me. "Yer not part of the company."

"I'm new here. I came with Captain Wythe."

"Where is Captain Wythe?" the cook pressed.

"He left again."

"Not seen him." The man ran a finger across the undercarriage of his nostrils. It was smeared against his backside next. My mind questioned whether it should listen to my stomach.

I forged ahead anyway. "We've been here a few days."

"Have you coin?"

"No—"

"Move on."

"But," I cried. I was getting desperate.

"Get Captain Wythe to vouch for you. Else, move on."

"I can't get him to vouch for me. He left!" I shouldn't have raised my voice because it made my head swim.

"I said, move on," the man raised his voice in turn.

Handsome Interloper joined the fray. "What seems to be the trouble, Private?" He glanced at me, but I was distracted by his admirer, who was just realizing she'd been abandoned by taking the chair offered to her. A decided pout was clear despite the distance.

"Nothing, Doctor," the cook answered.

"Excellent. You may give this woman her due rations."

Okay, he'd figured out I was a woman, though it was obvious from the slack-jawed stare it was news to Typhoid Martin. The cook abandoned the gender conundrum and stuck with the company line of, "Cannot be feeding beggars, Doctor."

"I'm not a beggar," I protested. Yeah, maybe I was, but…

"Why should you think she is a beggar?" the doctor continued to question the cook.

"Is not one of the camp followers," he replied.

"I arrived a few days ago," I said to the doctor.

"Captain Wythe brought you?" the doctor asked.

"Captain Wythe is not here, Doctor," the cook interjected. "There is none can vouch for her."

I took a pass at responding but was getting too woozy to make much headway.

"Are you faint?" The doctor caught my elbow with his free hand. "I will vouch for her. I saw her enter the camp, accompanied by Captain Wythe, two days prior."

Something Jonathan had said floated around in my brain. It was lost in the fog. What was it?

"Sir."

"The woman's rations, Private."

The cook grimaced at the doctor's authoritative tone. Snatching a trencher from the basket at his side, he dumped a quick scoop onto it, not caring whether the mess stayed on the bread or slopped back into the pot. The trencher was thrust into my hands, and the next person in line ordered forward. I fumbled with it, the spill-over stinging my fingers. The doctor took it from me by catching the whole thing in his bowl.

"Come. Sit." Glancing at the woman pining for him from the chair, the doctor then led us in the opposite direction. Oh, she gifted me with such a nasty look for it.

The doctor settled us onto a roughly chopped log near an open fire, then offered me his bowl with orders to eat. We took turns tearing pieces of the bread with our hands and using them to scoop the mixture. Starvation got the better of my manners. I'd wolfed down more than my share long before I realized what I'd done.

"I'm so sorry."

The doctor laughed. "I am only too glad, as you appear to be recovered."

"Yeah, thanks. It was nice of you to come to my defense." Under normal circumstances, I'd bristle at the idea of a woman needing to be rescued by a man. Problem was, I was embarrassed at having hogged the food, not to mention the guy was good-natured about it, far more than I deserved.

"Not at all, Mistress…?"

"Moore. Savannah Moore."

He seemed relieved to have learned my name at last. The intense observation of me relaxed, anyway. "It is a pleasure to meet you. Auden Cole, at your service."

"A doctor," I added.

"Yes," he acknowledged with a dip of his head. His cheeks flushed in the process. Too great a selling point to the women in his life,

I imagine.

"It's nice to meet you too. Can I ask you something? The woman from the lunch line, over by your tent…"

His attention flicked over to where she was gossiping with another camp follower. "You were not interrupting."

"Oh, I think she very much thinks otherwise."

"Please, pay it no mind."

"Well, I would, but I doubt I'll have a choice," I half-joked. "You just earned me a new enemy today, and I really don't need more of those. This being a war and all."

"I had not considered…"

Doctor Cole mouthed a protest when I waved over to the women to join us. Fortune was on his side, though. The doctor's admirer jumped up in a huff, and I'm not sure, but I think she stamped her foot. Her companion fell in, after being pestered to, her Razzie-contending sigh notwithstanding. They picked the longest street possible through Tent City to ensure we'd see them sashaying away together, the doctor given the most direct view of their derrieres.

I raised my eyebrows at him. His head sunk into his shoulders, and he busied himself with his meal. "Coward," I teased.

He looked up, startled. "Yes." He shrugged. "Perhaps."

I had a near-miss of stew when the moistened bread broke under its weight to slop past my leg. "This isn't easy to eat." I chuckled and sucked the spill from my palm.

The doctor relaxed again as I laughed off the mess I was making and offered me the last piece, but I declined. He set the bowl on the ground between us rather than finish it himself. Unsure of what to say next, he fed another log to the firepit at our feet, then rubbed his hands together to wipe off the debris. There was dried blood under his nails.

He noticed my observation and sat on his hands, hiding the troubling evidence. I followed his example of wiping my hands together to clean them. The dancing light entertained us during a quiet interlude.

"Was it true, what you said?" I asked. "You saw me with Captain Wythe?"

"I believe it was you. Your hair looks to be the same." Something like wonder tinged his voice. Before I could question him about it, he continued, "I fear I owe you an apology."

"Why?"

"Captain Wythe brought you into the surgery, but I was… engaged in a pressing matter. I could not spare his request much thought, as to your treatment or what to do with you, hence why I bade him to care for you. I intended to examine you, but I have been kept quite busy.

You were not seriously injured. I was kept informed." My attention drifted to the doctor's bloody attire visible through his unbuttoned coat. He responded by clutching the folds closed. After a long study of the logs spitting sparks into the air, he added, "I hope I have not upset you."

"No." Though I wasn't sure if my drawn-out answer was as honest as I would've liked. "It's just... I haven't made peace with everything that's happened yet."

"You are welcome to tell me if you wish."

So, I told him. I didn't mean to, but once the dam broke open, the spilling of my story couldn't be allayed. Sometimes the words flowed freely. Other times, the hostile memories threatened to suffocate me and halted me in my tale.

The doctor stifled a gasp, his expression assuming a deep grimace afterward, when I described how I met Jonathan and his knife. Still, he was attentive throughout, interjecting an audible response at the appropriate places. Not once did he try to interrupt me or interject attempts to downplay my version of events or make false efforts at comforting me.

"Sorry. You didn't expect to be playing a shrink today, huh?" Unloading days' worth of trauma on someone I'd just met wasn't my classiest move.

"You have nothing for which you should apologize," he said. "It sounds as though you have had a harrowing experience."

"We aren't at war with anyone. Back home, I mean. I've read about the war here," I hurried to address his confused glance, "but reading about something isn't the same thing as living it."

"Without question," he agreed. "You are not from the United States, I gather."

I stared, not sure how to answer when he didn't say *Colonies* like I kept expecting.

Expressing concern again at the alleged gaps in my memory, he shook his head before asking, "What did you mean when you said 'playing a shrink'?"

"Um, acting as a doctor to my emotions." I couldn't think of a better way to explain it when put on the spot. Doctor Cole repeated the phrase, and I could see it resonating in his mind. "We call it psychology," I said.

"Tell me, are you versed in ancient Greek philosophy?"

"No. Why?" I asked with my own surprise.

"The Greek word 'psyche' means the soul. The ancient philosophers such as Aristotle, for example, wrote about the mind as the rational soul. He described the two different forms of intellect—the possible and the agent intellect. Hippocrates—" He stopped himself.

"Creator of the Hippocratic Oath. The father of modern medicine," I prompted him, though my use of *modern* was ironic, given how I'd been displaced.

A broad smile accompanied his saying, "You cannot be interested in such things."

My turn to be coy. "I can't?"

Our conversation was cut short, however, because Jonathan and Alexander stormed past us. I excused myself to race after them.

Chapter Thirteen

The men were glowering at Jonathan's tent by the time I caught up with them, neither speaking. Just staring. I wondered what they were up to. "You're back."

Jonathan fingered the red fabric on the tent's rope. His other hand hovered near the knife strapped to his side. "What is this?"

"It's from my shirt. I was having trouble remembering which tent was yours."

Alexander glared a warning shot at him.

"Remove it," he ordered.

"O-kay." I complied while I asked, "Why are you mad? What's going on?"

"It is no concern of yours," Alexander snapped at me.

"It is when I'm getting yelled at for no reason."

"Wanton baggage, you have no business here."

"Who the hell do you think you are, barking at me like that?" I fired back, charged with fury.

"Enough," Jonathan shouted at the both of us. "We are not *back*, Miss Moore, as you inquired. We have not yet begun."

"You haven't?" I was taken aback because I was pretty sure Jonathan had mentioned something about a tight schedule. Without my phone, I had no real sense of time, but several hours must've gone by since we last spoke. What had they been doing?

"We need the other men for cover," he complained.

"Well, the fool isn't going to give them," Alexander said.

Jonathan sighed at the ground. He raised his eyes to me, his head pitching to the side as stared.

Alexander scowled. "Do not think it."

"We have a small window of opportunity, Alexander."

"Which can wait until morning."

"When our chances of success will have diminished. At least with Miss Moore—"

"We need trained soldiers. Not strays like the cabbage farmers the major has the nerve to call militia." Alexander may've been referring to any of the rough-and-readies who comprised the majority of the men wandering the campgrounds, but the insult was flung in my direction.

"She *is* capable of combat. I have seen it," Jonathan insisted.

"Uh, wait a second," I piped up.

Alexander didn't care about what I'd said and bulldozed his argument right over me. "You involve her, you shall go without me."

Jonathan's mouth parted in surprise. "You would disobey your commanding officer?"

"I do not know what fabrication you told DeForest to keep this creature here with you, but understand me. I will not allow you to endanger us by involving a woman—a demi-rep, I would have you consider—on any of our missions."

"She is not the first." Jonathan's voice softened, his words grown dull. "And I was speaking of the general."

"At least she was one of our kind," Alexander said to Jonathan's lowered face.

Doctor Cole was hovering across Forest Thoroughfare, looking uncertain about approaching us. He'd said something about examining me when I ran off to get sucked into this mess. I hadn't realized he meant right away. I shook my head at him and escaped into Jonathan's tent.

I touched a hand to my cheeks. They felt flushed. It didn't know why it bothered me that Doctor Cole had witnessed the whole fiasco. I wasn't going to stick around long enough for anyone's opinion of me to matter.

The flaps parted, somewhat hesitant at first. It was only Jonathan. When I was sure no one else would be joining us, I informed him how I wanted no part in whatever his mission was. The red strip was still in my hands, the fabric twisting with my nervous energy. It wrapped around the fingers on my left hand, binding them. I released them again to wind the fabric back the other way. Several passes left reddened indents to crown my knuckles before Jonathan responded, "You may not have a choice. Major DeForest ordered you accompany us."

"He *ordered* you to take me with you?"

"Not in so many words. The major makes his commands known without stating them outright."

"Do you have to take his orders? Or just this general's you keep referring to?" I wondered which general he reported to. There were several: Phillip Schuyler, the Marquis de Lafayette, and even—before his betrayal—Benedict Arnold.

Jonathan's thoughts weighed on his tense shoulders and expression before he answered, "The general's instructions override any conflicting orders given by Major DeForest. We are not one of his number, although we assist him and his men."

"You and Alexander?"

"Captain Brott, correct. And now, you."

"Jonathan, it's not like I don't want to help—"

He nodded. "No woman should be forced to do what is asked of you."

"Women can be soldiers. Plenty of them are. I'm just not one of them!" I collapsed onto my cot and gave in to feeling lost at sea again. "I have to get home."

He gave a small, sympathetic smile, then grew flustered when his mouth opened and closed with nothing said. Turning to his trunk, he withdrew a key, suspended around his neck, from where it was hidden under his shirt. The cherrywood box was retrieved from its confines. An extended accompaniment composed of the camp's daily pursuits filled the prolonged silence in the tent. Jonathan stood, leaning over his desk, hands pressed on either side of the box, neither opening it or moving.

"We shall leave you here," he decided. "Let us hope none take notice."

I was stunned. "You're talking about disobeying orders."

"I see no alternative. I will not force you to assist us if you do not wish it."

Oh hell.

What was I supposed to do? I didn't want to go off on the *Mission: Impossible* the guys were planning. But I was also afraid of what would happen if I was left behind. Trying to manage on my own in Jonathan's world was difficult beyond reason, not to mention what if we lost track of one another? It wasn't like I could message him to ask for updates on his whereabouts.

But damn it, to risk being discovered by Major DeForest. It could destroy the impression we'd left with him about my also being an agent of the unnamed general. What would the major do to me if he *did* find me? To Jonathan? We'd already established disobedience was grounds for flogging.

Jonathan's voice startled me. "Take heart. We shall not leave until morning. I will be here to protect you through the night."

"No." I jumped up to face him. He was making decisions based on my being part of the equation. I couldn't let him. For the future's sake—my son's sake—I couldn't let him. "I'm sorry. You need to forget I'm here. Forget me. Do whatever it is you'd do if I wasn't here."

"But you are here," he said simply.

"I don't want you choosing because of me."

"I vowed to protect you. I have to take you into account."

"No! I… I release you from your promise."

Oh fuck, no. What did I do?

What chance of survival did I have without Jonathan's promise to get me home? Only he knew where he'd found me and how to get back there. But I couldn't allow history to change because of me.

He remained quiet. At his deep exhalation, I opened my eyes to see his face settle into the decision he'd made. He surprised me by taking my hands in his.

Something passed between us. Like an electric spark without the sting. Instead of it repelling me, though, I was drawn in. As, it seemed, was he.

"I shall honor my vow, Miss Moore. My assistance and protection are yours. If it gives you any comfort, then know this. Whilst I do believe you would have been useful to us, I would rather wait until tomorrow morning when Major DeForest will spare us the number needed for our success."

His fingers trailed along the backs of my hands as he withdrew, taking the red fabric with them. The sensation of his touch lingered, and somehow, even though it didn't last, relief—like finding a memento I'd thought lost—lightened the worries and fears burdening me.

Jonathan stepped outside. When he returned, his hands were empty.

"You have strength in you," he said, addressing my curious stare. "You have proven yourself more than capable."

"You obviously haven't been paying attention," I scoffed.

"Begging your pardon, madam, but it is *you* that has not been paying attention."

Chapter Fourteen

I didn't see much of Jonathan until dusk. The only request I made, before leaving him sole possession of the tent, was to avoid mentioning me in whatever he was writing. Although I don't think his mind returned to whether I was a British spy, he paused in his careful staging of inkwell, paper, and quill to give his full attention to me and ask why.

A little verbal fumbling of my own followed. The best reply I had was, "I shouldn't be interfering in your affairs," then I hightailed it out of there before things got weird in Awkwardville.

The red fabric floating in the breeze stalled my hasty retreat. He'd returned it to its post on the tent's cord. It was a touching gesture that tickled in my chest. Thanking Jonathan would have to wait, though, at least until after I'd concocted a better excuse for why he shouldn't tell his superior officers about me. Lingering could only invite disaster.

Next came the problem of what to do with myself. Circle the camp to get the lay of the land? Maybe learn about what life was like there. My father would've been in seventh heaven. Of course, he'd want to poke his head into every nook and cranny and explore each living artifact in microscopic detail.

Suspicious-looking much? Never, right?

Thoughts of home opened a painful rending in the middle of my chest. How had Evan managed the last few nights without me? I was supposed to pick up Good Dreams Spray. We were running low. It was just linen spray. Apple Cinnamon. Sometimes Candy Cane for the holidays. To Evan, each fragrant spritz was magic loosed to ward against monsters, bad dreams, and even coyotes. Something my mother did for me as a kid.

What would Justin tell him? Sentiment and childish things weren't worth much in his books.

But what if the twenty-first century wasn't carrying on without me? What if, instead, it was waiting? Holding a place for me in the lineup of time?

Smearing away tears with my palm, I vowed to hold on to my theory of a temporal pause and keep it close. I had to survive first before I could worry about making up for everything I was missing with my son.

Exploring the camp promised to be a worthy distraction. *If* I was careful not to look suspicious to those who might be inclined to think of me as the enemy. Friend Alexander was a worthy contender. Charming man.

How did someone like Jonathan befriend someone like Alexander? It wasn't like he didn't make valid points. I had no business going on a dangerous mission with them. It was the rudeness in his refusal that galled me. What had I done to rub him the wrong way?

Speak of the man.

Alexander was saddling a pale-yellow horse at the opposite end of Forest Thoroughfare, securing the strap from under the horse's belly. The black tricorn hat crowning his head meant he was getting ready to leave.

Oh, what the hell? Since Jonathan had decided they could wait until morning only moments earlier, as Alexander had urged, I figured I'd pay him the courtesy of letting him in on Jonathan's decision. Maybe it would help ease whatever ill-will lay between us.

Hope can be flighty, and mine threatened to migrate to more hospitable climes. I refused to be deterred by Alexander's condescending glare as I approached or subsequent refusal to acknowledge me, though his flinging his leather bag off his shoulder at an angle calculated to thwack my arm with it on its way to the saddle came close to convincing me.

On my third attempt to address him—I did call him Captain Brott and not Alexander—he turned on me with a, "What?"

"I was talking to Captain Wythe. He agreed your plan of leaving in the morning was best." There, see? I could be political.

"Did he now? And he has sent you as his little messenger?"

"No, but—"

"Exactly," he answered with full satisfaction at having won the day.

Except he lost me. "What?"

"You are not one of us."

"Like it was in doubt." Though *what* he'd picked up on regarding our differences was unclear. Was it the fact I wasn't a local? Or did he suspect something more serious?

"It is no concern of yours what we do," he said.

"Agree with you there," I responded. The slap of the leather strap to accentuate his feelings on the subject was… a touch. "Nice" not being the word choice I'd go with. "Hey, I'm just trying to be helpful. I saw you prepping your horse and thought I could save you some time."

Not willing to let me have the final word, he interrupted my dramatic exit by calling after me, "You should leave."

I swung back on him. "Believe me, I'd love to."

"It is within your power. Go."

"Now, what would you know about that?" We glared at one another. Did he know something about my kidnapping? Getting nowhere, I focused on regaining control of the conversation. "Captain Brott, I don't know how long I am going to be staying here. Hopefully not long—"

"Truer words have ne'er been spoken."

Frustration was gaining ground on me. I bit down an angry retort and tried to stay the course. "We may be seeing each other for a bit. You don't like me? Fine. But don't you think for…" I almost called him Jonathan again but caught myself. "…Captain Wythe's sake, we might call a truce and at least be civil to one another?"

"That would imply you are to be tolerated."

"I just want to go home. Captain Wythe is helping me."

Why is this so painful?

"You may have bewitched my friend, but it shall be undone." Not knowing whether Alexander's accusation of witchcraft was sincere, I found myself dumbstruck. "Burden someone else." Having spat his final blow at me, he flung himself onto his horse, then galloped off into the woods.

I stared after the ass and his horse long after they disappeared. There was no chance of anyone mistaking my subsequent meanderings for information gathering because the world around me was just background noise to my agitated mind. Nothing registered, other than my boots as they trudged through the trampled weeds and tripped over the occasional root bursting through the campground at random intervals.

How had things with Alexander gone so wrong? Sure. I was one more mission Jonathan didn't need. Understandable. I could maybe even respect his defense of his friend for it. If he wasn't such an unbelievable jackhole! The man could be the literal death of me if he decided to escalate the whole bewitching Jonathan thing to the next level.

This adventure was rating a one-star and dropping.

Chapter Fifteen

Someone grabbed my elbow. I swung around, ready to clock my attacker with my free hand. Fortune smiled on the parties involved, though, and I recognized who it was before my fist connected so I could pull the punch. Otherwise, it would've been *me* administering first aid to the ringing bell of Doctor Cole.

"Sorry." Deflated, I dropped my stance.

A chuckle off to the side highlighted how the almost scuffle had drawn a small audience of onlookers, including the chuckling Wall. Nice to know I amused someone.

"No harm done," the doctor replied, though he said it a step farther away from me than before. Only for a moment. "You are troubled."

He returned to holding my elbow, worry in his drawn expression despite my attempt to self-defense his face with my fist. My head jiggled yes, and my lip quivered without my meaning to. Traitors.

"Come with me." He gestured toward the massive tent he appeared to call home. The chair given to his testy admirer at lunch was resituated to where he could guide me to sitting in better light. "Captain Wythe informed me of your injuries," he reminded me with an inclination of his head. "Have I your permission to examine you?"

Amber flecks caught amid a jade-green sea—

"Mistress Moore?"

I gestured to my throat in response. A bent knuckle lifted my chin, exposing the cut on my throat. Eyebrows furrowed, he paused at my jawline, however. His fingers grazed an irritated spot. The Mascara Incident. Once resigned his services could do nothing there, he moved onward, a displeased sigh rumbling in his chest. His exploratory prodding of the area around the knife wound inspired a sharp intake of breath from me. The doctor checked to see if I was okay.

"Do you have any rubbing alcohol?" I asked.

"You wish to rub…?"

"Yeah, alcohol," I said the word along with him. "To clean the wound."

"The wound appears to be clean." He tilted his head, searching below my chin. "A scab has formed. There will be discomfort for a few days more."

There wasn't any heat coming from the area when I raised my own fingers to the spot. "Is it puffy or radiating red from the scab?" I asked, wanting to be sure since mirrors were in short supply.

"Radiating red…?" he repeated. His head cocked to the side again as he checked. "No. You are familiar with healing?"

"A little." Thank goodness the cut hadn't become infected.

"Were you injured elsewhere?"

"Nothing major."

"Then, I have your permission to examine you further?"

I shrugged. "If it makes you feel better."

"I had rather hoped to see you feeling better." He leaned in, a friendly smile to encourage me.

I'll say this: Doctor Cole was thorough. Having received my consent, he studied me piece by piece, moving with the precision necessary to conduct actual surgery. Asking if my fingers were paining me, he cradled my right hand while he tested them between his thumb and forefinger. The increasing ache he drew out of the joints—the worst from my little finger—had me straightening in my chair. I'd accepted the soreness as the natural aftermath of Round One with the Eighteenth and never bothered looking. An actual examination showed my pinky was red and swollen.

Sensei would kick my ass if he knew I'd thrown a bad punch.

The doctor made some passing comment about my having a high tolerance for pain. His grumbling didn't make it seem like he was impressed. As if to test me, he continued meddling with the aching finger before informing me he didn't believe anything was broken. There might be a reason Ph.D. types say the treatment was worse than the disease. My eyes were watering.

Once finished, his professional demeanor dropped, and the man I'd laughed with over lunch returned. A kind smile melted away the intense, jade stare. He gave my arm a reassuring squeeze before disappearing into the tent at my back.

With the obligation to avoid disrupting history, I sat and allowed the past to unfold through the ebb and flow of the daily workings of the people around me. At one point, Jonathan hurried by in the distance, guided by his own pressing concerns. I had to resist the temptation to jog after him and offer to help.

A group of young women crossed in front of me, each carrying an impressive collection of firewood. They separated, going their own way with a nod goodbye and a bubbling of laughter. One woman slowed to admire a man seated on the ground. A stray, dark curl peeked out to play along the back of her neck from the colorful fabric wound around her hair and up, under her straw hat. She was pretty.

The recipient of her attention paused in cleaning a musket to grin at her. Extracting a metal brush from its end, he laid it in the grass alongside the weapon and rose from his spot to receive her collection. She smoothed an apron the color of buttercups along her thighs, wiping her hands as she did, while he deposited the firewood near the entrance of his tent. The man mirrored her actions, dusting his hands across the sides of his pants before reaching around her head to pull the woman in for a lengthy kiss. She laughed at his maneuver, melting into him.

It was heartening to witness something familiar and undeniably timeless. Two people who loved one another. I found a random stone by my feet to study instead, giving them the privacy they deserved. Never had I felt so alone in a place filled with so many.

Doctor Cole reappeared at my side. They'd married before the year's campaign, he shared. When her parents learned of the young man's plan to enlist, they moved up the wedding with their blessing.

"Tea," he said, in answer to my blank stare at the tin mug he was handing me. A meaningful smile accompanied his whispering, "She would have followed him anywhere. Wedding or no."

The first sip was too hot to drink. The tea, although weak, still did the job of soothing me. I wrapped my hands around the mug, grateful for its warmth.

The doctor returned to his spot, kneeling in front of me. "Mistress Moore."

"Savvy," I corrected him. "It's what my friends call me."

"Savvy. Savannah." He compared the names, rolling them around in his mouth, an apparent thought-filled habit of his. "I like it."

"Thanks."

"Savvy, you journey with Captain Wythe. Do I understand your situation correctly?" I was slow to respond. His easy acceptance of using my nickname was unexpected. "If he has abused you or violated you, arrangements can be made for your protection. Such conduct is not tolerated by the militia."

I must've looked worse than I thought. Since it was Jonathan who'd cut my throat—albeit not seriously—and bruised my jaw, Doctor Cole's concerns weren't unwarranted.

"He isn't hurting me," I reassured him.

The truth was, I liked Jonathan. He might be temperamental, but if one considered what *I'd* endured over the previous few days was a mere fraction of what *Jonathan* must've experienced and had weighing on him, then a little stress-induced temperamentality could be forgiven. Goodness knows, the promises he'd made to help me weren't lightly given or simple ones to keep. Besides, he was kind and contained what I suspected to be a fount of humor begging to break past his reserved exterior.

But there was something else I'd yet to put my finger on. Something drew me to him, even though he was only a step beyond being a stranger. Different from a romantic attraction. Okay, it may've played a part, too. Only a small part. Jonathan was good-looking, best seen when his laughter chased away the frequent worry creasing the ridge between his brows. This thing was… almost physical, in a way I'd never experienced before and couldn't explain.

"Savvy?"

"You're not drinking," I said.

Doctor Cole smiled. "May I have the honor of joining you?"

"I don't want to keep you from your work," I backtracked the unintentional invitation.

"I should be grateful for the respite."

It would've been safer to push him away, but I was lonely, and sitting with the doctor—with his familiar green eyes looking out for me—felt a little bit like home. I found myself saying yes and thanking him. He smiled again, then armed himself with his own mug and second chair from inside the tent. Set a respectable distance apart, we sat, passively watching the activity around us.

"I hope I have not offended you," he said. "The tea. I cannot seem to acquire the taste for coffee."

"Why would tea be offensive?"

"You are not from America." He nodded to himself. "I suppose it has a different meaning for you. Drinking tea marks one as a royalist. Though I assure you, I am not one of those. I adhere to the boycott of other English goods. You see, it has become fashionable to drink coffee instead."

I buried my head in my cup. "You're lucky."

"Lucky? How?"

"You're better off without it. Coffee, I mean. I'm addicted to the stuff." An exchange of smiles passed between us.

The second sip was cooler, though just as weak. I checked inside the mug. No teabag. Of course, there wouldn't be. Centuries too early for those. Doctor Cole answered my asking what kind of tea it was, naming some blend of oolong I'd never heard of, then apologized for its watery quality. "This is the last of the brick, I fear. I have no other." Another example of what happens when supplies run short. I hoped bullets weren't in short supply.

He leaned forward to rest his arms along his legs and swirled the contents of his mug while he commented on the temporary citizens of the looming woods surrounding us. Sharing their names and connections to each other, he knew pretty much everyone. A whole catalogue was maintained in his mind of interesting details about their lives. He was the camp's living memory.

Sometimes, we just sat in companionable silence. I liked how he never pushed me to talk when I fell quiet, my thoughts trailing after the daily routine of those born centuries apart from me. If she was right about nothing else, the woman from the lunch line was correct in admiring the doctor. He had a gentle, pleasant way about him, and if he had half the skill to match his bedside manner, it meant he was a fantastic doctor. Goodness knows, he was easy on the eyes.

"What is it?" He laughed.

My face burned at him noticing the amusement flirting across my lips with the preceding thought. I breathed a laugh myself, searching for a response.

Doctor Cole rose from his chair, looking out at the camp. I followed his gaze as he said, "Captain Wythe. I took the liberty of examining Mistress Savvy. The wound on her throat is healing well. There is some swelling and discoloration on her right hand, however."

Jonathan turned to me. "What has happened?"

"From the soldiers," I told him.

"Show me." He held out a hand to receive mine.

The same magnetic spark from before danced on my skin when my fingertips alighted onto his palm. I tried to catch his eyes to see if he felt it, too, but he avoided looking at me, keeping his focus on my fingers. Taking my lead from him, I carried on by showing him both hands, allowing him to compare the two, and outlining the damage to the expanse of my pinkie.

"What is to be done?" he asked. The worrying crease returned, though he didn't demonstrate an overwhelming urge to prod the injury like the doctor. A full three hundred, sixty-degree review in slow-mo was sufficient.

"The bones are sound," Doctor Cole replied. "There is not much to be done, though she should avoid use of the hand for a time."

I groaned at the recommendation. I already had plenty of nothing to do while everyone else bustled around me. Jonathan sympathized, his expression softening despite his obvious concern about the state of my fingers.

"I'll soak my hand in the stream a couple of times. It's cold enough. It'll help reduce the swelling."

His thumb drifted along the length of my forefinger. The doctor, meanwhile, repeated my prescription to himself and nodded in approval. Jonathan took in the exchange without comment and released my hand.

"There is also bruising across her jawline from misuse," Doctor Cole continued. His tone lacked an outright accusation, but he scrutinized Jonathan's reaction as he relayed the last of his medical findings.

My worthy protector didn't offer the doctor any satisfaction for his trouble. He searched my eyes for permission before presuming to examine my face. His shoulders relaxed a fraction at my nodded assent, the only evidence he was aware of the cause of my injury. Placing the tips of his fingers under my chin to guide my head, he reviewed the marks a section at a time, assessing whether he still had permission to touch me in between.

Again, if the doctor caught the unspoken confession, he gave no indication. I made a mental note to never play the Eighteenth's version of poker with either of them.

"I won't be soaking my head in the stream, however," I joked. Both men offered a hint of a smile, perhaps out of courtesy because neither's expression registered their being amused.

"What of the lady's missing memories?" Jonathan asked, turning back to the doctor.

"Definitely not soaking my head in the stream." My efforts to distract them earned me a thorough ignoring by both men. Never mind *my* being the subject of the discussion, which morphed into supposing whether I'd hit my head. The doctor asked Jonathan if he could examine me. "I'm fine," I insisted.

"She was knocked to the ground and rendered unconscious." Jonathan steamrolled over me.

"Where was she struck?" Doctor Cole asked him, scanning my hairline and also neglecting to address the conversation to me.

"I am not certain. Mayhaps the back."

"Okay, guys, calm down. First, I was not struck on the head." I directed my initial point to the doctor. "Second, I didn't lose consciousness right away," I corrected Jonathan. "Because third, we both continued fighting, remember?"

"Though Captain Wythe did carry you into the camp," Doctor Cole said.

Oh good, I exist again.

"It's called fainting. I fainted," I countered the doctor. "I can't believe I just admitted… Uh, no." I generously donated several more noes to the cause as they closed in. I had a more-than-sneaking suspicion they were contemplating holding me down so the doctor could paw through my hair.

"We are concerned for your well-being," Jonathan said.

"Yeah, I know."

"Please allow Doctor Cole to examine you." he persisted.

"No. Thank you."

"Why do you protest?"

"I don't want to be man-handled, for starters." They had enough good manners to look embarrassed at my accusation. Neither was placated, though.

"Savvy—"

"Miss Moore—"

They'd addressed me at the same time. Jonathan's brow furrowed at the doctor's second use of my nickname. Doctor Cole gave the male-dominance floor to Jonathan, waving a hand for him to proceed.

He did, saying, "What if you have suffered an injury to your head? Do you not wish to know the cause of your missing memories?"

"Memories get repressed for a reason," I explained, since the doctor had intimated that psychology resided more on a philosophical spectrum in his century than that of every day medical science.

"Do you not want them to be restored?"

"No!"

We were left dumbfounded, as if actual raw sewage had spewed from my mouth instead of brain garbage. I'd invented the lie about missing memories to explain away why I couldn't tell anyone where I was from. It should've been just that. A lie. Whatever magical event or supernatural phenomenon took place in those woods, they flung me back in time. The end, no more. Off to bed, the tale was done. I wasn't willing to entertain the possibility of my mind keeping something more serious from me. The notion was terrifying.

Both men reacted to my distress and paused in their onslaught.

"You remind me of my sister," Doctor Cole said, easing us from the reprieve. "She is equally stubborn."

Jonathan felt the need to agree with the doctor's description of me, though his expression grew wary. The ball was back in my court.

"Well, I'm sure your sister loves being remembered for her stubbornness," I said with quiet sarcasm.

"She has other admirable qualities." Doctor Cole smiled.

"Admirable?"

"Please, Miss Moore," Jonathan interrupted the friendly exchange. "It would relieve me to know that you were not harmed further."

If I persisted, I imagine Jonathan would've accepted my resistance and dropped the subject. However, the other truth staring me in the face was he'd asked little of me in return for his promises. It would be heartless to deny he'd already faced some backlash for sharing his tent with a woman. A serious violation of the Colonies' social mores. Alexander was living proof. As, likely, was Major DeForest.

I relented.

Jonathan was a relentless supervisor, hovering while the doctor searched my scalp for trouble. Self-conscious from the sensation of the doctor's fingers combing through my unwashed hair, I was restless in the chair. What I wouldn't have given for a shower.

Multiple admonitions to sit up later, the doctor pronounced me whole except for a small bump on the back of my head. Since the other bumps and cuts and bruises and scratches and whatever else were from the fight as well—because they couldn't have come from anywhere else—what was one more? My latest mantra to keep the new worry about repressed memories at bay.

The men responded to my blasé attitude with a quiet grumble from one and a shake of the head from the other, but they didn't challenge me. Watching the concern cross their respective faces, I was relieved to know at least two people cared about my well-being in those backward circumstances.

With a final prognosis of a recurring case of Life—notwithstanding the side effect of Mild Stress—and my expressed gratitude given in return, Jonathan guided us away from the doctor's tent, past Center Square, drawing us behind the row closest to the woods, where no one would see or hear us. He shifted his weight back and forth as he struggled to find the words he was looking for, blushing about something.

Avoiding my inquisitive expression, he said, "I am truly sorry," indicating with a finger to the place on his own jawline corresponding to where he'd bruised me on mine. "I vow it shall never happen again."

"Thank you." I appreciated him acknowledging his culpability, but when he was able to look at me, I said, “No, it won’t.”

He bowed his head, admiration present in his subtle smile. Our firm hands-off policy established, he gestured for me to lead the way back into camp.

Chapter Sixteen

Another fiery sunset burned along the horizon. The camp's inhabitants packed away their daily routine and settled into the ritual of getting dinner and circling the various, open fires.

Jonathan wanted to find Alexander. He was surprised to learn I'd seen his proverbial comrade-in-arms and even spoke with ole' Alex long enough to tell him about the change in plans to a morning departure before he left by horseback. Jonathan digested the news and swallowed whatever other emotions had been brought up. Because something troubled him, judging by the wide-eyed search of Tent City.

He stated, "Even so, Alexander should have returned by now," and took off in the direction of Alexander's temporary residence, leaving me to puppy-dog after since I'd need Jonathan's help to get dinner for the foreseeable future. A repeat performance of the lunch debacle with the cook wasn't my idea of a good appetizer.

His friend's missing horse was waved off as being hitched somewhere else, and he barged into Alexander's tent to find a scruffy tentmate—only slightly more clothed than his companion of the female variety—who confirmed in brisk terms what I'd said.

Jonathan hurried back to my side, perplexed, scanning the vicinity; his knuckles white as they gripped his knife's hilt, cheeks flaming red.

I wondered why he seemed lost without the arrogant Alexander. "Are you okay?"

"Why should he not tell me?" was his only reply.

"Maybe he'll turn up later."

"It grows dark."

"Did you want to go look for him?" I asked, uncertain.

"To what end? I know not in which direction he went." When I pointed out the path I'd seen his truant buddy take through the woods, Jonathan remarked to himself, mystified, "He went into town."

The natural question of, "What town?" fizzled on my lips. What did it matter? We were downstate, far from the ancestral equivalent of my hometown. The answer to the only mystery I should've cared about lay on the hillside in the woods where Jonathan and I met. That was the only *where* that mattered, I reminded myself.

Having rekindled the flames in his cheeks when he glanced toward Alexander's tent, Jonathan brooded with hands on his hips, chastising his boots with drawn brows. When he raised his head in the direction of the unknown town again, something else crossed his face, and a different worry distracted him.

Maybe I wasn't the one folks should question about being a spy.

I forced myself to dismiss the idea. I hadn't been there long enough to draw such a conclusion and shouldn't be petty by voicing such a damning suggestion about Alexander just because the guy was a dick. I also didn't want to subconsciously look for ways to prove the inadvertent theory, which might force me to a crossroad where I'd have to decide whether I should disclose what I learned. Such a revelation could upset history by uncovering a spy never meant to be discovered. The opposite choice would mean keeping it a secret from Jonathan, which reeked of injustice. He'd saved my life and volunteered to protect me, which merited some…

I wondered at my allegiance to Jonathan, concerned I was already too invested in the lives of people I never, by all rights, should've met.

He broke from our respective meditations first. "The light fades. He is like to stay the night."

"Which disrupts your plans."

"Aye." He sighed.

Well, it explained some of the anxiety. Something told me there was more to it, though.

He revisited the tentmate by calling through the barrier of the tent canvas, for decorum's sake, rather than interrupting the crescendoing *pas-de-deux* in-person to ask when Alexander was due back. The volume used by the man, who panted his ignorant response in a staccato rhythm, drew nearby snickers. Jonathan bolted down Forrest Thoroughfare, displeased.

"Do you know where he's staying?" I raced after him. Another aye was let loose. "We could go get him," I suggested.

He jerked to a stop. The desire to agree was clear in his hopeful expression, but then his face darkened as he reviewed my jaw, then neck, then borrowed clothes. The weight of his resignation when he said, "Nay," dragged on his body as well as his spirit.

As much as it bothered me that my presence was the reason for his decision to stay, I was secretly relieved when he declined my offer to hang out with the doctor so he could go alone. At least, I hoped he didn't see the relief. I followed as far as his tent's entrance but elected not to go in with him.

Somewhere, someone piped a quirky tune on a flute or a fife. Voices talking and laughing blended into the mix. Riding the cold evening breeze, woodsmoke and cooking smells warmed the camp and chased off the baser odors of sunbaked horse manure and filth. Why wasn't anyone concerned about giving away our location with all the happy noise and firelight?

Scanning the darkened trees, I shivered. It felt like something was watching from a distance. Waiting. The call of company, even if only as an outside observer, and the promise of food made the risk understandable.

There was a different cook on ladle duty. Same dish as lunch, I was disappointed to discover, only thinner. Young laughter caught my attention as I waited. One of the major's teens was teasing the other, whooping about a letter the recipient held away from him. The boy whipped it closed to shove it into a fur-covered bag slung across his chest, trying to avoid his friend's grabbing hands and kissy noises. His face, a deep red, matched his auburn locks. The first scooped him up and dragged him, arm in arm, toward another station dealing mugs of rum.

The evening cook was much more congenial and laughed at the boys as only a more senior compatriot can. He accepted my explanation of being in the camp with Captain Wythe and asked if I was planning to bring the captain his supper. I wasn't sure what Jonathan's plans were, but since I hadn't seen him stop once to eat, I said yes.

One serving was twice the size of the other and contained a heartier quantity of beans. An indignant gripe burned on my tongue, except the history lessons reached the front of my brain before I could embarrass myself. Camp followers were given half rations.

Suck.

The Red Cloth of Truce made it a breeze to find Jonathan's tent, though I paused and wondered for the first time whether it threatened our safety to stand out from the rest. Deciding I had enough to worry about—he wouldn't have returned it to the tent's ropes if it did—I elbowed the flap open and accomplished the extraordinary feat of passing through without smearing the entrance with our dinner.

A sheath of paper was stretched open on the desk, held in place by an inkwell and a sizeable penknife. It was empty of any news or other markings. A straw-colored candle in a clay holder burned with a less-than-pleasant odor emanating from the dripping wax. A true indulgence for a camp whose supplies were overdue. But Jonathan wasn't at his desk. He sat on his cot with his head in his hands and didn't seem to register my entrance.

"You okay?"

"Miss Moore! Oh, here." Roused from his contemplation, he noticed the food in my bare hands and stood, scanning our surroundings several times before his attention landed on the foot of his cot.

The key was withdrawn from its hiding place under his shirt, which—with a soundless twist—unlocked his trunk, where he retrieved another key lacking any attachments. This he used, after moving the wad of filthy work clothes to the floor and a little fiddling with the mechanism, to open the trunk at the end of my cot.

It was stuffed full, as if a lifetime was crammed inside. Jonathan located a wooden bowl amid the compressed wardrobe and held it out to me. When I went to add the second trencher, he grabbed it from my hands, trading the bowl for the bread, and declined my offer to share.

"But you gave me the bigger piece."

"Nonsense." He shushed me and shoved a portion into his mouth before I could insist on swapping servings.

The maneuver of sealing the trunk and ignoring my telling him he didn't need to return my clothes to its surface was masterfully performed while balancing the trencher and its soupy topping in one hand, all without spilling. He didn't know what to do with the second key and resolved the question by leaving it on his desk.

"Thank you for bringing this," he said, toasting me with his dinner.

"It's the least I can do." I shook my head, amused yet resigned.

"Truth be told, madam, the least you could have done would have been nothing."

I wasn't sure if he was serious or not but decided to go with not and see what happened. "Oh, well, it's nice to know I'm improving in my usefulness."

He settled onto his cot with a brief smile, leaving me to return to my earlier spot, near mine. "Here now, you cannot sit on the floor."

"Sure, I can. I just did."

He rose and dragged the chair away from his desk. "Sit. I insist."

"Not going to happen," I teased and dug into my dinner. His

body waltzed in place while he was jostled between being flabbergasted, amused, and subsequently torn. "You don't have to sit on the floor because I am," I reassured him. It was obvious from his scrunched-up nose how repugnant the act was to him.

"Could you not sit on your cot?"

"Nah, I'm good."

"Nay, madam. You are incorrigible," he said, though not unkindly, and lowered himself to the ground. He rocked side-to-side several times, trying to settle himself. "This is not comfortable."

"If only you had a cot or a chair to sit on," I teased. "And please don't call me madam."

"Oh? Is it not appropriate?"

"No! No way," I said in mock offense.

A smile wanted to make itself known, breaking through his efforts to press his lips together. Another mouthful passed with him continuing to take me in, as if he were gathering measurements in his mind to paint my portrait. I leaned forward, fist resting under my chin in full Thinker mode, and returned his stare.

"I come to believe, lady, that you are a martyr. You slept soundly on yonder diabolical cot, untroubled by its wretched size. Wounded, yet you did not complain. None else could suffer such as this." The fledgling smile grew at his gesture to the hard, wooden floor beneath us.

I laughed, enjoying our banter. "You live in a camp. Are you telling me you've never sat on the ground before?"

"Not by choice." After a pause to take a bite and study me further, he asked, "Mistress…?"

"Just as bad."

"How *shall* I address you?"

"Savvy."

"Ah, once more. The inept term of friendship. Nay, I shall hold with 'Miss Moore.'"

"Inept?" The melodrama continued.

"Indeed." He grinned.

"Shows what you know… stick in the mud."

"It is a marvel how words masquerading as those of the English language flood the air around you, yet I wonder if you do speak the language." A volley of laughter passed between us.

Jonathan turned his head to his dinner and asked the slop, "Why is the term 'madam' displeasing to you?"

His innocent vocabulary begged for a good ribbing, but he'd played it off cool and casual, trying to hide his shyness about asking, I didn't have the heart. Of course, it didn't stop me from blurting out,

"Because a madam is the owner of a whorehouse."

He choked. Flying to his feet to plop the remains of his soggy bread on the desk, he thumped on his chest with his fist. I bit my lower lip, trying not to laugh. He wasn't in actual danger of choking—wide eyes and a paled complexion, his only real concern—so the sputtering was kind of funny.

When he regained control, he dropped to his knee and apologized, but I waved him off. He was spared having to ask the follow-up—the words tripping him up as he tried—because I explained, "A mistress is the woman a married man has sex with when he's cheating on his wife." A memory's sting came for a quick visit. Jonathan's face grew red with mortification, so I couldn't help adding, because his reaction was adorable, "Unless the woman is a madam, then she's just a whore."

His jaw bottomed out. I lost it, which became infectious. Soon Jonathan's rich laughter filled the tent, too, his head shaking in disbelief, and his shoulders bouncing in unison. When he regained his composure from our humorous digression, he concluded, "As you are unabashedly amused by this… disjoint in our communication, I shall assume this means that you are not offended."

"I'm not offended." I dried my cheeks with my sleeve, giggling. "Sorry."

"Hmm. Your apology is accepted in turn."

He retrieved his dinner from the desk, still humming with amusement. My serving gone, I stood and offered him the bowl. "You would not mind?" he asked.

"Of course not. It's yours."

Something in his lack of response while he took up residence on his cot made me wonder about its vacant companion and trunk. I reached through the tent's entrance to wipe the crumbs and dried sauce from my hands, sending them tumbling into the darkened grass outside, and debated whether to comment on it. My whole body spasmed, the pronounced shivering growing uncomfortable. The April chill was settling into my muscles, making my swollen finger ache. I flexed it a few times, which didn't help much.

Curiosity got the better of me. "Is it your only bowl?"

"I do not have one."

I yanked the blanket off my cot. "You don't have a bowl? Whose is—?"

"You are cold." He stood, abandoning his dinner, and began removing his coat.

"I'm fine."

"I insist." He continued to unbutton.

"Nope. I'm good." Flinging the blanket around my shoulders like an old-time movie villain, I hopped onto my cot.

It gave a startle as the legs threatened to collapse under me. We both held our breath. When the danger passed without me landing on the floor in a pile of cot rubble, I laughed at my own recklessness and laid down.

"Incorrigible." He shook his head with a smile. It fell when he disparaged himself, saying, "I have been a terrible host."

"You've been a little busy."

"A poor excuse. Please forgive me. Upon my return…" He nodded once. I did, as well, acknowledging the mission he didn't want to name aloud. "… I shall endeavor to do better."

I rolled onto my side, grateful the cot held its ground. "You're forgiven, but if you'd like to make it up to me, there are two things you could do for me." I trailed off, giving a playful smile.

He was game to play along some more. A smile mirrored mine. "Dare I ask?"

"You're the brave soldier."

"Mayhaps you were misled."

"Too bad. I'll tell you anyway." He chuckled. "One," I said, "you could get me home."

"Miss Moore, I—"

"I know." I waved off his serious reply. "Two: in the meantime, if it's possible to find me a coat, and maybe a gun, I'd appreciate it."

"I will do what I can, though you should not require any weapons."

"You do recall how we met, don't you?"

"Indeed." He cleared his throat. "Now that I am resolved to protect you, you need not take up arms again. Unless you wish it."

"Well, no. I don't wish it, but you kinda mentioned something about having to go run some errands…" I hoped the euphemism might ease the folding of his brow. He dipped his chin in response. "And leaving me here to defend myself and your…" I gave a dramatic sweep of my arm over the tent's paltry decor. "… many, many belongings. I think a gun is in order. Don't you?"

Jonathan's head dropped at the reference to how few possessions were present. I chided myself for being insensitive. I figured he owned a house somewhere, bountiful with all the trimmings and expensive knick-knacks and baubles a man with such perfect diction and proper attitude could desire. Alexander wouldn't have goaded him earlier if he was actually homeless, right? I glanced at his fingers. No ring.

He was good enough to shuffle the conversation along. “Mayhaps, we could both benefit from your assisting me with a task.”

“Sure. Okay.” My curiosity was piqued. I wondered how my asking for things could connect to doing him a favor.

Metal scraped the surface of his desk as Jonathan gathered a small object to give me. The key to the second trunk. “You would do me a great service if you would take possession of the chest and its contents. Whatever is in there is now yours.”

“Wait. What? Whose is it? Won’t they want their stuff back?”

“It was my task to dispose of it. Now, I give it to you.”

“But I don’t understand. Whose is it?”

Jonathan answered with no emotion, “He died.”

“Oh.” It took me a moment to recover. “What about the man’s family? Won’t they…?”

“He had none.”

“I’m sorry.”

“Most kind of you, but do not be. He was no friend of mine. Major DeForest insisted that the camp was too crowded for me to receive sole use of a tent, let alone an officer’s tent. In truth, I was shackled with the major’s spy. The man was ever in my way, trying to read my correspondence or sift through my belongings.”

His mild undertone of bitterness troubled me more than his words. Life and death. War not peace. Such was his reality and—considering the war was entering its fourth year—had been for some time, to the point where it passed by unnoticed. There was no romance or cinematic beauty to it. It was an ugly reality, trudging along until for someone like the anonymous tentmate, it ceased to exist.

“Do you think he left a coat?” I felt kind of mercenary asking. It sickened me. There’s a reason I never enlisted. People died in my world too. Sometimes by violence. Didn’t mean I wanted to see it happen in either world.

Jonathan had stopped giving me his full attention. The malodorous candle was tilting, creating a flood that was advancing on his paper. So, he didn’t notice my reservation during his rescue attempt of the page and answered thoughtlessly, “It was ruined when he was shot.”

And there it was.

There was little light left because the candle was coming to its own demise; the now-repugnant “task” more ominous in the shifting shadows from Jonathan’s efforts to clean his desk. I set the key on top of his trunk and sat back on my cot, trying to put as much distance between it and myself.

"Oh, Miss Moore."

Attracted by the sound, he crossed to kneel in front of me, sympathy in his eyes. We had a minor struggle, though there was no real fight in me, as Jonathan pressed the key into my palm. Both hands encircled my uninjured fist, locking the key inside, when he said, "Please do not trouble yourself. Others would help themselves to whatever they need in your place. This is simply the way of things."

I shook my head in resistance.

"If only I could offer you better." He sighed. "Believe me. I am in earnest when I say you would be doing me a kindness were you to allow me to give you this."

There was humility in his face. To refuse risked insulting him, as if I were ungrateful for the many compromises he was enduring because of me. I swallowed the sour taste in my mouth and nodded.

Satisfied by my assurance I was okay, he brushed his thumb across my knuckles before stepping away. From his own trunk, he retrieved yet another handkerchief—the man was made of them—and drew from its confines a robin's egg blue ribbon. It looked like silk.

Another sigh caught in Jonathan's chest as he admired it with a sad expression, caressing the length of its delicate fibers. The refolded handkerchief was tucked into a pocket. But then the sadness was replaced by quiet resolve.

Focusing back on me, he asked for the key. The blue ribbon was woven through its eye and knotted closed, forming a necklace much like the one he wore. A moment passed before he offered it to me. "You would do well to keep this hidden."

I clutched the key in my hand, whispering, "Thanks."

He returned to dealing with the waxy pond on the desk's surface and announced how he would leave in but a moment so I might ready myself for the night. Since I had no pajamas, no make-up left to remove, and not even a toothbrush to my name, I declined and laid down. Rolling toward the tent's canvas to give Jonathan some privacy of his own, I closed my eyes for the evening just as I was.

Chapter Seventeen

Morning arrived with specters of frost drifting through camp. Even still curled in a tight ball on my cot, I felt their presence. Trying to unravel the blanket twisted underneath me so I could drag it over my head, I noticed a second blanket had been draped over my legs during the night. I checked Jonathan's cot to make sure he hadn't sacrificed his own—which he had—and was sleeping in nothing but his coat, which he wasn't, because he wasn't there.

A swell of voices carried from outside. From the sounds of it, Alexander had returned. Jonathan answered, no doubt discussing the final arrangements for their errand, as I preferred to think of it. Mission may've been a more appropriate word, but the danger and potential outcome of Jonathan facing such danger was something I was trying not to dwell on.

My boots had been removed for me and were waiting, side-by-side, at the foot of my cot. It'd been a long time since someone had looked out for me. I couldn't help but take a moment to revel in the tiny bit of comfort being cared for brought. Tucking the sensation away for a rainy day, I sat up to retrieve my boots, sending an object clattering to the wooden floor.

The key.

Ambivalence came for a visit. I showed it the door. I wasn't going to hurt Jonathan's feelings by refusing his gift. Taking possession of it didn't mean I had to use it.

The metal had absorbed the cold morning air.

It was intricate for a key to a soldier's trunk. The shaft was long and thin with decorative bands crowning the teeth. There were only two.

Together, they formed a square peninsula, the cut-out in the middle creating a cross in the hollow space.

I wondered who was sadly associated with the silk ribbon and whether seeing me wear it would bother Jonathan. With it wound around my neck, under my shirt to hide the key as he'd advised, the metal resting between my breasts was a firm reminder of winter's hold looming outside the confines of our tent.

The swelling in my little finger had gone down, due to the cold, but at the cost of my hand being stiff and sore. It made it difficult to slip my boots on. After a quick stretch to get my body moving, I folded Jonathan's blanket and returned it to his cot, a smile warming me.

Silly.

My own thread-weary excuse gathered around my shoulders, I hesitated at the tent's exit. My teeth were fuzzy, which meant my breath was less-than pleasant. Running a finger over them rated Bad Idea. It'd been an age since I'd washed my hands with municipal water and soap. A fresh set of clothes would've been nice too. Rummaging through the dead roommate's trunk, however, was unappealing, no matter how desperate I was. At least the whole camp population was in the same proverbial boat of old clothes and no showers.

As cold as the tent was, the open air stung even more. A deep shiver traversed the length of my body when it hit me. Skipping breakfast and jumping back in bed seemed like a reasonable alternative. Except the fires, and thereby any hope of getting warmer, required getting a move on.

Both men noticed me stamping my feet, bouncing my weight between them to try to warm up. Jonathan's face brightened, so I decided it might be safe to wander over. Having wished them both a good morning, I damn near died of shock from the absence of smart-ass retorts by Alexander, who graced me instead with a head nod of recognition. He then excused himself to finish his preparations.

"Someone had a good night," I observed.

Jonathan and I watched his receding back as he strode toward Camp Central. It was unintentional, but I'd leaned into him to make the aside and was finding it difficult to resist the continued warmth his body offered. He didn't move, instead giving a quiet hum. Worry crowded his face. A tinge of sadness too.

I touched my fingers to the back of his hand. "For all the good this does asking: are you okay?"

He looked at me for the first time since Alexander had walked away. The worry faded while Jonathan studied my features, my hair, the blanket stretched around my shoulders, then returned to my eyes. "Aye."

The corner of his mouth rose for a fraction of a second.

"You still leaving?" I asked, knowing full well he was. Jonathan mumbled an affirmative. "Do you have everything you need?"

"The major has held true to his word. The men are readying themselves now. He is always more receptive when it is Captain Brott who makes the request."

"Why? He's such an asshole." I then apologized for the slip.

"As you are here under my protection," Jonathan said, "you should be advised. There are many who believe me to be a spy."

"For… the good guys, right?"

"It is a matter of opinion, would not you agree?"

I lowered my voice. "You don't work for the British, do you? I mean, I won't give you away, if you do. I… It's not my business. I guess I just want to know what kind of danger I'm in."

"Forgive me. I should not have answered you in such a manner. All spies are detestable, even those who serve on the same side," he explained. "My name should grant you some protection. Only do not expect it to curry you any favor. Do you understand?"

"Yeah." Unexpected, not to mention unsettling as confessions go. I thought it was an empty snipe by DeForest. Captain and Major couldn't have just hated each other?

"Come. You are shivering, and I must prepare." Jonathan lighted his fingers on my elbow to invite me to go ahead of him. It was a relief to escape the frosty open air and return to our… *his* tent.

"What can I do?" I asked.

"You can avoid trouble whilst I am away."

"Ha ha. I was being serious."

"As was I." Damn it, he was. "It is a terrible thing to ask; nonetheless, if you would remain unseen, I would be grateful."

Remembering he was disobeying the major's direct order by leaving me behind was sobering. "I'll do my best."

"You have my thanks." He dipped his head to me. "Take heart, Miss Moore. Though there are no guarantees, it is safest for you here amongst the major's numbers."

Having made his record-shattering entry for World's Most Reassuring Remark—for which I was, at least a tiny bit, grateful—he busied himself with his trunk, surveying his supplies.

"Did you have breakfast?" I asked.

Though obviously absorbed with his preparations, he mumbled something about there being little time. An additional, sheathed dagger was removed and tossed onto his cot, followed by a rectangular pouch on a strap. The latter was situated across his chest, rather than cast aside, to sit on his hip. A quick look inside when he opened it to count its contents revealed paper cartridges of gunpowder for the pistol ever present at his side. It wasn't even half full.

"Why don't I get us some breakfast?" I suggested.

"We leave soon."

"You can take it with you."

"You expect me to eat while I ride?" he scoffed.

"I eat and drive all the time." Clutching the wheel and a power bar wasn't the same thing as handling a horse's reins and the latest from the pot, but I was getting antsy about his impending departure. "There must be something I can do."

"There is nothing."

"Something. Something, so I'm not constantly mooching off you."

"What, pray tell, is mooching?" he asked. The steady *schlick* of his knife being drawn across a rectangular stone distracted him.

"It means taking without giving anything in return."

Jonathan paused in his preparation, then separated blade from stone before meeting my anxious expression. He didn't speak. His face told me he understood and even sympathized with my predicament. Not only to my hurt pride, it was like he was staring right through me to expose the worry gnawing at me.

What will I do if he dies?

Soldiering on, I nodded toward the supplies on his cot. "Do what you need to. If you're still here when I come back with breakfast, it's yours."

"If I am not?" His knife dangled from the hand at his side, forgotten.

I was worrying him. Not where his focus should be. "You're going to be gone until dinner, right?"

"Miss Moore—"

"Jonathan." I didn't want to be placated. I didn't want to be pitied. I just… "More for me," I joked, but my heart wasn't in it.

"Such being the case," he said, "do not look for my return until after nightfall." His kindness caught in my chest.

"I wish you'd call me Savvy. It'd be nice to know I have a friend who…" I'd already gotten too close to him. He was right to keep some distance between us.

"Whatever my words," he replied, his voice hushed, "you shall not be forgotten."

His eyes…

The moment was too brief, then it passed, and we returned to our chosen tasks.

The bowl from dinner wasn't on Jonathan's desk. He caught me looking and directed me to where it was stationed on my trunk. I'm not sure what disturbed me more—his calling the trunk mine or his having undergone the entire process of removing my boots, tucking me in, washing the bowl somewhere not in our… *his* tent, and placing it on top of the trunk, done without disturbing me while I slept. If someone decided to march in in the middle of the night to murder us, I'd be dead long before I even stirred.

Jonathan finished with his preparations; the sharpened edge of the spare blade having met his approval. A messenger bag was in place along with the cartridge bag, one on either hip, their straps crossing his chest in an 'X.' He checked his pistol.

The should-be simple task of fetching breakfast intensified the assault on my nerves, and I hadn't even left yet. It also distracted Jonathan, whose process slowed every time our eyes caught. I retrieved the bowl and raced from the tent in search of food.

Damn. It hadn't gotten warmer.

Homing in on the first sizeable plume of smoke, I hurdled through the obstacle course of camp life toward a cooking mound. And damn some more. It was the cook from my last solo attempt. There were other food sources, but since I could hit as much static from someone I'd never met before, not to mention I didn't want to lose any more time searching for and risking a longer line, I decided to hope for the best.

The cook didn't acknowledge me as he smacked a serving of porridge into my bowl, at least until I mentioned getting breakfast for Captain Wythe, as well. He sniped at my single status, questioning what I planned to put it in. I had to admit I was otherwise empty-handed. Duty done—from his apparent perspective, anyways—he ushered me along, then ignored me when I asked whether there was bread or something portable to bring Jonathan.

The next man in line took his cue and circled around me, bowl first. I hesitated as my overwhelmed brain struggled with non-existent options since porridge was it and I lacked the means to carry a second serving. Frustrated, I hurried back.

Jonathan wasn't in the tent. Mixing with the morning bustle, his voice filtered through Forest Thoroughfare from Alexander's side of the tracks. I rushed to the far end in time to see him mount a black horse with starry-white sides. Alexander was already restless in his saddle, chomping at the bit more than his horse. The three uniformed men in green waiting with them looked unconcerned either way.

Jonathan's shoulders settled when our eyes connected. I didn't want him to leave. I also didn't dare delay him. I held my ground and returned his nod, trying to give him reassurance I didn't feel with a smile.

Alexander flashed a grimace at him and shouted, "Get up, now, afore Hell takes us all!" He spurred his horse through the tree line, with Jonathan and the other men galloping after, heading in the opposite direction of town. It wouldn't be a quick errand.

There I was, a lonely statue in a whirling scene of eighteenth-century productivity, foolishly clutching a wooden bowl smeared with a thin glop. It was only a camp follower's half ration. I couldn't even manage to get Jonathan provisions. Then again, I don't think either of us had much faith in my ability to help.

Recognizing that hurt until I forced myself to remember—I wasn't there to help. My mission was to stay out of the way of history until I could find the means to get home.

Chapter Eighteen

As soon as Jonathan rode off, everything shifted, and any illusion of security vanished. The wind whipped up—torn from its sleep with full fury—and pursued them down the path. A cloud of leaves chased after. Sunlight paled under the cover of dark clouds racing in. Scanning the woods, I felt the ominous watchfulness from the previous night creep closer, hovering along the camp's borders. My body shied away even before a voice inside me whispered, "Hide."

Our Red Flag of Truce was being lashed so violently by the onslaught of the wind, I started to check the knot but had to abandon it when my blanket was ripped off my shoulder. I snatched the wayward end, winding my torso underneath its frail enclosure, before the whole thing was lost. Voices from the camp broke apart on the rushing air. Their fractured shouts hurried after clothing and possessions being stolen from them.

The wind wasn't pacified by my efforts to escape. It tore at the tent's walls as I fled inside. The noise of the flax sheets, whipping in its fury, echoed in the enclosed space.

Within a heartbeat, the world stilled, and the canvas dropped, limp. Silence pervaded the camp, and the watchful presence made its move. It approached, as if pressure from the stormfront had amassed at the edge of the woods to single me out. It started at the area over Jonathan's cot. The linen pressed inward. Four indents in a semi-circle with a fifth to the side, reaching through the fabric. They dragged toward the corner, rutting a pathway around the post. A trail of frost broke across their wake.

I flung the bowl onto the desk, desperate to reach the tent flaps in time to yank them closed. Fumbling with the strips, I twisted them into a terrible knot I wasn't sure would hold.

The presence paused at the front corner, running a finger down the length of the post. A fingernail scraped in a quick *ziiip* away from the cloth as the presence continued circling. I crouched low, telling myself it was so I could reach the third tie at the bottom. It lingered right in front of me. Canvas, and nothing more, separated us. Ripples of frost seeped through the flimsy barrier, about mouth-height, as I wrenched the final tie shut, cutting off my sole source of light.

Trapped alone in the dark, with no way to defend myself, all I could do was tremble and wait. I was a child again, scared by a midnight thunderstorm. Only I didn't have the comfort of my father's arms to protect me from the darkness. Needles bristled on my skin, goose flesh creeping upward as a chill worked its way inside me.

I pursed my lips, forcing the air from my lungs. Drawing in a slow, deliberate breath, I focused on the pounding of my heart. The mounting panic attack threatened to unbalance the defensive position I took.

It waited.

I wish Jonathan was here.

As if in response, the air warmed, heat building from an unknown source to rival the iciness outside. It felt electric, snapping against my skin. When the presence didn't move, I allowed the blanket to slip from my shoulders. Shoving it under Jonathan's cot with my foot, I resituated myself to regain a defensive stance, unhindered.

My thoughts turned to Evan, and I found myself imagining his apple cinnamon linen spray. The sweetness as it'd burst into the air, chasing away his fears and bringing a dimple to his cheek as our bedtime ritual cheered him. Kisses on our faces and hands and hair. The way it'd trail with me through the rest of my nightly routine, long after the evening's pirate ship had sailed toward its next adventure and the covers of another storybook closed.

The presence fell back, retreating into the depths of the woods; the wind shouting after it. I relished the release of tension in my chest. As the trembling slowed, I vowed I would never let Evan run out of Good Dreams Spray. I never wanted him to be afraid of the dark. Like many promises made in the heat of the moment, it was a promise I'd failed to keep.

Chapter Nineteen

The violence of the storm outside eased, as did the fear it invoked. I opened my eyes and wondered if I'd fallen asleep. The air was freezing again. Maybe I'd gotten sick without realizing it, my body fluctuating between a fever-driven dream and reality. Or maybe my panic attacks had discovered new and terrible ways to torment me, reviving old childhood nightmares, thanks to my current, terrifying circumstances.

Leaning against Jonathan's cot, I reclaimed the bowl, hoping eating would take my mind off the sense of abandonment and residual fear. Nope. The contents weren't in the least appetizing; congealed porridge was better when it was warmer. I tried to imagine it hot. Steaming hot, with the sides of the bowl chasing away the frozen ache from my hands. Smooth and gooey, and perhaps with maple syrup. My imagination decided it didn't want to play along.

Some company and a friendly face were what I needed. There was the doctor, though the man literally dealt with life and death, and any distraction from his duties could have huge repercussions for what should've been my present, the distant future. The exact opposite of my *laissez-faire* mission regarding history's passage.

There was the possibility of finding a fire and people-watching… The last trouble Jonathan needed to rain down on him was word reaching the major.

Which brought me to the trunk. Dancing outside naked held more appeal. Still, I longed for something to pacify my pacing mind.

I reclaimed Jonathan's blanket, layering it under my own. The banal act alone, of letting the wool embrace me, helped soothe my fears.

I ignored the temptation to wonder why.

It let in a horrible draft, but I used his trunk to shove the hem of the canvas away from the wooden floor, at the back of the tent, where no one would notice something was amiss. The opening allowed a shaft of light to make its way inside. No one came to question the scrape of the second trunk being dragged to the center of the tent, either. As I withdrew the key from its hiding spot, my body heat radiated from the metal. I held it to my face, wishing the thing was a tiny furnace I could press against my skin. Instead, the metal cooled within moments.

The lid was smooth under my passing hands, covered like the rest of the trunk in a soft leather of a browning yellow. Brass tacks lined the edges and decorated the front panel, looping like garland on a Christmas tree. Steadying my hands against the front plate, I slid the key in. It took a little effort to figure out how far in it should go, but then the lock released with a satisfying click.

A bundle of clean, grayed cloth covered the contents. Wrapped inside were my afterwork clothes. Homesickness swelled in my chest, chased by the ghosts of the men I'd killed when I wore them last. I rewrapped them and chucked the whole thing under my cot. Out of sight, out of mind.

Continuing my survey of the trunk's stocks revealed… clothes. Linen shirts, matching pants. Several sets of what looked a little like women's bloomers, a fact which made me smirk. Spare pair of socks.

Hallelujah!

A cloak.

I tossed my blanket onto my cot—Jonathan's blanket was treated with more care—and briskly donned the heavy wool garment. Chocolate on the outside and lighter within, its hem brushed inches above my knees. A second layer draped from the shoulder to the base of my ribcage like a cape, and the entire thing clasped at the neck. I'd never seen anything more magnificent than the much-needed cloak.

Further in was a collection of random items of varying usefulness. A bone cup and a knife with a similar handle. Its wide, metal blade was kind of like a frosting spatula topped with a large coin soldered to the end. There was also a simple, tin box loaded with a fine, brown powder. The emanating fragrance had a nutmeg-like undertone. Snuff. The dead roommate had some money to his name.

Next… a wooden-handled straight razor and a brass canister of some sort. The canister was long and oval, with decorative ridges orbiting its center. After a little playing, the lid slid off, exposing two empty holes flanking a corked third one in the middle. A gentle shake told me it contained liquid. The smell of ink coming from the cork suggested it was a portable inkwell. The other holes were meant to hold spare quills, then.

Oddly, the trunk was devoid of paper. Unless you counted a copy of *The History of the Decline and Fall of the Roman Empire*. Not a lot of light reading there.

Only one other item lined the bottom. Another box carved from stormy-gray soapstone. A muscular horse, shown in an open gallop, raced along its side. Popping the box open revealed it wasn't hollow like I expected. Rather, it resembled a solid brick cleaved in half. Bored into the inner portion was a series of equally shaped bowls. When the two halves were placed back together, tiny holes led from one side of the exterior to the bowls hidden within. I jotted a mental note to ask Jonathan about it when he returned.

Something wasn't right about the trunk. I couldn't put my finger on what it was. Unlike the outside, the inside was bare, which meant the wooden frame of stacked boards was visible. The bottom, however, differed. It was one solid piece, the grain threading a courser pathway than the boards. Whatever the wood was, it'd drunk the paint. A deeper blue resided there.

Changing position to peer in at an angle did the trick. There was a decided space between the visible bottom and the ground. I ran my hand along the inside edge and was rewarded with a splinter for my trouble. As I yanked my hand away to inspect my finger, a bit of twine caught my eye. It was subtle, blending into the wood perfectly. Easy to miss if you were looking into the trunk from the front.

Pulling the twine revealed the false bottom for what it was. Three more treasures came to light, nestled in the secret compartment. A long, black leather wallet with a Continental dollar and multiple pieces of silver coins.

My father's love of history meant he collected a plethora of knick-knacks. For years, it revolved around the Jacobite Rising. One day, when I was eight, a package arrived. The door to his study remained shut for days while he was engrossed in its documents and other artifacts, including a legitimate Continental dollar. When he emerged, we learned the American Revolutionary War was his new obsession.

How he loved to pour over that coin, turning it around and around in his hands. I caught him in the act one day, his eyes watery. He called me into his study and pressed the coin into my hands, asking me what I felt.

"It's just a coin, Dad." I'd laughed at him. He smothered me with a fatherly bear hug before reclaiming it and letting me flee from the drudgery of another history lesson.

Even without a history buff in the family, it would've been hard *not* to recognize the coin because it was good enough to identify itself with the words "CONTINENTAL CURRENCY 1776" stamped into the metal. Tracing the path of the sun's rays toward the sundial and Ben Franklin's admonition to "MIND YOUR BUSINESS," I felt the memory of my father's arms wrapped around me.

The silver wasn't as recognizable. There were nine pieces in total. Truly. In pieces. Because none of the coins were whole. They were cut into halves or quarters, imperfect puzzle pieces that didn't align to form a whole. Some had numbers carved into them. Twos and fours. A small fortune, I hoped.

Also hidden in the compartment was a sheath of paper, folded inward from every side, top, and bottom. Its wax seal was broken, an emblem of a bee stamped into the hardened goo. The gentle wavering of the pages under its weight whispered their temptation to open it. It seemed like a sacrilege to read someone's private letter. But then again, wasn't this what my father's collected writings were? The correspondence, journals, and essays from our Founding Fathers.

No names. No locations, either, written anywhere in the scrawled lines. Worse, most of it didn't contain words but numbers in sets of three, separated by a period between each set. I threw the damn thing into the trunk. I *so* didn't want a piece of this action. Jonathan was closer than he realized when he described his former roommate as a spy.

Freaked out by the cloak-and-dagger stuff I'd stumbled on, I abandoned the final item without looking at it. Whatever it was, it was well-wrapped in linen.

I huddled by my cot, listening to the wind playing with the canvas. Somewhere off in the distance, a tree shed a branch, sending it crashing through remaining limbs to the ground. A much scarier sound when there was only a fabric roof for protection. Closing my eyes, I pulled the cloak tighter around me and waited for the manifestation of something driving the wind, but I was alone in the billowing darkness of the tent's canvas. Exploring the final hidden object was worth the distraction.

My fingers recognized the shape of the gun before I unwrapped the weapon to look at it. It was beautiful. If an inanimate object could inspire sensations, then my hands felt electric as I explored the piece. Gold inlay crowned the top of the barrels with a series of blooming flowers and dancing leaves. Even the wood itself, mahogany in color, was carved with scrollwork along the grip and boasted a gorgeous applique of vines and leaves encircling a sunburst of bright silver. The name *Canon Tordu* was painted in gold, parallel to the barrels' center line.

What surprised me most were the double barrels. Two triggers with matching firing mechanisms. I didn't think such a thing existed outside of bad, Saturday afternoon-type movies of swashbuckling pirates and French musketeers. There wasn't any ammunition. Gone, along with the previous owner.

Overall, I was pleased with my new treasures. The cloak was a worthy ally against the cold, and having a little money and a gun was reassuring. Someone would have to teach me how to use it. Pistols from the Eighteenth weren't supposed to be accurate at any distance, but something about this particular pistol made me confident it would fire faithfully. Plus, the extraneous stuff, like the straight razor, equaled currency in the form of bartering materials.

I tucked the money and pistol back in the hidden compartment, taking care to keep the twine from the false bottom positioned along the front ledge, in easy reach for those in the know about its existence. The coded letter was the only damper on my spirits. I knelt closer to the sliver of light leaking in from under tent's canvas.

What to do with it? If I hid it and Jonathan learned about it later, not only would he be justified—from the eighteenth century's perspective—for being angry with me but also for accusing me of collaborating with the enemy. On the other hand, just because turning over the letter could mean giving valuable information to the Americans, it didn't follow that the decisions based on such information by the muckety-mucks would have a positive effect on the War. Soldiers might be shifted to other places, causing losses never meant to have occurred or vice versa, those changes altering how other battles were fought, lost or won.

A scratching sound behind me interrupted my dilemma. A knife was being thrust in and out between the entrance flaps. The tie snapped apart with a final pass of the blade along the severed threads. The blade returned, preceding the spread of fingers through the newly made opening to divide the flaps and allow a man's head to peer inside.

"What're you doing?" I exclaimed at Jonathan. "I could've opened it for you."

His eyes burst wide with surprise—not expecting to find me there, it seemed—then they dropped to the letter folded in my hand. Those same eyes narrowed when the seal was taken in. The knife blade stabbed in my direction as the man demanded, "Give me that."

I bolted to my feet. "You're not Jonathan."

It was his eyes. They weren't the same cobalt blue. The ones running the course of my body were duller, grayer. His hair, lighter.

The man's head jerked to the side to stare down Forest Thoroughfare. He growled a sigh. "Give me what is in your hand, and I shall not kill you."

"Fuck off."

He cocked an eyebrow, sizing me up one last time, then retreated in the opposite direction from whatever caught his attention. A flash of a red uniform glared at me from under his cloak as he fled.

What the hell?

The man looked so much like Jonathan, it was unnerving. Obviously, he wasn't, or he wouldn't have been surprised to see me. And he wouldn't have fled. And he wouldn't have menaced me with a knife over a letter. Even though he'd be awkward, like a freshman asking a girl to the prom, Jonathan would have found a way to ask.

Who knows what possessed me? Some brilliant refusal to let the man get away with breaking-and-entering. I had to know who he was and what he was doing there, trying to force his way into Jonathan's tent. I concealed the incriminating evidence between the pages of the Roman tome, then thrust the book and letter under the false bottom, letting the wood panel clatter back into place. Clothes and such were dumped on top. The trunk had me swearing while I struggled to find the right depth for the key inside the lock.

The guy would be long gone if I didn't hurry!

Adrenaline—nature's perfect ingredient for firing up muscles in preparation to chase after an imposter also shuts down the ability to think logically. I whipped apart the middle tie to spill through the tent's entrance, catching the tail end of the redcoat disappearing into the woods. He was heading toward the stream.

Only after I'd charged through the tree line, in hot pursuit, did I realize—I'd forgotten the pistol.

Chapter Twenty

The foreboding presence lingered even though there was nothing obviously wrong, other than my complete stupidity in chasing an enemy soldier, unarmed and without backup. The trees rustled in the wind, leaves collecting at their bases before continuing their journey along the forest floor. Branches creaked as they collided, jostled by the rushing air. Otherwise, the woods appeared empty.

I'd lost sight of the redcoat.

I wished Jonathan was there. It should've been him on the wild goose chase instead of me. Or maybe he would've had some sort of rational, let's-sit-back-on-our-cots-and-chat kind of explanation.

Explanations didn't matter, rational or suspect. It wasn't my place to interfere with the intrigues of history. I just had to survive them.

I should go back.

The stream wasn't far ahead. I promised my smarter self I'd stop there. A quick look. I could decide later what to report to the camp's inhabitants, if anything.

Sanity having found me, I moved into the undergrowth, away from the path, squatting low to conceal myself. A careful review of the clearing made it seem like I was alone. The water burbled along carefree. Its only concern was reaching its final destination.

Weaseling between my shoulder blades, burrowing in between my vertebrae, a cold itch crept up my spine. I was being watched. Searching my surroundings, even swinging to check behind me in case I'd been followed, showed barren trees and snarled vegetation. It made me question if what I'd experienced in the tent had been real.

Right around the point when the nagging voice inside had

convinced me to return to camp, a sound pricked at my ears. A mourning dove, emitting a long, low coo. Sort of.

The random note troubled me. Not so much because there was a mourning dove. They were as plentiful as any other bird where I lived; their song was as typical as the roar of a car engine, which was why it hadn't registered at first. Something about this particular specimen set it apart from the ordinary.

I listened hard, concerned by the pregnant pause between the last call and the eventual series that followed.

Not overhead. It was close, somewhere beyond the bushes, where my unwanted bathing adventure occurred. Except, the clarity of the tone was off. It was like… It sounded like…

Wait.

Only one note again. Not a dove's usual three with three repeats.

A second answered. The responding call came from farther downstream, also near the ground, and also not the correct number of notes. Two, nothing more.

A chill ran through me. No other birds were singing.

Oh, not good.

I debated what to do. Should I go for help?

A twig snapped. Everything went still, as if the whole of creation was holding its breath.

The first shot shattered the silence. A man's voice cried out as the bullet found its mark. The camp came alive: voices yelling out the source of the gunfire, rushing into the woods, tearing through the underbrush.

Me? I was a sitting duck, right in the middle of another battle. My gaze flew over my surroundings in a panic. If I ran for it, I might encounter any number of awful, enemy-entrenched scenarios in the woods. Never mind how I could very well get lost.

Damn it!

Up. No one ever looks up.

The tree I was crouched by had good, solid branches. I grabbed the first one within reach and climbed. Shouting and the exchange of gunfire continued from the area downstream. The same area where I'd heard the would-be mourning doves. Smoke mushroomed in clusters. Men splashed through the water, bodies forcing their way through the deeper flow. Yelling, screaming. The reek of sulfur swelled.

Hoisting myself higher with my forearms, I wound toward the far side of the tree, grateful the ancient trunk was twice my size.

I slipped, the limb I'd been holding onto flying out of reach. The underside of my arm caught in a lower branch, stopping my fall. Slick moss kept me from getting a firm hold with my feet. It tore with each attempt, uncovering rot beneath its roots.

A redcoat spotted me. He'd been reloading his musket when my floundering stripped the branch of its carpeting and sent the moss plunging to the ground in filthy clumps. Dark eyes calculated the distance to my location. Only several yards away. The ramrod was withdrawn. Both hands gripped the gun. Gaze raised to mine. My breath caught.

He was dead in the next moment as a bullet flew through his chest, knocking him over in a half-spin.

Relief, then horror, flooded through me.

Move!

My feet got a grip, and I resumed climbing, desperate to hide from the remaining soldiers fighting below. My breathing was coming in clipped bursts as I pressed my back against the trunk and held on for dear life.

Another redcoat ran past me in full retreat. He was flung forward when a round tore through his ribcage. Particles of dried leaves rushed from under his body as he landed on the clay-packed earth. He gasped. A hand trembled as it clasped at the open air. There was nothing there. Wet burbles saturated each breath he struggled to take in. The forest floor lazed on a subtle incline underneath him, noticeable only because of the deep red oozing across the leaves.

Quiet followed. And lingered.

A militiaman wandered by to inspect the body. He helped himself to the contents of the dead man's cartridge bag and pockets. A letter was flipped over and back again before it was rejected. No official seal to make it of interest to anybody. It was discarded, flung onto the redcoat. He collected the available firearm lying several yards away and left.

My eyes wouldn't obey my command to look away. Stillness, except for the letter. The edges lifted with the passing breeze, but it wouldn't leave its owner. Its center dampened with blood.

Sounds retreated. The borders of trees, outlines of leaves, horizon, and sky melded together. I cupped my hands over my mouth and forced myself to slow my breathing. Four counts… breathe in. Four counts… breathe out. The world darkened with only the glow of the sun reaching me through a growing tunnel of night. Four counts… breathe in. Four counts… breathe out.

Everything slid into focus, and I was able to take my hands away from my mouth to steady my perch in the tree.

The militiamen searched the area and helped the wounded back to the camp. The dead were gathered after. Two green uniforms passed under my unintentional post. One of them peeled the letter from the body, glanced at both sides, and tucked it into his satchel. Together, they lifted the redcoat by his arms and legs to carry him away.

I kept hidden, determined not to betray Jonathan.

The aftermath took far longer than the actual fight. In the heat of the moment, every second felt like a lifetime, especially when I'd been discovered, trapped with no way to run—the prey waiting for the hunter to finish loading his kill-shot.

Considering how few soldiers engaged the militia, I wondered if they even meant to engage. A brisk mission to retrieve a spy's letter didn't require multiple men. It would've been easier to sneak in and out if only one man went… Unless they were the back-up, it occurred to me. Like with Jonathan and the few men he took with him for cover.

Or, judging from how quickly the fight ran its course, it may've been another series of scouts, like what Jonathan and I found ourselves in the midst of on my first day. But where there were scouts, there was a British unit not far behind, waiting for the flushing out of hidden rebels to kill. It was only a matter of time.

Next, the hard part—getting down. The wool cloak kept snagging. No wonder the previous owner had it stored away. I removed it and let it drop to the forest floor. It landed without catching on anything, but it was such a long fall, my breakfast contemplated making the journey before the rest of me.

You can do this, I coached myself. You have to.

A few deep breaths to refocus my confidence brought me to the ground, relatively unscathed. I'd acquired several new scrapes along the way. Nothing major, other than my little finger throbbing again. The skin bulged over the curve of my knuckle with renewed force.

I leaned against the tree and breathed through the pain.

Why is this happening to me? I shouldn't be here. Why am I here?

Focus, Savvy, focus.

The woods returned to normal. Birdsong resumed, a chirruping descant to the tamed wind and the babbling tune of the stream. Whatever had been watching must've been the scouts, though… maybe not. It was faint—the breeze having carried away the worst of it—but gun smoke and death haunted the air, and the same ominous presence that'd scraped along Jonathan's tent was lurking in the shadows. I could feel it. A whisper of laugher rustled through the trees as it receded into the distance, satiated by the carnage but not truly satisfied. It would be back.

Chapter Twenty-One

The Wall brought me up short. He was blocking the pathway back to camp. A long gun sat in front of him, the butt planted on the earth and his hands folded over the barrel. His focus wasn't on me, though. A scrap of mauve fluttered in the tangle of bushes and weeds where he was scowling. The hem of a skirt, caught in the undergrowth. Snippets of brown shoes and white stockings were visible, crumpled as they were in the fabric.

"Doctor Cole," The Wall said. A glance in my direction was the first outward sign he was aware of my presence and had been speaking to me.

My feet carried me closer, unbidden. I didn't want to look. I couldn't stop myself. Each step brought the body further into view as I moved to The Wall's side, near the break in the undergrowth where the woman's fall had divided a patch of wild berries. The edge of a silver-colored cloak clung to a branch, winging up and away from her side. Smears of dirt sullied her white apron. Ragged scratches from the thorns trailed along her arms.

A cruel overkill to an unnecessary end. The rusty puddle of mud meant the bullet had lodged in her lower back. Not a quick death. There was no exit wound. Lacerations crossed her cheek, more of the wilderness's brutality.

The woman from the lunch line. The woman who pined after Doctor Cole.

My breath caught in my chest.

Why? I didn't like the woman. Actually, that wasn't fair. I didn't even know her. My one experience of her was her dislike of me because the doctor had chosen to avoid her and have lunch with me instead. It wasn't something I'd asked for, serving as a convenient excuse for Doctor Cole to escape her attention. The doctor was an attractive man. I could see making an attempt for him. Pretty daring for an eighteenth-century woman, something someone as unassuming as the handsome doctor might find off-putting.

But it didn't mean she was a bad person, and she didn't deserve to die.

A bucket rested near her feet, filled to the brim. We'd somehow missed each other on our respective trips to the stream and both gotten caught in the melee. Only the shooting sent me flying for the trees instead of back to camp, whereas a bullet prevented her return.

The Wall held out something. I stared at him, dumb with shock.

This wasn't right. I never had a chance to explain, to try to convince her I wasn't interested in the doctor. Not like she was. Maybe it could've been a foundation for us to build a friendship on. She'd be an ally, one to teach me about life at camp and how to do the everyday things she knew and I didn't. Or maybe her hatred of me would remain, and a perpetual, angry glare to serve as my constant companion. There were infinite possibilities, never to be. She was dead, and I didn't even know her name.

The Wall took in my general state before answering the question when put to him. "Molly Pitcher."

A wooden object was pressed into my hands, along with a long gun. Her bucket. He'd collected it without me noticing. His steady look told me it was time to go back to camp.

Should it matter to me that she died? Thousands of men and women died during the war. Nothing was going to change that fact, not even me.

The problem was… these weren't nameless, faceless people. The countless everyday people—at best, forgotten by the twenty-first century. Or else, reduced to a tally mark in yet another battle's death toll—were no longer history. I was living among them, learning their stories and experiencing their struggles. They were increasingly, and for the foreseeable future, my present, everyday companions. It was impossible to stand apart, aloof, as if nothing happening to them mattered.

How did the men and women of the Colonies do it? To march into battle, see their friends and loved ones fall around them, and carry on with their lives, doing it over and over, again and again. Did they get close to one another? Could they avoid it? I'd tried. It hadn't worked, even when I didn't know their names.

The Wall didn't know her name, either. *Molly Pitcher* was the moniker for every woman who assisted the men on the battlefields. It meant the same vivacious spirit that led her to pursue the doctor drove her straight into the fray, as well. She wasn't a lowly camp follower who cooked meals and sewed clothing, passively waiting for the men to return.

She saw open battle, yet volunteered time and time again. She deserved far more credit than she was given, and it grieved me she would never receive her own place in history for the courage that called her from the safety of her home and a simpler life than freezing in the wilderness. Just so she could die alone in the bushes.

Chapter Twenty-Two

There was a flurry of activity back at camp. Multiple people, men and women, crowded around the various open fires. Weapons were being cleaned, supplies surveyed, and an increased number of soldiers patrolled the perimeter. I met one such young man when I emerged from the path, who yelled at me to, "Halt!"

Everyone froze like deer spotted in the woods. Their attention flew to where we faced off as they stood ready to leap into action or flee.

The guard didn't recognize me, even after I identified myself. His rifle jumped to take aim when I searched for The Wall behind me, wishing I wasn't carrying his firearm. Another man jogged over and chastised the guard, pressing his rifle toward the ground, saying, "Tha' is the cooler what joins giblets with Captain Wythe."

The second man ordered me on my way, and I rushed off with head ducked, dismissing questions about what he'd said. Better not to know. The rest of the camp went back to its feverish tasks.

Sounds of pain broke through the sides of the medical tent. I placed the bucket in the grass with far more care than necessary as I procrastinated about going in. The smell was terrible. Horrors of every kind—blood, fear, disease, tension, filth, and death—swarmed together in a festering oppression to smother the inhabitants. I held the tent's flap open wide, trying to let in some light to help me find the doctor while I turned my head toward better air.

The scene drew me in.

Multiple cots filled the space, housing men in varying states of injury with old bandages and new scars. Closest to the entrance were the recently wounded. The doctor was working on one of them. Another perched on his elbows, lifting himself as far as his injury would allow, to spew a curse word and yell across the expanse to the doctor, demanding he hurry.

A dark-haired woman moved between the rows, apron splattered, basket in hand. Toward the back of the tent lay the sick and deceased. Kneeling in a shadowy corner, an older woman held the hand of an unconscious man with a shaky prayer on her lips.

"Mistress Moore, you must leave here." The doctor's voice was lightyears away.

"I…"

Doctor Cole left his patient to stand in front of me, blocking my line of sight. My eyes followed the path down his chest to an explosion of glistening red staining his apron. "Mistress Savvy, are you injured?"

My own fresh trauma, compounded by the gruesome scene laid out in front of me, left me shaken. Would the gunfight have happened if I hadn't been there to stop the letter thief and trail him to the stream?

"You must leave," the doctor insisted. "Several of the men are abed with smallpox. You have not yet been inoculated."

"Am… I am."

"You are?"

"Back home." Focusing on the doctor's face helped. "I was vaccinated for smallpox, when I was home, as a kid, when—"

"I require your assistance." He grabbed my wrist to pull me into the tent after him.

The slick of blood smeared onto my skin, along with the stench enveloping us, turned my unhappy stomach.

Doctor Cole released me when I resisted to hurry to his patient and the unholy mess at the man's left, lower quadrant. "If you cannot assist me, then you should leave."

"Right. Okay."

The scene receded, even though I wasn't fully aware of taking the steps necessary.

I shouldn't have been a part of this. It was wrong to interfere.

Whirling around during my effort to escape sent me colliding into The Wall, who pushed into the tent at the same time, carrying the Molly Pitcher in his arms. Knocked off balance, I grabbed the outer edges of a rickety cot frame to save myself from crashlanding onto the inhabitant below. The long gun I'd been holding clattered to the ground in the process.

Glassy eyes floated open. The stench of stale beer broke loose when the man's mouth slackened. I stuttered an apology too late. His eyes rolled heavenward, behind his lids, before closing. Sour acid flavored the back of my throat. There was a putrid, blood-soaked bandage swaddling the stump where his arm once was.

Doctor Cole glanced at the fresh burst of sunlight and directed The Wall to a place for the newest patient but stopped when he recognized her. Shock didn't keep him from asking who it was. The Wall returned the doctor's stare, still cradling Molly in his arms.

"It's what I came to tell you," I managed.

The doctor was visibly torn between going to her and continuing with the man he was already assisting. "Is she…? Does she…?"

The Wall shook his head no.

"I'm sorry." My voice was thicker than I would've liked.

The doctor's gaze fell to the stomach wound in front of him. His hands drifted, lost for a purpose despite the gruesome task in need of their skill. At the patient's groan beneath him, Doctor Cole returned. He set his shoulders and resumed his work by digging into the wound with a large pair of metal tweezers. The groan morphed into a wail.

The Wall carried Molly's body toward the back of the tent and settled her near the other corpses littering the ground. His bulky fingers proceeded to slip her shoe dangling over her heel into place, then drew the lace into a delicate bow. It wouldn't come loose again.

He paused on his way out to retrieve his gun from me. A damp stain of muddied brick-red had seeped into the sleeve closest to me. He cleared his throat, pulling my attention from the blood. Patches of strawberry whiskers, pale with age, were tucked into the back corners of his grayed beard. I'd never noticed before.

The Wall nodded toward the doctor.

Doctor Cole's head was turned toward the canvas rather than to confront the expanse of patients crowding around him. A stain, almost like coffee with soured cream, had leached from the lower hem to beyond the tent's equator, spreading in mildewy tentacles over the area where the doctor was facing. The withering pile of dirty snow, the likely source.

He dabbed an eye against his shoulder before facing his patient. Grief clung to him, though, thickening his breathing and stiffening his limbs as he pressed his arms to his torso to steady the shake in his hands.

A burst of cold air urged me to follow The Wall outside the billowing tent flaps. I wanted to follow. Instead, my focus returned to the doctor.

Doctor Cole's head ducked low, staring into the hole violating the man's body. The tweezers slid out. A scrap of shredded fabric was caught in their clutches. The tips of frayed white fibers wilted as blood invaded them to dye the whole swath bright red. It was a piece of the man's shirt, ripped loose and driven into the wound when the bullet penetrated him. The doctor shook the tweezers several times before the fabric became unglued and dropped into a tin pan at his feet.

The sound of buzzing flies vibrated through the din of the angry patient's yelling, another man's moaning, and my own blood rushing through my ears. Louder. The din was getting louder in my head. The patient was writhing and shoved the doctor's instrument away. Doctor Cole stopped working and stared at the man, adrift again. The man became delirious, his words morphing into an amalgam of sounds gone hoarse.

I surprised myself, crossing toward the opposite side of the cot, and clasped onto the man by the wrists to restrain his arms. My mother would've been proud.

The doctor didn't resume working, though. Emotion filled his eyes. Amber-flecked eyes, just like mine. I wished I could take his hand, but with the patient still struggling, I had little chance to offer him even a sympathetic glance in return, let alone find comforting words. Twenty-first century platitudes, as empty and meaningless for moments like this, even before they were coined.

He dropped his chin, then resumed searching the man's wound. I averted my gaze. Photos of gunshot wounds don't compare to the separation of flesh by metal instruments as they sift through torn muscle and blood flow, the victim still screaming throughout.

A fly buzzed at the man's hair. He didn't notice and struggled with dying strength.

"Has he been given anesthesia?" I soothed with my voice, knowing my words wouldn't reach the man but the tone might.

"What is anesthesia?" Doctor Cole responded.

The fly abandoned us to zip off farther into the tent.

"Medicine. For the pain."

"If you know of any such medicine, I would be grateful to hear of it."

Oxycodone, acetaminophen, ibuprofen—the stuff of the distant future. What did they have?

"What about morphine?" I asked. "Laudanum?"

Too Jane Austen?

"Laudanum?" Doctor Cole turned the word over. A clang in the tin pan meant he'd found the shrapnel he was seeking. "Laudanum is for the treating of dysentery and sickness."

"And pain," I countered.

"I suppose."

"Do you have any?"

"I have not had the ingredients necessary to prepare a tincture for some time."

The fly came out of nowhere to slam into my cheek. My hands flew up on reflex, but the fly was gone long before I could swat at it. My stomach lurched. I swiped at my face again, grossed out and itchy where the fly had hit me.

The man went limp, the agony too much.

The cursing man waiting in the other cot was still with us and cussing the open air, oblivious to how the hands of the woman working on him had already stitched closed the chasm in his thigh and was wrapping the area with a bandage. The mug of beer she smacked into his fist before moving on to the headwound sitting stoically two cots over required further consideration on his part. His curses went on mute while he assumed his new assignment.

Irritation crossed Doctor Cole's face. He peered into the weeping belly wound, prying the flaps of skin wide with tweezers.

"You should clean that," I directed toward the ceiling.

"I have already removed the ball."

"I meant the instrument. But yeah, you should clean the wound too. Flush it with alcohol."

"Are you a doctor, Mistress Moore?" Doctor Cole asked, though he didn't deliver his insincere inquiry with a full dose of even-temperedness.

"No, but… If you don't want my help, then you shouldn't have asked."

Shrill warning bells sounded in my head, and guilt reverberated along with them for snapping at him. He was right. I had no business telling him what to do. Plus, I risked the future, trying to teach him about painkillers and the prevention of infection. Irresponsible, beyond a doubt. Who cared whether I was troubled by the hopelessness of a medical tent lacking medicine or any of the other emotions I was drowning in?

Since the patient had ceased thrashing and I didn't want to add to Doctor Cole's stress—or my own, really—I bolted from the side of the cot toward the exit.

"What help is it you are attempting to offer, Savvy?"

My own temper flared, though my more-rational side perked up, as well, and noted the genuine interest shown when he spoke my nickname.

When I pursed my lips, frustrated, he pointed out, "You sickened at the sight of the wound."

"I did." I sighed. I wanted to do more, but he'd hit the mark, and I had to own it. Treating patients wasn't going to be one of those things.

"What then?"

All the What Ifs—the philosophical debate plaguing me from the moment the Eighteenth made its presence known—joined together at the inevitable crossroads I'd done nothing to avoid. Truth be told, I'd run toward it. The question wouldn't be dismissed this time, and it wouldn't be dissuaded. It glared at me with each proverbial tick of the clock, demanding to be answered: Should I help the people around me or step aside, a silent witness to their struggles?

"I already told you." I swung the tent flaps open to leave.

"Show me."

Frozen by his words, my mind went blank. I couldn't answer, and I couldn't leave.

Evan's face appeared when I closed my eyes. How his sweet smile would turn mischievous when he'd choose the same book about pirates, night after night, and I'd tease by groaning and suggesting fairytales with purple unicorns instead. The curl of his lips into a pout first thing in the morning as he buried himself deeper into his covers and stuffed animals. The way he lapped up my father's stories, in ways I never could as a child, about "hidden treasure," buried in a wooden chest of historical knickknacks in my father's study. Evan loved the Continental dollar. My father promised it would be his one day.

Mother always indulged him during our shopping trips, serious in her habitual lecture about eating healthy as we'd enter our local café, even though she'd tell him to choose a cupcake from the dessert counter. A rare treat for the daughter of a doctor. The chocolate raspberry was his favorite, piled high with buttercream and a sprig of mint tucked under a fresh berry.

What about the world surrounding me?

The man with the headwound was kissing the hand of the nurse, offering his thanks. She rewarded him with a warm smile and a final check of the lengthy, linen bandage cocooning his scalp. The cursing man finished his mug.

He noticed his fellow soldier's gratitude, then shifted his weight, grabbing at his bandaged leg as he did. He didn't complain. The grieving woman's head dropped onto the unconscious man's chest. Her prayers failed her.

The tent was overwhelmed, bodies clumped in miserable, closed quarters. Together, though, it kept them warm. Then there was Molly.

My chest constricted.

I can't just do nothing.

I willed myself to breathe and, remarkably, my lungs behaved.

While searching for answers, I'd noticed a small desk in the center of the tent. There was an empty tin mug on top. I took it outside to rinse it with water from Molly's bucket.

There wouldn't be rubbing alcohol or iodine.

My thoughts turned to Jonathan.

"Do you have any vinegar?" I asked as I reentered the tent.

Doctor Cole considered me, then pointed to a small barrel at the front corner of the tent. A pip of protest from his direction on the subject of waste sounded and died when I swirled a sampling inside the mug and dumped it outside. Instead, he continued wrapping a bandage around his hand, forming a square. Without an actual measuring cup, I had to guesstimate the correct amounts of water and vinegar to pour into the mug.

A fly was trying to crawl into the man's wound. The doctor waved it away, then pressed the prepared bandage there. I swallowed hard and offered him the mug. "Pour this over the wound to flush it clean."

He looked skeptical of the mixture inside. "What will this do?"

"Well, if the patient was awake, it would sting." The attempt at lightening the mood fell flat, but at least he was still listening. "It'll also wash out any debris caught in there and reduce the risk of infection."

"Reduce the risk of infection," he pondered. "You have seen this done before?"

"Not with bullet wounds, but for minor cuts and scrapes, I have. With rubbing alcohol, I mean, but you don't have any. Vinegar should work, though."

"Where did you learn such as this?"

"My mother."

"Your mother?" he asked, surprised.

"My mother's a doctor."

"A woman doctor." He peeled away the bandage and grimaced at the gray tinge to the blood there. "Was she a doctor of emotions?"

"A psychologist?" I reminded him. "No. A surgeon, actually."

He avoided looking at me and handed back the mug.

"What?"

"You were not in earnest."

"I am."

"Would you use such a treatment on yourself?"

It was a challenge, issued using the doctor's calm, rational tone. My brother would act the same way, especially when I'd rail about my ex-husband. It always made me pissy. "Seriously?"

His voice softened. "Your wrist is covered in blood."

I lifted my left arm and showed him, "You mean where you

grabbed me with your bloody hand?"

"No, Mistress Savvy. The other one."

Yet again, the man missed nothing. I had to twist my arm around to see how the underside, already ripening into an impressive plum color, was only the opening act for a dramatic climax eclipsing the bone of my outer wrist. Damn. I'd dismissed the ache once the skirmish ended and thought I could leave it behind at the waterside by ignoring it. Time to acknowledge how serious the gash was. I offered a rueful smile.

Doctor Cole was decent enough not to say anything and returned to checking his patient's stomach wound, trading the old, soaked bandage for a new one.

Pressing my back into the tent's canvas to keep it open so he could watch, I doused the gash on my wrist with the vinegar mixture and squeezed my lips together against the pain ripping through the wound. The doctor's eyes burst wide. After a decent shake dry, sending mud and crimson rain splattering to the grass outside, the gash was easier to see.

Despite me insisting I was fine and moving closer to him to display how non-oozy my forearm was, the doctor grimaced. "Was that wise?"

"My mother always says the sting lets you know it's working. Kills whatever might cause an infection." He tilted his head. "I don't know how to wrap a bandage the right way," I confessed. "Will you help me?"

Doctor Cole rose from the side of the cot, abandoning the latest fabric square stuck to the stomach wound by the slow spread of fluid. It still wasn't wrapped with bandages.

"It can wait until after—your hands are filthy!" I shied away from the doctor's efforts to seize my wrist and examine it. Blood filled the natural crevices of his skin, creating a webbing of deep red. An occasional flake fluttered from the more heavily coated areas where it'd already dried. "I'll get you some more water and vinegar to wash up."

"She must be a formidable woman, your mother." He was offering a truce. It rubbed funny against the raw part of my heart where the homesickness was festering.

"A force of nature. If she was here, she'd take one look at this place and march to Philadelphia herself. Barefoot, if she had to. She'd tear into every congressman and wouldn't leave until she got you the supplies you need." I blinked against the moisture spilling onto my cheeks. "Of course, she'd also shove you out of the way and lecture you on the right way of doing things."

"That does sound formidable," he concurred. Fresh tears trailed my first. Doctor Cole leaned forward with a sad smile. "However, I foresee a problem, should one such as your mother attempt such an act."

I forced a smile in return when I said, "A woman wouldn't be allowed to run a surgery?"

His gaze flicked over to the nurse rebandaging the armless man. "If your mother could accomplish such a thing as procure the supplies needed, I should gladly make way. No, Mistress Savvy, it is this. The Congress fled from Philadelphia in September. She would have to journey to York town."

A breath of surprise escaped me, then his peace offering won the day. I stopped crying and allowed a little laughter to break through. Even through his own grief and hardship, his kindness and warmth were never shaken. "Thank you." I sniffed. "I'll grab the vinegar."

The doctor nodded and accompanied me outside.

Relief spread across his features at our escape into the open air. He tilted his face skyward and inhaled, filling his lungs and arching his back with an audible pop as he stretched. The tension returned to his face when he noticed the bucket in my hands, held ready.

It occurred to me to ask if he had any soap. Like Jonathan, he was without. Simple water, then, to assist him with washing up. We repeated the cycle with vinegar.

The man with the bullet wound… I focused, instead, on explaining the one-to-four vinegar-water mixture as we approached him.

"You pour this into the wound?" the doctor asked, trying to work through the wisdom in the suggestion. He swatted the same pesky fly bombarding the man's loose bandage. Nasty, disgusting.

"It'd be best if we could turn him onto his side. The idea is to wash out the wound, not flood it with dirty liquids."

"It seems sound." Doctor Cole sighed. "Very well."

I balled my cloak and deposited it on the ground, out of the way. The pan was shifted to where we wanted the vinegar rinse to drain. Then came time for the doctor to roll the man onto his side and for me to irrigate the wound, since he was the stronger of the two of us. He moved into position, but when he did, the bandage fell, revealing the damage underneath.

I was glued to the floor; the gaping wound, a blackhole I was being sucked into, unable to look away or escape. The doctor saw I was having a hard time trying to not to be nauseated and took over. Scooting around the head of the cot, he continued balancing the man on his side, circling until he broke the spell by blocking my view.

I hurried to replace him at the man's back, freeing the doctor so he could flush the wound. It took several cups, because of the wound's depth, to ensure the blood was clean of debris and residual gunpowder.

Once we finished and the man's belly was stitched shut, I rushed outside and fell to my knees, clenching the pressure point on my wrist to drive away the urge to vomit. Usually, it helped. Not that time.

Chapter Twenty-Three

The sun had broken through the clouds and was a welcome contrast to the chill in the air. It continued its march toward late afternoon, undeterred by the frenetic activity in the camp. I remained seated in the grass, semi-aware of its passage and grateful for the breeze carrying away the last of the nausea.

At the cooking mounds, people swiped up meals and jogged to their next stop, eating as they moved and worked. A lot of gear was being moved around, too, bundled high in people's arms. Horses were being watered and readied. Near the open fires, men were making and distributing what I later learned were musket balls. Tiny glints of light from the fire, shifting on the dark metal balls, peeked out from their hurried hands now and again.

Doctor Cole emerged from the medical tent behind me. Water splashed off his hands as it tumbled from the bucket. A smack of canvas followed. Not long after, footsteps crunching through the matted grass wandered to where I'd landed. Chocolate wool billowed around me as he lowered my cloak over my shoulders.

He hovered while I drew it closed before sitting on the grass next to me, pulling his legs toward his chest and wrapping them with his arms. The tin mug was passed as he did. A glance inside showed it was clean. No floaters or color. It carried the faint, telltale odor of vinegar, so I reasoned, as Jonathan would've said, the water was potable. Still didn't tempt me.

"When did you last eat, Mistress Savvy?" the doctor asked.

"I left breakfast on the lawn. I don't think I'm going to manage much of anything for a bit," I said, handing the mug back to him, untouched.

He fingered a dent in its side. "It *was* you."

"It was me. Technicolor yawn and all."

"Tech- what?" A tick of his mouth upward coincided with a glance in my direction.

A soldier raced by, dropping a wooden rod from a towering bundle at our feet. He reclaimed it with a brisk apology. It occurred to me I'd been sitting out in the open for too long. I risked being spotted by the major.

Turning to the man slumped at my side showed just how tired he was. The eyes examining me were red, the area underneath streaked with purple. His profession nagged at him regardless of his fatigue.

"How about you?" I asked. "When did you last eat? Or sleep?"

"I have not had the time," he admitted to his mug.

"I wonder why you'd offer treatment you won't use on yourself."

Doctor Cole nodded, accepting having his challenge turned on him, and even mirrored my half-teasing smile. He grew serious when he said, "My patients have needed me."

"You're no good to them dead."

A weighted sigh followed. "You are probably right."

"I'm always right. Sooner you realize it, sooner you'll save yourself some aggravation." As drained as we both were, his momentary shock at my declaration turned into a decent laugh for us. Fatigue made the joke funnier than it was.

"You are so like Sarah." Doctor Cole shook his head as he finished chuckling and emptied the mug.

He shifted his weight to get up with me when I rose. I pressed my hand against his shoulder, taking his mug with me. "The stubborn sister?"

"Yes." He smiled and resettled himself, after I promised I was only visiting the cooking mound. Watching his head collapse onto his folded knees, I hoped the food line took a few minutes. He needed the rest.

At my stated intentions, the cook squinted toward the doctor sitting alone on the grass. A full serving with bread was offered without hesitation. Though hurried, he was nice enough to ask whether I was eating too. My stomach was still queasy, either as an after-effect of the slasher-film worthy medical procedure or else from being empty. I accepted a portion of bread for myself, anyway. There was always later.

The good doctor was upset at how small the serving was when he thought it was meant for the two of us to share. Notably, his distress was for those around him, how such thin rationing would affect the camp's inhabitants, and not himself. It took a little convincing that I didn't want my share from the pot and would try to settle my stomach with the dry bread. When I left open the possibility of going back for more, he finally agreed to eat. Didn't stop him from eyeing me as I picked at my medicinal carbs.

Several swallows later, he mumbled, "Thank you, Mistress Savvy. For all of your assistance."

"How about just Savvy?" His lowered chin told me he wasn't talking about holding down a difficult patient or fetching him something to eat. I added, "I'm sorry about your friend."

Doctor Cole's voice was strained when he said, "I *was* a coward."

"No. Oh please. I was only teasing you."

"Our families are old friends," he plowed ahead, not acknowledging my apology. "When my sister married, Nell was pleased because her family's property was adjacent to Sarah's new home. They became inseparable evermore, or so bemoaned Petrus, my brother-in-law. At least until this last autumn." The remnants of his mug once again served as a means to leave the world behind.

"Her name, it was Nell?" I encouraged him back. "What happened?"

He brushed his eye against his shoulder before continuing, "Their homestead was burned. Soldiers came in the middle of the night along with a posse of local Tories. The entire family was driven from their beds and dragged out of doors with barely a stitch to protect them from the cold. They were made to watch as their farm was looted and set ablaze. Nell's father and older brothers were taken captive. Theirs was one of several attacked. From what information we have gathered, the men of age were bound and marched south to be conscripted into the Royal Army."

"And the women?" I asked.

His voice hitched when he answered, "The women were abandoned."

"That's awful!"

"It was a mercy they never went as far west as Sarah and Petrus's home." Doctor Cole paused. "Will you not eat, Savvy? I could fetch you—"

"No, thanks. The bread helped, but I don't think I could eat any more right now."

His mug rotated several times in his hands, but he left it at that.

A draft of woodsmoke drifted over our humble picnic, warming the silence between us and carrying the doctor's sad tale with it once the breeze shifted. It was a relief to sit, just the two of us, and to cease to matter—even if just for a moment—in the whirlwind surrounding us. Our quiet sojourn was short-lived.

"Begging yer pardon, Mistress," the auburn teen called as he raced over. "Major DeForest does want to have a word with ye."

A futile surveillance of the moving bodies and equipment didn't turn up Jonathan. "I'll catch the major later," I said.

"Ah… but Major DeForest orders ye to come now."

"Well, I'm busy right now."

The poor boy's mouth dropped farther and farther with each turn of his head in the direction of the major's tent, to where I was stationed in the grass, and so forth.

Doctor Cole broke the silence by standing and brushed away scraps of dead grass from his backside. A hand was extended as he spoke to help me rise. "Mistress Moore." His tone was gentle but nonetheless chastising. I didn't like where things were going. "I should return to my patients and detain you no further from your own duties."

I wanted to protest like it was nobody's business, but I couldn't fault the doctor. In his world, orders had to be obeyed, a reminder he'd kindly worded. I gave his hand a squeeze, reconciled to the pain to come, and offered my condolences again. The doctor blushed at the continued contact, embarrassed as much as the teen whose entire face colored during the display, saying, "And I am sorry you have not the comfort of your mother to assist you."

On his way back to the medical tent, Doctor Cole paused at its entrance before sharing another regretful smile. I returned his farewell, then allowed myself to be dragged, yet again, before Major DeForest.

Chapter Twenty-Four

"Miss. Moore. An hour prior, though by some accounts it has been two, the *patrol* marked you entering the camp." The emphasized word was directed toward the auburn teen. Blinking at both Major DeForest and me, the boy mumbled something about returning to his post, then retreated from the tent with a lowered head. The major continued, "Yet, when I sent men to the tent of Captain Wythe, he was not there. Indeed, none can find Captain Wythe. Perhaps you would be so good as to inform him how I am eager for his report."

Which meant no one else had run into Phony Jonathan.

"No problem. When I see him again, I'll tell him."

"You have not seen him," the major said.

"Not… since we separated."

"When was this?"

"Earlier today."

"Were you not to accompany Captain Wythe?" the major continued with somewhat contained irritation.

"I returned to camp before him." Not a complete fabrication. The words were true, if you counted my roundtrip to the stream coming in first, while Jonathan completing his errand took second place.

"Why should you return without him?"

"It was strategically the best decision."

He was a military man. He'd buy that, right?

"In what way?" he questioned, each word getting more pointed as he spoke.

"I learned redcoats were nearing the camp, but I wasn't able to warn anyone in time." Also true words, if misleading out of context.

"Why not?"

Oh, brother.

"Because they were ahead of me. I had to be careful to stay out of sight."

"Why was that?" the major persisted, his gaze burning.

"Why was what? Why were they ahead of me? Or why'd I have to stay out of sight?"

"Both."

The exchange was getting annoying, and I wasn't sure even my words were true anymore. He was fishing, using the tactic of intimidation via steady pressure and little communication from his end. I gave into my irritation. "Major, say what you mean. I'm done playing."

We squared off, each with our arms crossed in front of us, scowling across the no-man's-land of the major's desk. The chaotic scattering of documents, maps, letters, etc., etc., previously camouflaging its surface were missing. In fact, most of the major's belongings were missing. Only the chairs and a letterbox remained as an additional barricade between us. It was tempting to ask about the redecorating. Doubtful the inquiry would be welcome.

I said nothing.

The long silence was tense.

I refused to back down.

A man dressed in a similar cloak to mine—gray, not brown—entered unannounced, heedless of the battle of wills he was disrupting. He delivered a bulky letter to the major and bolted.

The wax seal was checked, then hidden. DeForest scrounged through the letterbox and circled the desk, holding the pewter knife he'd selected in front of him and jostling its weight in his hand. I refused to back up but kept a careful watch on the major's blade. He *hmphed* at my unsubtle shift into a defensive position.

Leaning against the desk, he snapped the seal open with the knife. "You come by way of an accident?" The major gestured with the letter knife to my hand and its red, swollen pinky.

"No, I meant to introduce my fist to the redcoat's throat. It didn't land right in the heat of the moment, but he's dead, so what's it matter?" The words were more flippant than I felt. The conjured memory started a churning in the pit of my stomach.

The major paused and read his lengthy letter.

"How do I know you did not lead the attack to us?" He charged into a new and speedy line of assault.

My stomach lurched again. "If you mean what happened earlier today by the water, you can ask the patrol. I wasn't with the redcoats."

"You were not?"

"No."

"Before this afternoon's attack?"

"You mean when I first arrived in the area? Ask Captain Wythe. We met in the middle of the woods. We were both attacked *by redcoats*, and we both defended ourselves. It's how I injured my hand."

"And had your throat cut."

"And had my throat cut."

"What mission is Captain Wythe on?"

"An important one," I parried. Being well-versed in the same technique of setting a rhythm of questioning to elicit an unguarded response by a sudden shift in topic, I was skilled in avoiding the trap the major had attempted.

"I do not appreciate games either, Miss Moore. Where is Captain Wythe?"

"He will inform you of everything he is free to. Take it up with him."

The major raised his voice and pointed the letter knife at me as he thundered, "I am taking it up with you!"

"Well, I can't help you!" I returned with mirrored volume and intensity.

"You are here in my camp, under my command. You will answer my questions."

"I'm not under *your* command, and I can't tell you what I don't know."

The major and I stopped yelling and returned to seething at one another. He stalked behind his desk, wiping spittle from the side of his mouth, flown loose with his temper. The letter knife was slammed onto the desk's surface. Everything around us had gone quiet, the outside frenzy paused, listening in.

I lowered my voice to volunteer, "My part wasn't the same as Captain Wythe's. I had my own tasks and wasn't informed of his."

"Why should this be?"

"So I can't be made to confess what I do not know," I spelled it out for him like he was an idiot. The major scowled. My tone wasn't appreciated, but truth be told, I didn't care what DeForest appreciated right then and was ready to suggest he could go do something to himself that was anatomically impossible.

"You surprise me, Miss Moore."

"Oh yes, please. Go ahead, launch into a speech about how disappointed you are in me. How you expected more. Someone of my obvious brains and abilities. Dazzle me with rhetoric about loyalty to the

Cause and how you thought I'd understand and just do what you want because you want it. I've heard it all before. And by the way," I cut him off with an open palm in his reddened face before he could unload the monstrous piece of outrage he was working up. "I don't play games. I *am* on your side. I'd give you a hand, if I could, but I can't tell you certain things, including what I don't know."

I finished with less smart-assery and was sincere about wishing I was free to swoop in with an assist. Maybe not the major, specifically, and his political in-fighting with the other Americans, but the War for Independence? How could I not want to help? I just hadn't worked out what kinds of things were safe for me to do. When the fighting started again, was I supposed to stay out of the way or jump headlong into the fray? Holding down a patient who was already being treated was one thing. Taking a life was another.

DeForest eyed me, weighing my words with a grumble. My less-confrontational offering didn't satisfy him. Doubtless, he didn't trust me. Or at least, not completely. He did relent in his direct assault on my allegiance. There was no fruit to be had, either, regarding information about Jonathan.

He sat, continuing to eye me. I remained standing, trying my best to give the impression of waiting without a care. Someone hit play again on the outside world.

The major leaned back, balanced his foot across the opposite knee, and cradled his hands behind his head as he engaged in a new tactic. "The camp is breaking. You may have noticed." I had, though I hadn't put two-and-two together until the major pointed it out. I assumed the activity was preparation for a possible future attack. My mistake, not his business. "As you and Captain Wythe will continue your post with us…"

"I haven't heard otherwise."

"Of course. I have taken the liberty of ordering your belongings—those being Captain Wythe's belongings—to be stored on one of the wagons. Have your own been delivered, Miss Moore?"

"Captain Wythe has possession of what I brought."

"I see. As I have said, they have already been collected. To save you the trouble, Miss Moore, of having to disassemble Captain Wythe's tent and hauling its contents yourself."

He was up to something. I was being walked into a trap but couldn't see what it was. "How thoughtful."

DeForest smiled at my reply. He knew damn well I realized he was bullshitting me, and I was powerless to do anything about it, especially as he launched into the *coup de grâce.* "Captain Wythe will need to be informed of our relocation, and since neither of us knows the captain's orders… That is correct, Miss Moore, is it not? Neither of us knows Captain Wythe's orders?"

"It is," I answered through a forced smile.

"Other than the plan to break the regulars' line so as to escort you to a rendezvous point, correct?"

"I couldn't say."

"You could not say. Naturally, I would not wish to inconvenience Captain Wythe by requiring him to travel in the opposite direction."

Here it comes.

"As such," the major continued, "you had best inform Captain Wythe of the camp's departure yourself. We shall leave you here. I will send word to Fort Clinton as to our location. I trust you will not share such valuable information with the enemy, Miss Moore. The regulars and their like?"

"Of course not," I was forced to agree with the major, yet again, while he glossed over his plan to abandon me.

"Because Fort Clinton is well-fortified," he persisted, staring at me.

"No doubt."

Satisfaction crossed his face. He had the answer to some unspoken question. What it might be, I had no idea. I had to rally, or I'd lose the match. "Let me save you some trouble, Major. You can leave our belongings here."

"Private MacCraith!" he bellowed. The unexpected volume change was rattling, to say the least.

The auburn-haired teen burst inside at being beckoned. "Aye, Major DeForest?" His face paled, his gaze darting back and forth between the major and me. He was aware of the tension in the room, having probably heard our entire argument. Most of the camp had.

"Is Captain Wythe's property stored on the wagon?"

"As ye have ordered, Major."

"Seems there is no trouble to be taken," the major smiled at MacCraith, then me. Correct answer achieved, the teen breathed a sigh of relief.

"We'll need access to our supplies, however." I returned the major's bullshit smile right back at him. "I'll unload our trunks myself rather than waste any more of your men's time."

"Quite impossible, my dear Miss Moore. Your trunks were amongst the first to be loaded. They are like to be buried under many others by now."

"My gun is in there!" The panic in my voice was difficult to hide. The major was serious about his plan to abandon me and steal Jonathan's belongings for good measure.

"You do not carry your weapons on your person? Foolhardy practice to—"

"It's hardly good practice to carry weapons into a medical tent." It was the first excuse I could think of. I kept going with it. "Those men are tired, in pain, and not in their right minds. You want a man half-crazed grabbing a weapon while the doctor and I are trying to treat him?"

"You were assisting Doctor Cole?"

The question was meant for me but was directed at the private, who was cowering at the tent's entrance, wavering between staying and trying to slip away unnoticed. The shock of realizing he was being addressed, as he discovered both the major and me staring at him for confirmation, brought both feet back into the tent and his body to attention. "Miss Moore was with the surgeon, Major."

"Private."

"Aye, Major?"

"Fetch Doctor Cole."

"What? No, wait," I interjected, hoping to reason with him.

"Now, Private MacCraith!" the major snapped.

"A-aye, Major DeForest." A quick salute, then the teen rushed from the tent, undoubtedly thrilled to be away from the major, even if only for a minute. I know I would've been.

"Major, please don't send for the doctor. This is ridiculous," I said.

"You are honest. Are you not, Miss Moore?"

"Of course, I am, but—"

"Then why should I not send for my own surgeon?"

"Because he's exhausted. Not to mention, he's treating patients, in case you hadn't noticed. Please, for his sake. Not mine."

How the intrigue twisted the major's smirk. He returned to reclining in his chair to study me with arms behind his head. "We shall take but a moment of the doctor's time," he decided with false charm.

"Major—"

"Please, sit, Miss Moore. You must be exhausted as well from assisting him."

I wanted to punch the man. Would've even offered up my injured hand to have done it. No wonder Jonathan held him in bitter contempt. The major belonged in a courtroom. Or in politics. I sank into the chair, frustrated.

The minutes stretched on, and not just because I was anxious to get out of there. Doctor Cole was likely working on one of the wounded from earlier. Or anyone in the camp, come to think of it, who'd taken a turn for the worse. Surgery can take hours. The major filled the interlude by scanning, rearranging, and muttering through an assortment of papers from his letterbox.

For lack of anything better to do, I took to examining the silhouettes of twisted branches jumping along the canvas walls. Jonathan's doppelgänger crossed my mind again. I wondered if I should tell the major what I'd found in the dead roommate's trunk and how the redcoat had wanted it. Maybe it would earn me a little goodwill, I reasoned. It would've meant confessing to being in the camp longer than the major knew, though. It also meant risking his focusing on our disobeying his orders. Worse, what if it threw further suspicion onto Jonathan somehow being complicit with the redcoat's presence there?

Ugh. It was like some stupid TV drama.

A passing thought of all the shows I'd been building up in my queue to binge-watch during downtime made me chuckle at the cruel irony. They'd go to waste if I never made it home again.

The major barked up some phlegm to accompany his glare at the noise.

I really might not survive, I realized.

A scene of ice cream oozing from its container flooded my imagination. A sticky, mint sludge filled with islands of softened chocolate, swallowing the countertop alongside Evan's Plain-Jane vanilla. It was the mountain of toppings he liked.

Which detective would they send to search my house when people realized I was missing? I hoped for Garza. He was good with kids. He'd know what to tell to Evan. He knew how to handle my ex.

Doctor Cole ducked through the tent's entrance and caught me wiping away tears I was trying to conceal from the major. "What is this?"

"Sit, Doctor." The major gestured to the open chair next to mine.

"Thank you, sir. What is the meaning of this?" The doctor appeared to have some skill with the major because he remained standing and wouldn't be swayed.

"I wished to inquire after the wounded you received this morning."

"Why is this woman crying?" His concerned gaze returned to me.

The major adopted a kinder tone. "First, I need to know what you did this morning, Doctor."

I spoke, instead, when Doctor Cole paused. "Please answer Major DeForest's question."

A surprised sound caught in the major's throat. It morphed into a rumbling passage-clearing. His recovery wasn't quick enough to avoid Doctor Cole's notice, however. The doctor seemed to grasp the gist of what was going on because he answered, "I treated the wounded, of course, with the assistance of Miss Moore."

"As I have been informed." The major nodded. Doctor Cole further demonstrated his skill in handling the major by remaining politely yet unflappably mute. DeForest was left to prod him. "Miss Moore was telling me of her nursing skills. I was impressed."

There was no way to intervene. If I gave the doctor a warning look, how it was a bait, the major might view it as a potential set-up, something the doctor and I had concocted to conceal whatever nefarious movements the major would imagine. I couldn't justify the risk to Doctor Cole's reputation. I studied my hands clenched in my lap.

"She was very helpful," Doctor Cole answered before asking, "What troubles you, Miss Moore?"

DeForest jumped in, saying, "Miss Moore was saddened by the death of… who did you tell me, Miss Moore?"

"Nell, Major. Nell died," I shot back at the arrogant bastard before I could stop myself.

Horror at my blurting about the death of Doctor Cole's childhood friend for no other reason than to take a swipe at the major—and worse, in front of him—was quick to overwhelm me. The doctor's expression showed a similar shock. It fell away as grief marched in. I swore and rushed to hide my face.

A tentative hand lighted on my shoulder before pressing a comforting weight there. The doctor's kindness was too much. It only made the tears fall faster.

DeForest mumbled something to the effect of not having gotten that far into the conversation or some such bullshit. His embarrassment didn't distill me with *schadenfreude*, though. The rest of the exchange between the major and the doctor passed without my hearing it.

Doctor Cole squatted in front of me. "Shall I send for Captain Wythe?"

The major fought to keep his interest hidden at my saying, "He isn't back yet."

"When do you expect him?"

"Tonight. Though he said there's a possibility he won't be back until tomorrow."

Doctor Cole gathered my good hand from my lap to encircle it in his own. A promise of future exploitation of our conduct resided in the heart of DeForest's condescending sniff. Doctor Cole ignored him.

"I travel to a flying hospital stationed several miles from here. Accompany me. You would be well-looked after."

"Captain Wythe and Miss Moore have their own orders," DeForest informed him. "They are due at a rendezvous near here."

"Major DeForest's ordering me to wait here for Captain Wythe, and he's holding our stuff hostage," I whispered to the doctor, though the major heard, given the close quarters and his subsequent grimace.

"What? Alone!" Outraged, Doctor Cole shot to his feet. Or with as much outrage as a kind-hearted man can muster. He didn't have the callousness of DeForest, but his stern tone and clipped words made his anger clear. "You would abandon a woman, alone?"

"This woman is a spy and quite capable of taking care of herself," the major said.

"Unarmed and without supplies? We are surrounded by war parties and enemy scouts."

"I see she has made short work of you already, Doctor."

"What's wrong with you?" I demanded while the doctor challenged simultaneously with, "How dare you?"

Several tense moments passed before Doctor Cole broke the stare-down and turned back to me. "You do not have to stay here. Come with me. You may travel under my protection."

"You do that, Doctor," DeForest warned, "and I will report you the Board of War and Ordnance for harboring spies and disobeying a direct order from a superior officer."

"Write to them, Major," Doctor Cole challenged, "And *I* will enlighten them as to how you abandoned a camp follower, empty-handed, to the wilderness and threat of enemy attack on nothing more than a baseless, hollow suspicion."

His bluff called, DeForest's cheeks became inflamed. "Private MacCraith!" he roared. The teen's auburn head poked its way into the tent. The major turned to address Doctor Cole, leaving the boy confused about whether he should come in or run for cover. "As Captain Wythe is fond of reminding me, he and Miss Moore take their orders from the general, Doctor. We cannot disrupt the *general's* orders, Doctor, even if we may want to."

The doctor and I exchanged looks to see who would take the lead in responding. It didn't matter because DeForest continued without us, saying, "You are to travel with the wounded. You know your orders from there. Private MacCraith will naturally stay with Miss Moore as her protection," he dragged out the last part, "until Captain Wythe returns. Have your supplies ready, Private. The camp breaks in one hour."

When the teen froze in shock, the major barked a direct dismissal at him. The boy jumped and rushed to obey, though, from the shuffling noises outside the tent, I imagine he had no clue about what he was supposed to be doing.

Two-to-one, him being the major's guard, the boy was "privileged" enough to have his gear already stowed on a wagon. Stuck in the middle of nowhere with nothing but the clothes on his back.

We were both screwed.

Chapter Twenty-Five

I didn't wait to be dismissed. There wasn't much more Major DeForest could do to me. Not without taking direct action against me, and he'd been hesitant to step too far afield. I barged through the tent's flaps before anyone could stop me. No angry commands bellowed, demanding my return. I tore past Private MacCraith, who sputtered a few unintelligible words, bogged down as the stupid boy was with his own predicament.

Doctor Cole was right behind me. I broke into a run, anxious to learn whether everything was truly gone. It didn't take long to confirm MacCraith had been telling the truth. Most of the tents were missing, including Jonathan's.

At the sound of my name for the second time, I snapped at Doctor Cole, "Leave me alone."

"Savvy."

"Just leave."

"I am concerned for your welfare. You cannot remain here."

"What am I supposed to do?" The mounting worry made my voice pitch higher.

"Come with me."

"I have to find Jon… Captain Wythe."

Despite his use of my first name, the doctor scowled at my use of Jonathan's. "What is he to you?"

His challenge stumped me. Not because I questioned my relationship with Jonathan. Well, I did, when I stopped to think about it. But I wondered why it rankled Doctor Cole. My voice trembled when I said, "He's my ticket home."

"Speak plainly, madam. Why is it you would risk your life by waiting for him, alone, in the wilderness, when there are ways for you to be reunited in safety?"

"I think you meant to call me Savvy."

Doctor Cole closed in on me. "Are you a spy?"

"I… support the Colonists, Doctor."

"You have not answered me."

"I'm not a British spy."

"But you are a spy." His solemn conclusion hinted at disappointment.

"I'm…" I didn't want to contradict whatever perception Jonathan had created of my role in the camp, even with someone as harmless as Doctor Cole, but… How did everything become so complicated? "I'm just trying to get home."

"Getting yourself killed will not see you there," he lectured me with some heat in his voice. "I shall remain with you."

"No. Your patients. You can't disobey the major's direct orders."

"The major is a scrub. He can go hang."

I had no idea what his outburst meant, but I was both grateful and unnerved by the fierce devotion Doctor Cole was showing me. "You've only known me for a day, Doctor."

He reddened at my reminder. "I apologize, Mistress Savvy. I should not have spoken in such a manner. The major was right," he said to no one in particular. "You have made quick work of me."

"I'm not what he told you. I'm not trying to manipulate you, I swear." The doctor nodded but didn't say anything. "And I'm sorry about Nell. I shouldn't have used her to try to stick it to the major."

His voice caught when he said, "You are forgiven."

"I, um… thanks." It felt like there was something else I should say to apologize. Rather than wait for him to repeat his invitation, I instead confessed, "I am afraid, but my only hope of getting home is finding where Captain Wythe met me. He's the only one who knows where that is. I don't dare leave here, since this is where he'll be looking for me."

"Utter madness." He shook his head. "I cannot abandon you."

"You have to. You've been ordered to… a flying hospital?"

"It is a temporary hospital. Savvy, my orders return me to the militia once I have seen my patients safely delivered. All I ask is those few days' time."

"Which Major DeForest says is in the opposite direction from where I need to go."

Even in the middle of nowhere, I lawyer everything. Why can't I just agree with him?

I backed away. "Believe me, I am grateful for your friendship and your difficult-to-resist insistence I go with you. But I want nothing more than to go home, as soon as possible. Captain Wythe's supposed to be coming back here, to this spot, any minute now. And I won't risk you getting caught disobeying a direct order from the major. There are serious consequences. I couldn't live with it."

"If you should be killed? You are asking me to live with your death, as well."

"You keep overlooking Private MacCraith being ordered to stay behind to protect me."

"*You* are more capable of protecting him." He swallowed, twisting his head to the side, grimacing, before he burst out with a warning. "Captain Wythe, it is said, is a man not to be trusted. Have a care, or the same shall be said of you."

When I stared in return, shocked speechless, Doctor Cole grumbled and started to leave several times, warring with himself rather than me. A hand raised to emphasize a point without the rebuke being spoken. His fist pounded onto his thigh on another pass. Done with pacing angry ruts into the earth, he stormed off.

I sank to the ground and clutched my knees against my chest. Somewhere, the practical part of my mind was urging me to stop wallowing and plan for how I was going to get through the night. The sun was slipping behind the treetops, its descent visible. Fewer and fewer people hurried by as the minutes dragged on. Their preparations led them to the far end of the camp's soon-to-be-former site, so I heard Doctor Cole return long before he reached me.

He knelt in front of me and earned permission to take my right hand with his. A dampened cloth was pressed to my injured wrist. The sting of the vinegar bit my nose and torn skin, but I refused to allow the pain to drag my spirits down. With each pass of the fresh linen strip the doctor wound around my wrist, I imagined myself stronger and more secure, like the bandage knotted in place. I was going to survive.

"Savvy." Doctor Cole hesitated, then said, "I apologize."

"Thank you."

"You are too much like Sarah." He sighed. "Truth be told, you look a great deal alike. It is uncanny." Studying the green eyes staring out from a face that—I had to admit—resembled my brother, Stephen's, I wondered about the connection the doctor and I shared. "Perhaps I should be a better guard of my own well-being," he said. "Though, were you truly the Crown's own, I do not believe you would have refused me.

Savvy, please. You are still one of my patients. The bandage will need to be changed and more vinegar applied. You lack supplies for your own care and have told me you cannot do it yourself."

The justification, allowing Doctor Cole to take me with him despite the major's orders, was like a siren's call. Would the few days' delay in reuniting with Jonathan matter? Who was to say the major was being truthful about the camp traveling in the opposite direction? But like Odysseus bound to the mast of his ship, I was restrained from following such temptation by the many fears of what my interference could mean for the future I'd left behind. I determined I had to stay and let the camp and the good doctor go back to their own lives without me.

"No, Doctor."

At my quiet but firm resolution, the doctor acquiesced. "Take this."

Doubt prodded my resolve as he handed me a leather sachet. At his insistence, I opened the flap. Obvious, despite being tucked among the contents, was a silver pistol. "I can't take this."

"Are you armed?"

"No, but *you* might need it."

"You will take it. There are plenty of soldiers with arms to protect us. Take it, or I shall disregard your wishes and remain here, whether you will it or no." Though said out of kindness, Doctor Cole's declaration was adamant.

"Okay… Thanks, Doctor."

Studying the bandage on my wrist became a focal point for him when it was difficult to look at one another. I pressed the bag to my chest as the finality closed in on me.

"Auden," he shared.

"Auden?"

"It is my given name. You insist I call you by yours, yet you do not return the act of friendship upon me."

"You're right. Auden," I repeated. It had a pleasant lilt to it.

"It means 'old friend.'"

I gave a small laugh. "It's the perfect name for you."

From our first lunch together, so long ago as the day before, he'd been my unwavering friend from the eighteenth century whose memory I'd cherish for the rest of my life.

"Be safe, Old Friend," I said.

He gave me a sincere yet sorrowful smile. "And you, Savvy."

Chapter Twenty-Six

The camp's inhabitants took the overgrown route toward town, racing against the shadows as the last of the sunset dissolved into the horizon. A dangerous time to move three-hundred-some-odd people, wagons, and horses. A handful of British scouts would make far less noise and be more easily concealed amid the trees than a large caravan on an uneven, wooded path. But who was I to judge? I guess the major had been more troubled by the scouts finding the outskirts of camp than he was of the danger of moving at night.

Oh crap!

More soldiers would be there, right there—I realized—before dawn, at my very location where the militia was abandoning me. Doubt flooded through me, the doctor's warning sounding in my head. My gaze flew to the tail-end of the convoy. Uniformed soldiers on horseback brought up the rear, spears in hand. Foot soldiers preceded them, a long gun stationed against their shoulders with bayonet in place. Armed and ready.

If I followed, tucked away, hidden among their numbers, under cover of night, far from Major DeForest who led their crazed parade, it would be hours before I'd be discovered as a stow-away on their flight. I *could* follow. Face the music, if and when it came. Or only as far as…

The future wasn't mine to gamble away. It had to come first, and the countless reasons for not interfering, for needing to find Jonathan right away, and for avoiding trouble by trailing the major's men demanded I stay.

But what if I was wrong? What if none of it mattered, and I was—?

It woke.

The ominous presence that'd laid low all afternoon roused. A stirring in the atmosphere as the familiar pressure focused and grew deep within the night-laden forest. It advanced, circling around the former site to the broadside of the caravan, dragging leaves and debris along the forest floor as it kicked up an angry, frigid wind. The trees groaned in protest at the presence shifting through them. My muscles tensed, the urge to flee overwhelming. I searched but couldn't see anything.

When the last of the soldiers vanished, swallowed by the noise of the agitated trees and the blackness of nightfall, the presence remained. It refocused, the watchfulness glaring into the clearing. Something about the site drew its attention. It surged toward me like a tidal wave bearing down on my chest. My heart froze. The presence ground to a halt at the edge of the tree line, brooding from within the shadows.

It was far too familiar. I longed for my father's arms around me.

Suddenly, it spirited away, flying along the parallel of the path with a hiss sounding an awful lot like "Wythe!" The wind tore after it, the landscape adopting an eerie quiet, the air gone stagnant.

Private MacCraith shivered next to me, his hands shaking. I worried about the pistol trembling with him. He couldn't have been more than maybe fifteen or sixteen.

"Private?" He didn't respond. "Private MacCraith," I tried a little louder.

The boy jumped, eyes wide. "Do... do na' ye worry, Mistress Moore."

"Okay."

"We have none to fear. Ye will see." The trembling hadn't stopped. For me, either.

An enormous form loomed from the blackened cluster of trees, silent and steady in its approach from the direction of the stream. MacCraith gasped and took aim, yelling for it to halt. The boy had the right idea. I followed his example and snatched the silver pistol from the doctor's satchel.

It paused. The shadowy length of a long gun was placed butt end on the ground. There was something familiar... I exchanged a look with the boy, who demanded the figure identify itself.

"McIntyre."

MacCraith beamed at me and ran toward the hulking man. The woods around us remained otherwise quiet and—I hoped—empty. Catching up with my youthful guard, I recognized our companion. The Wall. I don't know what possessed the man to stay with us, but seeing the relief in the private's features, I whispered a genuine offering of gratitude to the skies.

He was busy examining the boy's flintlock when I joined them. Consternation on the older man's face worried me as he fingered the shiny-new weapon. He pointed the pistol off to the side, toward the ground, and before I could protest, pulled the trigger. The jaws of the hammer snapped forward. Nothing else happened.

The man stared at the boy, who looked shocked then cowed. With a tilt of his head, he bade MacCraith to inspect the useless weapon with him. I leaned in as well, and though The Wall glanced my way, he didn't discourage me. It reminded me of my father's replica. He fingered the empty jaws of the hammer. No flint to light the powder in the pan.

"Huh," slipped from my mouth.

The boy wanted to protest and declare his innocence, or something along those lines. The Wall silenced him with a stare. "Aye, sir," MacCraith mumbled instead.

"We should find cover for the night," I said to save him.

The private went back and forth, seeking further instructions from The Wall and me. The older man scratched the corner of his jaw.

"I will fetch us wood for the fire," the boy offered, starting to slink off.

"No, don't."

"'Tis cold," he whined. "Ye canna wish to freeze."

"You light a fire, and every scout within miles will see it and come for us." Poor kid. I didn't dare tell him my full suspicions of the danger we were in.

"A'right." The boy trembled again, scowling.

The Wall regarded me through the exchange with what appeared to be approval. A smile threatened to overtake the corner of his mouth, though he grew serious as he returned to his persistent watch of the surrounding area.

Since he was the most capable of the three of us, I asked him, "Where do you suggest we sleep?"

A dip of his nose pointing away from the stream and forest roads marked his suggestion.

"A'right, then," the private said. "Right." He continued muttering to himself as he made his stunned passage across the clearing where the camp once resided.

"I'm Savannah Moore." The Wall nodded in reply. "Your name's McIntyre?" When he nodded a second time without further comment, I asked, "Do you have a first name or a rank I should use?"

He declined to answer, scanning my appearance instead. I

couldn't help but wonder if he was enjoying my physique again. His review paused at the doctor's satchel, my wrist, and—longest—at the pistol tucked along the length of my leg. He was taking stock of our situation.

His attention returned to my face, and with a shrug, he said, "Promised the lad's *máthair*," before he followed the boy into the woods.

I de-cocked my pistol.

Looking around, I wished there was more moonlight to fill the darkness between the trees. Distant towns meant no ambient light to chase away the fears only night can conjure.

Would Jonathan risk traveling at night? Doubtful. Unless someone had invented a way to message him about the camp's departure without my knowing it, he was blissfully unaware of my predicament, figuring I was safe and well-guarded. No reason for him to hurry back. We'd have to stick it out.

The question was: what if he did arrive and search the area without our noticing? Several horses traveling what counted as roads would be hard to hide, but what if they sent a scout ahead on foot? If they did, would the scout bother inspecting the vacant campsite long enough to make his presence known? I had to hope he would.

Jonathan would want to look for clues to determine which way the camp went. But I didn't want him tracking the militia. What sort of clue could I leave him? It had to be something to make him linger so we could find one another.

My hand had inadvertently traveled to the key, and I was swinging it back and forth along the ribbon's length. At the discovery of what I was doing, a stray thought crossed my mind about the red fabric from our tent. I unwound the ribbon from my neck and hoped it wouldn't tear to pieces as my fingernails struggled with the knot.

Once freed, I dropped the key into the satchel at my hip for safe keeping. Staking a nearby scrap of kindling into the ground, about mid-clearing, I added the ribbon to the top, allowing its length to hang loose. Our truce of red, now a sign of allegiance in blue floating delicately in the night air.

Pulling the cloak tighter against the cold, I worried how it might affect Jonathan to discover the ribbon that held some sad meaning for him left out in the elements, tied to a dirty stick. I had to let it go and worry about myself for the time being. Begging forgiveness could happen later. If I lived long enough.

Resolved, I turned my back on the silk memento and joined my two companions. MacCraith was tucked behind a tree, keeping watch, several yards from a thick undergrowth where McIntyre, The Wall, was hacking a space in the middle with a cutlass. The man was impossible to read. He eyed the clearing in the distance more than once. As usual, he didn't say anything. No objection, ribbon sustained.

He pointed the cutlass at a pile of evergreen branches. Taking my cue, I collected the cuttings for him, which he spent some time arranging into carpeting for the landlocked beaver's dam he was creating. A sizeable pine tree stood guard over the space, separating the makeshift enclosure from the clearing where the camp had been. It also meant it blocked the view of anyone who might be looking for us.

Although it was difficult to see much of anything in the dark, I scaled the pine to assist with the watch. A scritch of McIntyre's fingers over his beard was aimed at my perch, then with a swift hoot like an owl to the private, he tilted his head skyward. The private eyed both of us and took to the trees, as well.

Having completed a futile search of the surrounding area, I pulled the doctor's bag onto my lap and wondered how Auden was managing with his patients. I hoped the flying hospital was where he expected it to be.

The leather satchel was soft with age. I glided my fingers along a pattern of scrollwork tooled into the flap. A brief panic chilled me when I reached inside, unable to find the key right away because it'd made its way to the bottom.

Further rummaging uncovered an apple, judging by its telltale shape and size. Auden had also packed some bread and what felt suspiciously like a dog chew, both wrapped in cloth. The final object was a tin box. I planned to inspect it in the morning and hoped it contained packets of gunpowder and balls.

McIntyre gestured for me to climb down. I made it maybe two branches before the wool cloak snagged and I fell to his feet.

Half the man's size and I still managed to make twice as much noise.

He did another review of our surroundings, indulging in a throaty chuckle, nonetheless, at my expense. "Sleep," he ordered, pointing to the enclosure he'd built.

"I can help keep watch."

"Third watch," he said and crossed to the base of MacCraith's tree.

Their subsequent exchange was too far away to hear. The boy risked a glance my way and shifted in his tree before returning to his study of the woods.

McIntyre, meanwhile, disappeared into the darkness. I wondered which of the two of them was taking first watch and which the second, but since I wasn't planning on letting anyone down, I decided to take his suggestion to call it an early night.

It took a little work to find a less-uncomfortable way to lay on the branch mattress. But just like with the miserable cot in Jonathan's tent, once the fullness of the day overcame me, I fell into a deep, though dream-infested, sleep.

Chapter Twenty-Seven

A man coughed. I jolted upright, scratching my face on a branch. Several moments passed before the grogginess and confusion born from a restless night faded, and I remembered where I was. Cursing to myself, I tested my forehead with my fingers for blood. Everything about the Eighteenth was hazardous.

McIntyre stood near the opening of the make-shift den, surveying the general direction of the old camp and reminding me in his silent way that it was my turn to take watch. A swig from a canteen containing a twist of something infinitely more potent than vinegar was offered as I emerged. Potable, yes. It burned my throat straight through to the other end. Coffee would've been a better wake-up call.

With a nod, he walked off, away from the clearing, and found a fat tree to lean against. He chucked a pinecone from under himself, then settled, arms crossed, eyes closed.

A pale glow of amber along the horizon hinted at the sun's imminent arrival. Further review of our immediate surroundings showed Private MacCraith asleep in the tree where we'd left him. I wondered how long he'd lasted and whether McIntyre had gotten any sleep.

I inched toward the camp's clearing, pistol in hand, taking only a few steps before pausing to look around and listen. A mourning dove nearly stopped my heart. My thumb sought the hammer on the silver pistol, and I held my breath. A few more calls convinced me it was a legitimate bird. Tracing its song through the evergreens, I found its silhouette before it took flight in a succession of cooing and heavy flaps of its wings. Its mate followed.

Rather than continue forward, I backtracked to the tree I'd slept under. There was plenty of time to wander into the woods to do a more thorough check of the area, but I lacked McIntyre's skills of moving silently. It wasn't worth the risk. Instead, I climbed, higher than the night before, and did a regular, slow scan of the woods, scrutinizing each portion with methodical precision. For good measure, I also searched for anything even pretending to be the hillside where Jonathan and I met. No such luck.

Purple sky transformed into a wash of royal blue, the amber light melting into a creamy haze peering above the eastern horizon. Tufts of clouds navigated the breeze in blazing pinks and reds. The sky was a living canvas, growing brighter and bluer before succumbing to a white brilliance as dawn burst in full upon the skyline. The lingering gray of winter was no match for the sun that day.

I lamented all the early mornings, darkest during the winter months, trying to squeeze in some yoga in the family room before the rush to serve breakfast, and fix lunch, and find Moosey Moose, and limit Evan's plastering Moosey with a zillion kisses goodbye, in the hopes of still catching the bus and my first cup of coffee on time. Rarely did I stop to enjoy the breathtaking birth of a new day.

I'd completed several visual laps of our surroundings before MacCraith woke with a startle. A garble of words burst from his lips as his limbs jerked outward. He was lucky they did. He seized onto the branch he was sitting on, arms and legs enveloping it in a death grip, when he found himself airborne. The private's gasp woke McIntyre, who swung toward the sound, musket first.

Trees, trees, trees, trees, and trees. Nothing was moving in on us.

McIntyre checked the opposite direction. I shook my head no when our eyes met in the middle. Calculating the hour to be early enough, judging by his review of the sun's climb, he returned to his position behind the tree to sleep.

The boy was sheepish, his cheeks burning, when I offered a reassuring smile. Deciding to get a move on, he climbed from his perch and wandered in the opposite direction of the clearing. He paused, looking lost as he studied the side of a tree, then me, then his surroundings, before starting the cycle again. Several more steps led to another pause.

When his embarrassed glance returned to me, I caught on to his dilemma and circled to a branch on the far side where he couldn't see me. The splatter of urine hitting the forest floor soon followed, making me aware of my own urgent needs.

The debacle of descending from my perch without falling and

breaking my neck was no picnic because my ass had gotten sore. I limped in the general direction of the latrine. The boy jogged over to suggest I stay close, but once I explained my intensions, he backed off, leaving me to my own devices.

The damn thing was gone, disassembled, and the wood carted away, the foul ditch buried at last. Not a corncob in sight. I never thought I'd miss a latrine. A plethora of fat trees, willing to offer some privacy in its place, was mine for the choosing. Hooray.

What I would've given to wash up at the stream. A literal Continental breakfast was waiting for me to fish it out of Auden's bag. Well, apples and bread, anyway. Only the lifelong, in depth, gruesome lectures on the workings of feces-induced diseases in the digestive track prevented me from digging in. Lacking reinforcements within shouting distance made any waterside fieldtrip a stupid idea of epic proportions. Food had to wait until after McIntyre woke and we could go together.

MacCraith was leaning against the base of his tree when I returned. Cradled on his lap was a letter. The private's fingers were tracing the graceful looping of a signature. His mouth worked as he drew out the sound of the name enrapturing him. It was snapped closed and tucked into his bag when I sat to face him.

"Is she pretty?" I asked, referring to the secret missive.

"Och, aye," he said, hesitant. "How did ye know?"

"How did I know she was pretty?" I teased.

"Ah, no." He was slow to warm to me. "Tha' it 'twas a lass tha' wha sent me the letter?"

"I saw you last night with your friend. He was teasing you about it, or one like it. Then I saw you here, now, looking fondly at it." He blushed and couldn't look at me. "You don't need to be embarrassed. We've all been there."

"Been there?"

We were already keeping our voices low, but his shy whispers were difficult to hear. I scootched closer. The private's back went ramrod straight with concern, stopping me.

"How long have you known her?" I asked from my original spot.

"Several seasons." The joy blossoming on his face made the whole rest of the world disappear.

I smiled. "What's she like?"

"Like?"

"What sort of things is she interested in? What does she like to do?"

"Oh... ah... I do na' rightly know." Such a question was a novelty to him. His eyes widened with amazement. Memories of their time together colored his freckles while he contemplated how he might answer.

"Well, what does she write about?"

He eyed me with sudden suspicion. "Why is it tha' ye are asking so many questions?"

Caught off-guard, I smiled and retreated from my habitual lawyering. "I was curious. It's nice to see someone in love."

"Are ye na' in love with Captain Wythe?" The suspicion still resided in his look.

"I… barely know him."

"Yet," MacCraith blushed again and whispered, as if the trees might find our conversation obscene, "ye and he do run tame."

"Uh, we share a tent, if that's what you mean. For protection. Doesn't make us lovers."

"Then… 'tis the doctor wha' ye are in love with?"

"Okay. Interesting. What makes you think I'm in love with anyone?"

"Well, what when the doctor did take yer hand, ah…"

It was my turn to be embarrassed. "I met the doctor, like, a couple of days ago. We're just friends."

The sound of a woodpecker filled the void in our conversation. I took refuge in following the direction of its insistent tapping.

"Major DeForest says ye are a spy," the boy told the sky. After he tried and failed to look at me, he picked at a thread he'd worked loose from the top of his gaiter.

"And it's your job to report back to the major what I do and say, right?" The boy paled and stared. "A lucky guess on my part. Major DeForest doesn't like or trust Captain Wythe, and thereby me."

"Aye. Oh… Well, I canna read," he blurted. "So, I could na' say what 'twas in the letter." The bluster of courage failed him, and MacCraith grew quiet again. He leaned forward and started in on the bottom of his gaiter.

"I can read. I'd be happy to read it to you," I offered.

He brightened for a moment, then darkened. "Major DeForest said ye were a clever one. Tha' ye would try to trick me by pretending to be kind."

"Offensive much?" When the boy didn't respond, I got up and brushed the leaves and dirt off, my solitary sky-high duty suddenly promising far better company.

"'Tis what he has said, is all," MacCraith called after me.

"Whatever."

My butt protested resuming my treetop post. Too bad. I stayed there, grousing long after MacCraith had wandered into the woods, always within sight of McIntyre. Yeah, it was the major who was the problem, poisoning those around us. I sighed. Temporary. Everything was temporary, until I get home.

I shouldn't have snapped at the boy.

We kept to ourselves as the sun climbed to its peak. I raised my face to meet it, thankful the day was warmer than any of the previous since I'd arrived. McIntyre disappeared. MacCraith wanted to follow but was ordered by the older man to stay. He shot an anxious look in my direction. After stalking the base of his tree several times, MacCraith braved the climb back up, as well.

I couldn't stand it anymore. Expecting to find sanitary conditions again was hopeless. I devoured the bread and apple from Auden.

After the second or third time MacCraith's stomach gave an audible growl, it occurred to me I hadn't seen him with anything more than his fur satchel and weapons. He eyed me as I crossed to the base of his tree and began climbing. The hand on his non-functional pistol tightened. I offered an apologetic smile and, wrapping my arm around a branch to keep from falling, handed up the mystery-meat jerky from Auden.

The private hesitated, but in the end, he accepted my offering with a meek, "Thanks to ye."

I nodded and, once earth-bound again, headed for the clearing. My body revolted at the idea of more tree hugging. The several days-worth of unfamiliar tasks and limited amounts of food and water were wreaking havoc on my muscles. I attempted to alleviate the kinks by stretching, reaching upward and enjoying the release from my clenched lower back.

Unrestrained, now Tent City had moseyed onward, the previously comatose grass perked up with the spring sunlight. A survey of the forest's borders showed we were very much alone. The breeze stirred, and the blue, silk ribbon lazed in its wake.

Birdsong, composed of a rapid, repeating phrase of twittering, breezed by the treetops. The source was a cobalt-blue bird, the size of a wren, as it passed the former campsite. When it reached the far end, it circled back to glide over the area again then touched down in an evergreen, near the road leading away from town, before it took wing. It flew in low and landed next to the Stick of Allegiance.

I inched closer, trying not to make a sound. Another scan of the woods showed nothing else moving.

The bird lifted itself with a fluttering of its wings and hovered inches from the stick. As it did, it pecked at the ribbon. Bad enough it had been left out during the night, I couldn't let a bird destroy it or make off with it for its nest. How would I explain to Jonathan?

I ran into the clearing, withdrawing Auden's pistol from my bag as I did. The bird rushed into the air at my approach. I knelt on the ground, my fingers trembling during my rescue attempt, knowing how exposed I was in such a wide, open space.

A rustle of feathers brought the bird swooping to perch itself on my hand. I stifled a gasp. The fearless thing steadied itself on my upturned forefinger. I didn't dare breathe, unsure what it was doing as it ducked its head, peering at the bandage on my wrist and taking in its length spiraling up my arm. A tiny shiver whispered along my finger. The bird's black upper beak separated from the lower half of a pale yellow. Most of its feathers were blue with swaths of pewter streaks peppered in, including through its cute, stubby tail.

Amused by the idea of my unexpected friend trying to claim a piece of the bandage in lieu of the ribbon, I jostled my hand and encouraged it. "Go on."

A little resituating was all the bird cared to do.

It looked like a regular bird. The way my skin tingled at its touch made me wonder. It cocked its head. Shining black eyes took to examining my face, focusing on my forehead. I leaned in for a closer look.

A swift fluttering of its wings sent the bird on its way. Reminded of the need to hurry, I searched my surroundings while I finished working the ribbon's knot loose. Brilliant sunlight and occasional puffs of clouds filled the sky. My feathered friend, however, had disappeared.

The ribbon slid free from the stick. I tucked it into my bag and ran back into the safety of the woods. Twittering kept pace with me.

The little blue bird was sitting on a branch, behind me. As innocuous as it should've been, the bird's watchful eye made me uncomfortable. Our odd exchange ended when it took off. It circled the camp's borders once more before it disappeared.

Chapter Twenty-Eight

McIntyre returned sometime after my strange encounter with the bird, carrying roasted meat, skewered on two wooden spits and seasoned with actual herbs. It didn't seem like he'd been gone long enough to hunt and prep a meal. The man was a marvel. More marvelous was how it tasted.

Once Private MacCraith had finished sucking the bones clean, McIntyre gestured for the boy to surrender his deficient weapon. A suitable piece of flint was selected from his bag.

Flintlocks and a fireside barbeque. Just like pirates. A dream come true for Evan.

Nope. Treetop watch for me. A short-lived arrangement in the end. It was hard to concentrate because McIntyre's repairs of the pistol were fascinating.

He spent little time focused on what his hands were doing as he chipped away at the stone's edges—our surroundings, his constant concern—until he'd crafted it into the correct shape and size to fit the jaws of the hammer.

After screwing them tight around the flint, McIntyre—aware of my involuntary study of his every move—gestured for me to come down and observe.

MacCraith supplied him with a paper cartridge, which the older man ripped open with his teeth. The hammer was pulled back one click, about halfway. Most of the powder was poured into the barrel and *tap, tap, tapped* further inside with the gun's ramrod.

Digging into the cartridge, McIntyre withdrew a lead ball and a bit of fabric. He wrapped the ball in the fabric, which he also tamped down. The remainder of the powder was fed into the flash pan before he de-cocked the weapon and returned it to MacCraith.

McIntyre held out his hand to me. It took a moment to realize he was offering to check mine too. Other than his initial raised eyebrows, his thoughts were unreadable when I retrieved the silver-colored pistol from Auden's bag and informed McIntyre of whose it was. They didn't betray surprise. Just what did the camp's inhabitants think of me and my fledgling relationships with Auden and Jonathan?

McIntyre turned the piece over in his hands, and—as I hadn't taken time to inspect it before—I admired it along with him. Unlike the private's weapon with its typical wooden grip, Auden's pistol was made of steel, tip to stern. The grip wasn't smooth, either. It ended decoratively with two strips curling back in and around toward a metal stem, like the bottom portion of a four-leaf clover. Instead of a trigger and finger guard, there was some sort of knob.

No wonder it felt funny the couple of times I'd handled it. Stamped into the side was a daisy enclosed in an oval.

"Black Watch," McIntyre said. "Seven Years' War."

He determined the gun was unloaded by using a cleaning brush's handle to measure the available space inside the barrel. It filled the entire length, straight to the pinhole. No ball.

I fished out the tin box, where Auden—indeed—kept a few cartridges. McIntyre snagged one and passed it to me, ready to guide me through the loading process.

A twig snapped.

My gaze flew from the sealed paper cone to find McIntyre staring in the direction of the stream. A flash of red ducked behind a tree.

Oh shit!

Metal *c-lick-ked.*

McIntyre's massive arm swept around me to shove himself between me and the former campsite. If a barrage of profanity would've saved us, I'd have let loose. MacCraith squirmed on his perch when I glared at him. It was his pistol making the noise.

Peaceful, inconspicuous woodland scenery stared back at us with Bambi-like innocence from across the clearing. A woodpecker knocked, somewhere a squirrel chittered, but additional manmade noises? Absent. Not even a soldier's mount. The redcoat was there, though, no doubt.

My throat tightened. I still hadn't worked out if I should fight, if pressed, or bow out and watch. Would it even be an option? I counted each breath—ten, then fifty—struggling with my disobedient lungs as I worried about the consequences of each choice.

McIntyre hadn't moved, so neither had I.

Another fifty. Counts, more counts. I lost track.

Somebody, do something.

A few more breaths before McIntyre reached around with a massive hand to guide me toward the base of my look-out. Once I was hidden behind its trunk, I exhaled, and resumed counting, the numbers three and perhaps seven next finding its way into the descending tally.

Focus, Savvy.

I squashed my back into the bark and searched the woods surrounding us. The steel pistol was in one hand, the paper cartridge, intact, in my other. But my mind was blank. I couldn't remember the steps I'd just watched to load the pistol.

McIntyre edged backward until he was facing me. I mouthed no, there weren't any soldiers behind us. He slipped into the bushes. Four fingers raised to MacCraith. The private nodded. With his eyes, McIntyre ordered me into the branches above. I agreed whole-heartedly, tucking Auden's pistol and the paper cartridge in my leather bag to begin climbing.

The first branch was on the side farthest from the clearing. To get beyond reach, though, I'd have to circle the tree, making me visible to the redcoats. I sought guidance from below, but McIntyre had vanished into the undergrowth. Deciding it wasn't worth the risk, I pressed my chest into my only source of cover. MacCraith snuck a peak. The way he darted behind the trunk wasn't encouraging.

A shot rang out.

Fuck.

It tore through the leaves to my left, the opposite side of where the private stared back at me, eyes wide. MacCraith was about to swing around the tree to return fire. I shook my head at him wildly. There were only two of us. If there was a similar number of redcoats to the ones from the day before, we stood no chance in a gunfight.

Where the hell is McIntyre?

I tucked the steel pistol under my cloak to mask the sound of the hammer. A cluster of leaves bobbed in the breeze. I held my breath and waited.

Quiet.

Nothing else moved.

I tore the cartridge open, ready to pour the powder into the barrel when a nagging feeling stopped me. Something wasn't right. I'd missed a step, maybe? MacCraith showed me his pistol, mimicking de-cocking the weapon. I shook my head, confused. I needed to load it. He repeated the motion.

A call like a mourning dove filled the air. Only three notes.

I squeezed my eyes shut.

I'm not going to die here. I have to see my son.

I took a deep breath and tried to focus.

There was only the one shot. Nothing else had followed. It'd gone wide, making it hard to tell if we'd actually been spotted or if the redcoats were tempting us to reveal our location by firing back.

A sound choked off, close to where we were hiding. There was the whisper of undergrowth being displaced. I couldn't tell if anything else happened. My heart was pounding in my ears.

If I couldn't steady the trembling in my hands, I risked the pistol rattling its way free and careening to the ground.

MacCraith gestured again, and I figured out what the problem was. I'd pulled the hammer back too far. Clicking it to the halfway point, I braced my arms against the tree trunk as I struggled through the novel steps.

I did it!

A man's voice seized in pain. A shot cracked, sending a body crashing into the bushes. Someone rushed through the trees. Another shot followed. It had to be McIntyre. It sounded like he was trying to lead the soldiers away from us.

MacCraith fired toward the clearing, in the direction of where the redcoats had given chase.

For Evan.

I thrust my arm as far as I could reach past my hiding spot and ducked my head out to find a target. There were only two. I tugged on the trigger. The knob jammed at first, breaking loose the next. The hammer snapped forward, sparking the powder to life.

My eyes slammed shut at the burst of light and smoke. A painful cry meant I hit the guy! Not something I celebrated for long.

Shots were exchanged from near the forest road. A musket ball pierced the foliage within a foot of where I was cramming my forehead into the tree trunk, trying to balance on the branch and fumble with another cartridge of powder.

MacCraith got off another round. I readied myself with a deep breath. The private raised his palm to stop me before I could take aim. I glanced at my pistol. It was loaded correctly. But he was staring toward the clearing.

We waited.

Nothing happened.

For an eternity.

No more gunfire. No other sounds or movement.

MacCraith descended from his perch. I followed his line of sight to where McIntyre was approaching. He did a visual check of both of us, top to bottom.

"We leave at dusk," he said before disappearing.

Chapter Twenty-Nine

The sound of riders approached as the afternoon sun was waning. A speckled horse led the way with a pale yellow at his side. Both were carrying men of blue. Three mounts carrying green uniforms stayed close to the break in the woods, behind them, not moving beyond the relative cover of the trees. Only the black with starry-white sides strode forward, stopping next to the Stick of Allegiance stationed at its center.

The man dismounted and headed toward our former hiding place at the far end of the clearing. McIntyre had since moved us to the corner farthest from the stream and the bodies he'd hidden in the underbrush.

I damn near fell in my rush to run out and meet Jonathan, wondering only for a moment why he chose to look for us there. I was that painfully relieved to see him. He needed a bath, in an it's-getting-important kind of way, and looked weary to the bone, but he was otherwise in decent shape. No signs of blood or anything else indicating he'd been caught in another skirmish.

"What has happened?" he asked.

I reassured him we were fine before it occurred to me—he wanted an accounting of where the camp had gone, not knowing about our afternoon encounter with the redcoats. Before I could get far, though, he took my hand and showed me my own bandaged wrist.

"It's nothing."

"This is hardly nothing, Miss Moore."

"Sure, it is. I scraped it climbing a tree."

He wouldn't let me reclaim my hand, clasping it between both of his, low, out of sight from the others. I followed the path of his eyes, which remained fixed on the thumb wandering the curve of mine. A sensation like a ray of sunlight reaching from behind a cloud danced along my skin at his touch. It twirled up my wrist, soothing away the sting.

"I just bandaged it. To keep it clean." My words were unsteady; the feeling as it intensified, a distraction. Jonathan released my hand during my second attempt to separate us. The warmth disappeared, and the sensation faded.

"And here?" He swept aside the loose hair dangling against my forehead.

"A… scratch from a tree branch."

"It looks to be more serious than a mere scratch."

"Does it? That's not good."

He sighed and scanned the rest of me.

"I'm fine," I told him. "Are you?"

"Evidently, you are more trouble than I imagined."

"Not answering my question, I see."

"Unlike you, I am unharmed."

"How nice for you," I joked, though I doubt he missed the unintentional sigh of relief mixed in with the sarcasm. "Do you have some of your vinegar water?" He affirmed he did by handing over the canteen at his hip. "And a clean handkerchief?"

Jonathan raised an eyebrow at the request but pulled one from an interior pocket. It needed a quick shake, then to be turned inside out—he'd smeared it with his fingers—before I could apply the mixture. "Allow me," he offered.

My answer consisted of returning his canteen, though I did thank him. Dodging his hand, I pressed the cloth to my forehead. A sharp sting meant I'd found the right spot.

"I can see better," he said and made a second attempt at claiming Chief Resident of Wilderness Hospital status.

"I got it." I inhaled sharply when the struggle squeezed some of the vinegar into my eye.

"Woman, you are making a mess. Allow me to assist you."

"*Man*. You're one to talk. You're filthy."

"I have ridden all day in search of you. It is to be expected."

"In search of me*?* I haven't gone anywhere, remember? And you smell like a horse's ass. I'd rather nothing get into the cut and infect it."

"Yuh… er…" Jonathan wrestled for a response but came up short. He eyed the trees and leaned in to keep his exclamation from potential eavesdroppers, "God's teeth, but you are impossible."

"Thank you," I answered, sugar and pie at him.

"Do not think it," he said, fighting the game I was tempting him to play. "It was not a compliment."

"I only accept compliments from you. So, thank you."

"Indeed." His mouth twitched. "I suppose you would have me accept your claim that I smell like a horse's... backside with your compliments?"

"Only a true friend would be this kindly honest with you."

He sighed and smiled, frustration lost with our banter. "Incorrigible."

His hands were so close to mine as he gathered and eased the handkerchief free, the memory of his touch floated along my skin. The fabric stretched between us. Jonathan's forefinger closed the distance, finding the back of my own.

"We stand here exposed." Alexander's interruption startled me, and our hands separated, leaving me the victor of our funny little game. "Time runs out." With a glare at me, Alexander returned to the other soldiers. I hadn't even heard him approach in the first place.

The green uniforms stood at the edge of the road, stretching and rubbing down their horses. McIntyre and Private MacCraith were with them, the herd noting our exchange with varying degrees of interest and smirking.

Flirting? You can't flirt with him. What the actual...?

I became self-conscious, both at my conduct—had I fractured my brains when I fainted?—and about the response Jonathan was giving me. Despite the reprimand from his buddy, he continued to smile at me. A sense of peace rolled off him, inviting me in.

Maybe it was the relief of him returning whole and healthy, but standing close to him, aware of the heat rising from his body and the way he drank me in with his eyes, it felt vaguely familiar. Safe.

He offered to treat my face again, right around the time I shoved the handkerchief at him. Not meaning to accept his offer, I jerked back, surprised, when he raised his hand to my forehead. "My pardon. I, ah," he managed.

"It's fine." I forced a quick smile before escaping in the direction of our amused audience.

Jonathan stopped me by calling, "Miss Moore, would... would you be so kind as to see to my horse?"

"Um, sure," I agreed and received the reins from him. "What do I do?"

"You jest."

"Nope."

"In truth? You have never tended to horses before?"

"Do my words not sound like the English language again?" I

joked.

His laugh was incredulous. An eyebrow raised, a seeming "huh" in the twist of his head as he shrugged it off. "Come," he said. Together, we walked toward the edge of the clearing, where the men had gathered. "I shall teach you when I return." He gave his horse a loving pat on the neck, instructing the animal to "keep watch o'er the lady," then he glanced my way, adding a mock warning. "Beware. She is a hopeless maiden of misfortune."

"Uh-huh. Where are you going?"

"Not far. I would speak with you about certain matters. First." He leaned close, which amused the herd, even if they couldn't hear what was said. "As a friend has kindly informed me, I needs must attend to my toilet."

It took me a moment to translate—he wanted to clean up. "Wait! There're redcoats near the stream."

Jonathan's brows raised in surprise. He called to the others. "You encountered regulars?"

"Tha' we did," MacCraith acknowledged. "Hell mend 'em."

Alexander took charge, saying, "A scouting party was discovered surveying the major's numbers. They were tracked less than a mile westward to an encampment perhaps twice that of our own. DeForest donned a white feather at the sight and fled."

"Major DeForest is na' a coward," MacCraith challenged him. Alexander indulged in a smirk to Jonathan. "Ye canna expect us tae stand in the open agin so many." Captain Condescending's smile lost its smugness.

Wow. I was wrong. The private did understand, better than I, how dire our situation was.

Slapping his reins off to the private, Alexander moved closer to Jonathan and thereby me. MacCraith was surprised by the treatment, staring at the leather straps. When he raised his eyes, determination filled them. His puffed-up chest dropped at a subtle shake of McIntyre's head, outranked as they were.

Alexander relayed what he'd learned of the skirmish earlier in the day. I nodded, verifying what was said.

"You were to be kept from harm's way," Jonathan muttered at the ground. "It was wrong to leave you."

"Don't be ridiculous. You had your mission. It didn't include me." Pointing out how his being there wouldn't have made a difference—I was in danger no matter where we went—fell on deaf ears. It caught Alexander's interest, though. A once-over of my appearance ensued.

Jonathan shook his head to himself before asking, "Are you aware of the major's current location?"

"He said he'd leave a message at Fort Clinton about—"

"Fort Clinton?"

"Naturally." Alexander's comment was flippant, which he paired with a knowing look to Jonathan.

"In which direction did the militia travel?" Jonathan pressed.

"That way," I said, indicating the path toward town.

"That way leads north," Alexander said with derision, "away from Fort Clinton."

"But once near town," Jonathan countered, "the road branches back southward."

The news was troubling them. Something other than the camp breaking without them. I wished I'd asked Auden more questions about where we were and how to find his final destination.

"He did say the camp was traveling away from… what we discussed," I added. Once again, the need to coordinate stories frustrated me. I wasn't sure what Alexander had been told or if I should keep to the spy story we'd left with the major. "Though it might've been a lie."

"What under the Heavens would cause you to suspect that?" Alexander turned away from me, shouldering Jonathan until he'd cut me out of the conversation. "Send your scout."

"The light soon fails us." Jonathan glanced over his shoulder at me as he spoke. "And it may be for naught. The roads could very well have been seized by now."

"The dark matters little. It is better to know for certain."

"We should not remain." Jonathan nodded in agreement.

"We shall have to leave the men behind. Their horses are spent."

Jonathan nodded again, eyebrows furrowed. Alexander clapped a hand to Jonathan's shoulder, then moved off to speak with the soldiers.

"There's more to your mission, isn't there?" I asked.

"Aye, and time closes in on us."

"But—"

"A moment." Jonathan lifted a hand to the small of my back, leaving it to hover there without touching, and guided me away from the others. "Forgive me, Miss Moore. It is imperative that I bring… that I reach my destination. My contacts are expecting me, else Captain Brott could travel in my stead."

"Just tell me how to find the hillside. Please."

"I could not in good conscience allow you to travel without protection."

I stared at his boots, not wanting him to see the purse of my lips as I wrestled with how to respond. Jonathan sighed, then considered Alexander in the distance. "You seek the wooded region between and to the south of New Cornwall and the Landing. East of here. There are no roads to lead you there directly. If you come with us, I make for New Windsor, to the North. There, we might receive word of the number and movement of the regulars."

The Highlands of New York, so-called because of the Scots and English who settled there a century earlier. At least, now I knew where I was.

"I have to get home," I whispered.

"As such… it would be safest to leave in the morning. We shall need the light if we are to journey through the forest."

"We? But, your mission? You said time is running out."

"I have sworn to protect you," he answered, as if it were as simple as wishing me a good night, though he added before I could object further, "You will not absolve me of my obligation. I should like to see you restored to your family myself."

The forested area to the East was densely packed with an impossible undergrowth of tangled bushes, vines, thorns, and the unknown. Jonathan had said the hillside where we met was overrun with redcoats. Our eventful afternoon had proven the area to the West was overrun, as well, with far more. Staring up at him as he asked if I needed to rest, I didn't doubt him. Not his words when we first met or the danger he feared was surrounding us.

"I can't let you abandon your mission," I said. "We'll go to New Windsor."

He touched a hand to my elbow. "You are certain? I would guide you east if that is your wish." After I confirmed I was, he said, "I am most grateful. As soon as it is reasonably safe to do so, we shall journey there."

"Okay. Thanks."

We exchanged a brief smile before he asked, "Now tell me true. How were you injured?"

I filled him in on what'd occurred at the water's edge and my involvement in the day's skirmish, though I downplayed how scared I was. Better believe I didn't mention the nightmarish presence. Jonathan was troubled enough. His doppelgänger trying to break into our tent, however, was something I knew I shouldn't keep from him. He wasn't happy, to say the least.

"Did he harm you?"

"No."

"These injuries, they are not from the regular? He did not attack you?"

"No. Promise," I said, hoping to allay his dramatic response to the news. "The guy ran off."

"Ran off?" A finger was thrust into my face as he accused, "You followed, which was why you were at the water's edge. God's teeth, woman!"

"Yeah, I know. In hindsight, it was stupid."

"You could have been killed."

"Maybe. I mean, I thought he was you. He's kinda like you."

"Miss..." His voice was full of warning.

"He certainly has your grumpy—"

"He is *not* me," Jonathan persisted.

"Yeah? Who is he, then?"

Jonathan seized his hips with his hands. He glared at the ground when he grumbled, "What did the man want?"

"Who *is* he?"

"He is... one of many complications."

"I bet."

"Only let us make certain that he does not capture you. For both our sakes."

I tensed at his warning. Complications with Jonathan were something I definitely didn't need on my quest to get home.

"I have frightened you," he noted. "For which, I apologize. Nonetheless, it is imperative that you understand the danger in which you have placed yourself."

"That's just it, isn't it? I don't understand." Jonathan turned silent. I shook my head, frustrated, when I said, "It's not my business what side you fight on, but it's impossible to protect myself when I'm left in the dark."

"He is loyal to the Crown, and now he has seen you in a rebel camp." He stared, waiting until I was staring back before he insisted, "Never forget. Would you, I implore you, answer my question?"

I could've lied. Told him I hadn't a clue what the guy was after. I wanted more time to think things through. What was the most likely outcome if I'd never been there and Jonathan had been left with the trunk? Expecting intel on my uninvited guest was pointless. I'd witnessed my self-appointed protector, doubling as a potential spy, in action. Mute in the line of verbal fire was his *modus operandi*.

Aggravating as it may've been, Jonathan was willing to sacrifice his entire mission for my sake. I realized I didn't want to lie to him. Not this time.

"A letter," I replied.

"A letter?"

"I found a letter hidden in the trunk you gave me. I think he saw the seal on it when I was holding it."

"Did you read its contents?"

I shrugged. "It was mostly a bunch of numbers."

"What is this?" Alexander demanded from behind my shoulder and continued past me to stand next to him.

"Where is the spy's letter now?" Jonathan asked.

Alexander shot a look of surprise at him.

"Hidden," I told them. "In a secret compartment in the trunk."

"You were supposed to leave protections," Jonathan rebuked Alexander, who was taken aback and glanced my way. He didn't seem to share my confusion about what Jonathan meant but rather why it was said in my presence.

He recovered and gave a lackadaisical shrug of his shoulder. "The major's cabbage farmers can look after themselves."

Jonathan glowered at him, then turned on me with no less ire. "You should not have waited for me. You were safest with the major and his men. Did I not tell you as much?"

"It's not like I had a choice," I retorted, irritated at becoming the target of his bad mood.

"Explain yourself."

The story of being summoned to the major's tent and outplayed was dragged out of me, stunted by my keen desire to confess to only Jonathan what'd happened. My request to speak with him in private was overridden by both men. It left him grumbling.

"I'm sorry about your trunk," I added.

Alexander crossed his arms. "Snatch cly?" he asked Jonathan.

"More like to strike at me. Where are the ribbon and key?" Jonathan demanded.

"Here." I reached into Auden's bag to show him. Jonathan swept them from my hand and tucked them into the pouch on his hip. "Hey!" I snapped at him, insulted I was no longer entrusted with the key to a trunk he'd given to me. "It's not my fault the major stole our stuff. What do you expect me to have done with it even if he had left it with me? We're in the middle of nowhere."

"You shall have it back," he softened. "For now, I have need of it."

His change in tone didn't pacify me, though. "You're going to unlock a trunk that isn't here?"

"Do not," Alexander warned. It wasn't me he was chastising.

"Some of us keep our word," Jonathan answered him.

"Some of us are not so foolish as to give it needlessly."

Jonathan's horse grew restless at the bickering and pawed the ground, forcing me to retreat or else endure being trampled. I made room for him without arguing, who then moved to the animal's side and whispered in his ear, soothing him with several strokes to his muzzle.

"Walk with me," he ordered Alexander.

Staring down their backsides as they crossed to the far end of the clearing, leaving me holding the reins, I worried maybe time was running out for me too.

Chapter Thirty

Jonathan and Alexander's voices carried during their absence; their words muffled by the distance, but not their anger. The rest of us grew nervous. The soldiers readied their rifles and searched for possible danger; their respective fatigue set aside out of necessity. McIntyre signaled for Private MacCraith to follow, and they disappeared into the woods to assess the area on their own. I wanted to stick with McIntyre, but he used an actual word to voice his disapproval, ordering me to "remain."

Left Alone with Three Armed Strangers takes the gold for awesomest circumstances. They kept an eye on me during the lengthy silence that followed the supposed friends' outburst. One in particular got testy when the steel pistol made its appearance so I could conduct my own examination. I put some distance between us during the process.

When the cranky captains deigned to return, they donned matching scowls and refused to look at each other. Alexander stormed past me to retrieve his horse from where we'd hitched the animals. The green uniforms had long since gathered at the road's entrance to light a fire. A flask was being passed around when he approached them. None of them rose to stand at attention. One man spat on the ground in Alexander's general direction while his back was turned. Another chuckled under his breath at the insubordination.

Alexander either didn't hear or care. He ripped his horse's tether loose and mounted before charging off toward the northern road. Jonathan called to him as he thundered past. "I will return for them in the morning," Fair-Weather Friend shouted, disappearing into the trees. The uniforms scoffed at the notion of them needing chaperoning from the condescending prick.

Jonathan huffed a sigh, exasperated. Must not have been the plan. He didn't criticize the expletive I used to describe Alexander. It was infuriating to be caught in the middle of their constant fighting, especially since it related to me yet was hashed out during my absence.

Orders were growled at me to wait where I was. McIntyre and MacCraith rejoined the group from the depths of the woods when Jonathan approached the soldiers, and the testosterone meeting began without little womanly me.

To hell with this.

I marched toward them, but they broke before I got halfway, ensuring my continued exile from all useful information. Jonathan returned with his horse in tow and thrust the reins into my hand, not even slowing as he stalked past me to retrieve the stick from the center of the clearing. It was cast to the side. The other men stamped out the fire, scattering the evidence of it having been there.

Smothering my frustration as best I could, I raised a hand to wave goodbye to McIntyre and MacCraith. The private looked at McIntyre, who gave me a nod of farewell.

MacCraith ducked his head. "Black-Eyed Susans," he announced. "The lass cares for those."

Chin held higher, though his cheeks were freshly flushed, the private followed the other men onto the southern road, the one that'd delivered them to the former campsite only an hour or two earlier.

Jonathan yanked the reins from my hand on his return visit. "Come."

I wasn't thrilled about being treated like some precious, itty bitty lap dog to *come* or *sit* or *stay* as he pleased, but it hadn't escaped my notice how he was eyeing the general direction of our redcoat problem.

He crossed the line, though, after we were tucked into the protective cover of the woods and he demanded, "Mount."

"Are you asking me or telling me?"

"I have not the patience, woman." He kept his voice under careful control despite the anger simmering underneath.

"I'm not taking orders from you."

"Then you can remain here," he grumbled.

"Some man of honor you are."

"I am not to blame for your presence here!"

His declaration surprised me. It made me wonder what horrible words had been exchanged with Alexander. It also helped quiet my anger as I told him, "I never said you were. Look, I get I'm inconveniencing you and your mission. I also get it's causing some consternation between you and Captain Brott, and I'm sorry." But Jonathan didn't answer. His brows had slammed together, and he seemed tongue-tied. "What is it? What's wrong?"

I swung around, expecting trouble. Only the wilting glow of sunset was there. Turning back to him, I discovered he looked perturbed and a little ill. When he lowered his head, silent, I placed a hand on his cheek. His skin burned, but instead of looking flushed, he was pale.

"Are you okay?" I scanned his body, worried he was injured and I'd somehow missed the signs.

It took him a minute to find his voice again. The strange look on his face, however, remained. "I do not know how it is you were brought here."

"I know. Here, why don't you—?"

"Nay, ah." Efforts to lift the canteen from his side were resisted. "I have promised to do all that I can to restore you to your home." Concern crowded his face. "Do you believe me?"

"I trust you."

Exhaustion weighed on him. "Mayhaps, I am not deserving of your trust."

"W-what do you mean? Because of the redcoat?"

He gathered my injured hand in his, careful to avoid the pinky. A grumbling in his throat accompanied the way he studied the increased swelling there. Touching a fingertip to a freckle, close to my thumb, he traced its circumference, circling attentively, as if trying to balance on its tiny edge, then followed with his palm sliding over top to rest there. For several moments, he held onto me with eyes pressed close.

Jonathan's horse snorted and shifted its weight, causing the branches of the undergrowth to scratch against each another. A bird perched in a tree overhead. Its twittering added to the tiring accompaniment of daily birdsong. His features softened. Peace of mind warmed his expression, and it radiated through our joined hands, calming me, as well. I found myself relaxing into him, my face right below his when he returned to me.

"I will do what is right by you," he vowed.

"I know you will."

Our physical closeness caught his attention, and he ceased his exploration from the flush of my cheeks to the shape of my mouth. Clearing his throat as he stepped back, he commented on the setting sun and the need to leave before night was upon us. A huge sigh escaped him. "You have told me before that you are unfamiliar with horses. I should have remembered. I can teach you how to mount."

"I know how to mount a horse," I said kindly.

"You do?"

"I just don't know how to care for horses."

He watched as I approached the animal and placed a steadying hand on its flank. Instead of mounting, though, I ran my fingers over its dusty coat. "I never *obey*," I attempted to lighten the mood with my tone, "but I do listen to the advice of my friends. Especially when I know they're just looking out for me."

"It is good of you to… I should not have… Thank you." Jonathan welcomed the attempt with a smile. "I shall take it under advisement." For a moment, we took each other in, grateful to have reached an understanding.

"What's a snatch…?" I couldn't remember the rest of the phrase.

"Snatch cly. It is a man who is so low as to steal from a woman."

"Oh." I patted the horse again before I fitted my foot into the stirrup to pull myself up and into the saddle. Saddle bags and a rolled cannister sprouted from every corner, which didn't leave a lot of space in between for riders. "Did you want me in front of you or behind?" I shifted my weight forward, smooshing into the attached luggage.

"I shall walk," Jonathan informed me as he gathered the reins. With a click of his tongue, he encouraged the horse onward. The unexpected departure temporarily unsettled my balance.

Once recovered, I leaned closer, over the bulky leather roll, and followed his example of keeping my voice low. "We can share the horse. There's room."

"It will not be necessary."

"You're tired."

He started to answer but cut himself short.

A violet sliver of sunlight twinkled amid the passing trees. The woods had already closed behind us, the former campsite well out of sight. Jonathan never stopped scanning the area around us when he spoke. "It would not be proper."

"Proper? We share a tent, for goodness' sake!"

"But we do not… we do not touch," he insisted.

"You've touched me before."

"Only when I was trying to heal you. Not as…"

"What?"

I wasn't really keen on his failure to expand on something this important, especially because he was refusing to look back at me. Flinging my cloak to the side so it wouldn't catch, I then swung my leg around and slid to the ground. Jonathan's cheeks were flushed when I jogged in front of the horse to face him.

"When you were injured," he stammered in frustration at the

sudden hold-up, "Your throat, there. When… Must you argue with me?" he pleaded with me. "We must move on."

"Well, then." I gestured to the horse's saddle.

"A respectable woman would never ride atop the same horse as a man," he murmured.

"There's no one here to see."

"I shall see."

I bit back a retort and glared, then I twirled around to continue down the road on foot. His words stung, which only irritated me more. I knew what the social conventions in the Colonies were. Of course, he was embarrassed about taking my hand earlier. Why did it bother me?

"Miss Moore," Jonathan called softly from behind me.

I refused to acknowledge him. Frustration at myself, him, and the whole situation drove me forward. The sound of the horse's hoofs crunching on the leaf-strewn path didn't carry. I checked to be sure they were following.

With no way to resolve the issue without one of us giving in, we kept our distance and held our tongues for another mile or so. But the farther we went, the angrier I became. "You're placing our lives in danger and slowing us down by refusing to ride with me," I complained.

Jonathan's longer stride caught up with mine. "You are offended?"

"Yeah, I am."

His shock only fueled my irritation. I picked up the pace, hoping to end the subject. I wanted to brood rather than take my frustration out on him. He matched me and mumbled about needing a moment so he might find the appropriate words before explaining, "I was reminded that I have been negligent in protecting your virtue. I merely seek to rectify—"

"I don't care what Alexander thinks. I only care about staying alive. If it means sharing a tent with you so I don't get attacked in the middle of the night or sharing a horse with you so we can escape the redcoats closing in on us, then damn it, that's what I'm going to do." He was lost for words, and I was too anxious to let him off gently because, without intending to, I snapped at him, "You said yourself you're concerned the road might be seized." Rational would have to wait until we were safe again, I guess.

"Aye," he admitted.

"You'd rather die than ride a horse with me. Can't imagine why I'm offended."

Storming off without making noise was impossible. It forced me to slow. The distance between us was sizeable, nonetheless, by the time

I realized I'd resumed our journey but he hadn't. Jonathan was standing where I'd left him with his head leaning against his horse's neck. Since the sun had long since made its exit, I couldn't tell what he was doing. A bird darting from his general vicinity interrupted my private debate about whether I should walk back and apologize. It flew overhead, choosing the same path we were following.

Jonathan raised his head and looked over to where I was waiting. I didn't know how to respond. Where were the words I needed to make things right?

He resumed walking, slow and silent. His head hung until he reached me. Sympathy filled his eyes, and we just regarded one another, uncertain how to proceed. He was trying to be considerate. I was trying to do the same. Problem being, our respective upbringings were clashing.

He spoke first. "It was not my intention to offend you."

"I know."

He held up a hand. "My horse has ridden since morning and cannot carry two."

Embarrassment heated my veins. The animal's condition had never once entered my mind. "Will we make it in time to where you need to go?" I asked, humbled.

"I cannot be certain. What is more, there is a small contingent of regulars who are monitoring the town through which we must pass."

"How do you know?" I whispered, searching the darkened road.

"The town is more than half a mile ahead. We will rest here for several hours and pass through once it is quiet." He waited, looking at me for agreement.

"Okay." It was hard not to be skeptical, let alone unafraid. Danger lurked in every direction, watchful for prey like us. I had to trust his experience and, thereby, judgment.

Jonathan found a thinned spot in the undergrowth where we could force our way through. It was a slog, even though most of the greenery was still waking for the season. When he figured we'd gone far enough from the road, he stopped to remove the horse's tack. Fatigue was wearing on him. He fumbled with the strap. I touched my good hand to his, and he surprised me by letting me finish for him.

The horse shook the dust loose from his coat once the saddle lifted from his back and nosed the forest floor in search of spring grass. His chomping made me acutely aware of the gnawing of my own stomach on nothing. At least one of us turned up something.

Jonathan passed me the horse's blanket. "We will not be able to light a fire."

"It'd attract attention for miles," I agreed.

"Aye." He gave a grateful smile.

"You aren't worried about him wandering off?" I nodded toward the horse.

"He is a faithful companion. He will not go far." Jonathan leaned against a tree. Exhaustion flooded his face. He closed his eyes, mumbling to himself.

"What?" I asked. A pocket of warm air floated across my face.

"You should rest. We shall not make the attempt for several hours."

"I'll be fine for a while longer. Why don't I take first watch? You can get some sleep." I held out the blanket for him.

He waved it off. "It would... hardly..."

"You look like you're about to fall over," I told him. "Please."

"You must stay close."

"Don't worry about me."

"My manners are not what they ought to be," he chastised himself, relief in his expression nonetheless. Bags and weapon holsters were stripped and dropped to his sides.

"Tell you what. When we're back in polite society, we can each play our expected parts and use our best manners. Okay?"

Jonathan eased himself to the ground in unsteady fits and bursts. "As you say." Sleep was pulling him under.

A question tickling my mind trickled out before I could stop myself. "As what?"

"W-what say you?"

"You said we don't 'touch as.' You didn't say as what."

"As man and wife."

Having mumbled his response, Jonathan went out cold. His head eased to the side, and his arms, which had been crossing his chest, slackened. Faithful Companion gave a final shake of his mane before he, too, lowered his head in repose.

A shiver coursed through my body. Winter seemed determined to reclaim the night as its own. Kneeling next to Jonathan, I extended the saddle blanket over him. He didn't stir. Strands of dark hair, having worked loose from its tie, trailed along his cheek and danced with each exhalation. I reached out to brush them away but stopped myself, afraid it might wake him. Instead, I watched the slow and steady rise and fall of his breathing.

This moody, handsome, complicated man frustrated and moved me in ways that amazed me. Exhausted to the point of dropping and assaulted with demands from all sides, he still felt guilty for failing to meet his own standards of what was appropriate treatment of a woman.

We barely knew each other, and yet, every argument seemed steeped in his efforts to take care of me. Even at their best, no other man had ever treated me with such loyalty or selflessness, and huddled there, guarding over him, uncertain of where we were going or what was in store for us, I found I was grateful he was in my life.

Then I burned with shame for being drawn away from my home and everything and everyone who was waiting for me there. I rose to begin another long watch in a nearby tree.

Chapter Thirty-One

Jonathan didn't wake the first time I said his name. I touched his knee. A gasp answered the third attempt, and his hand shot to the spot on his hip where his knife usually resided. I withdrew in case he took a swing at me by accident. The sound startled his horse, who whickered a complaint.

When recognition showed in his eyes, I apologized for disturbing him. "I can't stay awake much longer."

He searched the sky. "It nears two in the morning."

My gaze followed his, astonished he could estimate the hour from the stars. Constellations, whose names I didn't know, danced among threads of clouds. Still, they were familiar, even centuries before my birth. "Is it too late?"

He was studying my face when my attention returned to Earth. "Now is ideal." His smile faded. "Fear not. I am rested well enough to see us safely there."

"Just tired. Makes me cold."

"Ah." He eyed my wool cloak billowing as I shivered.

"Maybe scared. A little."

My prolonged yawn muffled whatever he said next, but I heard something involving "courage" and "virtues."

"What?"

"Can you ride?" he asked.

"I'll do whatever you need me to."

Supplies were gathered and repositioned over his chest. He checked his pistol before holstering it and reaching for the horse's saddle.

The sound of Jonathan speaking pulled me back awake. My mind struggled to understand what he was saying. He had to repeat himself, his fingers sliding across my arm, urging me to follow him to the road. Once there, he held the reins, encouraging me to mount. Assured I was settled, he advised he would need me to remove my foot from the stirrup. The poor animal groaned at the extra weight when Jonathan joined me in the saddle.

With a jolt, I fell against his chest as the horse leaped into action, hurtling us along the wooded pathway at a good clip. I struggled to balance myself, then skootched forward to give him space.

His arm wrapped around my front. "Be still, Miss Moore."

Any concern I had for respecting his society's rules about men and women's physical interactions fell away at the invitation breathed into my ear. I sank into him, drained, and settled into the rhythm of the horse's gallop. Countless trees raced by at a hypnotic rate.

We came to a stop near the town's outliers. The change yanked me into consciousness. Jonathan was surveying the sleepy houses, snuggled amid the trees. A frosty cloud gathered around my cheek when he said, "I must ask that you keep quiet as we pass through. Say nothing, and do as I ask without question. Will you agree to this?" I nodded. Whispering, almost to the point where I couldn't hear him, he sounded like he was praying. "*Et nos vidimus et testificamur*."

Icy particles floated, only to dissolve as his words warmed the night air. He closed his eyes while he continued softly. Too tired to pester him about maybe not taking a 2 AM meditation break in the middle of Redcoat Central, I allowed myself to drift as the stillness tempted me to sleep. Somewhere a bird was twittering.

It's too early to be morning already.

Jonathan's voice resonated through his body. "*Nos ex Deo sumus non qui non est ex Deo non audit nos*."

Warmth rose along with his words to wash through me. Abandoning any last effort at caring, I turned my body as much as the saddle allowed into his and pressed my cheek to his chest. He tensed, but cleared his throat instead of stopping me, and repeated his prayer.

When he was finished, he tapped the horse's flanks with his heels, and we moved toward the outskirts of the town. I pried my eyes open. A white saltbox slept in a muddy field, its windows dark except for the hint of firelight playing along the edge of a curtain. I tracked the light long enough to determine no one was watching us from inside the home as we continued past.

Two men talking in hushed tones drew me awake. They were moving away from us, slipping through the space between houses.

Bayonets pointed toward the stars. They were also in uniform. Red uniforms, peeking out from behind their lengthy overcoats. British soldiers.

I gasped and bolted upright on the horse. Jonathan's arm flew across my chest to clasp my shoulder. He pressed me close, securing me against his body, as he whispered in my ear, "Be silent. They shall not see us."

Multiple houses went by during an intolerable number of minutes as we rode onward. Through the narrow alleyways, other redcoats hid among the shadows, surveilling the sleeping town and watching for traitors.

The forest was right there. It stood ready to swallow the road and us with it. We couldn't reach it fast enough. Another horse and rider rounded the corner of the final house. The man's red uniform shone like a blood moon even in the dead of night. Concentrated calm controlled Jonathan's features, who continued our slow and steady gait toward the approaching rider. The redcoat was unperturbed by us and instead scanned the nearby trees.

Fear threatened to sabotage my efforts to mimic Jonathan's demeanor. I slid my fingers from their clasp on his arm to my bag. The steel pistol was so close.

He released my shoulder. Fingertips glided over my forehead and across my cheek, luring my eyelids shut as the warmth from his touch calmed me. I fought the sensation tingling along my skin. The redcoat was almost on top of us. He'd shifted his search to the space between the houses, looking toward the center of town instead of at us.

The leather flap was ridiculously heavy. My efforts to slip my hand inside my bag faltered. Jonathan traced his fingertips over my face again. Warmth cascaded through me, flooding my senses and drawing me away from myself like pebbles from the shore. A peacefulness welcomed me as I drifted with the tide.

Chapter Thirty-Two

Sunlight invited me to join the day. The room was cozy warm. It tempted me to laze in bed. I couldn't remember the last time I'd slept so soundly or woken feeling refreshed. The smell of wood smoke was what encouraged me to open my eyes. I didn't have a fireplace in my room.

Simple, white walls I didn't recognize greeted me. I bolted upright in a sprawling four-poster bed, softer and far more luxurious than anything I could ever hope to own. There was a single window with oak shutters tucked against the wall to my right. Late morning shone in crisp rays, highlighting tiny pieces of wood ash floating in the air. An expanding circle at the center of the window's pane, like ripples on a pond, spoke of hand-blown glass.

Rather than contain a typical corner, the opposite side of the room bulged inward at a forty-five-degree angle, shrouded in oak paneling. Red clay tiles encased an enormous fireplace at its center, and a steady fire, fed by a fresh pile of logs, crackled inside.

I'd been stripped of my clothes in favor of a fresh nightgown woven from coarse, white cotton. My panties remained. Everything else of mine was gone. Fresh linen bandaged my wrist. The swelling in my finger had all but disappeared. I stretched and squeezed my hand several times, more assured with each motion. There was little tenderness.

Searching the room for my clothes added to the mystery. I rifled through the waist-high dresser. Blankets and linens. I even checked the desk, resembling a giant cigar box on carved legs, lying within reach of the bed. Writing instruments, spare sheaths of paper, a handful of poetry books, and a decided absence of my belongings.

Looking out the window didn't reveal much about where I was. Numerous branches of a two-story lilac bush, dressed in young leaves and buds anxious to burst open, splayed over the glass. Beyond, a large yard stretched outward toward a stone wall encircling the property. Countless evergreens flooded the wilderness outside. Chickens with black tails and white-mottled breasts wandered the grounds, mixing with a smaller brood sporting varying shades of red feathers.

But there were no people.

And no redcoats, I was happy to discover.

A beautiful, pale green gown, lush with strawberries and vines twirling across the fabric, was draped over a ladderback chair. Forest-green trim graced the collar and twice encircled the edge of the sleeves.

Having glanced at the door without hearing anyone, I risked holding it against my chest. Something I'd never be permitted to do in my own time. The length of soft spun cotton flowed through my reverent fingers.

Returning the gown to its spot, I continued exploring the collection displayed on the round table snuggled between the chair and its mate, fascinated to see not a reproduction costume but clothing worn by real people. A folded, green quilted petticoat to match waited on the wooden seat.

Two strips of red fabric were arranged in a neat pile on top of a pair of heavy, gray thigh-highs. Not sure what the loose fabric was for, I twirled the strips around my fingers, wondering if they were left as a joke by Jonathan.

The sound of a door closing downstairs interrupted my musing. Someone started puttering at the far end of the house. I searched the room again, including under the bed. No sign of my clothes, boots… or Auden's bag. Which meant the steel pistol was missing too.

I grabbed a water pitcher from the dresser top, relieved it was sturdy clay. Someone's head was getting it if they tried anything.

Nervous, I crossed to the jolly-red bedroom door and pressed my ear to the wood. The puttering continued without voices. Easing it open, I discovered my room lay at one end of the house. Taking care to proceed first on tiptoe, I relaxed my entire foot, walking with a normal gait as I progressed farther through the hallway, grateful the large plank boards were accommodating by keeping quiet.

Peeking around the railing to the floor below brought into view a blue-and-gold floorcloth leading from the front of the house toward the back.

The stairs weren't as gracious as the quiet floorboards, though the sounds below continued at a marked pace, undisturbed, as I descended. As I reached the ground floor, an expansive lawn showed through the sidelights of the main entrance. A butter yellow parlor lay open to my right.

My only option was to wrap around the stairway toward the left. A grandfather clock with a solid, oak case flanked a second parlor. This one had the chaotic air of a private retreat, whereas the yellow was more welcoming for guests.

I caught a glimpse of myself in a gild-framed mirror. My forehead wasn't *that* bad. Examining the expanse of my throat, I noticed there was only a suggestion of pink without a scab. I shook my head, chuckling at Jonathan and Auden's overreaction.

A woman's voice singing the Eighteenth's rendition of a country song joined the sounds of her movements. I tracked it to the back of the house. A dining room faced me, and a second hallway, running perpendicular to the first, led to two other sun-infused rooms to my right. The area underneath the stairwell, to my left, was separated from the rest of the downstairs by an open door.

A woman with red, curly hair peering from under her white cap was crouched in front of an enormous kitchen fireplace. She was stirring a copper pot set on the hearth. The hem of her white-and-gray striped gown was bunched in her free hand, away from the open flames.

Steam rose in fragrant threads from the contents of a cast-iron cauldron suspended over the fire. It made my mouth water and my head swim.

She hopped to her feet, wiping her hands on a deep rose-colored apron as she did, then turned to the sizeable table in the middle of the room. A tray prepared with a tea pot, covered plate, and pewter cup was waiting alongside a massive kitchen knife.

Swiping the utensil of culinary mutilation, she then jumped at noticing me in the doorway with the pitcher in my hand. "Bless me! Are you a mad woman?"

"Excuse me?"

Her demeanor was pleasant enough, but I backed-up when she smacked the knife onto the kitchen table with a heavy rattle and came toward me to chide, "What are you doing walking around naked? What if the mistress should come home and see you as such?"

I was dumbfounded and stared at my nightgown.

She snatched away the pitcher before I could react. "Go upstairs. I have a tray started for you. I shall bring it along with the water. Go. Go on now!"

Her last command, though delivered with a kind, teasing undertone, brooked no refusal. I wound my way back around the stairway toward the front of the house and returned to my room. Not sure if I should close the bedroom door because I was deemed naked or leave it open as an invitation to enter, I settled on leaving it cracked.

I risked another look out the window for signs of anyone coming. It faced the back of the property and the forest beyond. No telling whether the mistress of the house was on her way or not.

With little else to do but worry about what'd happened to Jonathan, I took to examining the painting above the fireplace and had plenty of time to linger over the details. Breakfast, apparently, had gone out for a dawdling, country stroll. A white, Dutch colonial surrounded by a stone wall was so prominently featured amid the painted river valley and distant homes, I figured it must've been the house I was in.

"Ah, there you are," the woman said as she entered with the tray and pitcher.

I wondered where else she supposed I might've gone off to, though in a moment of light-headedness while I'd waited, my mind hiccupped—my meager lunch with McIntyre and MacCraith, an age ago—and I'd considered escaping to find a drive-through. Realizing the impossibility of such a quest almost broke my heart.

The woman bustled to the table and brushed aside the clothing left there to make room. The items were then relocated to the bed. Unclear about whether she was friend or foe, I avoided using his rank when I asked where Jonathan was.

"Ah, now, do not you worry about him," she said. "You are to eat, then I am to draw you a hot bath."

The woman's casual attitude about Jonathan was a good sign, and the promise of a bath was like winning the lottery, but I was still anxious from the previous night. How could I have fallen asleep? My heart had been pounding a mile a minute. I was convinced the redcoat riding toward us would've stopped us.

The woman clasped my arm and escorted me to a chair when I asked about Jonathan again, scolding me during the journey in her mock tone by saying, "Captain Wythe said you would like as be trouble."

Relieved to hear her call him Captain, not to mention the familiar, teasing label, I countered, "I'm not trouble. I just need to speak with him."

"He left you a message, he did. Said I was to give it to you if you were to argue." A sheath of fine linen paper, folded inward then halved, was handed to me.

Would she have given it to me if I hadn't "been trouble"?

No wax seal. My curiosity itched to learn how Jonathan stamped his letters. With his writing box elsewhere, under the determined custody of Major DeForest, I shouldn't have been surprised.

Though it was only a few lines, his handwriting was beautiful. Neatly spaced letters curled and looped in decorative flourishes. He wrote: "*To the Maiden of Misfortune, I must attend to another errand, but look to return before supper. Please accept the arrangements that have been made for you as a token of my friendship. With my compliments etc., JW*"

"Jerk." I laughed. Only Jonathan could find an eloquent way to use my words against me to say I smelled and to do it in perfect calligraphy.

"Ma'm?" the mystery woman asked from the fireplace where she'd been stirring the logs.

"Nothing. A joke."

"Ah." She caught me with my hand resting on the note, long after I'd refolded it and set it on the table next to me. "He is a right handsome one, that Captain Wythe."

"Is he?" I demurred, unwilling to go on record with my opinion.

"You have laid eyes on the man." She returned the poker to its place against the wall and crossed to the table. "I could do with a guardian the likes of him," she prattled on without any assistance from me and prepared a cup.

I damn near cried. Actual coffee! The woman was pleased with my reaction as I breathed in the aromatic brew and lingered over my first taste. The blend was silky smooth and a hint bitter. Perfection in a pewter wrapper.

"I shall come to fetch you once the bath is poured."

"Wait." I stopped her from rushing off. "I didn't catch your name."

She was good enough to repeat it so I'd remember: "'Tis Éabha. Éabha Carroll, ma'm." Though if she thought spelling the Gaelic helped… well, I got the feeling she was razzing me when she did, honestly.

"*Aw*-va." I took a stab at the pronunciation and was told close enough. "My name's Savvy."

"Savvy? 'Tis a right funny name." She smiled.

"It's short for Savannah."

"Cannot say 'tis much better," she teased and shook her head. "You had best eat. Skinny thing such as you."

"Wait," I called. Éabha was already half out the door again. "I don't even know where I am, whose house this is, where Captain Wythe is…?"

"Ah, such a fuss. You are a welcome guest in the home of Master

Johannes Cloet of New Windsor. Now, see to your breakfast. I expect the family to return in good time."

"And Captain Wythe?"

"The master and your Captain Wythe will be along." She smiled, scurrying from the room and closing the door behind her, leaving me alone with only my thoughts for company.

Chapter Thirty-Three

Éabha, for all her friendly chatter, was as frugal with useful information when she returned as before. It began when I told her I needed to use the bathroom. She led me down a back stairwell, which groaned with every step. A single window provided light for our descent. The kitchen, she pointed out as we passed the sealed entryway, lay at the bottom of the stairs to our left. She ignored another to our right, opting for the one facing us.

The whole process was done with a pleasant, “Of course!” and upon throwing open Door Number Three, a prideful, “Here we are.”

What a dramatic change from the wintry camp. The room with its blazing fire welcomed me with fragrant arms. Éabha escorted me around a multi-paneled screen blocking the view from those entering the room. A large, metal bathtub sat near a window on the other side.

Much like when I’d made a similar request with Jonathan, it took a little language negotiating to learn I needed, what in the Cloet household was called, the necessary. Then came the debate about my going outside naked, which Éabha opposed. My bladder was cheering on any solution, really, ready to relieve the situation. A chamber pot was offered and refused. The rest of me had my pride to consider.

We settled—or more like I insisted by barging into the hallway to try the unidentified doorway, forcing Éabha to follow, protesting—on my using the outdoor necessary, but only if I wore a borrowed cloak that fell to my feet and was to be clasped closed to avoid exposing my indecency to anyone wandering the grounds. When asked who else was on the grounds, she admitted the workers were not like to be seen the whole day long but could possibly return. You never do know.

The necessary was a round, stone building painted white, set back several yards from the house. Vines grew along the exterior and wove up Grecian columns standing sentinel on either side of the doorway, which—upon later inspection—turned out to be wooden. Another established lilac bush shielded the western side from the sun.

Éabha shared with pride how the structure had been a wedding gift to Mistress Cloet, along with the metal bathtub in the additional room off the kitchen. Mistress Cloet came from money, you can be sure, and Master Cloet was determined she would not want due to her situation as his wife. Or that was what I was told as I hurried to use the necessary while Éabha jogged after, overseeing my progress and keeping a lookout.

The picturesque scenery was lacking in signs of a returning Jonathan.

My subsequent thanks were received with a hurrying of hands to scurry me back into the house and then into the "bathing room" before anyone could see. After the chill of sitting in the stone building on a wooden box to do the necessary things one does in an outdoor privy, the sauna-like conditions of the bathroom were glorious.

Éabha's friendly bossiness resumed, and she directed me to the tub. Only the bottom half of the mustard-colored shutters were closed. Rather than risk her refusal, I began and was permitted to close the tops, though there may have been a humorous remark made at my expense about how I would willingly go out-of-doors naked but refuse the heavens into the room when no man was around. She kind of had a point. We were left with only the varying firelight to see by.

A small table and chair, with what passed as a towel of sorts laid over the back, were set by the tub. And on the table, a real bar of soap! It smelled like honey, speckled with some herb I couldn't put my finger on.

"The mistress made it herself. Bought the oil, special, from Manhattan." Éabha beamed at my pleasure. "Course, 'twas before."

A rope drawn near the fire was covered in, what appeared to be, the clothes I'd inherited from Jonathan's dead roommate. Éabha was lifting and flipping each dampened article when I asked. "No need to fuss," she answered. "Give the water a feel. See if 'tis to your liking."

"Where's my bra and boots?"

She flustered and only looked at me askance. "Ah now, what will Captain Wythe say if I cannot get you to do as he asked?"

"My bag? The leather bag I had?"

She turned full on me. "Captain Wythe has your bag. Took it with him, he did, for safekeeping and such. None to worry. Now, if you would see to the water. I have plenty to do before the family returns. Go on."

Curious, I asked, "Where is the family?"

"Bless me, ma'm. At services, of course."

"Services?"

"It being Sunday," she prompted. "Palm Sunday, at that. You are not one of them pagans, are you?" she asked at my surprised look about the date.

"No, I'm not a pagan." Not a churchgoer, I mused, but not a pagan either. "I guess... time got away from me."

"How careless. The bath, if you please."

Éabha carried a black pot from the open flames and was bogged down with its weight. The woman knew how to drive a conversation to where she wanted it. Clucking her tongue, though insincere in her censure because I believed the water was a little cool, judging by her sideways smile, she poured more from the steaming pot into the tub. A dunked arm to give it a swirl told me it was spa perfect. I smiled my approval.

She replaced the pot over the fire and returned to unwrap the bandage from my wrist. Remarkable. The gash had faded to a pale pink, as if weeks of healing had passed in hours. Éabha balled the bandage and pocketed it into the folds of her skirt. She then seized the lower hem of my nightgown, flying it above my hips.

At my insistence of my taking things from there, she shook her head again with more laughing disapproval about how much trouble I was before dashing from the room to putter around in the kitchen.

Chapter Thirty-Four

The bath was heavenly, soothing to every muscle protesting the last several days, washing away my every care with mind-numbing bliss, and dreadfully short-lived. Only a mild wrinkling was rippling over my skin when, with an announcement of her entrance by a series of items being banged around and the door flying open, Éabha reappeared to tell me the mistress and children had returned.

She directed me to hurry myself and dry off by the fire because she would be back for me once she saw to the mistress. Within seconds, she was gone, and the tranquility I'd found trailed after her, a ribbon of woodsmoke from the hearth caught in her wake.

A quantity of grass and other evidence of my adventures clung to the skin of the water and along the sides of the tub. I extricated myself from Moore Marsh and scrubbed down again with soap, mindful of the household overture building in differing volumes and sounds as an increased number of bodies moved through the rooms and floors.

I didn't want to get caught in *flagrante delicto*, dousing myself with water I'd scooped from the hearth's kettle using a copper teapot I'd spied on a shelf, as I balanced over the tub, naked. The water may've been scalding when I rinsed, but totally worth it to be camp-life free.

Éabha's second entrance was preceded by the sounds of her rushing down the back stairwell. Warning enough to whip the towel from the chair and cover up. Not quite enough to replace the copper tea pot. She flew around the bathroom door, shutting it fast behind her.

With her arms flapping at her sides, she exclaimed, "Bless me! What have you got yourself into now?" At my explanation about needing to rinse off the soap, she asked what was wrong with the water in the bathing tub. My gesture to its debris-ridden interior was met with, "Well, you did see a spot of trouble on your way."

She situated the chair next to the fire and seated me in it, swiping the teapot from my hands by its wooden side handle. She withdrew a rectangular comb from the depths of her skirt and began working it through my hair. When she'd finished, it was tossed onto my lap. Carved bone teeth sprouted from a center bar and extended away from each other instead of standing single file like a modern comb. One half was wide-toothed, the opposite half, finer.

"Here you are." Éabha returned from the clothesline with a white garment. She clasped my hands to whip them through the sleeves before I even registered what she was doing.

"Is this the nightgown I wore last night?"

"'Tis your shift, ma'm. Yours to use during your stay here, anyways." She skewered the thing with my head and directed me to stand, allowing her to settle the piece of clothing being discussed into place. The towel was snatched from underneath.

Maybe someone should recruit Éabha as a spy. She's sneaky enough.

"I feel funny borrowing all these things," I told her.

"The comb 'tis yours now. Mistress has no need of it." She continued with pride despite my reluctance to accept it, "Master Cloet did give the mistress a fine, new set of brushes and combs of silver this winter. You ne'er did see such a thing. Shines like the sun in her hand."

"That's nice."

"Right pleased she was, I dare say." Éabha nodded, assuring me in case there was any doubt. "Hasn't touched this old one since. None could blame her. Right, let us get you above stairs. Mistress has a lovely gown set aside for you."

"I could just wear the clothes I came in," I offered.

"Oh, you very well could not! Be seen in this house in man's dress? Whatever would possess you to scour such rigging?" she chastised. A long, pink bathrobe of satin was whirled around my shoulders.

"My clothes were ruined when I was attacked."

"Bless me." Her bossy manner softened. "You, poor soul." She gave my arm a gentle squeeze, then took my hand with a, "Come along, if you please," and guided me from the bathroom, up the back stairwell. Éabha paused at the top.

Once assured the coast was clear, we continued to the room where I'd awoken. Closing the door behind us, she reclaimed the comb, leaving me standing in the middle while she placed it on the dresser and closed the oak shutters.

"The mistress prefers to dress above, you see, rather than have her gowns brought below and through the kitchen or back stair. Better to keep them clean," Éabha explained with a note of apology. I reassured her it was okay. "But of course, it is. Mistress Cloet has plenty of good sense, you wait and see," she promised.

The fascinating process of dressing me began. As awkward as I felt about having someone do it for me, I was grateful for the help because some of the pieces eluded me.

Éabha wound the red fabric strips around my legs, just above the knee, to tie the gray stockings in place. "The mistress has her own side of mischief, not unlike yourself," she teased.

A flicker of disappointment pestered me. They weren't from Jonathan.

"I don't think I'll need that." I laughed when she approached me with something akin to a corset.

She was amused, but not deterred. "Of course you do, ma'm."

"I thought you said I was too skinny."

"Oh, 'tis not to do with your lack of girth." She chuckled at my fashion ignorance and wound it around my torso, lacing the ribbons only tight enough to keep it from tumbling free. "The stay is to hold you in place. Best to keep you sitting a'right, you shall see."

She continued to ramble—merry smiles and playful teasing throughout her dressing me, welcoming and familiar as if I'd been visiting the family for years—promising they would fatten me, none to worry. A petticoat of unadorned white, other than a gray floral band at the hem, was added on top of the shift and stay. The quilted petticoat was laid on top. The pale green gown crowned them all. After the mountains of layering, I doubted women ever got cold in the Eighteenth.

"You will naught see gowns such as these elsewhere in the precinct," Éabha told me, full of pride, while she buttoned the front of the gown in place. "None else gift their wives the likes as does Master Cloet. Such fine buttons."

The lower portion wrapped around three-quarters of my legs, leaving an open front panel so the green petticoat could be seen and admired. She collected gray, fingerless gloves, whose knit length would climb above the sleeves cascading beyond my elbows and reviewed her work. "Are you warm enough, ma'm?"

"Yeah, thanks."

"You look much improved, indeed. The bath has returned your color to a heathy fashion." Turning to lay the gloves on the dresser, she announced, "There are mitts here if you need them."

I fingered the folded note from Jonathan.

I should burn it, I realized, along with any other evidence of my having been here.

But I couldn't bring myself to do it. Perhaps it was because he made me laugh when I needed it, and I didn't know how long I was going to keep needing it. I decided to hold on to it for safekeeping rather than risk it getting misplaced. I could always give it back to him or destroy it before I went home, I reasoned. Would it matter if I secretly kept it and brought it home with me?

Éabha was contemplating my neckline with the profound dedication of a scholar slaving away on a dissertation. At my questioning look, said she would need but a moment. She tugged on the shift to evenly display the lacy edge above the gown's bodice and, with a smirk, snatched the folded note from me to tuck it into the front of my stay.

"I have naught a spare pocket for you, ma'm." She shooed my hand from her handiwork. "And you should keep this close to you, would not you agree?"

Once released from her meddling clutches, I searched the folds of the gown to find an opening but no liner forming a pocket. My hand passed straight through. Lacking a viable alternative, I agreed with Éabha and accepted my additional paper stay, its soft linen curving between my breasts.

Oh, stop smiling, Savvy.

Éabha pulled a chair from the table, gesturing for me to sit with my back to the fire. Using a series of unseen bobby pins or hair clips or good, ole-fashioned wishing—who knows?—she managed to style my hair into a pouf. Despite her parting shot of my being "such trouble," I won the verbal duel about wearing a white cap. It was left on the dresser. Simple brown, satin shoes with a low heel were tucked over my feet and tied with ribbons for me. They were tight on the sides, but otherwise wearable so long as hiking wasn't on the agenda.

With a final smile of triumph at my transformation, Éabha drew me to standing and declared me fit to meet Mistress Cloet.

Chapter Thirty-Five

Mistress Anna Quakkenbosch Cloet sat at a writing desk in the yellow parlor with her back to the door. At the announcement of my arrival, she set aside the letter she was composing and rose to greet me. Her peach petticoat, embroidered with gold brocade, swished against an outer gown of cornflower-blue cotton when she moved. I was relieved to see her head was bare except for a fat, peach ribbon twisted into the height of her golden hair. It was left to cascade, along with her curls, behind her shoulders.

There was an awkward moment when Éabha made the introductions. Out of habit, I reached out to shake hands, and Mrs. Cloet glanced at me with confusion. A fleeting rush of annoyance at her refusal to touch my hand unnerved me.

Women don't shake hands. What's your deal?

I couldn't imagine where it came from. I dropped my hand, feeling oddly unsatisfied.

Mrs. Cloet gave me a tentative smile and directed Éabha to see to the writing desk. Éabha curtseyed, then busied herself with dusting the letter and caring for the quill and silver inkwell. The flounce of Mrs. Cloet's sleeves floated gracefully around her elbow, though they seemed bare without lace or other accessories, as she invited me to sit at a round table in the center of the room. I sighed, since I was in no position to argue when she claimed the ladderback chair facing the front of the house.

"I hope you have been made welcome in my absence," Mrs. Cloet said. Her voice was melodic in tone, to the point of being hypnotic. It welcomed you to like her from the first moment.

"Yeah, thanks. Your home's pretty."

Painted wood paneling filled the entire far wall and embraced an active fireplace. Its enormous mantel reminded me a little of a piano keyboard, its dentil molding carved in alternating blocks, some rising in height above the others.

I couldn't resist checking the front windows behind me, showcasing way too much scenery and not enough Jonathan. Lovely greetings aside, being paranoid I'd say or do the wrong thing and cripple his mission, made me antsy. I hoped for a rescue soon.

"*Bedankt,*" Mrs. Cloet answered during my search. "It is small, yet I pray you will find it to be as comfortable as do I."

"It is." I recognized I had an obligation to pay attention to my hostess and turned back to say, "Comfortable, I mean."

"My husband will take great joy in hearing of your approval. Do forgive the informality. As it shall be just us two, I thought it would be pleasing to us both not to wear Sunday attire."

"Uh, no. It's fine." I leaned forward to examine the floral motif etched into the silver buttons on her gown. If the many layers of gorgeous dresses weren't Sunday-best, what must the good dresses look like?

Mrs. Cloet reviewed my borrowed outfit in return. "Are… you warm enough, Miss Moore? Would you care for another log on the fire?"

"I'm fine."

"I am glad. My husband worries so for the comfort of those who honor us with a visit. Captain Wythe has been a particular friend to us."

"I can't wait to meet him. Do you expect him soon?"

"As I said, it shall be us two."

"Oh."

I'd tried to mask my disappointment with a nervous smile but was unsuccessful because Mrs. Cloet added, "You have nothing to fear here, my dear. You are safe."

Éabha was sent for refreshments, although we were warned that dinner might be in readiness at any time; however, Mrs. Cloet preferred to wait to sit to a full meal, and I was too preoccupied to mind. Early afternoon sunlight was streaming through the window. It was going to be a long day.

"You are not from the American States, I understand," she said. "It must be difficult being far from home."

"Yeah."

How much could Jonathan have told her, and when? It was roughly two in the morning when we started the last half mile into town.

"Do you have a family of your own?" she continued.

"When do you expect the men to return?"

She was kind, and her voice soothing, but the way she drew me in with an almost magnetic pull—like Jonathan did—bothered me. Not because I was afraid of her, but because she made me a little afraid of myself and how I was tempted to... be near her? No, there was more to it. I just didn't know what.

"Please be seated, Miss Moore." A window shutter bounced off my back and into the wall. I'd stood and backed away from her without even noticing. "No one will harm you here," Mrs. Cloet reminded me, her face concerned. "You are amongst friends."

"Sorry. It's just... everyone keeps telling me Jonathan's fine, but where is he? How do I know he's fine?"

"You have had his letter, have you not? Éabha was to give it to you."

I interrupted her calling for Éabha by saying, "I have it. She gave it to me." I touched the front of my gown where the paper was pressed against my skin. "I... I've never seen his handwriting before."

The excuse for my increased nervousness wasn't holding up. I cringed at the undertone of distrust it conveyed, especially since I had no doubt the letter was from Jonathan. But I didn't know what my role was there. Drink coffee and make small talk? What explanation had he given for my presence—or *his* presence, come to think of it—or for any of it?

This wasn't like waiting for him at camp, passing time along the fringes of life there. Not that my hopes of keeping to the sidelines had worked out very well. Traveling with Jonathan meant I was now in the midst of his mission, not certain who his contacts were or what dangers there might be. I think I preferred freezing in the woods. At least there, I knew Trouble was showing its ugly face because guns were being drawn.

Éabha came in with a silver tray. Mrs. Cloet gave a reassuring smile while Éabha laid her offering on the table. Not bothering to fight the urge any longer, I turned toward the front window.

A kitchen garden of young herbs and early flowers sprouted close to the house. Coursing down its middle was a stone pathway, extending about half an acre until it reached the stone wall circling the property. Mature apple trees ran parallel to the wall and dirt road. Guests were welcomed onto the grounds by a wrought-iron gate, framed with a large vine-labored arbor. The road yawned off to the left and into the extended fields before disappearing into rolling hills but curved at the front of the house and melted into forest several yards away. Neither direction revealed Jonathan's approach.

"Have the children taken refreshment, Éabha?" Mrs. Cloet asked, giving me the time and space I needed.

"Aye, Mistress." Éabha poured out two cups from a copper pot with a wooden side-handle suspiciously identical to the one I'd used earlier in the bathroom. "Matilda has them in the kitchen with her. Jacob asks if he may go to the Iron Works to see his papa."

Mrs. Cloet glanced in my direction. A slight frown dipped then vanished before she answered, "Not today. Master Cloet and Captain Wythe have business that needs minding. He may ride the pony if he wishes."

Éabha set the pot back on the tray and placed a cup with saucer in front of each seat, saying, "Ah, he shall be right happy, I dare say."

"Indeed, he shall. *Bedankt*, Éabha," Mrs. Cloet warmly dismissed her.

"Mistress. Ma'm." We were given a curtsey at our respective address. She closed the door behind herself, shutting me in with Mrs. Cloet.

With a nervous glance, I made another search of the roads. Mrs. Cloet sighed. I turned to apologize, but she was praying. Out of respect, I looked away and waited until she was done. A draft traveled from the chimney to breeze the heat from the fire across the room. It trickled over my bare arms and face. Except…

No smoke.

"Please, do sit," Mrs. Cloet invited. The musical lilt was more pronounced. "There is chocolate and biscuits to satisfy us until dinner is ready."

The shift in her tone worked its magic because I laughed at the treat being offered. "Dessert before dinner?"

"What else would we have to satisfy us?" She returned the laugh.

A tiny voice inside noted I was being influenced. Realizing how close to the table I'd come, I became wary, not sure what the random thought meant.

"Perhaps it would provide you some comfort were you to call me Anna," she suggested.

"Yeah. It would." I was slow to accept and wished I wasn't being so rude.

"What is more, I shall tell you where Captain Wythe and my husband have gone, though I know little of my husband's business, mind you." Her eyes were a captivating ice blue.

"Yeah. Yes, it would make me feel better."

She gestured for me to sit, and I did. "There you are." Anna smiled and took a sip from her cup.

The hot chocolate was rich, warmed to perfection, and tickled my tongue with a hint of bitterness. Exactly how I liked it. It soothed me from the inside out, spreading its sumptuous heat like a heavy mist rolling along the surface of a tropical waterfall. My body tingled with pleasure at the sensation, and a sigh escaped my lips as the last of my hesitation vanished. We both laughed and relaxed into our chairs.

"What shall I call you?" she asked, holding out the plate of biscuits for me.

"My friends call me Savvy."

"Savvy*?* What a lovely name."

"It's short for Savannah. This is really good," I said, having taken a bite of the biscuit. It was some sort of sugar cookie, light and sweet. "What is it?"

"They are drop biscuits," Anna told me and bit into her own. "Savannah is also a lovely name. Why do you shorten it?"

I was touched by her sincerity. "A friend, a good friend, came up with it. She…" Sadness seeped through my newfound serenity at the reminder of my best friend. We'd planned to meet two days after my disappearance.

No.

I reminded myself of my determination to believe the twenty-first century was simply paused, waiting for my return. I wasn't gone or even missing. Only venturing on a mere sightseeing trip through time.

Anna's expression flitted from surprise to sympathy. I apologized, but she declared there was no need and asked, "What is your friend's name?"

"Sorrel."

"Like the flower?"

The napkin I'd neglected to lay over my lap caught my eye. I struggled to set the cup and saucer down without rattling them to collect it.

"I am certain your friend misses you, as well," she said.

I smoothed the rose-colored linen several times, chasing the wrinkles down my legs until they vanished. A golden-threaded tulip bloomed from a single corner.

Anna sipped her hot chocolate and allowed me to compose myself. Needing a distraction, I enjoyed another taste from my cup and found it just as calming as the first. I gulped the rest, hungry for the soothing sensation it offered. It didn't disappoint.

She became alert before the sound of the front door reached me. Éabha was rushing through the hallway, greeting Master Cloet and Captain Wythe as they stomped their way into the house.

"Stay, Savvy." Anna shushed me because I'd risen. "Let the gentlemen come to us if they will." She was cautioning me to follow some gender-related custom I was desperate to ignore.

"Miss Moore is with Mistress Cloet, sir," Éabha answered Jonathan's inquiry. "I have seen to your requests, and she is in a state of undress. They are in the parlor, there."

At the comment, I compared my gown to Anna's, wondering how I was about to unbalance Jonathan again. Éabha's mischievous smirk when she'd dressed me came to mind, as did Anna's apology for informality.

Before I could solve the Which-of-These-Things-Is-Not-Like-the-Others, the door opened, and the two gentlemen walked in. I sat back demurely in my chair, hoping no one would notice me.

"Ah, *liefste*!" Mr. Cloet crossed to Anna, who rose and received his hands in her own, along with a kiss on her cheek.

His navy-blue suit coat, adorned with gold buttons atop the vertical pleats and front facings, swayed around his knees as he did. A matching ribbon held back the hair of his gray wig. His gold-threaded vest matched Anna's petticoat, and his entire outfit complimented hers to perfection.

"You return so soon?" Anna asked him with a look at Jonathan. She welcomed him with a nod. "Captain Wythe."

He masked it well—his voice was warm and polite—but anxiety buzzed the air around him as he said, "Mistress Cloet. We come only from the church."

He'd changed into a handsome, black vest and suit. Silver buttons reached his throat and lined both sides of his suit coat, which remained open. A white neckcloth peeked from under the height of the vest. It was a wonder he could breathe.

Only Jonathan's knife, tucked in its place on his belt, and the usual knee-high boots were the same, though they'd been buffed. His hair was also washed, brushed, and held back in a black ribbon.

"You have not yet dined, have you?" Mr. Cloet asked, tugging at his own crisp, white neckcloth to free it from behind the brocade vest so it could hang loose against his healthy middle. He selected a cookie from the dessert plate and indulged in a satisfying bite.

"*Nee*, but we did not expect to see you until evening," Anna replied.

"We shall go tomorrow." Mr. Cloet laughed and turned to Jonathan for confirmation as he told his wife, "The reverend, he did capture us as we made to depart and would not let us be until he had his say, else we might have accompanied you home." He offered the plate of cookies to Jonathan, who declined. "The man can talk and talk. You would think Judgement Day was well at hand!"

"Ah, Johannes," Anna exclaimed and crossed herself before she dutifully took the plate from her husband to return it to the table.

"*Liefste*, you worry so." He kissed her hands one at a time. "'Tis for the best. As the man has stirred the soul with his preaching, so has he stirred the appetite with his ramblings. We shall eat together as it should be." Mr. Cloet toasted her with the cookie before devouring the rest of it.

"*Mijn lieverd.*" She shook her head, smiling at him. "Captain Wythe, you have arrived in good time."

"I am glad to hear of it." Relief relaxed his stance. "We have had success of late."

"Splendid!" Mr. Cloet remarked, lifting his nose from its inspection of the hot chocolate pot. "Let us to dinner, and we shall discuss it."

You'd think Captain Brott-hole would want to be here so they could celebrate his role too.

He offered his elbow to his wife, who beamed at him as she received it and allowed herself to be led toward the parlor door. She slipped a smile to Jonathan as they passed.

But Jonathan tensed, his expression grown anxious again, and stopped them. "I should like to see the work's progress, Johannes. The general would be most grateful for word."

"There will be none to give the report, for it is the Lord's Day, as well you know. But worry not. That *Captain Machin* has sent many a courier. The general would likely be grateful for less word, not more." Anna drew a casual finger meandering down her husband's arm.

As she reached for the back of his hand, Mr. Cloet's tone—which had sharpened with the mention of the other captain—returned to his original, jovial tone. "We shall make the inspection tomorrow." Then, he exchanged a loving smile with Anna and led her into the hallway.

Jonathan would've exited himself after them had I not spoken his name. I guess I overplayed my part of the humble, society woman with the good manners I'd promised him because the three of them turned with surprise to see me rising from the chair I'd been occupying during their conversation.

"*Zegen mij!*" Mr. Cloet remarked. "I had not observed you there. How could we have missed such a lovely creature?"

Anna and Jonathan appeared mystified. Jonathan recovered—after a shocked glance toward Anna, who subtly shook her head at him—and introduced me to Master Johannes Cloet.

Our host approached to collect my hand in his, though he paused in the midst of a half-bow to consider me. Leaning in, he whispered, "I sense, my dear, that we are kindred spirits, you and I."

"In what way?" I asked.

"What say you, mine own?" Anna called from where she was waiting in the hallway.

Mr. Cloet studied me further before replying, "Captain Wythe is an old friend. Many a time, he has dined with us. I trust you will understand when I ask: What are your intensions toward our friend?"

I looked to Jonathan for help. He filled in, saying, "Miss Moore is here under my protection and has delayed her journey for my sake. I serve her as escort."

"Is this true?" Mr. Cloet questioned me. Despite his pointed look, he was still smiling.

"Yeah." I laughed, nervous.

"Johannes?" Jonathan's voice registered the same confusion I felt.

"I'm on my way home. Captain Wythe is helping me."

"Be it so," Mr. Cloet dipped his head to pronounce, "you are most welcome among us." He gave my hand a friendly pat, then released it. Jonathan received a clap on the arm as Mr. Cloet exited the room, declaring, "Come, let us to the dining room."

"Jonathan?" I desperately wanted to talk with him before we sat down to dinner, which, no doubt, would involve more questions I'd be expected to answer.

Some coaching was long overdue. I didn't want to blow whatever cover story Jonathan had created, plus I wouldn't have minded answers to some questions of my own.

"*Lieverd.*" Anna stalled Mr. Cloet in the hallway. "Would you be more comfortable if you were to change your attire before dinner? There is time."

Mr. Cloet reviewed how each of us was dressed. "*Ja. Ja*, I do believe I would. Most considerate. You do not mind?" he asked Jonathan, disappearing upstairs partway through Jonathan's response.

Anna closed the parlor door behind them, leaving us alone. I loved the woman right then and there.

Jonathan blinked toward the door, then turned halfway to address me, making his own subtle review of my gown from his periphery.

His cheeks flushed, and mouth flapped while he struggled for something to say until he landed on, "Miss Moore, how do you do?"

"I'm fine, thanks."

Confused at the formal greeting, but fine.

"You?" I asked.

"I am well, thank you." He looked trapped, kind of like how I felt when first closed in with Anna, finding the floor to be safer ground for study. If only the awkwardness could've been blamed somehow on the parlor.

"Jonathan, I need your help."

Called to a potential purpose, he cleared his throat and faced me to bow at the waist, saying, "How may I be of service, madam?"

"Savvy," I corrected him, indulging his slip with a head shake and a small laugh.

He looked sunburnt when he blushed deeper at the reminder. Having enjoyed the special treatment of receiving a bow, I wondered if I was expected to curtsey. I decided, why not, and gave it a funny go.

The glimmer of a smile broke through his awkwardness. "Miss Moore."

"Could you fill me in a little on what's going on here?"

"I do not understand your request."

"Tell me what you told the Cloets about me, what I'm meant to be doing here, how I can help you. Anything would be good."

"There is nothing you need do here."

"Jonathan, please," I begged.

"You are a guest in this house." He leaned toward the closed door.

"I know, but—"

"Arrangements have been made for your comfort during your stay here."

"I'm not comfortable staying here by myself," I insisted.

"It is what I require of you."

"Jonathan—"

"I know of no other way to assist you. You did not wish to accompany me on my mission. Now you reject the efforts I have made to see you safe." He bolted for the door.

"Jonathan," I called after him.

"What do you want of me, woman?"

"Savvy!" I snapped the reminder.

Jonathan sighed. He appeared just as lost and frustrated as I was. The crackling of the parlor fire filled the emptiness for several minutes.

"There is a danger," he admitted, his words slow and deliberate. "One I dare not tell you, but it is real, and it pursues us." For the first time since I'd known him, fear showed in his eyes.

My thoughts returned to the presence haunting the woods around the militia's camp. "It?"

He paused before responding. "He."

"Please tell me something," I implored, closing the distance between us.

He invited my hands into his, lightly tracing the space surrounding my forefinger with his thumb. The familiar tingle danced along my skin with his touch.

His quiet confession, hushed to the point where I need to lean closer, was troubling. "Captain Grey. His men seek my capture." Hands gripped mine. His gaze penetrated straight through me when he raised his head to meet my eyes. "It would relieve me to know that you are kept safe."

The battle for my freedom was losing ground to serving his fight for independence. "How long are you leaving me here?" I asked, resigned.

"Only until my mission is complete."

"How long?"

"Depending on the state of affairs, it should be another day or two." He looked as if he wanted to say more but didn't. Instead, he apologized by squeezing my hands before letting go.

"This danger…?" I ventured, wondering if I should risk telling him about the strange presence and seeing what he'd make of it.

"Now is not the time or place. We shall speak," he promised. "Please, will you not accept the arrangements made in your behalf?"

"I wasn't arguing with the arrangements, per se. Getting clean was awesome. And I like Anna."

"I am glad." A relieved smile returned.

We were back in tune.

"It's just… I'm afraid of screwing things up for you," I whispered. He didn't understand the phrase. "I'm afraid of endangering your mission. I don't know how to behave here, what things the family's been told that I have to be careful not to contradict, how to not embarrass you."

"You do not embarrass me," he reassured.

"I don't?"

"Have I done something to—?"

"What's wrong with my dress?" I rushed to ask.

"Your… dress?"

"Yeah."

The tension left him, and he laughed freely. "All of this over your attire."

"It's not the only thing bugging me." I sulked while he carried on at my expense. "Hey!"

"I am sorry, madam."

"*Savvy*," I reminded him.

Jonathan cleared his throat in an attempt to become serious. "Pardon. Miss Moore." He smiled as he inspected my dress for trouble, turning me around to be certain before concluding, "There is nothing amiss with your gown."

"I don't understand. Why did Éabha say I wasn't dressed?"

"When was this?"

"Earlier in the hallway."

Confusion filled his words. "She never—"

"When you first came in and asked where I was, she said I wasn't dressed," I prompted.

Realization dawned on his face. "Nay." He laughed again. At least the awkwardness was gone. "She said you were in a state of undress."

"There's a difference?"

"Undress means you are not in formal attire, as you would be if you were to accompany me to a ball or dinner."

I hesitated to ask. "Aren't we going to dinner?"

"A society dinner," he explained. "Here, we are amongst friends."

"Oh." I deflated, embarrassed by how lost I was in Jonathan's world. "You're not going to take me to a ball or society dinner, are you?"

"Do you wish it?"

"No!"

Jonathan chuckled again, letting me in on the joke.

I shot him a sarcastic look before informing him, "There's more."

"We shall be late for dinner."

"What happened with the redcoats?"

The humor fled from his face. "Redcoats? What redcoats?"

"The ones from last night. When we passed through the town."

"Ah." He brushed warm fingertips across my forehead, as if chasing away a stray lock of hair there. "You do not remember redcoats."

"Yeah, we…" The certainty it was a memory and not a dream crumbled. I stared at him, confused and a little light-headed, struggling to remember what I'd seen.

A knock at the door announced Éabha's entrance. Jonathan stepped back to a respectable distance as she informed us, "Dinner is set."

"I still have questions," I insisted.

"They shall keep." Jonathan offered me his arm. I wanted to argue, but it would've been rude to hold up our hosts, and my thoughts were swirling in my head, anyway.

We entered the hallway, my arm threaded through his, and we followed it past the stairs and to the left. The hall clock was nearing three in the afternoon.

As we approached the dining room, he asked, "Are you warm enough?"

"Okay. Why has everybody asked me that?"

"Ah." He cleared his throat. "You do not wear a fichu."

"Do I need one?" I froze. I wasn't sure what I wasn't wearing, but such repeat concern meant something noteworthy was afoot.

Jonathan urged me onward despite my resistance, causing my shoes to skid on the floor. "I thought mayhaps you might want one. Nothing more." His tone wasn't convincing.

"I wasn't given one," I said. Éabha gave us an innocent smile. Leaning close to him, I whispered, "You said the dress was fine."

"It… is."

"But?" I questioned his hesitation.

"The gown is…" His eyes fell to my exposed chest and lingered there. Heat crashed over his cheeks as he struggled for an appropriate word. "… becoming."

Jonathan escaped in the direction of the dining room without me, leaving me dumbfounded and a tiny bit at sea. He swayed, having succeeded in entering the room but rocked backward, into the hall, rather than continue. The risk of further unintentional study of my gown kept his chin glued to his chest while he gestured from the doorway for me to proceed him.

Éabha leaned from behind my shoulder to whisper in my ear, "Do not keep the gentleman waiting."

"There you are, Jonathan!" Mr. Cloet had called to him unseen from within the dining room during Éabha's smirking. "Gracious, man, are you alone?"

"Miss Moore is joining us," Jonathan replied.

"*Is goed*. It goes not well for a man ever alone."

Jonathan gave a polite smile in Mr. Cloet's direction and held out his elbow.

"I'm not going in there looking like a cheap whore," I responded to the invitation to take his arm. Irony being, were I in my own time, I wouldn't have thought twice about walking from one end of the beach to the other in far less.

With a little help from Éabha—who would've been a master insurance fraudster—managing to cut in front of me when I rushed for the stairs before she slammed on the brakes, Jonathan caught me by the elbow. “Come now, Miss Moore.” His smile turned playful, though his eyes remained fixated on mine. “I would never have mistaken you for cheap.”

I couldn’t tell you who was more shocked by his quip, him or me. The issue was resolved by my returned smile before I gave him a smack on the arm, which earned me a genuine, if not relieved, laugh. He linked his arm through mine and led me—practically pulled me, more like—into the dining room.

Chapter Thirty-Six

The dining room was white, made brighter by the afternoon sun gleaming through the numerous windows onto a large, gold floorcloth. Various patterns were painted throughout of swooping, dark-colored birds and lush vines, spotty with scarlet berries, overflowing from antique vases. A rich wine color flowed along the wood of the chair rail and crown molding.

Our hosts welcomed us to join them around a rectangular table, dwarfed by the sprawling expanse surrounding it which could easily entertain two dozen or more people without feeling cramped. Multiple mahogany chairs stood ready for those dozens, lined up as friendly sentries along the walls.

"It is the fire, you see," said Anna, gesturing to the interior corner farthest from us. "If we open the table to its fullest, those seated closest burn while those nearest the door find they are in want of heat."

"*Ja*," Mr. Cloet added, "We must play Trip to Jerusalem to see us through the courses in comfort." He'd exchanged his suit for an opal-toned dressing gown, left untied and draped loose over his shirt and short pants. The gray wig had also been abandoned in favor of a matching silk cap, adorning a close-cropped patch of stark-white hair.

"It is a game," Jonathan provided as translation. He escorted me from the doorway, which opened at one end of the room, to the table at its center and pulled out a chair for me.

"Alas," Mr. Cloet continued, leaning across his place setting toward me, "we have no musicians to tell us when we must *lève cul*."

"Oh, Johannes." Anna sighed.

Jonathan cleared his throat as he seated himself to my left, embarrassed, and rather than answer when I sought further translation, supplied instead, "When the music begins, the players dance, but when the music stops—"

"Musical Chairs," I exclaimed.

"What is this?"

"We have the same game. When the music stops, the players run to take a seat, but there's always one chair missing. The person who doesn't get a chair is out."

"Precisely so," Mr. Cloet interjected. We all smiled in perfect harmony.

Éabha served dinner from a long sideboard residing on the wall behind me, beginning with Jonathan. Small pies, one for each of us. The flaky top crust had worked loose, aided by a dark filling bubbling up and over the edges.

"Lovely, Éabha," Anna said as she complimented her.

"*Ja, ja*," Mr. Cloet concurred. "You keep us well. What would we do without her, *liefste*?"

"I dare say, we would not get on."

Éabha's face glowed at the praise.

I turned to Anna, tickled by the playful nature of our hosts and their dietary choices. "More dessert?"

"Ah, *nee*, Savvy. This is winter pie," she said, though the explanation was lost on me.

Jonathan was enthusiastic about the dish, a wide smile breaking as he inhaled the rising steam. Hard cider was delivered in pewter mugs.

Jonathan and Anna bowed their heads. Our hostess led the table in a Latin prayer, Mr. Cloet nodding along in agreement, fingering his silverware as he did, most grateful when the prayer concluded and he could dig in with gusto.

"The last of the turnips, I'm afraid, mine own," Anna informed him.

"Dear me, well. How unfortunate. We must ever on, I dare say." Despite his show of sadness and subsequent bucking up, Mr. Cloet lacked any true sign of being upset, particularly when he winked in my direction. "Are you warm enough, Miss Moore?" He gestured to me with his spoon. "Perhaps you should care to sit nearer to the fire? *Liefste*, shall we dance without the music?"

"I'm fine." I sighed at Jonathan, the joy at finding common ground over the game diminished.

He chuckled, though his demeanor altered in a flash. His eyes had traveled for a lengthy holiday too far south. He diverted them to his dinner, cheeks crimson.

I solved the How-Savvy-Is-Embarrassing-Jonathan-Again riddle. Anna was wearing a simple, white scarf wrapped around her neck. The tied ends were dressed over half her front, covering her chest. My napkin became equally embarrassed from too much attention as I contemplated whether hanging it over my cleavage would be worse.

"Ah well, *is goed*," Mr. Cloet carried on with his meal and chatter. "I do insist to my dearest wife, Miss Moore, that I would tear down these walls, only too pleased to do it, to build her a proper dining hall, with the fire in its rightful place, would she but allow it."

"How could I allow such a thing, *mijn lieverd*, when our home is perfect in all its ways?" Anna worked her charm on him. "Do we not sit in comfort, in intimate intercourse with our friends?"

Although I knew from my father's history lessons her words meant we were enjoying a private conversation, the playful expression on her face as she gave a pretty smile to Jonathan and me made me wonder.

"Are you well, Miss Moore?" Mr. Cloet asked. "You appear flush."

"I dare say," Anna added with exaggerated concern.

"Perhaps we should dull the fire."

"No, it's okay!" I exclaimed. "I'm fine. Just fine, thanks." Camp life sounded better and better.

"Ah, *liefste*," Mr. Cloet piped up. "I must tell you what the reverend did say—"

"Johannes." Jonathan flashed a look at Anna. "Was not the telling once enough for our ears?"

She picked up the cue. "He is not a man of few words, dearest mine. Best it be shared between us two, after dinner. We should not wish to bore Miss Moore."

Mr. Cloet laughed. "The man does ramble on. It is a wonder he does not run out of air."

"That he does, dearest. That he does."

"Perhaps, Miss Moore, you shall see for yourself. We would be most happy, Jonathan, if you would partake in the Easter meal with us. It has been too long since you have stayed at any length with us."

"It sounds great," I intercepted with as much warmth as I could. "But I'm expected at a rendezvous and wouldn't wish to overstay my welcome."

"You could hardly do so," Mr. Cloet declared, "and we should like to know you better."

"I'm afraid I can't interfere with our schedule." The last part was directed to Jonathan. He dropped his head; the message was not lost on him. This was one battle I refused to lose. I was going home.

"Come now, Jonathan," he persisted. "The general would grant you leave, were you to ask it of him, to celebrate the most holy of days with us."

"I—"

Jonathan's fingers lighted on my knee, shocking me into silence, while he smiled to the Cloets and said, "Your invitation is most tempting, Johannes. I shall know more in a day or more what lies ahead of us." Withdrawing his hand, he withdrew into himself too. Éabha's appearance to take his empty dish didn't register.

Mr. Cloet took a deep draw from his cup and signaled for more as he changed the subject. "We had the most pleasant of news, *schat*. It should make the way easier for our Jonathan and his fair lady. The regulars have quit the Heights."

Jonathan's head snapped up. Frustration was heavy in his tense expression.

"Indeed." Anna eyed her guest before giving her full attention to her husband. "Such excellent news."

"*Ja, ja*. The reverend did observe as much for himself, for he was traveling from Firthcliffe before the dawn, having been sought to anoint. But then, you know, the wretched man did not die! The reverend was called out for naught."

"Perhaps it was the reverend's prayers that did heal the man," Anna offered.

Mr. Cloet turned his attention to me, smiling. "My wife, you see, is always trying to convert me to become a better man. Though I pray, I am irreverent and must strive to become a holy man by her guidance, as she did not have the good fortune to marry a reverend man herself." He chuckled at his own wit. Anna humored him, joining in. "But I have been distracted from my news," he remarked. "The regulars have moved westward."

"Westward," I repeated.

"Most like to join the camp there," Jonathan explained, looking displeased.

Mr. Cloet agreed. "The good reverend did see them quit the place himself, fleeing from God's holy rays as the sun did rise and into the darkened woods toward the West, where the devil may take them."

"Ah, Johannes." Anna crossed herself, her lips pursing at his perpetual irreverence, which Jonathan mirrored. Mr. Cloet, however, winked at me, though I couldn't return his teasing smile. Auden's name escaped my lips.

"What say you, ma'm?" Éabha asked while she leaned close to

serve me a bowl of stew, thick with meat and a heavy sauce. The others turned their attention to me, as well. I shook my head and fell back into my cushioned chair.

The men continued to discuss the activity of the redcoats sighted throughout the region, though Jonathan eyed me with concern more than once. The consensus of the locals was the North River had been the source of the invasion, somewhere between New Cornwall and New Windsor. When the British overran Fort Montgomery in the autumn, they took to raiding the areas surrounding the water passageway, striking as far north as the capitol in Kingston, which they burned. Those spotted in the weeks prior were believed to have remained rather than continue back south with the rest of their number.

The discussion turned to the British army's hold on Philadelphia, but I stopped listening and was trying to calculate where we were in relationship to the moving redcoats and my goal, the hillside near New Cornwall.

"Miss Moore, you are not eating." Jonathan dipped his chin in the direction of my untouched dish.

"Éabha," Mr. Cloet said, "Take away the bowl. Miss Moore does not want it, do you? Fetch the lady something else."

"No. Thanks. I'm not hungry." My mind was lost in a mix of emotions jostling me from one worry to another in a nauseating way. Thoughts of Auden skipped to Nell and her family's expulsion from their home by marauding soldiers.

"Mine own, perhaps no more talk of soldiers," Anna said.

"Quite right," he agreed.

"We are safe here." Jonathan paused, leaning closer. "This place is a safe haven."

"Right," I told them, feeling numb. Mr. Cloet continued his own examination of me, and I wondered what he was looking for.

"Her mind is on something else, I dare say, Captain Wythe." Anna directed her comment to just him. Some wordless understanding passed between them. "You spoke a name, Savvy. Whose was it?"

"Uh, it's nothing. I'm… I'll be fine."

Jonathan slipped his fingers under my palm and drew my hand across the table, cupping it between his. A sensation like butterflies playing on a summer breeze fluttered along my skin, his hands warming against mine. "Miss Moore, you wished to speak with me earlier. I did not hear you. Tell me now?"

He's willing you to confess, a voice inside warned.

I pulled away from him, confused, and knitted my fingers together in the center of my lap. My hesitation melted away, nonetheless.

"Auden. Doctor Cole," I corrected myself. "He was sent to a flying hospital along with the wounded. He didn't go with the major."

And he gave me his gun.

"It seems, Jonathan, you are too late," Mr. Cloet sympathized. "The field has already been taken." The man nodded in my direction, which only upset me more.

"No, I…" But there was no way to explain to Jonathan what I felt about Auden. What I suspected. He mumbled how he understood, though I wasn't sure if he did, and I didn't know what to do about it.

Mr. Cloet shifted the conversation when the table grew silent. "A flying hospital?"

"It had been stationed near Woodbury Clove," Jonathan said. "Orders have come. They are to aid in establishing a permanent hospital near here. Doctor Cole is the surgeon servicing the camp to which I was assigned. He attended Miss Moore when first she arrived."

"Ah." Mr. Cloet glanced at the wound on my neck. Self-conscious, I tugged at the wide collar of my gown. "Then, they journey north, to the church."

The table turned grim, which was when I put it all together—the flying hospital would be trapped between the British camp to the west and the contingent moving in from the east. Closing my eyes with the next wave of nausea, I squeezed the pressure point on my wrist. The pie stayed put.

Once I centered myself, I told them, "I'm sorry. I'm ruining everyone's dinner."

"Ah, my dear lady. Worry not." Mr. Cloet swept his hand across the terrain in front of himself. "We have had our fill, you see?"

A survey of the table confirmed it. Our places were already cleared.

"You are far from your friends and family, Savvy," Anna said as she attempted to comforted me. "Of course, you cannot bear losing others, even those you have met in but recent days."

They were exactly the right words. I allowed them to resonate with me and could find no fault with her assessment. A sad but relieved sigh—relieved someone understood—relaxed my shoulders. I smiled at her with gratitude.

"Do not despair," Anna continued, "It is possible Doctor Cole and the hospital met on the road and traveled northward before the Royal Army crossed it."

"I will send an inquiry," Jonathan offered. "We will learn what became of Doctor Cole."

"No," I murmured.

"If it would bring you peace of mind."

"It won't. If something happens to the messenger because of me… I'd never forgive myself." Inquiries also meant letters. Letters to be filed and kept for posterity's sake. Letters including my name in them.

"There are ways—"

"Don't. Please." I addressed my hosts, hoping to change the subject by saying, "Why don't we just enjoy dessert and talk about something else?"

"Is there dessert?" Mr. Cloet perked up. "This is a special day. You must come more often, Jonathan. We always eat well when you are expected."

Éabha made an unintelligible sound to Anna, who responded by laying a hand on Mr. Cloet's arm, stroking it as she announced to the table with enthusiasm, "Éabha has more *appeltaerten* today." Mr. Cloet grinned with identical enthusiasm.

Having put Éabha in an awkward position—ignorant blundering, my specialty—I felt compelled to interrupt. "Anna, dinner was wonderful, but would you mind if I went for a walk instead? It looks beautiful out."

"Surely there could be no harm. Do you not agree, Captain Wythe?"

"Would you accompany her?" he asked in return.

"With pleasure."

"Miss Moore, I must insist that you remain within the stone walls. As you heard me say, Cloet land is a safe haven. Such cannot be said for what lies beyond."

"Those of the town support us, Savvy," Anna explained. "Others in the precinct, I am sad to say, are loyal to the Crown."

Jonathan gave her an appreciative nod. His fear of Captain Grey hunting him was still fresh in both our minds, I imagined. And there was the dark presence in the woods…

The whole thing felt like a snare tightening its grasp, my hopes of finding a way home slipping beyond my reach. It weighed in my chest.

Anna seemed concerned. When our eyes met, she added, "If we are together, I can guide you through the region. Do not worry. Our land extends for a ways. You will have plenty to divert you."

The claustrophobia eased with her final reassurance. "Thanks, Anna."

"While we walk, Éabha can bring the dessert to Johannes's study." She turned to her husband. "You can advise Captain Wythe without further distraction."

Jonathan's good humor revived. He jumped on the opening.

"Thank you both. Mistress Cloet, Miss Moore. Your kind offer is most appreciated."

He faced Mr. Cloet with expectation but was met with a deep frown. "Jonathan, your dedication to duty is admirable, but it is a holy day. We cannot abandon the ladies, who are left too much without our company."

Anna shot a fleeting smile to Jonathan. She traced her hand along Mr. Cloet's cheek and gazed deeply into his eyes. "My own, do not think on it. You shall be free to serve the Cause, as you have done. Have no fear that I could ever be so callous as to give you pain for it. I bear well the deprivation until we may be together again, as we women must." Mr. Cloet's features relaxed as he was enthralled by her gaze. "We are strong enough. Do you agree, Savvy?"

Careful, the voice inside warned.

"Uh, yeah. Yes," I responded.

Anna stood and acknowledged Éabha, who was passing through the dining room door. "Please bring the tray to Master Cloet's study. The men must work. We ladies shall see to our own cares." Both men rose when the mistress of the house did, leaving them in no position to argue. She laced her arm through her husband's and escorted him to the door after Éabha. "Would you prefer wine rather than cider, mine own?"

"Whichever gives you greatest joy, my wife." He smiled.

"Come now, I would have *you* choose." She closed the door behind them.

I wasn't sure why I was being shut in until Jonathan turned to me, anxious. "Miss Moore, please, do forgive me."

"For… what?"

"You have seen too much of this bloody business as it is. Master Cloet and I should never have discussed it in your presence."

"Oh. Well, I'm glad you did."

"But we caused you distress. I would have told you what you needed for your journey. The rest, you should have been spared."

"Jonathan, I kinda need to know what's going on so I can survive. Leaving me in the dark isn't helping."

He frowned. He may not have agreed with me, but he nevertheless promised, "I shall endeavor not to conceal from you what information I am at liberty to share."

And what about the voice warning me? Did I imagine it?

"Besides," I studied him as I said, "you'd have me miss out on the fascinating romance between the Cloets? The way she got him to agree with her? Forget it. It was a dance worth watching."

"Johannes does appear to reside on Queen Street." He spoke in the direction of the floor.

"I don't know what that means."

"It is said of any man who is governed by his wife."

"Is… that bad?"

Jonathan shook his head to himself, though he smiled when he looked up and said, "It depends on the wife. Would not you say?"

The distance somehow closed. His face was hovering near mine while he searched my eyes. I wished I could reach inside of him and understand him.

"The winter pie was something else," I added, not quite ready to leave. "Can't say I've ever had anything like it before."

He was amused. "Indeed?"

"No. Jonathan?" A new wash of emotions lapped at me, hinting at a tide threatening to overtake me if I wasn't careful to move out of the way. "Thank you."

"Wherefore?"

"For everything," I answered, then I left the room and many things unsaid.

Chapter Thirty-Seven

Anna had the men settled in the dark-paneled parlor in short order. A white tablecloth billowed into the air like a sail when she swept it from the rectangular table, set in the middle of the room, so they'd have somewhere to work. Clusters of furniture—chairs and tea tables, a trunk, and an embroidered footstool—assembled around the perimeter. Mountains of ledger books and papers climbed over every available inch.

Éabha was directed to stir the contents of the corner fireplace and add a sprinkling of potpourri from a nearby bowl, and Anna declared she would plate the dessert herself. Her matronly eye on Jonathan, she dumped the balled linen into my arms, suggesting he assist me with folding the lengthy cloth. Mr. Cloet raised his brows at his wife, but held his tongue, and gathered the documents they required.

Anna studied me when I protested needing help, then she acquiesced with a passive, "As you wish," instead ordering Jonathan to fetch more wood from the barn, as they were likely to run out before the day was through.

He graciously accepted the task. Didn't mean he kept his opinion about being ordered around to himself. An air of feigned martyrdom, displayed so only I could see, had me hiding a grin while he fulfilled his duty to our hosts.

Upon his eventual return, his subsequent orders saw him holding the generous supply for Éabha, who transferred logs two at a time to the diminished store by the hearth. Éabha gave him a flirtatious twist of her lips with each pass, not bothering to hide her pleasure at the excuse for being in proximity to my protector, the distance diminishing in correlation with the number of logs in Jonathan's arms.

Throughout the entire, unnecessary display, he craned his neck around her to where Mr. Cloet waited with his display of reports spread across the table, looking a lot like a child counting down the final minutes until summer break. Anna forbade me from taking his place, as I was the guest. I dismissed the bristly feelings Éabha's antics inspired and focused instead on my amusement at Jonathan's pained look.

Released from his chore and having accepted a plateful of dessert, Jonathan dove into the reports. The apple pie was devoured, wine tasted over the examination of several documents on the table. It didn't take long for the men to become immersed in whatever business had brought us to the Cloets' door.

Anna waved us superfluous women from the room with a flick of her hands. Unable to help like any other stereotypical houseguest, I was left in the hallway while she disappeared into the bedroom at the top of the stairs and Éabha was dispatched with the tray and empty dessert dishes in the direction of the kitchen. She must've dumped them because she returned quickly to follow after Anna.

I was uncomfortable because the men's voices were carrying, which made it difficult *not* to hear the updates being given, so I ventured into the yellow parlor to give them space. A robin wrestling with a worm in the grass outside served as my entertainment. My efforts were thwarted, however. Mr. Cloet's voice resonated throughout the house.

The work, he explained to Jonathan, had been completed in Warwick, and the pieces brought in sets into New Windsor. The aforementioned Captain Machin was supervising the joining with the forge's owner, Samuel Brewster. Mr. Cloet believed the final links were to be assembled in the following days if Brewster's men had not already accomplished as much. The biggest question remaining, as far as Mr. Cloet was concerned, was whether they could get the thing downriver undetected, or were the bloody redcoats still rising from the depths of the waters like the plague they were.

Unable to escape the men's discussion, I decided to make my presence known by wandering back into the hallway, where I took to examining the clock outside their door. Mechanical ships tossing to and fro on painted waves marked the passage of time.

When Mr. Cloet reached his point of concern, I watched for Jonathan's reaction through the open doorway to see what it would be. He stroked the underside of his beard and accepted the refreshment Mr. Cloet was splashing into their goblets. He was an otherwise careful guard of his own thoughts.

"The number of trees that has been felled would astound you. It is a wonder you cannot see clear to the house!" Mr. Cloet eyed Jonathan.

"I know it disappoints you not to be there this day, but one cannot be on the workers every hour. They may escape ensnarement by the militia for the contract, but the forges go night and day. The Sabbath is their only reprieve. It is bad for the men. Bad for the morale."

"Of course, Johannes. No one is saying otherwise."

"That Machin may grumble. Sometimes I am complained of as being in his way. Others, I am never at his bidding when he wants. He has Brewster running hither and yon. The man does not know his own mind from day to day."

"Captain Machin is distracted by the concerns of the mission and has no actual fault with you, my friend," Jonathan said. "He is beholden to the Congress. Not an uneasy task, for the politicians are as much at war amongst themselves as we are against the king's forces. There are some who think the Works a waste of time and resources, given the difficulties of the Montgomery."

"One faulty link!" Mr. Cloet's voice boomed through the narrow hallway. "It was repaired, and the northern passage held for a year until the fort fell. There was much success on the river. It was want of the men's mettle, not the iron, that was the downfall of the Montgomery."

"Six hundred against five thousand trained regulars? There was no want of mettle."

"True enough," Mr. Cloet allowed. "True enough."

"Word has also reached us of a faction in the Congress, motivated by the contrivances of General Conway and others, sought to remove his Excellency as Supreme Commander. There are those who prefer General Gates for the command, including—it is said—the delegates from Boston."

"*Niet te pruimen.* Does not the salvation of our country merit higher claims on our citizens' hearts than their own jealousies and ambitions?"

A moment of silence passed between them.

"We are fortunate that Governor Clinton agrees with you about the attempt to regain control of the river." Jonathan glanced in my direction as he spoke.

Whatever previous hesitation he had about discussing the details and politics of his mission in my presence was ignored. A test, I guessed, of my loyalty and whether I was, in fact, not a spy for the British. Or else, an olive branch in response to my complaints about his leaving me in the dark.

I was grateful for the sign of trust, either way, but uneasy. Sure, I was curious about the "Works" and the dangers he was facing and when I could hope to go home. But if my experience with Major DeForest taught me nothing else, it made me nervous about learning anything of value to the enemy. This information crossed the line.

The noise from Anna and Éabha's heeled shoes coming downstairs distracted the men. A collection of fabrics and hats was passed to me as Anna walked toward them. With a quiet apology, she laid a hand on the parlor door's latch, offering to close the door on our frivolity.

Mr. Cloet clasped the front of his dressing gown with both hands and nodded as she did. Jonathan's thanks softened his expression when I wished them good luck with their work before he and Mr. Cloet were tucked away with their secret task.

Éabha scooped the collection from my arms and escorted me into the yellow parlor. A beautiful shawl of a soft, cinnamon-brown knit was offered to me. Lighter threads curled in a paisley pattern throughout. I was grateful beyond measure for the chance to cover up and hurried to Anna's side to receive it. Her brow creased as she fingered a threadbare section along the edge.

"Do you think you need it, ma'm?" Éabha swiped the shawl from Anna. "If 'tis but you and the mistress, that is. Why not let me darn the threads, and you can have it come evening?" With an almost sincere air of absent-mindedness, she tacked on, "Will the gentlemen be joining you for supper, mistress?"

"Would the sewing be completed if I said they would?" Anna challenged her.

Éabha didn't bother to hide her playful meddling with the open invitation. "Well, it would be difficult, what with there being more mouths to feed and there being more to do in the kitchen." I groaned at her. "It would be worth the wait 'til morning if it did. I dare say, Captain Wythe should not mind," she finished saucily.

"We just met several days ago." I shook my head at the women and tugged my shift higher, above the gown's swooping neckline.

"Ah, but the heart wants what it wants, even if it wants it in but a day," Éabha mused.

"I think perhaps we have teased Savvy enough on that score," Anna admonished her.

"As you say, mistress." She curtseyed in response. Her demeanor toned down, Éabha draped the folded shawl on a chair, then fitted me with a cerise cloak and a straw hat. The gray, fingerless gloves were also presented to me.

I asked about my cloak, the one I'd inherited from the trunk, and was reminded it was still drying, having only been laundered hours earlier. A hint of disgust was detectible in Éabha's answer. What she couldn't know was the woolen cloak was the closest thing I had to my own property. Playing dress-up was fun, but these weren't costumes in a museum to entertain patrons. Everything I was wearing was part of Anna's daily wardrobe, handmade petticoats and shifts, sewn from scratch or else purchased from overseas before the war. Wealthy or not, there had to be a limited number. It hated borrowing so much.

Once Anna and I were both bundled, Éabha excused herself.

Cool spring air breezed over us as Anna led us through the kitchen garden to begin our tour of the grounds. The sun kept it from being uncomfortable. Lavender plants bowed under her hand trailing overtop as we passed by. Their subtle sweetness lingered above the plump buds, eager for warmer days ahead.

She paused where a section had died and plucked off browned bits while she spoke. "Savvy, I want you to know we are honored to welcome you as a guest in our home. It is a difficult time here, when neighbors and friends find themselves at odds with one another, never certain in whom them may trust or whether danger will come to call. Too many a family has seen themselves torn apart, not only from the terrible news of a loved one having been killed, but from even its own members discovering themselves on opposite sides of the conflict."

I glanced at the men visible through the parlor window, flying their fingers along the table and debating what lay before them.

Anna passed in front of me to address me directly. "Jonathan told us of your meeting. That you were abducted and left abandoned in the woods with nothing. How you were forced to fight alongside him like a soldier. You are a woman of pride, Savvy. One, it is easy to see, who looks only to herself to make her way in the world. My husband and I are not part of the local militia, as are my brothers, but we do assist as we can. To aid Jonathan in his mission and to welcome you into our home during your time of need is our way of contributing to the battle against the king's aggression. It is our duty and our privilege, and I hope you can find some peace in knowing this."

Once again, she had reached to the heart of the matter, finding the perfect words to counter the oppression I felt at being dependent on others, with no choice but to accept their charity or else starve. I resisted, anyway, because it felt like I was forsaking my quest to go home. "I'm not here to make friends. I'm not even supposed to be here."

"Yet, you are here, Savvy."

"I'm not supposed to be."

I wanted to tell her the truth. Everything about her invited me in. She was kind and accepting, and I was so alone. At the same time, she made me wary. I was afraid of what might happen once the bell was rung and people learned I was from the future.

She answered my silence, saying, "I believe, in my heart, it is not possible to be anywhere but where God means you to be."

I could only stare.

My parents weren't particularly religious. Churches were for the study of history. Time held in place by wood and stone, stained glass and candle ash. Quiet reflection, now and again. Divine destiny or intervention or fate or whatever nonsense? Such a possibility was mind-blowing. How could I have been *meant* to be torn from my home, everyone I knew and loved, all the ways defining who I was, to spend the rest of my days in the past?

"Take comfort." She collected me in her arms when the first tears fell. "You shall know the joys of a home once more."

"You don't know that."

"Are you ready to abandon hope?"

"No."

"Then, believe it to be true." She squeezed me tighter, like a long-time friend.

When we drew apart, I couldn't look at her, embarrassed by the outburst that still hadn't subsided. She was compassionate and patient and so understanding. I vowed right then and there to do my best to banish the belief I was denigrating myself by accepting help from the Cloets. Or Jonathan.

Anna touched a hand to my cheek when I mumbled my thanks. "Let us come away from the window," she said.

Jonathan was stationed there, watching. Concern filled his face. I rushed to brush aside the tears, wishing he hadn't seen them. He jerked toward the door, but she signaled for him to stay with a shake of her head. Frowning, he did, his body returning to its post. Thoughts of the work with Mr. Cloet clearly abandoned.

Sweeping her arm into mine, she had us resume our walk. "He worries about you," she said once the side of the house blocked him from view.

"Because I'm a mess. It's ridiculous," I grumbled.

"Do not be so harsh." She stopped to face me. "Many a man who has seen bloodshed suffers from nostalgia. Why should you be any different?"

"Nostalgia?" I questioned the word, uncertain what she meant.

She guided us farther from the house. "You suffer from unsettling dreams, do you not? Perhaps not here, in the safety of our home, but out there, at the camp? In the forest?"

"How do you know these things?"

"I know because Jonathan knows," she told me with some hesitation. My cheeks burned. "Savvy, I am certain Jonathan would tell you as I do now. You have nothing for which you need feel ashamed."

I fussed with a loose finger nail. The tear was close to the quick. "Alexander was right."

"Alexander?"

"He warned Jonathan I was a distraction to him. Damn it, he's right. I *am* a danger."

"You speak of Captain Brott?"

"Yeah," I admitted, caught in a mixture of anger, embarrassment, and fear of what my interference could mean for everyone, including in my own time.

"Captain Brott is an unlicked cub whose only cares are for himself, his purse, and his power. You are not to listen to a word the man says."

Her declaration left me speechless. The harsh tone and what I assumed was a less-than-gentile insult seemed out of character. Then, laughter poured from both of us.

"I have no idea what an unlicked cub is," I told her, "But I have no doubt you're right!"

"Jonathan is a clever man," she spoke fondly of him, "yet there are two truths that elude him. It *is* possible to speak with women and the nature of Alexander Brott."

"He doesn't seem to have any problems with you," I noted, thinking of the many surreptitious looks passed between Jonathan and Anna.

"You, as well."

"I don't know. Things are pretty awkward between us most of the time, and we're just friends," I reminded her.

"I have known Jonathan for a few years now. He is awkward with every woman. It is easier for him with me because I am married and we share a common interest. You, Savvy, as you have said, you are newly acquainted with him, yet he speaks with you and cares for you in a way we have not seen in some time. It is why we like you so. Mind you, there is a lady we believe Jonathan does fancy. As is his fashion, though, he has not found his voice with her."

"I'm not staying, Anna. Here, in the Colonies. You should encourage Jonathan to like this other woman, not me."

"I do apologize. We should not have toyed with you." We followed the line of apple trees in silence. The implication of her words weighed on me. "I would ask you not to share this with Jonathan, as we are not yet certain." Anna paused until I nodded in agreement before continuing, "We believe she is now being courted by another man. At least, so it would seem, if the rumors are true."

"Then, I'm sorry for him," I told her. The green-eyed monster had no right to bother me.

"As am I." We reached the end of the stone wall. Rather than follow the turn in its path, we walked in the direction of the house, moving at an angle toward the backyard. Several outbuildings of different sizes sprouted up within the property's borders. "Would that you could stay."

"There was someone else, wasn't there?" I asked. "A woman from a while ago? Jonathan alluded to her when we were back at camp."

"Cordelia." Anna gave me a warning look. This was a dangerous topic of conversation. "He came to America for her, though he would never confess it. Cordelia was beautiful, lively, courageous, and owned his heart completely. How he loved her."

"What happened?"

"Her family came here from England. Jonathan convinced his father to purchase a commission for him. His choice in regiment granted him the means to follow. Though, of course, he hid his true purpose. I believe Jonathan's father had already made plans for him, including having chosen for him a bride. There remained only the introduction."

"Jonathan was a *British* officer?" I was shocked by the news, but the more I thought about it, the more it made sense. "No wonder Major DeForest thinks he's a spy."

"There are many who distance themselves from Jonathan." Anna stooped with pursed lips to grab a large rock and carried it to the stone wall.

Her troubled expression deepened when it wasn't apparent where the rock belonged. I searched beyond its border, through the miles upon miles of wilderness surrounding us, and wondered how far away the means to going home was.

"It took Jonathan more than a year to find Cordelia," Anna continued the story, leaving the rock on top of the wall. "He was stationed first in Boston. It was not until his orders sent him to Long Island that he learnt of her. Cordelia and her family were living in the Highlands, though her father conducted business on the Isle of Manhattan. Jonathan defected from his commission and met with her there in secret. I believe he may have played a role in General Washington's escape when the city was lost.

"Be that as it may. Cordelia made the introductions and secured his position amongst the ranks of officers within our army." Anna grew silent, grief written on her face.

"You were friends with her, as well," I realized.

"She brought Jonathan to us when his missions first began and convinced us to include him. For a time, we saw much of them. War or no, those were truly happy days."

"He told you this?" I looked to her for more, but her lips were pressed shut and her cheeks gone damp.

Rather than push, I admired the parade of apple trees, their branches bespeckled with podgy leaf buds and immature blossoms and gave her a few moments to herself.

Maybe it was because Jonathan and I were in the thick of something important or because we'd just met, but he was pretty guarded. I couldn't imagine him sharing intimate details about himself. Then again, the war could've changed him.

"Like a puzzle being assembled," she said, her voice still thick, "I have learnt the story over time."

Sounds of children's laughter bubbled from a white barn erected at a distance from the house. Outside the opened doors, a boy was riding a brown pony. Jonathan's horse, free of any restraints, whinnied and pranced alongside them. The pony snorted in return and attempted to nuzzle the dappled horse, who ducked away to circle the pony's other side.

A squat woman with salt-and-pepper hair falling in messy strands from her cap was hugging a little girl to her front and laughing with the boy at the animals' game. Upon seeing us, the girl cried gleefully, "Mama!" and rushed over to us. A generous bear hug, topped with a kiss on the forehead from Anna, greeted the child, who was introduced as Gertrude. Her older brother, riding the pony, was Jacob.

The natural inclination to ask her what grades she and her brother were in at school left me tongue-tied. Instead, I managed a generic, "It's nice to meet you."

At Anna's encouragement, Gertrude informed me in broken English that Jacob was eight years old, to which Gertrude added through her mother's translation, it was why he got to ride the pony first. She was only four.

Anna was about to lead us to the children's nurse, Matilda, when the little girl gasped. She ducked behind her mother's gown, clutching the cotton waves in tiny fists. Jonathan's horse reared, though I didn't hear him make a sound as he rose and landed, forcing the pony to ground its hoofs into place to keep from running into its troubled playmate.

"Lord, save us!" The nurse clasped her hands over her mouth and disappeared behind the giant horse, which was shepherding the pony and its rider toward the house.

Not sure what was going on, I lifted the length of my gown, ready to rush over to help them. Anna seized my wrist before I got far. She yanked me close until I was leaning against her side like Gertrude—who buried her face into her fists—and whispered, "Be still. Do not speak." She pressed her features together; eyes shut, mouth moving almost unperceptively. "*Nos ex Deo sumus non qui non est ex Deo non audit nos*."

A pebble skittered along the dirt roadway. Following the sound, my knees grew weak at the sight of several redcoats emerging from the woods. They'd forgone the open road and followed its path on a parallel route. Except having reached the bend, they'd chosen to leave behind the cover of the trees and were approaching the house. Bent forward, swinging their heads in one direction to the other, the tips of their fixed bayonets searched with them.

As they neared the stone wall, gazes scanning the Cloet's property, I edged backward. The house was almost a football field away, the soldiers less than half that distance from us. If we ran for it, could we reach the backdoor before they jumped the wall and caught us? Could we outrun their guns if fired? I cursed myself for neglecting to get the steel pistol back.

How could I have been stupid enough to think we were safe?

"Be still. Be silent," Anna ordered. Ice-blue eyes bored into mine. She was so sure, so courageous, her influence so strong, I couldn't disobey her, even if I wanted to. She tipped her head in silent approval, then faced the road to continue praying.

Fear was making me feverish. Pinpricks of sweat swelled from my skin.

The redcoats spread out to follow the length of the stone wall, continuing their scrutiny of the property. Their focus passed over us, searched the area around us, scanned back our way, then continued onward.

The pinpricks gathered along my sternum, reinforcing each other until they drooled from my chest toward my stomach.

He was there. Jonathan's double. Another redcoat waved him over to where the man had situated himself in front of us. They conferred amongst themselves, their words too far away to hear, while they continued to eye the Cloet's lands.

Anna's prayer grew more fervent, her hand hot in mine even through our knit gloves.

A third redcoat joined them. I didn't see what happened next. Jonathan's horse looped in front of Anna, Gertrude, and me, blocking our view.

"Come," Anna whispered. "Keep to Felaróf."

Following her example, I pressed my hand onto the horse's side. Heat, rising off the animal, coiled around us. No objection came from the redcoats as the giant horse herded us toward the back of the house. We were allowed to walk away peacefully.

Éabha met us at the backdoor and hurried us into the kitchen, bolting the door shut behind her. Anna crouched low to meet her daughter's tear-streamed face. She kissed the tears, one rosy cheek at a time. Gertrude flung her arms around Anna's neck, knocking her mother off balance.

"My brave girl," Anna soothed her. "You did exactly right."

"Bless me." Éabha shook her head, hand to her heart. "Regulars. Been a spell since we seen them. Ma'm?"

Anna raised her face upward to check on me. My body was unwilling to move, despite the corner of the doorway digging into my side. Jacob *thump*, *thump*, *thump*, *thumped* down the back stairway and flung open the door. The wood bounced off my shoulder, swinging toward him again. He gave it another shove and rushed to Anna, shouting, "Mama. Mama!"

"Have a care with the door, Jacob," his mother chastised. "Are you hurt, Savvy?"

Jonathan hurried through the inner doorway leading from the house, a pistol standing at attention near his shoulder. He scanned the crowded room, checking on each of us, finishing with me. "Are you well?" he asked.

Words eluded me. He stepped closer, unable to reach me, his path being blocked by the Cloets hugging one another.

"Did you see, Mama?" Jacob continued over Jonathan, undeterred. "The regulars. They were watching us."

"It is done, Savvy," Anna told me. A chill passed through me at her words.

Jonathan's brow furrowed when I shivered. "Miss Moore?"

"I'm… fine," I answered.

Anna, meanwhile, was talking to Jacob, saying, "*Nee, mijn poepie*. They did not see."

"Mama!" Jacob laughed at the endearment. Even Gertrude giggled from her stronghold on Anna's neck.

"They leave," Mr. Cloet shouted from the front parlor.

"There, see? All is well." Anna squeezed the little girl, though she caught Jonathan's eye. Then she turned to Jacob. "Return upstairs with Matilda. Take your sister with you."

Gertrude cried, "*Nee! Ik wil niet gaan.*"

"Master Jacob," Jonathan addressed the boy. "Be a good man and guard the women."

"Aye, Captain," the child replied, saluting him.

Jonathan hesitated, but nodded once more to me, then returned to the front of the house.

Jacob grabbed his sister by the hand, ordering, "*Kom nou*, Gertie," and tugged an arm in the direction of the back stairs. She squeezed the back of her mother's neck tighter.

"Oh, Gertie. I fear I must go with the children, Savvy." Anna sighed. "Would you remain with Éabha, least until I can calm Gertrude?"

"Sure," I agreed.

Anna smiled her thanks and stood, sweeping the child onto her hip. "Come, *snoepje*." Before she left the kitchen, though, Anna paused by my side and leaned close to me. "Please do not speak with Jonathan about Cordelia."

Despite everything with the redcoats, why she'd still remember to make such a warning worried me. "O-kay."

"Jonathan blames himself for her death. She died only last year."

"That's terrible," I whispered back.

"For a time, we did not hear from him and learnt he had volunteered for more than one mission near guaranteed to fail." The unusually solemn expression on Éabha's face, as well, when Anna said this meant she wasn't exaggerating.

"Have you talked to him about it? I'm sure you could help."

"I dare say I could relieve his mind," Anna agreed. "The problem is—I blame him too."

Chapter Thirty-Eight

Éabha *Oh my*'ed and *Bless me*'ed several times, fanning her heart with her hand as she circled the kitchen. After fiddling with a cluster of dried sage suspended from the rafters for the umpteenth time—though if it were me, the count would probably have bordered on ridiculous!—she locked her sights on me and rounded the table to plop me onto a stool, saying, "Come now, I have lost much time and cannot do it myself. Sit and peel these root vegetables. It will give you something to quiet you."

A pile of carrots was shoved across the expanse of the wooden table into my useless hands, a waiting knife pointed out.

"Turnip!" she exclaimed, startling me. My hands jumped, knocking everything over and sending the pile into shambles. "Oh, begging your pardon, ma'm," she apologized. "Looks to be another left." The celebrated ingredient was held up for show. "Must have been mistook for a carrot and stored in the wrong basket."

"I'll be right back." I bolted from the table.

"Come, now. I meant no harm."

"I know. I just… I'll be back."

Hurrying into the hallway, then around the corner, I stopped to lean against the wall and pressed my hand to my heart like Éabha had done. I needed a moment. Mr. Cloet caught my eye from near the window in his study, a long gun in his hands. He lifted his chin to the other parlor without having to be told who I was looking for. He knew before I did.

Jonathan was ordering me before I even reached the doorway. "Return to the kitchen."

"Are they gone?"

His focus was fixed eastward, down the long line of the road to the crest of the hill. "We shall keep watch, nonetheless."

He'd shed his black coat and vest. The neckcloth was missing too; his shirt open without its restraint, sleeves coiled around his forearms, past his elbows.

He glanced to where I remained tucked behind the solid wood frame of the parlor's entrance. "I should be grateful if you kept to the kitchen. There are no windows, and two doors lay between you and the grounds."

"Here, I thought it was because you wanted me to cook you dinner. Supper," I corrected myself.

Jonathan breathed a laugh. "Incorrigible." With his attention shifted to the western edge of the woods, I couldn't see his expression, but his words grew heavy when he said, "Mistress Cloet remains above to guard the children, as it ought to be. We may need your skills should the soldiers pass the property's boundaries."

"Was that Captain Grey? The guy who looks like you?"

"He would not come himself." Coldness rode astride the answer. It sounded personal, whatever drove the one captain to hunt the other. "Will you do as I ask?"

"I'd feel better if I had my gun."

Jonathan huffed a sigh. "I cannot leave my post to fetch it."

"Tell me where it is. I'll—"

"You would make the household anxious were to you carry a weapon."

"What the hell do you think you're doing?"

He paused before answering, "It is expected of me."

"Great! Soldiers break into the house, I'll have what? A kitchen knife? Awesome. Knives in a gunfight. What could possibly go wrong there?"

"I would not have you in another conflict."

"You just said—"

"I know what I said!" He frowned, then softened his voice. "Come here."

I didn't budge.

Jonathan sighed as I continued my stance in the doorway. After completing a scan of the surrounding area, he tucked his pistol into the strap at his side. With head lowered, he raised a hand, asking, "Please, will you come closer? I do not wish our words to carry." Not moving, he waited, hand extended.

The sounds of Éabha prepping supper carried through the wall, her knife progressing in steady slaps against the wooden table through bulky ingredients. Potatoes, probably. Mr. Cloet coughed from the other room. A chair was dragged along the floor somewhere above us. Tiny giggles trickled through the floorboard.

I gave in and slid my fingers into his upturned palm. The surface was dry, shielded with callouses. He pulled me around him, drawing me into the corner to where I'd remain hidden from outside danger, then he leaned back to conduct another sweep of the grounds.

Once reassured the coast was clear, he stepped closer, out of sight from passersby. "The children are anxious. Even the boy, though he hides it well. He will give his mama a devil of a time in the days to come once the threat has gone for certain. The other women are frightened, as well. If they see you take up arms, knowing how you have fought by my side, you will frighten them further. But if you station yourself in the kitchen and, indeed, prepare the evening meal along with Miss Carroll, it would calm the family. And me."

I understood what he was asking me to do. Be brave for those around me. I hate spiders. Evan hated them more. Whenever he found one, he'd scream for me, throwing a fit unless I… This wasn't the same thing. "Jonathan, I'm—"

"Only a fool looks death in the eye and grows not afraid."

I stared, trying to decide if he was confessing fear. The dip of his head was subtle.

Our attention fell to the thumb passing along the back of my hand. His other stayed close to the weapon on his hip. As the moments slipped by, our joined hands raised, the natural connection between us guiding us together, until the backs of my fingers were brushing against his chest.

Our faces were only inches apart when he breathed, "I have known none so brave as yourself."

The skin below his collar bone paled in the thin lines of a scar slicing from somewhere hidden near his heart, stretching toward his sternum. He caught me looking and, embarrassed, cleared his throat.

I lifted my eyes back to his. They were such a beautiful blue. His thumb continued smoothing the outer length of my hand, calming me. Even knowing from his words and expression he worried about being able to protect me, I still felt safe with him. And I welcomed it.

"Please," he asked, "will you not assist me in easing the family's fears?"

"Yeah, okay."

After a lingering moment of standing together, the rhythm of the household marching forward while we held still, caught, Jonathan pressed my hand in an embrace, then eased away. "We shall keep watch for an hour. If it remains quiet, we must behave as though we were never troubled. Aye?"

I agreed, wishing for more than I knew he would grant me and reluctantly wandered into the hall. Without meaning to, I caught a glimpse of him standing at the window as I reached the banister, but he wasn't looking out the glass at the rising dim of night. He was watching *me*. It made me a little dizzy. We exchanged a smile, then I rounded the stairwell toward the back of the house.

Mr. Cloet had moved into the chair nearest the window. A book was held up, as if showing its cover to the front yard, which gave him the perfect view of both the road and the words he was enjoying with a relaxed grin. The long gun leaned against the hinges of the open, wooden shutters.

"Miss Moore," he acknowledged me, then returned to his reading.

Without further ado, the family resumed life as normal. At least, until the next time danger came to call.

Chapter Thirty-Nine

At the children's begging, they were permitted to share supper with the adults. A great show was made of extending the dining room table to its fullest, with little Gertrude being granted the important task of dictating the seating arrangements. There was a heated debate, in alternating English and Dutch, about who would sit next to Captain Wythe.

The young Cloets were baffled when I suggested they sit one on either side of him. Gertrude mumbled, "*U bent zinj dame.*"

To which Jonathan proclaimed, "But you shall always be my best lady," before asking me with a decorous tone, "Miss Moore, would you be so kind as to allow Miss Gertrude to take your place by my side for the evening?"

I played along, mindful of Jonathan's request to behave as if nothing had ever spoiled the day, and answered with matching, formal grace, "I should be honored to see such a fine lady at your side, my friend."

The child's face lit up. She clutched Jonathan's hand and dragged him, laughing, to the table's center.

Supper was a lighter affair than dinner, though no less entertaining or delicious. Jonathan was happily engrossed with the children's competition for his attention, and the final fears of the afternoon were forgotten.

Stories were shared of the children's adventures with their friends, fighting pirates and regulars, or among the secret society of the *Kippen*. Anna informed me these were the family chickens.

Their chairs jostled as they bounced, ecstatic at Jonathan's promise to play pirates with them the next day. They begged him to tell a story right then and there. It took little effort to convince him, and the extended family retired to the sitting room.

Dove-gray trim swept along the crisp white walls. The corner fireplace was alive with stories painted on the Delft tile surround, and a collection of miniature hope chests filled the shelves of two alcoves climbing past the mantel. Each was a different size, yet all of them were intricately decorated, adding to the room's folklore.

I found my attention straying to the collection throughout the evening.

Portraits of the family's ancestors looked down approvingly on their descendants as we settled ourselves to hear Jonathan's version of Black Beard and his many horrific battles on the open seas.

Spiced wine for the adults and mulled cider for the children came and went, and the sun stained the walls with its dying light in an array of pinks and oranges until it grew dark. Anna made the first effort at convincing the children it was bedtime, but Gertrude was too enthralled by Jonathan's tale and announced she could not sleep because the *nachtmaar* would come.

Anna's denying any such thing would happen in her house, with her there, was overlapped by Mr. Cloet declaring, "Of course you cannot go to bed with your heads stuffed with such beastly tales! Gertrude, my girl, you must lead us in a game of charades."

Anna made a passing comment about the children's papa spoiling them. A tender look of admiration was offered as consolation.

Another hour passed with the game showing no sign of stopping. Éabha came in to freshen the fire and check the candles on the walls, tasks forgotten because she was enlisted by Jacob to assist him with his clue. After lots of plotting, the pair began.

Little Gertrude climbed onto Jonathan's lap, and he encouraged her to guess what her brother could be doing by whispering into her ear. A smile was never far from his lips.

Éabha had laid on the ground with eyes closed as part of their pantomime and clutched both hands to her heart. Jacob bent over her and with terrific theatrics of silent emotion was distraught at her lying there. A fist reached into his vest, removing an imaginary object.

As he brought it to his lips, a guess came to me, but before I could shout the name of the play, Éabha yawned and woke. She and Jacob playacted huge surprise with arms outstretched, then hands to cheeks, leading to a giant hug. At which point, Jonathan, through Gertrude, shouted the guess I'd dismissed at Éabha's revival.

Everyone clapped when *Romeo and Juliet* was declared to be the correct answer.

An announcement was made that it was, indeed, past the children's bedtime. Dual protests ensued, but Mr. Cloet didn't dare undermine his wife a second time.

Their nurse had insisted on going to her brother's home in town after the redcoats' disappearance, forcing Jonathan to escort her once the danger was deemed to have passed, despite the household's assurances she was safer with the Cloets.

Poor Éabha was left doing double-duty, foregoing the opportunity to spend the night in her own cabin on the far end of the property. She swept the children in wide arms to usher them to bed, giggling. Not a harsh jailer, though, she was easily escaped.

While the children bestowed extra goodnight hugs and kisses on their parents, Jonathan plopped into the chair next to mine. "What troubles you, Miss Moore?" he asked with a teasing expression. It was both strange and refreshing to see him content, every part of him at ease.

"Troubles me? Nothing. I'm fine." I'd been enjoying myself so much—the play of normalcy, convincing—I couldn't imagine why he believed something was wrong.

"You are not familiar with *Romeo and Juliet*?" His accusing smile was full of good humor.

"Oh no, I am." I laughed. Jonathan followed my lead to lean closer so we could keep our conversation from reaching young ears. "Last I checked, fate wasn't very kind to the lovers."

"Ah, it is because you are thinking of what Shakespeare has written."

"Who else should I be thinking of?"

"David Garrick, of course." His brows flew skyward when I stared at him, confused. He made it sound as if I'd asked whether the moon was a biscuit or the rain made of Merlot as he exclaimed, "David Garrick. His version is much preferred to Shakespeare. The indecency of Romeo's lust for Rosaline was omitted, and the ending you witnessed, portrayed better here than any the whole of New England has seen. Lady Gertrude!"

Even before Anna could instruct them to, the children had rushed to Jonathan, wishing him, "*Goedenacht.*"

He took a knee to receive a big hug from the girl then rose to salute. "Master Jacob. Excellent performance, my good man. I dare say. You have educated our Miss Moore. For she has never seen a proper performance of *Romeo and Juliet*." Smirking, he added in my direction, "Far more rewarding after a night's theatrics, would not you say?"

I was at a loss.

The boy swelled with pride. "We have come to bid you a *good night*, Miss Moore." He grasped his jacket lapel and gave me an adult-like bow, emphasizing the English words he'd learned from his mother moments earlier.

"I bid you a good night, as well, kind sir," I returned his formal wishes. "And you, too, my lady. Those were wonderful performances this evening. From both of you."

Gertrude grinned, for the first time appearing less wary of me than before, as she was added to the praise. "*Bedankt.*"

Anna reminded her English was to be used when there were guests. The little girl didn't attempt repeating her mother's translation. Instead, she blurted out a question that made the entire room freeze. "*Wanneer krijg je een meisje?*"

Mr. Cloet coughed into a fist rather than allow the bark of his laughter to stand on its own. He followed with a stern look at his daughter. Jonathan diverted his eyes, his cheeks aflame with color.

It fell to Anna to address the comment with a kind warning, first in English, then Dutch. "I believe it is too early to think of such things, Gertrude. We have only met Miss Moore." Her voice was full of apology when she explained, "She asked when you will have a little girl."

I felt my own cheeks come to life and breathed a laugh of surprise. It was the flush of Jonathan's and the shift of his expression from embarrassment to something like hope that made me realize the issue needed to be addressed. "I… can't have kids, Gertrude."

"Jonathan, did—"

Anna slapped a hand onto her husband's arm, silencing him, her focus on me, intense. It made me uneasy. I clutched the key through my gown, not comfortable calling her on it, either.

Jonathan searched between Anna to me and back again, his mood grave, though his thoughts were otherwise hidden.

Gertrude's face registered increasing curiosity, focused on the various grown-ups' serious expressions during the impending silence. Even Éabha, who hesitated in the doorway, was uncharacteristically mute.

So, the child asked unhindered, "Why?"

"Gertie," Anna called over to her. Another apology was issued as she held out a hand to the girl.

But she was distracted by Jonathan whispering, "The child asks why." His gaze never left the floor.

"Well," I explained, turning back to the little girl at my knees, "a few years ago, I had an accident. Kind of like I got sick, and my body got hurt. Now it isn't possible for me to have kids."

"Are you sad?" Gertrude asked.

I should've said no. It was the truth. Or at least, it had been. Instead, what came out was, "I don't know."

The girl's eyes quizzed me. Believe me, I was just as puzzled by my response.

Jonathan shifted his weight uncomfortably. He abandoned his lonely study of the floorcloth long enough to look past me to Anna, who shook her head at him.

What is it with them?

Éabha broke in to swoop down on Gertrude, tickling her and bestowing noisy kisses on her cheek. The girl's squeals filled the room as she melted with the affection.

"Oh, but see here, Miss Gertrude," Éabha teased, "Master Jacob has been forgot. He cannot go to bed without plenty of kisses too!"

Jacob screamed his protests, laughing throughout, while Éabha and Gertrude descended and chased him into the hall, leaving the adults to yell their wishes of "*welterusten!*" and "sleep tight!" as they fled. Footsteps thundered up the stairs and into the front bedroom, where the cries of "*Nee! Nee!*" were smothered with more laughter.

Gertrude's question lingered.

That year was a such a train-wreck, what with Justin's affair and the bitter divorce filing I didn't see coming, I never allowed myself to dwell on losing the ability to conceive. An ever-efficient corporate attorney, he had laid the foundation for his abusive conduct ahead of time. He tied up my bank account with prolonged discovery, then sold our home out from under me within days of the trial's conclusion, a ready buyer in his back pocket. It left me couch surfing with my parents for several months.

I hated the crummy, post-divorce apartment while I saved for a down payment on a house; its faults, real and exaggerated, were harped on at every court appearance during our custody battle. Justin was flush and the prenup binding. But I refused to accept more money from my parents than I had to.

His whore of a mistress married him anyway.

Sorrel told me more than once she worried when I didn't grieve. In reality, I felt relief. Laid up in a hospital bed, following surgery, I learned how alone I was.

Just after midnight, the doctor had wandered in to tell me my fallopian tube had ruptured from a pregnancy I hadn't even suspected. It wasn't the first time. She offered her condolences to my numbed acceptance of her words.

No one came to visit me. I told work I didn't feel up to it and never shared what landed me in the hospital. My parents weren't around, off instead celebrating their anniversary with a cruise to the Bahamas. My brother and his family lived in the Midwest. Even Sorrel was on the opposite coast at a rare conference.

Of course, the father of my doomed baby hadn't hesitated in abandoning me. Never cared to ask why I needed him to keep Evan for a few extra days, though he complained about it with smug glee tucked behind his words.

So really, there wasn't any point in asking anyone to sit with me. I did my time, I healed, then I vowed to always remember—the only person I could count on to be there for me was me.

Something between grief and horror filled Anna's face as she stared, which was beyond unfair. How could she have laid her hopes at my feet, after I'd asked her not to expect me to play any part in Jonathan's future?

Mr. Cloet patted her hand, choosing a thorough examination of the fire for his refuge. The painted garden on the floorcloth was Jonathan's. His hands were clasped between his knees, his face vacant.

"Okay, don't pity me," I told the room.

"Savvy," Anna began.

"There's no future for me here in the Colonies. None. I get it. Women aren't allowed to support themselves here. They have to have a husband. But a woman who can't provide sons? She's worthless. It's why I have to go home. I have a life there. Where no one gives a good God damn about whether I can have kids or not."

She crossed herself when I broke the ancient commandment about swearing and dropped her gaze to her lap. Mr. Cloet sighed, frowning at his friend.

"Jonathan." I rose to stand in front of him. Even after his chin lifted a fraction higher, he still wouldn't raise his head to look at me, and I… I needed him to.

The issue never bothered me before.

Evan. I have Evan.

My fingers longed to wrap themselves in Jonathan's. Instead, I concluded my speech to him with fisted hands. "Finish your mission. Do what you need to do. But please understand, I have to go home."

He turned to stare out the window. A knuckle was raised to his lips, crushing them. He didn't speak. I wished I could give him back the carefree evening he desperately needed. We both did.

So, I walked away.

Anna rose to meet me at the door, and I readied myself to withstand a barrage of sympathetic words. "There's nothing to say,

Anna. It is what it is." But the pity was gone from her eyes, and only friendship remained.

Whatever emotions had been stirred up, yet refused to identify themselves, simmered down as she embraced me. "May I accompany you, Savvy? I can assist you with undressing."

I hoped I wouldn't offend her when I answered, "No. Thanks, though."

With a final look around the room, I bowed my head, wishing them goodnight, then I sought the peace found in solitude.

Chapter Forty

A fresh fire was roaring in my room when I retreated behind the closed door. Undressing alone wasn't as easy as it should've been. Buttons, pins, several layers of clothing, the under-petticoat's laces—uncooperative and entangled menaces. It took a good dose of stubbornness and a dash of heartfelt profanity to free myself from the mess without having to search for help and risk bumping into Jonathan.

The stay, though not what I'd call comfortable, hadn't bothered me until it came time to take it off. The relief was immense, and I allowed it to fall, reaching my arms overhead, leaning to one side then the other, then I stretched my upper torso backward.

Something tumbled to the floor. Jonathan's note. I'd forgotten about it. The fibers of the paper were damp from having been pressed into my skin for hours. I unfolded it partway but stopped myself. Ridiculous to think I could hold on to it. It could only serve to damn me further. Written proof of my interference.

I refolded the note and chucked it into the fire. A darkened pit opened up as flame pierced the center of the paper and swallowed it, consuming it from the middle while the outer edges shriveled inward, until destruction marched in from every side to reduce his words to ash.

Regret filled my eyes, the tears splashing from my cheeks, and my heart ached, either from the loss of the letter or the long-ago pregnancy I hadn't cared to dwell on. I didn't know. I wondered if it'd been a girl. I'd never wondered before. Other thoughts of home soon joined the mix, leading me through the entire playlist of grief's emotions. Compounded by the events of the past week, it left me exhausted and numb.

The flames danced before my eyes for some time. Swirling, ghostly images of the light burned over my vision until I couldn't distinguish between what was real and what was residual memory of fire.

A great irony struck me. How many times had I wished I could turn back time? How many times had I wanted to change what'd come before? If I stayed in the Colonies, trapped because I'd changed the past and undone the future, leaving no home for me to return to, none of those moments would ever happen. Yet, I would never be free of them. Those regrets would always haunt me.

And I would never again hold my son.

Éabha came in to find me huddled by the fire, lost in a torment of *Would Haves* and *Should Haves*. A fresh gown and various, matching accessories were delivered to the table. "Are you cold, ma'm? The shawl, 'tis mended if you have want of it."

My brain kicked into gear, and I shook my head.

She scolded me for the mess of clothing strewn everywhere, flicking pieces from where they lay. I apologized and offered to do it myself, but she declined with a kind scoff, saying, "'Tis mine to do, after all, seeing to the ladies in the house."

Useless and worthless, I returned to the fire and my stormy thoughts.

Another log was laid, the flames leaping out of the way until it came to rest, then welcoming the addition in their embrace. Éabha leaned away from the hearth, eyes filled with sad resignation. Ignoring our earlier exchange, she collected the shawl from the pile on the chair and crouched to wrap it around my shoulders, dressing the front to ensure it encircled me.

"I'm fine," I told her, shrugging a shoulder.

"Of course, you are, ma'm." A hand, two hands, rubbed my arms, as if trying to brush away the sorrow with her kindness. "Is there anything else you are needing?"

Assured there was nothing, she gave my arms a friendly squeeze and bade me goodnight, pulling the door closed behind her. Out in the hallway, she spoke in a hushed tone I couldn't understand. Jonathan's rich voice answered.

The clatter of her heels soon faded toward the room next door. A metal latch lifted, followed by the swing of hinges squealing open and shut. Gertrude giggled, her voice whispering through the walls. Éabha laughed, shushing her.

Jonathan, however, lingered outside my room. A step away, followed by a returning step. A single sound, not quite a knock, was barely audible. I rose and resituated the shawl around my shoulders, preparing to face him.

He startled. His forehead had been leaning against the door when it opened.

"You know, some people find it easier to knock with their hands instead of their head," I said, though the delivery lacked energy.

He breathed a laugh anyway. "You are incorrigible."

"Always and forever." His suit jacket was absent, and the top buttons of his vest were undone, neckcloth removed. The scar was once again visible. Before my noticing became a thing for him, I asked, "What can I do for you?"

"I apologize for disturbing you."

"I wasn't in bed yet."

He followed the line of my body and noted with embarrassment, "You are not dressed."

"I'm not dressed, not in a state of undress, or formal dress—as a matter of fact—but I'm not naked, either," I verbally meandered.

His expression shifted several times. Despite the color in his cheeks and his studious attention to the floorboards, he hummed, as if tempted to enjoy the reference to my earlier folly, but there was something on his mind, and the hint of a smile fell. Torn as I knew he must be between propriety and achieving his purpose in seeking me out, his gaze skirted from my lack of attire down the hall. We were alone.

In deference to his plight, I layered the shawl across my chest, making sure I was covered. The stockings extended above the line of my shift, since I hadn't gotten far in undressing. No sinful flesh was showing as a result. By eighteenth-century standards, however, I was standing in the doorway in my underwear.

"Jonathan, I don't have energy for the whole awkward thing right now. Spit it out, please. What do you want?"

"Aye." He cleared his throat and lifted a hand to show me what was held there. Blue ribbon tumbled from his palm and drifted over the edges of his opened fingers. I recognized it by its ribbon. The key he'd taken from me. It had been darker then, not the shining silver being offered. "I promised that I would return this to you."

I was touched he would care about what his gift looked like, an item meant to be hidden. Surely his mission should've kept him too busy to waste his time polishing a simple key. Maybe he thought I was embarrassed by it. And I'd been mad at him for taking it back, thinking he didn't trust me with it after the debacle with Major DeForest.

My heart fluttered, and I found myself smiling at him until I realized, "There's no reason for me to have it. You're going to finish your mission here, then take me back to the hillside where we met, remember?" He didn't respond. "You promised."

"I also promised to protect you."

"Meaning what?" I crossed my arms in frustration. The shawl slid from my shoulder, threatening to fall to the floor. I stared at him, not caring, and demanded with my eyes he answer me.

"It means the forest may yet be overrun."

The news of further delays and possible danger lying between me and my son blind sighted me, though perhaps it shouldn't have, given our day's excitement. I allowed my arms to fall to my sides, overwhelmed. Jonathan caught the shawl's edge before it was lost and returned it to its place on my shoulder.

"I will keep my promise." He sought my eyes with a tipped chin, seeking reassurance I believed him. I wanted to believe him. I had to. "In the meanwhile…"

My inhaled hesitation slowed but didn't deter him guiding the ribbon around my head. His fingertips floated over my skin as he slipped them into my hair, lifting and freeing it from the press of the ribbon.

He glanced to where the key lay level with my breasts, then dragged his gaze to mine, not bold enough tuck it into my shift himself. "Please guard this until I ask for it again."

The key was hot. Not from being cradled in Jonathan's hand. It burned as if he'd kept it hidden in the fireplace for hours and it carried the flame within its metal. What was more, I swear the thing was vibrating, like a tuning fork sounding a note no one could hear.

Once it settled against my chest, the vibration altered as it synchronized with the rhythm of my heart. The heat faded until it was nothing but a shiny trinket on a ribbon.

I raised a cautious hand to touch it and searched Jonathan's face to see if he'd felt the same inexplicable sensations when he gave me the key. The sadness there made it seem as if he was unaware of anything out of the ordinary. A sigh lifted then dragged his shoulders.

I was caught somewhere between confusion and fear, unsure whether it'd been real. Or had the hour and exhaustion taken its toll on me?

He read my expression with curiosity, though it was fleeting and disappeared more quickly than my emotions tussling for attention. "Should you need anything, Master and Mistress Cloet sleep there." Having gestured to the door at the far end of the hallway, he paused, then indicated the door across the hall from my own. "I am here."

We stared at one another, lips parted. It felt like something more should be said, by one or the other of us, but I wasn't even sure what to think, let alone how to phrase the questions spinning in my mind. Instead, he wished me a goodnight, then vanished into his room, behind the closed door.

Left by myself, in the cool hallway, late at night, wasn't going to solve the mystery, so I returned to my room. The possibilities refused to coalesce into some sort of logical explanation. I shivered despite the lively blaze leaping chimneyward. Either there was something wrong with me or the history books didn't tell the complete story of what transpired during the War.

I unwound the ribbon from my neck and held it at a distance. The key remained passive and silent, dangling innocently from the silk ribbon. Firelight played off the polished metal.

It's just a key.

I ran a trepidatious finger along its side. Nothing happened. Still, the experience in the hallway made me unwilling to put it back on. Placing it on the dresser, I backed away. Quiet and passive, it sat.

I buried myself within the mountain of blankets on the bed and hoped to put the issue to rest.

Chapter Forty-One

There was screaming. I bolted awake, terrified.

Embers emitted a dim glow from the fireplace, low and deep red, too weak to reach beyond the brick hearth. Moisture pasted the shift to my body. The covers slid to the ground when I sat upright, allowing a chill to seep through the dampened linen to my skin.

Jonathan shouted my name from a distance, the sound growing closer, booming louder, as he repeated himself, then he burst through the door. Gertrude's voice cried for her mama from next door. Éabha's soothing filtered through the rise and fall of the child's shrieks and gasps.

A thundering of Dutch exclamations overlapped Jonathan's yelling, starting from the other end of the house. The light from a candle reflected off the wall outside, illuminating Jonathan's silhouette in the doorway as he scanned for me among the shadows.

"Jonathan," I whispered. The rawness in my throat meant I'd been the one who'd screamed.

The light swelled into the room as the candle was brought closer. Able to see better, he scoured the darkened corners, then peeked around the wooden shutters. Finding nothing, he hurried to my side. "What is wrong?"

Mr. Cloet rounded the corner with a pistol at the ready. At the commotion, Jonathan rose from the edge of the bed. Mr. Cloet's stare bounced back and forth between us. "What is it, man? What has happened?"

Anna forced her way past him. She, too, eyed the furniture, the walls, even ceiling to where there was nothing extraordinary.

"Have a care, wife. The candle! Do you want to light the

powder?" Mr. Cloet complained but didn't wait for an answer. He flew to the window to ease open the shutter. Lingering over the view of the grounds until, at last, he declared himself satisfied there were no external threats and banged the shutters shut to face us.

She ignored her husband's admonition, focused instead on Jonathan and me. "Jonathan, what is it?"

The cries for "Mama!" sounded louder.

"Wife, the child is in need of you," Mr. Cloet chided.

"Éabha attends her," Anna said. "Savvy, what ails you?" The candle trembled in her hand, a line of wax wending toward the pewter holder.

Casting an eye around the room myself, I found nothing wrong.

Jonathan gathered the brown shawl crumpled on my bed, his gaze concerned yet inviting while he sought an explanation I wasn't sure how to give. Cotton caressed the sides of my neck as the shawl drifted into place on my shoulders. Its weight nestled against my body as he wrapped me with it, the only embrace I could hope to receive from him.

Jacob shuffled in our direction, asking if there were soldiers. Mr. Cloet exited the room to answer him, "*Nee*, *maatje*. Off to bed," kissing the top of his head as he did.

Jacob's half-hearted protest was cut short by a yawn. Father shooed his son to bed again. Reluctantly, the boy obeyed, claiming he was not afraid. His feet thumped along the floorboards toward the other end of the house. "*Wees stil*, Gertie," he snapped, then thumped the rest of the way to the front bedroom next to Jonathan's.

"There are kinder words for your sister, Jacob," Éabha's voice reprimanded from the other room.

"*De vrouw heeft een nachtmerrie gehad,*" Mr. Cloet addressed his wife.

Anna clutched her shawl to her chest. "A nightmare?"

"She will be looked after. Come now."

She was frozen in place, staring at me as if she was waiting for me to speak. I didn't know what to say.

"Jonathan. Why are you dressed, man?" Mr. Cloet demanded.

"I found I could not sleep." His focus began with Mr. Cloet, but he finished by addressing Anna. "I thought to take a walk."

"Perhaps it is not the best night for such things," Anna said. From her pointed expression, there was no doubt he was expected to agree with her.

"Forgive me, Miss Moore." He buttoned his wool coat, pressing a hand to his pocket. Guilt lingered in his expression. "I regret that… my pacing did disturb you. You and the family."

Anna nodded an approval.

Their silent communication concerned me. She was dressed for bed, but I was sure she knew something more was at work.

What are they up to?

He grew self-conscious as I stared, confused and worried more and more, the longer I thought about the pistol and the residential knife on his belt he'd tried to hide from me.

"Be at peace, Savvy. All is well," Anna reassured me.

Gertrude whimpered from her room.

"For heaven's sake, Anna," Mr. Cloet exclaimed. "See to the child. Then, perhaps, we might sleep. *Jonathan*." The emphasized acknowledgement of Jonathan's presence meant I was his responsibility and, as such, his problem to take care of.

Noticing the dying embers, Anna insisted Mr. Cloet hold a moment so she could spark a bit of fatwood to life with her candle. The newly added log she'd tucked into the firebox didn't want to catch, though. Eyes low while he claimed the piece from her with a promise to see to it, Jonathan raised them and held her gaze, bidding husband and wife goodnight.

Mr. Cloet welcomed the invitation to return to bed, departing without waiting for Anna to follow. Heavy footfalls paused outside his daughter's room, from where he offered reassurances to the little girl inside. Anna's brows were knit with worry. Her meaningful exchange with Jonathan was interrupted by a muffled sob for "Mama!" leaving Anna to bid us a reluctant good night. It made me wonder what secret language they'd developed, requiring only silence and a stare.

The door was left open. Light from her candle played against the walls of the hallway until she disappeared. Soon, the soothing tune of a lullaby floated through the house.

A rustic-orange glow brightened the room until the rhythm of the flames in the fireplace settled into a steady crackle. Jonathan remained hunched by the hearth, facing the random snap and pop of the logs.

Something caught his eye on the dresser when he stood. The key. With a glance in my direction, he fingered the teeth, moving to stand next to where I sat huddled on the bed with knees tucked close. "You are safe here," he reminded me.

It wasn't nostalgia, as Anna put it, haunting me. When I didn't respond, he brought a chair to sit with me. "More dreams?" Reaching around my face to turn my head so we were looking at one another, he brushed at my tears with his thumb. The dampness tingled as it spread across my cheek by his touch. "Tell me what you saw."

"The boy… The boy I killed in the woods. He waits for me every night by the tree. But then it changes. This dream I used to have." I shuddered at the fragments of my childhood nightmare reawakening. "Darkness."

"Darkness?"

"It's searching for us."

Jonathan seized me by the back of the head. Fear ruptured in my chest. The intensity of his gaze boring into me when he asked, "What else did you see?" made me realize it wasn't a dream anymore. I recognized the Darkness. The presence that'd prowled the perimeter of the camp, taking sadistic glee in the bloodshed, that'd circled the tent when I was alone, and shadowed the militia when they fled. It didn't find what it was hunting for in their numbers. Numbers no longer hidden from its sight. Unlike in my dreams, it sought its true prey. It only wanted me to get to Jonathan.

"Don't leave me!" I begged, clutching his arms.

Like before, I could sense the Darkness off in the distance.

The key clattered onto the desk. Fingertips alighted on my brow, brushing the span of my forehead, rounding the curve of my temple, then tracing the line of my jaw. Warmth, like the joy of laughter with old friends, tickled along my skin. The panic fled, the tension in my body easing as Jonathan soothed me, his fingers retracing their path. Soon, only his arms supporting me kept me upright.

My hands slackened, sinking from their hold as he lowered me onto the bed. "Stay with me."

"I…" His voice was strained. His gaze shifted to the fireplace, in the same direction as the couple down the hall who'd generously opened their home to us and would have the most to lose if he was discovered in my room come dawn. "I will remain until you are asleep," he promised.

With each lulling pass of his hand, the last of my fear melted until it faded, taking the chill from the room with it. Everything was at peace, like the peace of closing my eyes into the sun on a warm summer's day.

The voice inside warned what he was doing to me. I forced my eyes to open.

He was still there, fingertips soft on my brow, smile reassuring on his lips. Our hands' embrace, comforting. "You are safe."

I told the voice I didn't care.

Chapter Forty-Two

The muffled resonance of male voices penetrated the exterior of the house. The wooden shutters barred the light from entering, but it had to be morning. Stretching my elbows to the side, then hands and toes reaching in opposite directions, I relished the glide of my limbs along the linen sheets. Curling up again, like a tomcat in a secluded garden, I lazed in bed, perfectly at peace, and enjoyed the flickering glow from the fireplace. Someone had refreshed the logs during the early hours without me knowing.

Mr. Cloet's voice was easy to pick out. It carried across the yard and into the house. He didn't sound upset, but his usual jovial tone was absent. The master was all business. Other voices answered, each unfamiliar. Jonathan's wasn't among them.

The key bounced against my chest with the movement of me swinging my legs out of bed. I laid a hand against it. Nothing. It was just a key.

A thought bubbled in my mind. Something had happened during the night. Try as I might, though, I couldn't remember what it was. Something with Jonathan?

I pinched the bridge of my nose as a headache threatened to pounce.

Once it dissipated, I shook my head at my own paranoia and tucked the key into the front of my shift, an act I found strangely comforting. The token of friendship, a reminder—almost like a belief—I was protected. Safe.

Opening a shutter released a blinding flood of sunlight. When my vision cleared, I spotted Mr. Cloet, his back to the house, discussing with a wide sweep of his arm the distant corner of the property with two other men as they moved in the same direction.

Surveying my options: on the one chair were the clothes I'd arrived in, on the other was an espresso-colored dress. An outer petticoat of pink with cream-colored, vertical stripes waited on top. Neither option felt right, and the bathroom was calling. I decided to make a run for it without getting dressed. I encased myself within the shawl I'd neglected to take off before crawling into bed instead.

An empty hallway greeted me. I weighed the risks of the noisy back stairs or the quieter front. Quiet was good, but the latter would mean streaking through the entire first floor to reach the backdoor. I leaned over the stairwell railing, listening to determine if the coast was clear.

Jonathan's voice slipped from behind the closed yellow parlor door. "I had thought to call on… It was a foolish idea."

"Do not give up hope," Anna answered him.

"She has made her wishes plain." He sounded tired.

"You have not spoken with her," she persisted. "You know not what has happened, why she acts as she does."

"It is not my place to know what you have seen," he warned.

"I have seen the two of you together. You must not be afraid to speak with her."

He didn't answer at first. "I think it is for the best…"

"Jonathan, I am frightened for you."

"I have given you cause," he admitted.

"No, hear me. Keep this woman by your side," Anna insisted.

His tone sharpened as he said, "As you keep Johannes? You renounced our ways."

"It is the duty of a wife to see her husband happy. I do nothing more. I do not take away his choices."

"Only influence them."

"As do you with Savvy. Do not think, Jonathan Wythe, it has escaped my notice how you exert your influence on her." Her tone grew critical with her final remark.

"For her protection."

"What of *her* choices?"

He sighed. "It was only the once at dinner. It shall not be done again."

Anna quieted then her voice caught when she spoke. "You were not here. You did not see him in the winter."

"Tell me."

"Jonathan… The pains woke him many a night. He was ordered to rest and turn over his shares of the forge to Mr. Brewster. But he was unhappy being away. He was so very unhappy. The doctor feared his heart would soon fail."

"*Wellaway.* Forgive me, Anna. I did not know."

"I seek a quiet life. It is right I should assist you, but you bring danger to my doorstep. I had hoped to leave such things behind."

"Forgive me."

"When you marry, I pray you do so because you cannot live without the other person. Then you will understand. You would do all in your power for them."

The friends grew silent. Guilt at eavesdropping on their private conversation prodded my chest. I hadn't meant to listen, but the revelation something may've happened with the woman Jonathan was interested in, if only he had the courage to speak with her, as Anna claimed, kept me from interrupting. Hearing myself brought into the mix prevented me further from making my presence known.

I eased down another step, grimacing at the tattle-tale creak. She spoke undeterred, "There is something binding her to you. It is the ghost of a memory that has not yet happened."

"Anna." He sighed. "I do not understand your riddles."

"Bless me!" Éabha jumped as she rounded the corner to discover me lingering on the stairs. A handbasket swung back and forth on her arm with the sudden movement. "I did not hear you rise."

"I… good morning, Éabha." She wished me a good morning in return and stared. "I'm not wearing any shoes, you know."

"Aye, I can see as much. Nor clothes to go with them." Arms crossed her chest in deference to the outrage her society meant her to adopt. She gave me an impish look before setting her basket on the floor to rap on the yellow parlor door.

"No, wait! I was just hoping to sneak to… to the necessary," I stumbled, trying to remember the correct term. "I can go back up—"

Jonathan's emergence from the parlor put a stop to my going anywhere. Éabha adopted a state of perfect female submission as she begged his pardon for interrupting, then led his gaze up the stairs to me. He eyed me warily. "Are you well, Miss Moore?"

"Yeah, great. You?"

Nothing out of place here, thank you.

He turned to Éabha for an explanation.

"I have told her before, Captain Wythe. She is not to go about as such." She feigned the humility like a pro, complete with downturned eyes, clasped hands, and softened voice.

At least until he resumed studying me. Then the smirk returned. So much for the Cloet household accepting my unmarriable status. She received a dirty look from me for her trouble.

He responded with a smile that didn't reach his eyes. "I doubt there is any who could tell Miss Moore what to do with success, Miss Carroll. I dare not attempt to influence her."

His word choice made me wonder if he was testing me. His focus was intense enough. I met his stare head-on with a silky smile. "I listen to what you have to say, and then I promptly ignore you."

"Indeed." The corner of his mouth perked up; however, he remained wary. "Miss Moore, Miss Carroll is correct. Several of the men from the Iron Works are on the grounds as we speak. It would dishonor the family for the men to see you as you are."

My attention flicked to the closed door before I could stop myself. Though he didn't voice it, frustration filled his expression, and he grabbed onto his hips. An actual confession was the only proof I hadn't flaunted in front of him that I'd overheard him speaking with Anna.

"The workers have left," I offered, hoping to snap him out of it.

His brows raised. "You know this? How?"

"I saw them through my window. Mr. Cloet left with two other men." Like a child caught with her hand in the cookie jar, I rushed to reassure them I hadn't disgraced the family already, adding, "I was covered. You couldn't tell I was undressed. Or *not* dressed, I mean."

"Did you see where they went?"

"Toward the far end of the yard."

"Not the path leading away from the house?" he pressed.

"Uh, no. They were walking within the yard."

"The men did come to ask what trees could be felled today," Éabha supplied. "Master Cloet had been looking to clear the Nor'eastern corner for field and like has gone there." She referred Jonathan back to me for confirmation. I could only shrug.

The parlor door swung open, and Anna joined us. Ever one for appearances, Jonathan grumbled a greeting to her, as if she'd emerged from somewhere other than the parlor he'd just vacated. Éabha didn't seem the least surprised her mistress had been in there, nor did she seem to read anything into Anna and Jonathan having been alone together, conspiring.

"Good morn, Savvy. Did you sleep well?" Anna asked.

"Yeah, very. The bed's super comfortable. I keep oversleeping. Please feel free to wake me with the rest of the family."

"What a relief you slept undisturbed." She glared at him after she spoke. The zigzag of the floorcloth's pattern was utterly fascinating to him.

Something in the back of my mind struggled to break free, like a painful itch pulsing against my skull. What was it?

"Oh, Éabha. Thank you for bringing my basket." Anna glanced in my direction when she asked, "Were you able to locate those items?"

Éabha also shot an anxious look at me before saying she had not.

"What's going on?" I directed to both of them. Jonathan appeared perplexed, as well.

"I do not wish to alarm you, Savvy. I am certain they will be discovered… Some of your belongings may have been misplaced."

"What belongings?"

"What is this?" he asked simultaneously.

Anna sounded worried, though she put as brave a face on it as she could. "Savvy's boots and… and a few articles are missing. Not your cloak or trousers, but other items."

"What about Auden's bag? The leather bag I had?" I hadn't considered how I might return his things to him, but at some point, I would have to. To have lost them outright.

"The doctor's possessions are kept safe with me," Jonathan reassured me, his voice grim, though. "They are in my room. I saw them there this morning."

"Okay, but my boots? Those are two-hundred-dollar boots. I kinda want them back." The hallway filled with hushed exclamations.

"Continental dollars?" He sounded unsure.

I had to admit I didn't know how my home's currency translated to theirs. The amount probably sounded astronomical.

"But they were of value?" he confirmed.

"Well, yeah." They had been a splurge and worth every penny. To Anna, I asked, "My belt?"

"The boots will be found, Savvy. All of it. Éabha?"

Éabha hurried off at Anna's direction. I scowled at my toes rather than at Anna for the non-admission of the leather belt being AWOL too.

She tried to rally our mood, saying, "As Providence would have it, we are to take coffee with several of the neighbors today. It is a lovely morning. We could walk if you like. Crabapple Field is not far."

"Oh, um… Well, what about Jacob and Gertrude?" I asked. "Éabha must have her hands full. Why don't I just stay here? I could babysit for you."

"Babysit?" Jonathan questioned the word.

"How kind of you." Anna smiled. "Matilda has returned, though, and shall see to their lessons."

"She has?" I turned to Jonathan. "I didn't realize you'd left the house to escort her back."

"There was no need," he said. "Word came in the form of the woman's brother returning her." Anna's fleeting frown suggested it wasn't a happy return. "As such, you are free to enjoy the pleasures society has to offer in town."

"I don't think it's such a good idea."

To go mingling in town? A multitude of things could go awry, setting his mission in peril if I said the wrong thing and got curious tongues waggling. Or even Anna's standing in the community because of my otherness. Plus, the thought of sitting for hours on end with a gaggle of women, who'd want nothing more than to gasp and giggle over the latest gossip but would feel stymied by my unwanted presence, was uncomfortable, to say the least.

"They are kindly women, Savvy," Anna reassured me. "You would be most welcome within our circle."

"It would do you good to be amongst the company of your own sex." Jonathan smiled. "The ladies sew, do you not, Mistress Cloet?"

"We do." She eyed me.

Like with Pavlov's salivating dogs, the inclination to cringe was automatic. I'd rather eat dirt than put hand to needle. My mother demanded at a young age I learn how to sew. It was part of her grooming me to become a surgeon like her. The day I told her in no uncertain terms I'd never study medicine saw a bitter, brutal battle that kept us from speaking for months on end.

I'd collected an armful of cross-stitch patterns and unopened sewing kits she gifted me from the stash hidden at the back of my bedroom closet and took a lighter to them. The smoke was overwhelming. The relief I'd hoped would rise from their ashes wasn't.

I missed whatever else was said until Jonathan made the mistake of adding with the self-satisfaction of everything working out fine, "Mayhaps something familiar would make for a pleasant day." Anna clapped a hand on his arm, drawing his attention. "It would be for the soldiers," he offered, completely lost. "You have said you wanted to help."

"Captain Wythe, I think it would be better if Savvy were to accompany *you* today," Anna suggested.

"Me?" he asked.

"Hold on," I jumped in, questioning why the sudden change in plans myself. "I'm sure your friends are wonderful, Anna, but it's been a terrible week. I'd rather hang out here by myself." He dropped his head. Baby brother, Guilt, poked me some more. I worried I'd hurt Jonathan's feelings or maybe embarrassed him, a talent I was developing some mad skills in. "I don't mean to be rude."

"It is not wise to hide yourself away," she said.

"I'm not hiding."

"You are," she said, her admonition gentle but certain. "Life must continue. Accompany Captain Wythe. There is much you can do to assist him."

He gawked at her with surprise. It was news to me, as well. "Anna." I shook my head. "We talked about this."

"You…?" He stared alternately between the both of us. "Far be it for me to intrude upon the confidences of women; however, if it might…?" Instead of providing answers, Anna joined me on the stairs. There was something in her paled expression I couldn't read. Concern, maybe, though there was a pleading in her eyes. It almost looked like fear.

She hid it to shoo a perplexed Jonathan on his way, then plucked me from my spot by an arm to guide me to my room. Uneasy steps shuffled back and forth several times below us until they exited out the kitchen door.

After she had closed the bedroom door, she stated without accusation, "I know you heard us speaking."

"I'm sorry. It wasn't intentional," I hurried to explain.

"This I know."

A quiet moment of regarding each other to ensure things were okay between us passed before we spoke. Despite my earlier reservations about her, I was grateful for her friendship. It made my time in the Colonies a little easier.

"Anna, I think you should stand by your own advice and wait until Jonathan speaks with this woman before you give up hope on her. She may be attracted to him, too, you know."

Her features widened in surprise at my comment, and there was, perhaps, a hint of amusement in her changing expression before she became serious. "I assure you. The suggestion you accompany him has nothing to do with any of that."

She sifted through the clothing on the chair and passed me clean undergarments. A new shift, as well. I was every kind of surprised, pleased, and grateful. She turned her back to gather the next article while I changed. I declined her offer to tie fresh stockings in place, preferring to do it myself. For the rest, I welcomed her help.

She wrapped the stay around my torso, her gaze falling to the key dangling against my chest.

"Jonathan," I confirmed the unspoken question.

Without pausing to ask my permission first, she scooped the

ribbon into her hands with eyes closed, placing one on top of the other to press the key in between. "He has done well by you," she approved before handing it back to me.

"I'm not sure polishing an old key to an army trunk constitutes doing well by someone." I laughed, a little nervous. "It does make for an unusual necklace." I rubbed a thumb over the teeth, all innocent and serene.

"He offers you protection, Savvy. In this, he does well."

"Is he… influencing my choices?"

Her attention remained focused on the laces of the stay as she wove them through the holes and tied me into place. "Jonathan is a good man, an honorable man, with a certain amount of charm. You need not fear, though."

The length of the silver key passed smoothly under my worrying fingers, but as I pondered Anna's words, I decided they felt true. He had risked a great deal to protect me already without trying to force me into a different decision from what I'd wanted: his reputation within the camp, and perhaps even with the woman he liked, by letting me share a tent with him; corporal punishment, when he let me stay behind rather than obey Major DeForest's orders to drag me along with him; his mission, when he offered to set it aside to guide me through the woods.

And it troubled Jonathan when he believed he'd failed me.

I found myself believing his promise not to use whatever charm or influence or what-have-you on me again, even though it was said to Anna, not me.

"I know you do not want our pity." She ignored my resulting protest and continued speaking. "Please allow me to say. You are not worthless here. Jonathan needs you. He needs your help."

"What could he possibly need my help with?"

The same indescribable look of concern filled her ice-blue gaze. "You will help him, Savvy, will you not?"

"I don't understand. Help him with what?" The under-petticoat was raised for me to feed my arms and head into. Linen rippled along my body as she tugged it into place. I looked over my shoulder to where Anna was tying the back. "I don't think I'm supposed to be interfering."

"It is not interference when you are a part of what is happening." She circled around to face me. "There are many things about you that cannot be explained. You have a secret. One you are afraid to share." How on earth had the woman known? Her perception was remarkable. "I believe you are here for a reason."

"Do you know something about how I was brought here? Where I'm from?" I challenged her.

"Only what you and Jonathan know. But..." She hesitated, fetching the pink-and-cream petticoat instead of speaking.

It was situated on top of the other petticoat. After fluffing the bottom until it laid flat, she rose and searched my face, but abandoned whatever explanation had started to form on her lips and turned back to the bed. The way she fingered the hem of the espresso gown, I wondered if it was her unspoken words or a memory occupying her thoughts.

Pale ribbons from her cap trailed across her shoulder when she turned her head, and a decision settled over her. The gown floated as she flourished its length in front of me, feeding my arm through one sleeve, then the other.

As Anna pinned the bodice shut, she whispered, "He will die if you do not act."

The world tilted on its axis. I felt rather than saw her react as she caught me. Everything progressed from a blue haze into sharper focus. Her gaze was latched onto mine. Once assured my equilibrium had returned, she slid her palms from my shoulders to grasp my hands in front of her.

My mind was racing, both as an aftershock from what she had said—the attitude of her prediction, solemn and certain—and from noticing the electrical sensation humming between us. There was far more to Anna than she let on. Once again, I was tempted to tell her the truth about home.

"You don't know what you're asking me," I chanced telling her. "What I risk losing."

"There is a time for loss and a time for joy. Ever spins the fortune of life. Do not lose all by fear."

What could I say? Like Jonathan, I couldn't understand the riddle she was presenting me. I wanted her to tell me more. Tell me anything that made any sort of sense. The vertigo of thoughts left me speechless.

Her mouth parted like she was going to give in to my silent wishes. She pulled away instead. "I will send Éabha to dress your hair. I shall be late if I do not hurry." Anna bid me good day and wound around the bedroom door with a swish of her gown. "Oh!" she remarked, poking her head back in. "Please say nothing to Mr. Cloet concerning Matilda's return. He is displeased with her for abandoning us last evening."

Before I could re-center myself enough to respond, she'd vanished behind the door and fled downstairs. I sunk onto the bed, unable to process what'd happened.

What had I gotten myself into?

Chapter Forty-Three

Breakfast was waiting in the yellow parlor since the family had already eaten before I'd risen. Jonathan was in the outer fields with the other men, Éabha shared, but only after we'd returned from the necessary and she was loading my plate. The much-anticipated trip to the Iron Works being delayed until the discussion of trees was resolved, she insisted I partake. He was expected to collect me after.

When he did fly into the room, he wanted to hurry my morning coffee, declaring how Mr. Cloet would be ready to leave in but a moment. I'd sat for so long, my mind lost upstairs rather than focused on the generous spread in front of me, I was just starting my first cup and refused to chug it no matter how cold it'd gotten. We exchanged a volley of words over Jonathan's failure to eat. Éabha had tattled on him before she left, among her many promises that my belongings would be found. A second setting was meant for him.

He groaned, eyes turning to the doorway and the mission waiting for him. Nevertheless, when he turned back, his tricorn was making its journey to the table. Perusing the choices, his gaze landed on the untouched plate in front of me. He pushed it closer, nodding at the offering of cold beef, corn biscuits, and apple.

A maelstrom of worries was churning in my empty stomach. I questioned the wisdom of seeing the secret mission for myself, fearful of the many risks—known and unknown to me—Jonathan was facing. Plus, I was rattled from my earlier conversation with Anna, her predication he could die if I didn't help him. I wasn't ready to be responsible for someone's fate. How could she have laid that at my feet?

Then, there was the realization all my missing possessions came from the twenty-first century.

"Miss Moore?" He tossed the preserves-covered biscuit he'd been wolfing down. He'd remained standing, so the distance to the plate was significant enough to make the pewter ring when the biscuit connected with its edge. I gasped at the sound.

"What is it?" He rounded the table and knelt in front of me, collecting my hand in his. Too agitated to say anything, I shook my head. "You tremble," he noted. "What troubles you? Have I done…? Have—What… what is this?" His efforts to comfort me were thwarted when his thumb skidded across my fingers, leaving behind a speckled arch of raspberry. "Oh! Forgive me. I, ah…"

He snagged a napkin from the table and brushed at a wad of preserves stuck to his thumb, flustered because he knocked my coffee cup in the process. The preserves held their ground, no matter how hard he scrubbed at them.

Lost for an alternative, he thrust the side of his thumb into his mouth to suck at the stickiness, then wiped it clean. Once the glop was gone, he grabbed my napkin and offered an open palm, saying, "Give me your hand?"

"You're going to use the napkin to clean my fingers, right?"

"Would that my lips had such courage."

My mouth dropped in surprise. Redness spread across his cheeks, as if the several swipes of the napkin had mysteriously transferred the color of the preserves from his thumb to his face.

"I-I… It was… was most, ah," he said.

A bubble of laughter multiplied and soon had me bent over, grabbing my stomach. Jonathan shook his head, chuckling along with me while wiping away the mess.

After we settled down, he returned the napkin to the table, then slipped a clean hand under mine. The other glided on top. "Is it the mission that frightens you?" he asked.

The question sobered me. The mission was a speck on a fragment of the tip of the iceberg. Some memory was trying to claw its way forward, wanting to be revisited, but I couldn't get a hold of it, and it made my head hurt to try. I let it go, since I didn't want to delay him by delving into everything overwhelming me, especially my unsettling conversation with Anna, which carried the aura of bad idea. Instead, I nodded.

"There is much at stake," he acknowledged and shifted his weight on his knee, bringing him closer. A bent finger lifted my chin to draw my attention toward his face. Compassion filled his features; the crease between his brows vanished. His eyes really were beautiful.

Following the striations of sheer blue, encompassed within the gray ring, I was soon lost in them.

"There is little danger in what we do today," he told me. "We are inspecting an order placed at the general's request." Again, I nodded. "Mayhaps it goes without saying, but please allow me these words of warning."

"Okay," I agreed with trepidation.

"As you are undoubtedly aware, what we do here is secret. Many a man… or woman," he allowed, "who was thought to be a trusted ally has been found to be a friend to the enemy. I must insist that you speak with no one about what you see here today, even if there is one who attempts to lure you into their confidence, using facts of which they already know. Do you take my meaning?"

"Trust no one."

"I fear it is the wisest course. The Cloets, you may trust, but we are always cautious of the workers, even though they assist the smithy with the task. One cannot be certain. Thus, we keep a close watch on them."

"I understand. Jonathan, thank you."

"Wherefore?" he asked with genuine confusion.

"For trusting me. For bringing me with you today instead of making me sit through a sewing bee."

He smiled, amused at the scornful tone automatically accompanying any discussion about required sewing. "You did seem opposed."

"If you knew my mother, you'd understand."

"Ah. Such is the way with mothers and daughters, or so I am told."

We both chuckled.

He let me choose, I realized. There were no attempts to dissuade me from going with him, and the voice inside me remained silent. He'd kept his word.

His gaze followed mine, studying our fingers interlacing. A sensation hummed between us, as if he were a musician, his caress drawing vibrations along my skin like song from the rim of a wineglass. It brought me peace. I wondered if he felt the same thing when we touched. We looked up at the same time, and the same calm filled his eyes.

"Once you are returned—"

"Jonathan!" Mr. Cloet barged into the room. "Oh well… Pardon me," he bumbled. Jonathan leaned back, starting to rise, but Mr. Cloet waved his hands at Jonathan to remain kneeling. "No, no, no. Carry on.

As you were. Carry on, my good man!"

He was giddy as he scurried off with news of his discovery, slamming the door behind him. We could hear him calling for Anna before Éabha's voice reminded him from the kitchen that she had gone to Crabapple Field.

Everything seemed settled until Éabha's heels clattered in the direction of the parlor and Mr. Cloet barked, "Stay away! Leave the young people to their intercourse."

I burst out laughing, my cheeks heating as I did, though it would've been worse if Jonathan hadn't laughed along with me, exclaiming, "God's teeth! There shall never be an end to it."

"Staying here through Easter is, uh…?"

"I dare say." He shook his head. "Will you take something with you?" We scanned the options on the table.

"Sure." Having survived such an ordeal as preserves and non-proposals, I figured I could handle a dry biscuit. Even corn. "I know you're anxious to get going. Goodness knows, you'll want to cut off Mr. Cloet before he announces our engagement."

"Assuming he has not already procured the reverend for next Saturday." He smiled and assisted me to my feet. After a moment's pause, he turned his back to fetch the cloak waiting for me. I confess, he surprised me when he returned with Auden's bag, as well. As I withdrew the steel pistol to check the flint, Jonathan mumbled, "There was little powder. I have given you more cartridges."

Wrapping my hands around the barrel, I was grateful for the ability to defend myself without having to rely on others placing themselves at risk on my behalf. "You were running low yourself, though."

"The regiment supplemented my supply. I pray you need not make use of it."

"Me too."

Once the pistol was stashed away and the bag strapped securely across my chest, he assisted me with the cloak. A straw hat was offered, along with my plate so I could choose something, then he invited me to proceed toward the door with a gesture of his hand.

Just as I rounded the corner, I noticed he hadn't followed into the hallway. He was fingering the brim of his own hat.

"I'll go speak with Mr. Cloet and set the record straight."

"Nay, madam." He stopped my leaving. "Allow me."

"Savvy," I gently reminded him.

Jonathan joined me by my side. "Miss Moore."

Chapter Forty-Four

The Iron Works were a half-mile north. I was brushing away the last crumbs from breakfast—a smile passing between Jonathan and me—as we neared the stone wall at the back of the house with Mr. Cloet. Jacob came running up, calling for the men. A crisp salute was offered to Jonathan.

"Now, what have we here?" Mr. Cloet asked his son. "Are you not meant to be studying your Bible today, my boy?"

"I am to study the Iron Works with you and Captain Wythe!" Jacob was puffed up with importance, hands manfully clasping the facings of his coat, the way I'd seen his father do out of habit.

"Are you now?" Mr. Cloet played along, feigning acceptance of the sly remark as gospel truth. He divided his cloak, allowing him to copy his son's stance.

"'Tis far more useful than Latin, Papa."

Jonathan laughed. "Oh, best not let Mistress Cloet hear you say such things, lad. I wager your mama would have a grievous amount to say about the importance of knowing the Vulgate."

"Too true, too true." Mr. Cloet agreed with a serious tone and added a surreptitious wink at me. The script had already been written, and the players knew their parts well. Amusement danced behind the adults' eyes, as they allowed the familiar scene to unfold.

"But Papa," the boy implored, "I can study the Bible any a'time. Captain Wythe is only here now. I want to see the chain with him."

"Ah, ah." Mr. Cloet wagged a finger at him.

Jacob clamped his lips shut at the reprimand and offered wide eyes to both men.

Jonathan received Mr. Cloet's approval to proceed before he leaned forward to address the boy. "What is the most important part of our work?"

The boy pointed at me when he blurted out, "Miss Moore knows. She is family, now, like you."

I stifled a surprised laugh, then raised my open palms with a *Don't look at me!* shrug to Jonathan. He chuckled and regarded me warmly. "That she may be, though we are not betrothed," he informed father and son.

Mr. Cloet threw up a hand and sputtered his lips.

Jonathan's good mood didn't waver as he continued speaking with Jacob. "Nonetheless, we know not who does listen and who is true to us. Aye? We must not speak of such matters aloud."

The boy answered, deflated, "Aye."

"Then we are in accord, *Lieutenant* Jacob." Jonathan stood erect to shake his hand. The boy brightened and gave his hero's arm a thorough pumping.

"A promotion, eh?" Mr. Cloet remarked, "Well done, *maatje*. Well done. But what are we to do about this business of your Bible?"

"It sounds like important business to me," I teased. Why should I miss out on the fun?

Jacob was appalled. "You never studied Latin, did you, Miss Moore?"

Faced with absolute certainty from the boy, it was shamefully fun to burst his bubble. "A little. I've studied many things." Surprised remarks followed from everyone.

"You are educated? I dare say," Mr. Cloet turned to Jonathan, "that explains a great number of things."

"Indeed," Jonathan concurred.

Before I could question what it explained, our attention returned to Jacob who declared, "Sewing dolls doesn't count."

"Sure, it does, but I've studied a whole lot of other things too." I could picture my mother's triumph about the pre-med inclusion, had she been there.

Jacob remained skeptical during my efforts to describe my academic transcript to an eighteenth-century child. Jonathan, however, appeared dumbstruck by its breadth.

Mr. Cloet was also awed when I told them I was an attorney. "You advise women of the law? My, my. What an interesting notion."

"I'm a prosecutor."

"Of women?"

"Men and women," I answered. The drop of his mouth was

endearing.

Jacob's eyes were enormous. "Even murderers?"

"Even murderers," I confirmed.

He turned to the men, already a master at the art of showing skepticism via a cocked brow. Perhaps Jonathan taught him, though their expressions as they stared at me were useless if he thought he might learn from them whether he was being tricked. I wanted to throw my arms around Jonathan and laugh. His eyes danced along the length of my body, as if the gears in his mind were spinning and spinning, not getting him anywhere in puzzling things out.

"Very well," Mr. Cloet told his son. "It seems there is a great deal you can learn from Miss Moore. Go and inform your nurse. You are to accompany us to the Iron Works." The boy whooped with glee and ran to complete his task. Of course, the adults never doubted he'd get his way. "Mind your cloak comes along, *maatje*!"

Éabha's exclamation of "Goodness!" as he burst into the kitchen and then admonition not to run through the house carried, earned him another round of amused chuckles from the adults.

Mr. Cloet and Jonathan exchanged raised eyebrows and glanced in my direction. Once again, Jonathan retreated into himself. Our host shook his head at his contemplative friend before turning an eye to the yard beyond. "Well, here is the great man himself."

Following his gaze—the vast acres were empty. Or at least, devoid of people. Only Jonathan's horse, which wandered over to nudge him in the shoulder, breaking his deliberation. Mr. Cloet gave me a *watch this* nod.

Jonathan greeted the animal as an old friend. He stroked the horse's muzzle and leaned in to advise him of our plans to go for a walk. A pause ensued, as if we were waiting for an answer. The horse raised his head and neighed, wandering off after Jonathan had promised he would be called if needed.

"What's his name?" I'd been too scared when we'd hidden from the redcoats behind our four-legged citadel to commit it to memory.

"Felaróf." He addressed my quizzical look by telling me, "It means 'very strong.'"

"What made you choose to name him that?"

Must be some epic backstory.

I wondered if he had brought the horse with him from England or purchased him in the Colonies. The subject, throughout our interlude, was busy at a nearby barn, helping himself to an early lunch from a store of apples left exposed. Or what was called dinner here, I reminded myself.

Mr. Cloet yelled in an attempt to shoo the giant horse away. Felaróf nickered an equine laugh before helping himself to another apple and trotting off in search of other misadventures.

Jonathan laughed right along with the horse. "It is his name," he told me without irony in his voice.

O-kay.

I'd never thought of horses as companion animals, though his fit the description. They were bred for racing in my hometown.

Mr. Cloet shook his head when I checked to see if he shared my amusement. "Never you mind Captain Wythe, now, my dear. A clever man he is, but also frightfully foolish."

Clever Man was drawn back into the conversation by the teasing. "Here now."

"Oh, fear not, Miss Moore. You can depend on a man such as Captain Wythe. He is brave and loyal, strong and courageous, and dreadfully good-looking. A soldier should not be so handsome, for then the ladies shall break their hearts over him while he is gone, and the enemy will rally to move in and take the spoils in his absence."

"Is he? I hadn't noticed." I shrugged a shoulder and found some fictitious thing in the distance claiming to be more entertaining.

"But, of course, you have not." Mr. Cloet enjoyed the joke and continued with, "My, my, Jonathan. Your skills are fading."

Which made him flustered. "I have no such skills."

I smiled at the rosiness blossoming through the dark patch of his beard. It was funny how a skilled soldier could become hopelessly awkward. The downturn of his eyes, which met mine before retreating to the ground in thought… The way he always kept his right hand at rest on his knife's hilt, where it could fly into action if called for… The burst of blue once he raised his eyes, ready to rejoin those around him… It had become so familiar, so soon.

I wanted to wrap my hand into his, to tell him he didn't need to feel awkward with me, but I didn't dare. Worse, I recognized how much I'd miss Jonathan once I returned home. I'd never see him again. He'd be long dead, but I'd have the rest of my life ahead of me without him.

It must've shown on my face because his amusement wavered when he did look up. Whatever quip inspired his broad smile remained unspoken.

"Ready?" I asked. Jacob had already run past us. I spun around and trailed after the boy, hoping to conceal the unwelcome dampness in my eyes.

Wild grasses shorn in uneven clusters by the family's livestock, some still dull from winter's reign, were flattened into a pathway leading away from the house. One particularly industrious goat was making good work of a fresh patch. It noted my presence and ruffled its coat before returning to its task. Jacob's shouts of, "I shall scout the path ahead for dragoons, Captain!" echoed around us as he bolted toward the woods on his own.

I glanced back to share the moment with the men, hoping the smile I was expecting from Jonathan would cheer me up. The boy's game went unnoticed. Jonathan was where I'd left him, head lowered. Mr. Cloet frowned at him, then nodded a suggestion for me to go ahead without them. The eventual sounds of footfalls through the leaf-strewn grass encouraged me to continue walking.

The iron gate guarding the opening in the stone wall was a wonder. Square posts of wrought iron were melded into the masonry. Between each vertical bar stood a half-bar with spearheads piercing a horizontal piece. Adorning the frame of the door were thick, carved rosettes staged between interwoven scrolls, vines, and sculpted diamonds. The theme of spears continued within the frame, interlaced with climbing metal vines. Such elaborate decor seemed more fitting for the front of the house, where guests were more likely to see it.

The metal's hidden secrets tremored at my touch, rippling against my skin while I ran a hand along the iron. I hesitated, wondering at the sensation. As I crossed the threshold, I was like a pin pushing through a balloon that didn't burst, though it resisted my passage and stretched with me until I reached the other side.

Outside the boundary of the stone wall, a perceptible chill clung to the air. By all appearances, the whole thing seemed benign and ordinary, but instinctually, just as I knew the sky was up or my life was finite, I knew something was there. I shivered and tugged my cloak closed tighter.

Jonathan was still lagging, listening to Mr. Cloet, though he noticed my study of the home's boundary. His expression shifted to concern, and he bolted forward, ready to leave our host behind midsentence. I offered a fleeting smile to reassure him, despite being shaken myself, and continued along the path before he could reach me.

The trodden grass way brought us to a large pond, where the sounds of spring peepers flooded the air. The tiny frogs rustled in the weeds, hopping away as I neared the water's edge. Jacob had already disappeared around a bend. A thick array of looming evergreens blocked the path from sight. Unsure how much further the Iron Works were, I stopped to admire the view and wait for the men.

Varieties of lily pads bobbed on the surface. A sizeable flock of gossiping ducks waddled along the grassy shore, picking at the ground.

They were unperturbed by our presence.

Jacob darted back and forth with his reports about the quality of the pathway ahead, the distances we had yet to travel, and the vast number of enemy soldiers he'd routed before his latest return. At his captain's inquiry, Lieutenant Jacob estimated we should arrive within a fortnight. Mr. Cloet encouraged his young soldier to spare no details of his last bloody encounter as they continued past me toward the fields of glory.

Jonathan paused by my side. "What troubles—?"

"You're so good with kids. You're going to make a great father someday."

He scrutinized my face, brows folded. I offered another smile to show I'd meant it. Or at least, I tried. Two ducks raised their voices, chests puffed forward, wings stretched to flap gusts of air at each other. I took the opportunity to escape while Jonathan's attention was pulled away by the commotion and followed the Cloets around the corner.

He shadowed me, remaining several feet behind. We continued in silence, keeping to ourselves, the voices of Jacob and Mr. Cloet drifting back on the chilly April breeze. The relayed adventure became more animated by the moment. The boy's pantomimed thrusts and parries showed practiced form as he used a stick to demonstrate the flourish that ended a British general. Father and son celebrated the victory with carefree laughter. The story might change over the centuries, but love like theirs was eternal.

"I'm looking forward to seeing…" Jonathan's warning to Jacob about not knowing whether someone could be listening came to mind. I choose my words accordingly. "… this project for myself. Though I admit, I'm a little nervous about being in the know. I hope our timing works out for you."

Several footfalls passed.

"You have nothing to fear," he finally answered. Disappointment, perhaps in himself—or even me, I suppose—was apparent. Our thoughts were moored at the water's edge.

There wasn't a good way to address it. I wasn't going to take back what I'd said. It was true. He *would* make a great father. If he was worried about missing his chance with the woman he liked, I guess my timing was pretty poor. I hadn't meant her, in particular, when I'd said it. Based on Anna's gossip, I should've cared about whether my presence was hindering his courting her. It troubled me to find I didn't.

Instead, I focused on the other subject facing us. "When I was questioned by Major DeForest, I was able to tell him the truth. I didn't know anything about your mission or where you were. The deniability kept me safe. It kept you safe." My voice failed as my mind struggled with what I was saying.

Jonathan seemed equally perplexed. "Were you not displeased when I did not inform you—"

"I was. I still want you to keep me informed." I paused, then sighed. "This place has me so confused. I don't know what I want anymore."

Jonathan grew quiet.

What with his entrée into the war as a British officer, fighting against the very men he now called allies, I could only imagine the battles he must've faced with himself, trying to decide what was right.

It struck me with heart-rending cruelty. Evan would love Jonathan. If only he was with us. If only going home didn't mean losing Jonathan.

Thinking of how seriously he took his promise to protect me with an unwavering devotion and how much I'd come to want that, I realized—in the end—he would fail. I was going to get hurt.

There was a break in the trees. Then we were there.

Chapter Forty-Five

"Have a care, Miss Moore," Mr. Cloet called. His lip turned in a dramatic sneer toward the ground. "You are walking the land of Murderer's Creek."

He encouraged Jonathan to take up the opening in its tale, but Jonathan was a million miles away. When he did notice where we were, he excused himself and hurried down an incline leading to the heart of the clearing.

Our destination, I discovered, was laid not in a field but rather the creek's bed. A thick gathering of trees huddled along the somewhat dizzying embankment, due to its plummeting heights in areas. Water cut through the middle of an uneven pathway, leaving a rocky shore on either side.

As the trees dissolved, a large wooden structure like a giant dock stretched from the break, partway over the drop. A stone building supported it from underneath. At its end, a sloping portion of the roof dove close to the ground. I accepted Mr. Cloet's invitation to join him on the dock. It was like crossing a home's threshold after a winter's excursion. The wall of heat rising from the area below us was palpable.

In the belly of the gully, Jacob was trotting alongside Jonathan. They were heading for the first of several buildings lining the water's edge. Mr. Cloet explained how the heat was from the furnace below where the iron was produced from the raw materials mined from the mountains to the South. But his words barely registered. I froze when I saw what was laid out on the lower embankment.

"Ah." Mr. Cloet noted my shocked expression. "Behold, the chain for the general. Is it not a wonder?"

"Yeah, it is," I voiced on a shuddery breath, awestruck.

If only my father was there.

It wasn't just any chain they were constructing. It was *the* chain. Three lengths, in fact. The Great Hudson River Chain.

"Five hundred yards in length, when all is said and done. Let us see the Royal Army take the North River then, eh, Miss Moore?"

I could only nod in agreement.

"She will be better placed than the Montgomery. Mark my words. Shall we?" Mr. Cloet offered his arm to assist me down a winding, rocky pathway that swung away from the ravine to a narrower descent. A soldier in blue acknowledged us from his post within the trees.

Anna's shoes were sturdy enough, but every rock made its presence known through the thin soles. Concern about my disappearing hiking boots troubled me, especially when I slid on a loose stone. Mr. Cloet kept me on my feet, though, and I pressed him to go faster, anxious to reach the trail's end.

Situated around us when we reached the bottom were several plank-board buildings with stone foundations rooted in the rocky creek bed. Mr. Cloet explained the layout as we approached. The first building was the forge. Not one but two waterwheels captured the power of the creek's flow to work the bellows and an anvil inside. The embankment swallowed most of the noise, but I scanned up and downstream, wondering how the mountains of smoke rising from its multiple chimneys could be missed by the redcoats. From the talk earlier, it sounded like construction had been going on for weeks.

A second, smaller structure with a single waterwheel was the Rolling and Slitting Mill. A Blacksmith Shop resided on the opposite shore, also protected from sight by the sharp incline of the upper embankment. Furthest downstream was the Iron Warehouse. The Chain extended the length of the creek, beginning at the forge to gather at the warehouse.

"Once completed," Mr. Cloet shared, "the Chain will be floated from here to the North River and, from there, to be anchored at a spot most strategic, for it will be well-guarded by many cannon held by the Continentals. Though, what good are the general's men without the militia assisting them! Captain Wythe excluded, of course." He winked at me.

We came to the entrance of the forge. Jonathan's raised voice, struggling to be heard by a uniformed man, filtered through the industrious cacophony being generated within. Mr. Cloet entered to join them, but my feet carried me further downstream.

As a teen, I'd gone on a fieldtrip to New York's capital. My father chaperoned, of course. I liked the Million Dollar Staircase best with its many carved faces in the red stone, including a demon said to have been added by an angry craftsman because the workers weren't paid enough. At least, according to my childhood memory of the tour guide's story.

We were gathered on the steps for a class picture, and though it took forever for the teacher and chaperones to corral the twenty-some-odd, angst-ridden middle schoolers into something close to respectable looking, my gaze kept me occupied as they wandered up, up, up the stairs coming and going in several directions, up the giant handrails, along to the balcony, up further along the columns to the gold chandeliers and wall sconces with dozens and dozens of glowing bulbs, to the peak of the arches, until the sunlight blinded me through the multi-paned skylight. A European castle on Albany's shores, waiting for the royal procession to begin.

But that wasn't my father's favorite part. At the top of an escalator, under a giant portrait of our first president, lay three rusty, broken links. My father was enthralled. He hiccupped with excitement as he explained the history of the Chain and its significance in cutting off British supply lines from Canada to secure the Northern Department.

I remember rolling my eyes behind his back. My friends were racing through the corridor toward better attractions—like something called the Assembly Chamber—and I was anxious to go with them. I ran off as soon as I could break free. When I snuck a peek back along the corridor, my father was still standing there. A look of longing filled his face as he stared at the portrait of George Washington.

I couldn't understand at thirteen what his deal was. As I allowed my hands to hover above two of those same links, each about two feet in length, new with crisp, thick coats of sealant, ready to be called into service, I understood the emotion that'd held him captive in wonder.

"You may touch it, if you wish," Jonathan said from behind me. My tentative fingers shied from the cold, rough metal worthy to one day belong in a museum. It felt forbidden. "You cannot break it." He began to laugh but was taken aback when I turned to face him. "Miss Moore?"

I followed the length of the Chain, stretching toward the river. The portion farthest from me lay waiting for the next phase of its journey into the history books. Enormous, wooden rafts were stacked outside the warehouse, ready to receive the Chain and keep it afloat on the river's surface. The two lengths closest to me were connected to the Boom, a second barrier also meant to be stretched from shore to shore, consisting of a series of roughly twelve-foot-long logs held together by a chain on each end, like a ladder with wooden rungs. Giant staples pounded into the sealed wood bound the chains to them.

In many ways, it was crude, the construction rushed. Each link was rough, imperfectly shaped, and differed in size from its fellows. Yet, it was the most marvelous engineering feat in American history to date, and it lay before me, inviting me to take it in and touch it if I wished.

I lowered a hand onto a swivel, which would allow the Chain to twist as needed with the current's flow, and let it rest on the gritty surface. "My father—" My voice hitched. "My father, he…" There was no way to explain to Jonathan what I felt, what the experience meant to me. "I wish he was here to see this."

"Does your father live?" he asked. "Do you remember him? Where he is? I could send an inquiry."

"No," I whispered.

"Have you any…?" He didn't finish the question. He didn't need to. I understood what he was asking.

A hand alighted on my elbow. My breath drew in with a shudder. Fingertips brushed my sleeve. Painful silence was taken to mean no.

I'd betrayed them. I denied my family's existence, even though I'd said nothing. Like I accepted I'd lost them. I squeezed my eyes shut, trying to push aside the disturbing thoughts, and acknowledged his condolences, numb and suddenly tired.

The wind shifted, and the smoke from the forge grew heavy around us. It stung my eyes, the resulting tears searing across their surface. He caught my arm when I jerked away from the source of the polluted breeze, causing my heel to slip on a stone. "Will you permit me to return you to the house?"

"You have work to do." I fought the urge to walk back by myself and keep going, to hell with the impossible landscape and roving redcoats and the mysterious presence and regret.

The temptation to blame him for the pseudo-lie he'd forced on me was making me itch to pick a fight with him. He deserved better.

Instead, I changed the subject by referencing the wonder next to us. "You made it in time. The Chain's still here."

"Ah, aye." His hand fell. "I believe so." His uncertainty seemed odd.

"Is there more to your mission? Before the Chain gets sent downriver?"

The reminder called Jonathan away. He risked the smoke and squinted toward the forge. Mr. Cloet was conversing with two other men on the opposite shore, near the blacksmith's shop. One was the uniformed man I'd seen with Jonathan. The other was one of the workers, judging by his attire. Mr. Cloet waved to us.

"You can go. I'll be fine here by myself." I returned the gesture, hoping the act would encourage him.

"It would be no bother to—"

"I miss home. It's..." The idea of losing him closed in on me again. "Please don't worry. I'm fine. I am," I reassured us both.

"As you say," he said gently, "though I should like it if you would do me the honor of accompanying me."

"Are you afraid I'll get into trouble if you leave me alone?"

"Most assuredly." He smiled.

As much as I wanted a little time to collect myself, the invitation to stay with him was more appealing. As it was, the rocky bed was difficult to maneuver, so in the end, it was a good thing I agreed. My arm linked in Jonathan's, we stumbled upstream together toward the shop. I wished I'd insisted on wearing the clothes I'd arrived in. I kept slipping on the smaller rocks, freeing the water hidden between their layers. Anna's shoes were soaked before long, and I worried her dress would get ruined too.

I tried to keep it casual as I voiced the question nagging me, "Will you need to see to the Chain's installation first? You know, before you can take me back to where we met."

"My orders led me here. I anticipate new instructions will follow once I have made my report."

"Are we far from New Cornwall? Will you be free to take me there while you wait?"

Jonathan paused, as if weighing his words first, before saying, "If you will allow me the impertinence in asking—what is it that drives you homeward if... you have no family there to receive you?"

I swallowed hard. "It's my home. Does it matter what's waiting for me?"

"I suppose not," he allowed, and we resumed walking. "At times, I miss my home. I wonder if mayhaps I should return to face whatever awaits me there."

"You mean England?"

"Mistress Cloet has been speaking of me to you."

I stopped us from continuing. As much as I shouldn't have delayed him from meeting with the other men glancing our way, I wasn't ready to share him with the rest of the world. It was selfish, and I needed to get home, but despite everything, I wanted more time with Jonathan.

"What do you miss most, besides your family?" I asked.

The question sent him miles away. A smile warmed his expression. "Malkin, my dog. She is old and would not have withstood the ocean's crossing, but nothing, not even age, keeps her from drawing out water fowl from the brook that cuts through my father's estate. We have enjoyed many an adventure amid the rushes there." The youthful memories stole back some of time's edge to the way he held himself. "What of you?"

"Bookstores. And macchiatos." The latter needed a translation. "There's this place, a couple of blocks from my house. It's called Madeline's, which is kinda funny because the owner is this guy who's single. They make the best pumpkin cake, every fall, with this simple, light drizzle of sugar frosting on top with a dash of nutmeg. I like to treat myself to a slice and a macchiato and scan the new releases. Mysteries are my favorite. Nothing too suspenseful. Something fluffy to take your mind off things."

"Bookstores." He laughed. "Aye, there are not booksellers for many a mile. I imagine it has been a loss to one such as yourself."

"Even though it's undesirable for a woman to be well-read?" I returned, cocking my head, half sincere, half full of challenge.

"It is true. Women cannot pursue the law." He dipped his chin. "Think you so little of a woman's life here, though?"

His question stumped me. Not all the women I'd encountered were living the kind of life I would've expected. I wasn't. "I've been rude to Anna," I chastised myself.

"Worry not. She thinks well of you. As do I. Captain Machin!" Jonathan raised a hand to the uniformed man, who returned Jonathan's greeting. "Come."

Captain Machin was only a few inches taller than I was. A white, circular ribbon adorned the side of his tricorn hat, and the color of his uniform reminded me of the typical blue-and-buff seen in reenactments, though Machin's was faced with trim that was yellow, once upon a time. His matching yellow pants and white vest were also dingy, carrying the odor along with the tinge of the forge's smoke.

"I was not aware you were betrothed. Congratulations," Machin welcomed us.

Mr. Cloet snorted. "You give Captain Wythe too much credit."

Jonathan sighed at him.

"Hi. I'm Savannah Moore," I said to introduce myself. "Captain Wythe, here, is my generous, humble, and *mistreated* protector. He's escorting me during my stay in the Colonies."

The emphasis was directed at Mr. Cloet, who waved me off congenially. "You are the generous one, Miss Moore."

Machin hesitated over my automatic offer to shake hands and turned to Jonathan for guidance, who passed off the entire issue with a gesture to be his guest. In the end, Machin wrapped an arm around his front and bowed. "A pleasure, Miss Moore. You are brave to have chosen such unsettling times to journey to these United States."

"Not by choice, believe me," I said. "Though, it occurred to me, this is a rare opportunity. I'd like to appreciate as much as I can while I'm here."

"Ah. Thus, you have come to inspect the work with Captain Wythe."

"I wouldn't miss it for the world. This is amazing," I directed my remark to the Chain spread below us. The men turned to admire along with me. Their pride was clear in their smiles and straightened posture. It was certainly deserved.

"We are well-pleased to have achieved much in these few weeks. Though the credit goes to Mister Brewster and the men." Machin gestured to the man at his right. "This is Samuel Brewster, Miss Moore. His family owns the forge."

Mr. Brewster showed me his hands, dark with evidence of his contribution to those few-weeks' labor, as if apologizing for not shaking before I could extend the offer. "Well now, 'tis an honor, you see, to be called into service once more." He eyed me. "Have you an interest in seeing the forge, mum? 'Tis loud, and the place not for the likes of so fine a gown."

A gunshot pierced the air.

Crows took wing in a cluster, further upstream, screaming their retreat to the South. We stared, listening hard as the echo died off the mountains. "Could be a hunter." Mr. Cloet sounded unconvinced, even though it was his speculation.

Another shot rang out, carrying across the miles, then the distant fighting began in earnest. Dozens upon dozens of weapons raged, their smoke unfurling above the treetops in giant clusters. Uniformed men hurried out of the forge and the surrounding buildings, long guns in hand, to encircle the structures.

"Papa!" Jacob screamed from the forge's entrance. A worker caught him by the shoulders to prevent him from running out into the open.

"*Blijf binnen. Opschieten!*"

The worker dragged the boy away from the door, back inside, crying, at Mr. Cloet's bidding.

The men grabbed for their pistols. "Mister Brewster," Machin yelled, "escort the lady."

"The lady," I answered, cocking my pistol, "isn't going anywhere."

His eyes widened. Only Jonathan reacted to the tremble in my voice.

Machin signaled for his men to climb the embankment, the better to spot danger should it travel as far east as our location and hurried toward the rise on the southern bank to claim his own post. Jonathan clasped my elbow with his free hand, and together we raced to the closest building. Mr. Cloet wasn't far behind.

With our backs pressed against the wall where we could monitor the northern and southern approaches, Mr. Cloet eyed the weapon in my hands amidst preparations of his own pistol and teased, "Protector, indeed, Jonathan."

A nod of readiness, following a survey of the woods, led to a dash into the forge. The workers surrounded the giant fireplace with whatever make-shift weapon they'd scrounged from the forge's store in their grasp.

Jacob was huddled among them, hands squashing his ears to block the sounds of the violence cascading through the Highlands. Seeing us join them by the fire, he broke loose from the worker holding him and clutched at his father's middle.

"*Houd moed, maatje.*" Mr. Cloet slapped the ramrod of his pistol back under the barrel. A strong arm wrapped around his son's small shoulders. "Jebediah accompanied Anna. The women are alone."

Jonathan nodded and listened. "The fighting remains to the west." He turned to me to explain, "If soldiers were to be discovered in the Cloets' home, the family would be in greater peril. Will you go with them?" Meaning Mr. Cloet and Jacob.

"Will you not come?" Mr. Cloet asked him, tipping his head in my direction.

Jonathan's expression became pained. His gaze trailed down my arms, where the trembling was the worst. I wanted him to say yes, but his focus crossed toward the doorway and beyond, passing along the length of the Chain, so close to reaching its destination on the river.

I answered for him, "His mission comes first. His place is here." That was how it was supposed to be. I wished the tightening in my chest would stop disagreeing with me. "Ready?"

Mr. Cloet grimaced. He spoke again to Jacob in their native tongue, then deposited the child's hand into mine, allowing him to take position by the forge's entranceway unhindered. The boy cowered into my side. I bent low, telling him, "We're going to go protect your sister and Éabha."

"*Ik wil mijn moeder.*" Jacob's words were smothered by the length of my gown pressed into his face, but I recognized "mother" and guessed the rest.

"Then, let's get you home so you're there for when she returns," I told him. Jonathan stood at the edge of the doorway, opposite Mr. Cloet. He waved me over, but Jacob stalled, scared. "The fighting's far away. We're just going to your house because it's safer."

"*Maatje!*" Mr. Cloet called.

The boy's head snapped up from behind his cotton hiding place, and he ran with me over to the doorway. We were about to hurry out when Jonathan stepped in front of me. Inches from my face, he simply stared, not speaking.

"You're making me nervous," I warned. Anna's prediction rang through my head.

Am I doing the right thing?

Jonathan leaned forward, his mouth close to my ear. "Keep to the house. Do not return here, please. If the regulars come, show your weapon only if necessary and there is hope of success."

I fought the sting in my eyes. "You'd better come back when this is over."

His cheek brushed against mine as he withdrew, the whiskers of his beard coarse against my skin. Still, the spark we shared when we touched made it hard for us to separate. His lips lingered near mine. The sweetness of preserves floated between us. I wanted to stay there, lost in the moment.

"It goes quiet," Mr. Cloet interrupted. "We must leave."

He was right. The gunfire had eased, the shots further apart. Not necessarily a good thing. We needed to go in case the fighting was coming our way as one side retreated from the other. Or in case other British clusters were rushing past us to reinforce their numbers to the west.

Jonathan's hand filled the space between us, above my chest, his eyes closing, as if he was measuring the pace of my heart without touching. Heat from his palm caressed me despite my cloak. The words of his prayer remained hidden behind the dwindling gunfire.

His eyes flew open. He grasped me by the shoulder and shoved me forward. We were in flight, racing across the creek's bed and up the winding path toward the woods. My moment with Jonathan faded into the distance.

By staying to the side of the incline's path, there was enough grass to keep solid ground underneath me. Jacob was quicker and ran ahead. The sight of soldiers scattered along the ridge with bayonets fixed on their long guns, even though they were on our side, stopped him short. I grabbed his hand and, after a look at his father, we hurried through the trees, back toward the house.

Anna's shoes were terrible for running. The heels grew wobbly from the stress, threatening to snap, the wet sides rubbing against my feet already leaving their mark.

We circled the pond. The ducks and peepers were hidden. Nature hushed, waiting for the thunderous roar of war to cease.

The path straightened as the trees thinned, closer to the Cloets' home. Jacob wrenched his hand free and bolted, shouting for his mama. The space between me and the house closed. I slowed to rest, placing my hands on my knees to catch my breath. The iron gate was right before me. The kitchen door opened, and Éabha gathered a weeping Jacob into her arms.

Mr. Cloet rounded the bend. Even across the distance, I could see him gasping for air, but he was safe. We'd made it without incident.

The same sensation of passing through an invisible skin slid over me when I sought to enter the backyard, though I met with more resistance than when I'd left. Once admitted, I whirled around, troubled, searching for some visible sign to prove whether what'd happened was real. Iron spears with twisting metal vines. Cold, sculpted roses. Nothing more.

As I turned toward the sound of Éabha calling me, something flickered in my periphery. A wisp of light, gone. "What are you doing, you daft woman? Get in here!" Éabha called from the doorway. I stifled a shudder and obeyed.

Chapter Forty-Six

There was little gunfire throughout the rest of the day. A random shot here or there, always to the west, followed by an eerie silence. Peace, however, wasn't yet restored in the Cloet household when we returned.

After Éabha reported there'd been no sign of the enemy, Mr. Cloet announced he would station himself in his parlor, as he had before. Jacob begged to go with him. Instead, the boy was instructed to seek his nurse. A task made moot by Matilda herself, who hurried down the back stairs, barging through the kitchen door in hysterics. Hands red from wringing, rims of her eyes matching, she screamed when she caught sight of the guns held aloft.

"Calm yourself, woman." Mr. Cloet attempted to reason with her. "It was merely a disagreement of weapons. Jacob, accompany your nurse above stairs."

"What if the regulars return? Or the banditti of royalists from Westchester, come to murder us?" She smeared her palm across her eye. "Nay, I will to my brothers."

"I cannot spare Miss Moore to escort you."

The woman was aghast. Her wide eyes darted over my gown and the firelight glinting from the steel pistol, especially when she learned Jonathan hadn't returned with us.

"Mama!" Gertrude's cries carried through the floorboards above.

"*Godverdomme!* You have left the child alone?"

"I… I…" The nurse backed away.

"If you wish to go, then do so, but do not look to return if you do. Miss Moore, you will assist me?" At the nod of my head, Mr. Cloet stormed to the front of the house.

I held out a hand for Jacob, who shuffled to my side. A spluttering from his nose smeared against my hip.

The nurse looked like a bird, her head flitting to and fro for guidance.

"Mathias would do no more for you, Tillie, than can be done here," Éabha remarked.

"True enough." She sniffled.

Tiny feet plopped down the top few steps. A sob called for "Mama!"

"Keep your place," Éabha encouraged. "You should miss the children if not. I shall bring you tea, as I can."

A nervous dart of Matilda's head in my direction led to, "Oh, but Mistress—"

"Never you mind, Miss Moore. She cares not a whit what you drink."

Matilda wrung her hands one more time for good measure. It must've done her good because she sniffed back her tears with newfound courage and directed Jacob to join her and Gertrude upstairs for their lessons. The little girl had wandered into the kitchen by then, whimpering, so the nurse cuddled her with reassurances her mama would be overjoyed to hear the song the girl was learning. They must go and practice it a'more.

"Singing songs is for babies," Jacob snapped at the nurse.

Éabha's fists dug into her hips when she barked his name to chastise him. From the way he eyed my pistol to the tremble of his lip at the reprimand, I knew he was acting out because he was scared, just as Jonathan had predicted.

"Captain Wythe would probably want to hear about pirates," I supposed. "Can you think up a new story to tell him?"

He shook his head no.

"Oh. Too bad. I thought you were going to play pirates with him. I guess Gertrude will have to do it."

Éabha was smirking when Jacob whined her name. She attempted a serious expression and nodded at the dough she was pounding, "Pink Beard, I should think."

"Girls cannot be pirates," he argued.

"Is that sooo?" Éabha stretched her words in feigned confusion. "Miss Moore?"

I examined my pistol, then sighed. "It must be."

Jacob's eyes rounded. He tore up the back stairs, his feet banging overhead until a bedroom door slammed at the front of the house.

Éabha laughed. "That was right, well done. A proper hand you have with him. A shame it is—" She stopped herself before the reason for my shame was named aloud.

I dismissed her apology—though I confess, it stung a little—and excused myself, claiming I needed to assist Mr. Cloet.

"Come in, Miss Moore," he invited from his post by the window. "*Goed zo*. There are some things I should like to discuss now the opportunity has presented itself. Dear me. You tremble. Have you courage enough to sit a while and keep watch with me?"

"I'm just a little cold."

"Ah, I see now. You are soaked to the hems. Take a place by the fire, and I shall be brief. Close the door, first, if you would. It is not proper, though, as you may have noticed, not all here is done properly! We do as we must to survive, *ja*?" He thanked me when I did and welcomed me to sit again. I chose a wooden chair rather than risk damaging its upholstered companion.

Mr. Cloet checked the view outside, then studied me. I wasn't sure what he was looking for. "Have you no questions for me?"

"About the Chain, you mean?"

"Hmm. I had not considered you would think on that. *Nee*. Have you no questions about my marriage to Mistress Cloet? Given the interest our Jonathan has shown you, might you not care to know how our peoples can manage it peaceably? I gather you have not yet told him what you are.

"Oh, I know the words you would speak to object," he cut me off before I could even find appropriate words to express my confusion at the strange turn in the conversation, "and I know my beloved wife would tell me not to press. But it is clear you harbor feelings as tenderly as does Jonathan. You do not mean him harm. Am I not correct in this?"

"Why would you think…?" I asked, uncertain.

"Can it be, your eyes have not yet opened?"

"Well, I mean… we like each other, but—"

He leaned forward. "Your abilities, Miss Moore."

My mind started spinning. Was he talking about an ability to attract a husband? Or was he referring, in some dated way, to my skills as a fighter? What did he think I was capable of?

"Ah." Mr. Cloet sat back, silenced by a revelation that eluded me. "I thought for certain when you had cloaked yourself from us the day you arrived… No matter." He resumed his watch of the front yard. "They shall one day. Soon, I imagine."

"I don't understand. What shall?"

After a moment or two of searching out the window, Mr. Cloet rose and opened the door to call for Éabha. "Miss Moore is in a dreadful state. See how she shivers? Draw her a bath before she catches her death. Never fear, Miss Moore! I shall take your place as guard and will disturb you only in direst need." He winked for extra effect.

The ruse worked because Éabha laughed before expressing dismay at the sight of my soaked attire, teasing me with blame for the disaster I'd made of the gown and shoes.

We'd only gotten a few steps when he called, "Oh! Go ahead, Éabha. I have forgotten a message I was meant to give Miss Moore." He waited for the sound of the bathroom door before he approached to whisper, "Know this. We need not accept their influence, you hear? It never lasts for long, if you do, and it only aides your abilities to grow stronger." Once again, I was speechless by the many riddles being thrown my way. "Best not discuss such things with Jonathan, though, until you are ready, *ja*?"

Mr. Cloet bade me go and get out of my wet clothes, closing the door in my bewildered face. I drifted through the kitchen toward the bathroom, struggling to make sense of what he'd been saying.

Exactly who *could* I trust?

Chapter Forty-Seven

The sounds of Jacob tearing down the back stairs to stampede into the kitchen broke the hypnotic lull of the fire crackling in the bathroom grate. Jonathan's voice consulting with Mr. Cloet carried through the wall, as well. A request for hot buttered rum was granted, all others denied. Supper would be ready before long.

"Where is Miss Moore?" Jonathan asked, a hint of tension in his voice. "She *has* returned."

"She is in the bathing room. Ah, ah. Do not think it!" Éabha barked at him. "Heaven knows what you have been accustomed to in the wilds, but there shall be no indecency here. You leave the lady be."

"I-I would never… How…? I do not understand. Did she not bathe when first we arrived?"

Éabha answered with a description of my sorry state following my flight from the Iron Works. Jacob's voice cut through whatever response Jonathan gave. The sounds of the wooden floor creaking under him as he bounced, highlighted his excitement. "Captain, you promised to play pirates."

Their voices quieted until Mr. Cloet's boomed, "Back on the horse, *maatje*! We must return atop when we are thrown."

Mr. Cloet snuck something tasty from the table. I didn't have to be in the room to imagine the scene of Éabha throwing her hands into the air, judging by the tone of her voice as she scolded him for it.

"Outdoors is, indeed, the best place," she exclaimed and shooed the intruders from the kitchen.

The boy's name was added to the reprimands about the nearness of supper and appetites. They disappeared into the front hallway, with

Éabha's melodramatic lecturing trailing after them.

She came into the bathroom shortly thereafter with a robe in hand. "Captain Wythe is anxious to speak with you. I fancy what he desires is to see for himself whether you are in health."

Claiming she was relieved when I said I didn't need help to dress, she tossed her instructions at me on her way to the door. Supper needed attending since we had missed dinner and would want to eat early. A mug of rum would be ready, if I should come to fetch it for Captain Wythe once I had dressed. There was a fresh gown a'waiting on the bed, especially.

Up in my room, I longed to throw on my pants and shirt, but my boots and underwear were still playing hide-and-seek. In the end, I settled on the "especially" laid-out, sky-blue gown with cherry-print and a navy petticoat. A gauzy, gray scarf was also waiting. Nice of Éabha to acquiesce and allow me some of the modesty expected of women. I wrapped the scarf around my neck, dressing it along with the key's ribbon into the front of my gown.

The impracticality of attempting an eighteenth-centuryish style on my own, even with the benefit of damp hair, led me to give the white cap a try. Somehow, I managed to whisk my locks underneath so they stayed in place. Brown shawl in case I needed it, a pair of blue slippers with silver, braided laces, and down the front stairs I went, since they were wider than the nosy back steps and easier to maneuver in all my layers.

Mr. Cloet was in his study, reading by the fire. He grinned when he spotted me. "Oh, Miss Moore. What a lovely color. He is outside. You can hear him now with Jacob. Quite a commotion they are making. The noise shall not carry, though. Fear not!" A wink followed.

Any thoughts I had of returning to our earlier, bizarre conversation were cut short by Éabha rushing around the corner with a steaming mug in hand, bidding me to take it and go serve Captain Wythe while it was hot. Mr. Cloet's nose was deep in his pages, leaving me to follow her instructions.

The kitchen herbs, already taller and lusher since our arrival, danced along my gown as I followed the path through the garden toward the side yard where a mighty ruckus was taking place. Jonathan and Jacob were engaged in a dramatic battle. The pair shouted taunts to one another worthy of any decent popcorn flick, flourishing swords fashioned from stripped-down sticks as they parried and thrusted, then circled, one foot crossing the other in well-rehearsed mimicry.

My heart warmed, seeing them carefree and happy, living a life that—even if only for a moment—was normal.

Everything was going well until Jonathan was facing me and, noticing me enjoying their game, lost his focus. His stance relaxed just as Jacob sliced the air. Too late to avoid it, Jacob's sword caught the side of his hand.

"Ha ha! I have you," he exclaimed, celebrating.

"Indeed, you have." Jonathan shook the pain from his hand. Pride in the boy still broadened his smile. After an exchange of head nods, reassuring the other we were fine, and a decline of the mug from Jonathan, my enigmatic protector resumed combat with his young opponent. "Not for long, you scurvy cur. You have breathed your last."

Gertrude was nestled in the grass with Matilda. A toy tea set made of tin was spread out but forgotten on the quilt where they cuddled. The girl hugged her doll to her body, fixated on the battle. I took in the beatific scene of Jonathan and the children playing and found myself in a wash of joy, then sorrow.

This is what family is supposed to look like. Something he could never have with me.

Though, I stopped to wonder, what sort of life was it Jonathan could offer in return? What sort of man was he if he could influence others? Will them to do things? Though I could resist, according to Mr. Cloet. Or grow stronger, if I chose to accept. If only I understood what he meant. What abilities would I gain?

Around the time of our flight from the Iron Works, the memory of redcoats had become clearer. Our journey through town hadn't been a dream. Accompanying the clarity came the knowledge that I had a nightmare only hours before. I couldn't access it—my head ached with the effort—but it was there, buzzing the back of my brain. He'd hidden these things from me, telling Anna it was to protect me. But no more, he'd promised.

My lonely reflection distracted Jonathan. He kept craning his neck, eyeing me with concern in between blocks and thrusts. Jacob whined at him for his delayed response to a whistling slash of the boy's sword. Enough riddles, I decided. Neither of us needed him sustaining more injuries from the game.

Matilda welcomed me to join them on the blanket and scootched over by rolling back and forth on her hips, Gertrude attached to her lap and hampering her progress, until she'd made a modicum amount of room for me. "'Tis all as it ought to be. Fear forgot and out of doors again, aye?"

It was easier to agree with her.

She nodded back, flitting a glance along the tree line, then encouraged Gertrude to pour a toy cup for me. The little girl shook her head and buried herself in her doll. "Come now, be a lamb and give the nice lady her coffee," Matilda urged. The girl was debilitated with fear. It broke my heart.

"Who wants to sit and drink coffee when there's pirates about?" I said. "What do you say, Lady Gertrude? Shall we show these silly boys how it's done?"

"Oh my," Matilda exclaimed.

Gertrude peeked out from over a sewn head of yarn. Jacob, meanwhile, stopped so suddenly in his bout with Jonathan, his captain almost cleaved him with a downward stroke. A look of exaggerated though sincere relief was telegraphed for my amusement. I stifled a laugh at the unintentional farce, the boy being oblivious to how close he came to being clobbered.

"Gertie cannot fight with swords," he protested.

"Oh, and why not, says Iiii?" My inner pirate was readying for the battle to come. I rose to the occasion, planting my feet wide, my hands on my hips, and my chin lifted into the air. "Some of the fiercest, deadliest pirates be us women."

No one chooses for me.

I indulged in a sizeable helping of Jonathan's rum. Sweet and spicy, like pumpkin pie. Decadent and rich. Another gulp was necessary to fortify me.

Finding a decent stick on the ground, I bowed it in the middle with a show of preparation, then—to Jonathan's amusement—flourished my shawl to the side to cast it onto the quilt. The ladies applauded me.

"Have at thee!" I proclaimed and slashed my would-be weapon in several arches through the air. I knew I looked ridiculous to Jonathan's trained eye, but who cared? We were having fun.

He laughed as he approached. "You will need better posturing, or the battle will be lost to you before you have begun."

"Oh, you think you have my number, but I'm full of surprises, sir. I'll run you through and send you to Davy Jones's Locker."

A gasp from Gertrude trailed my pretentious threat. Jonathan froze, eyeing the tip of my would-be sword aimed at his heart. "Full of surprises? Aye, most assuredly." A hint of concern carried on his breathy laugh. "Though I could do without talk of sea devils and their ilk."

A watchful eye tracked my movements while he helped himself to a serving of rum. Returning the mug to the blanket, he invited Gertrude to join us. She refused. Even offering her my stick garnered only a subtle shake of her head.

Matilda apologized, "The child has become quite shy of late."

No real wonder why, their world caught in the middle of its own undoing and recreation. Gertrude's face disappeared as she snuggled deeper into her doll.

"Name one," Jacob challenged. I stared at him, lost, until I realized he was still mulling over the female pirate debate.

"I'll do you better," I said. "I'll name you two. Anne Bonny and Mary Read. They sailed the Caribbean with Calico Jack until the day they were captured. It was the men who gave up and drank below, crying, 'Woe as us.' Not the women. They fought the soldiers until the bitter end."

"You know your pirates." Jonathan beamed with admiration in his expression.

"I... There's a boy I know from back home. He likes pirates too."

Homesickness tugged at my heart until Jonathan distracted me. It started at first as a hum in his chest, repeating and building until he was laughing out loud.

"What?" I asked.

"Jacob and I have discovered the answer to the riddle that is you, Miss Moore. You are a pirate. It is why you cannot tell me where you call home. You live by your wits on the world's oceans. The waves are your castle walls, and the winds of the sea, the lullaby that sings you goodnight."

"You have me. You've learned my secret." I chuckled. "I'm the greatest of pirates! Captain of my own ship, *Misfortune's Maiden*."

Jonathan laughed again.

"Of course, now you know the truth." But I stopped there, the threat on my lips fading.

He was inches away. The smell of soot from the Iron Works mingled with the sweat he'd worked up from his play with Jacob. A hint of spice served as his base fragrance. He was just standing there, grinning, and I wasn't sure what to do.

Without warning, Jonathan lashed out, stealing my stick with his left hand. Mischief played on his features. He'd caught me off-guard, but not when he followed with his right to take a playful swing at me with his stick. Then, it was Jonathan who was caught off-guard.

I stepped into him to block his arm with mine, continuing the motion to grab him by the forearm while I seized his waist with my other hand. His shock, presumably from both the unexpected block and my slamming my hip into his midsection, allowed me the time I needed to complete the maneuver.

Teasing a smile, I swung to face the same direction as him, then dropped my center of gravity and leaned forward. Hooking his hip around, as my legs straightened, I brought him up and over my back with a satisfying, "Wo-maaan!" until he landed in the grass in front of me.

Still grasping his arm—I admit, I was slowed by my amusement of him blinking away the impact to his side—I gripped the soft portions of his wrist between my fingers to keep him from misbehaving and lowered my knees onto the side of his neck and ribs.

It wasn't as easy as in class, given the yards of fabric swirling around my legs, but being the queen of all things magnanimous—at least, when it came to tossing my personal protector—I eased his fall to avoid his getting hurt. Well, his pride maybe didn't make it unscathed because, trapped between sky-blue cotton and spring-green lawn, Jonathan was helpless.

The children and Matilda were on their feet, Jacob screaming with excitement, "How did she do that?"

"I rightly do not know," the nurse replied. "Oh now, Gertrude. They are only playing. Such as you and your brother. She will hurt Captain Wythe none."

Enjoying the moment, I leaned forward to lazily drag a loose strand away from his flushed cheek. "What do you think, Lady Gertrude? What should I do with him?"

Jonathan attempted to slither the arm trapped underneath him free, but a little pressure to his other wrist encouraged him to cease. I tormented him further by trailing my finger around the edge of his ear. "What *should* I do with you?"

Our audience yelled their choices for his fate. He laughed, commenting on my incorrigibility before offering his surrender. Once reassured everyone could hear the humble submission, I backed off his chest and neck to kneel behind him.

Leaning close to his ear, I maintained a firm grasp on his wrist and asked, "Will you teach me?"

"Teach you? The art of sword play, you mean?" He attempted to rise, but I wouldn't let him until he agreed.

Satisfied, I darted away to put some distance between us, in the unlikely event he sought revenge. He swiped a hand at his pants, shedding grass from his side, and eyed me for possible future attack.

Jacob declared Jonathan had let me throw him. Gertrude asked Matilda, who admitted to the girl she was not at all certain.

Clearing his throat, the party in question called a truce, offering me his mug after he'd taken a swig. "Do you truly wish for me to teach you?"

I accepted another serving, grinning like a little kid at the toy store and saying I did.

He hesitated, weighing my request while I collected my stick from where it'd fallen and returned to my untrained fighting stance. "You would not seek to put such skills to use?"

"It's just in case," I promised.

After sighing at the ground, he positioned himself next to me and began explaining the proper stance. I followed his example by leading with my dominant foot and keeping my other perpendicular to the front. With my right knee bent, and my left hand pointing skyward in an arch behind me, I was declared ready to stand en garde.

The children quit long before we did. Even Jacob tired of watching Jonathan run me through my paces, working the primary and secondary parries into my muscles. They gathered the quilt, along with my shawl and the empty mug, and returned indoors for their lessons. The training session continued until I misjudged the proper block, opening a window for Jonathan's stick so it thwacked into the soft part between my neck and shoulder. Amazing how something as dull as a stick could drive through you like a knife when it struck the right place.

He paled with mortification. Voice throaty, he apologized and grabbed my arm, demanding he be permitted to inspect my shoulder. I brushed him off, saying I was fine, even though I turned my back so I could grit my teeth against the throbbing muscle.

He stole away our sticks and slammed them into a compost heap near the barn, grumbling he "never should have permitted such a foolish—"

"Will you stop? You make it sounds like it's the worst thing to ever happen to me."

"But it happened by my hand!" There was actual pain in his declaration. I almost laughed, thinking he was overreacting. The emotion overwhelmed his body, as well.

Cordelia. It has to be.

"Jonathan." It took several tries before he allowed me to clasp his upper arms to make him look at me. "Hey. I've studied Jiu jitsu for a few years now."

"What is Jiu…?" he struggled with the word. I repeated it for him.

"It's the self-defense classes I told you about. I've had my ass handed to me many times. A number of bruises and pulled muscles over the years. The worst was when this high-schooler was a little too enthusiastic while practicing a chokehold. I had a headache for days."

"It is hardly comforting to think that my actions have added to the litany of harms done to you."

"You aren't part of a litany of harms. It comes with training. Are you actually trying to tell me you haven't had your fair share of cuts and bumps and bruises along the way?" His shoulders fell. "Then please," I told him. "Try not to beat yourself up over this. I won't."

He nodded, visibly working to pull himself out of the guilt threatening to rout him. It dampened his eyes when he looked up. I found myself sighing his name, reaching to trace my fingertips across his forehead and along his cheek, the way he comforted me.

I know this man. It's as if I've known him my whole life. He believes in honor and promises kept.

And I realized, he would give his life for me if he had to.

His mouth parted, then his fingers slipped into my hair so he could cradle my head, his thumb stroking my cheek. Delighting in the sensation of his touch, I glided my hands to his chest to discover the rhythm of his heart quickening through the moistened linen. Fingertips explored the line of my neck.

My eyelids fluttered closed, a sigh escaping my lips as he eased the scarf aside to expose the place where I'd been struck. With each careful pass along the curve of my shoulder—flowing, drifting, ebbing—my skin flamed alive, the sting melting away.

On his final pass, he steered both hands toward my upper arms, thumbs drawing across the fabric there once as his palms embraced me, then released. I opened my eyes to question him when he stepped back, cheeks flushed even though the rest of him paled. Dust clung to the backs of his hands. He stared at where I enfolded them with mine.

"You are a remarkable woman, Miss Moore. In truth, I have never known your equal." He finished in earnest when I breathed a laugh, saying, "I do not jest."

"No, it isn't you. You reminded me of a joke my best friend and I have. Whenever she sees me, she says, 'Can you be Savvy Moore?' And I always say, 'Well, I can't be Savvy Less.'"

He hummed appreciatively. "Miss Moore…"

"I wish you'd call me Savvy."

"If I am true to no other vow, it shall be this. I will never call you by that name." The unwanted promise bothered me until he added, "Your name. Your *true* name is much as you are."

I studied his face, searching for signs he was teasing. "A dry, grassy expanse of wilderness?"

His head bowed. A self-conscious smile followed. "It is beautiful."

My wits vanished. Those castle walls he spoke of crashed through me with the tide I'd neglected to avoid. I was lost forever. And I simply couldn't breathe.

When neither of us could think of anything else to say, Jonathan welcomed my arm into his. I melted into his side and, together, we strolled toward the house.

Chapter Forty-Eight

Jonathan and I freshened up in our respective rooms. Hot water for a sponge bath was the rationed luxury I was permitted, another bath being out of the question. I was informed in no uncertain terms, before I could even think to ask—I would not be sullying a third gown in one day. A little rosewater was slipped from Éabha's pocket into the basin, though, her habitual smirk present as she did.

After dressing, I hurried downstairs to find Jonathan deep in discussion with Mr. Cloet about the final steps for assembling the Chain. He invited me to join them, and I did for a while, until even the forced excitement of hearing first-hand reports of the project staled from the tedious accounting of this estimated amount of some variant of iron to be refined to form *X* number of pins for the clevises and binders required to fasten the Chain to the Boom. And so on, and then some, and more to follow.

Besides, I was a distraction to Jonathan. When his gaze wasn't lingering over my skin, a stray finger would flirt with my hand or the linen on his hip would kiss the cotton of mine. He'd become self-conscious and stop until some other means of connecting happened upon us. We were never out of contact for long. It got to the point where Mr. Cloet stopped trying to hide his amusement.

I cursed my heart for betraying me, taking refuge by the parlor window in the hopes a little space might help. A cloaked woman was walking the perimeter of the Cloets' property, off in the distance. Probably Anna, but the angle obscured her face and gown, so it was hard to tell.

Curious, I told the men to carry on without me—receiving a

regretful farewell from Jonathan, along with a reminder to stay within the stone boundaries—and escaped via the front door.

Her hands were resting atop the wall when I rounded the garden. Concentration filled her features. She was praying. Not wanting to disturb her, I held back until she finished. A look of satisfaction dissolved when she realized she wasn't alone. She begged my pardon. Another task could not wait. She raced toward the backyard, leaving me feeling awkward and alone.

With her company an apparent impossibility and the children busy with their studies, I walked several laps before seeking sanctuary from my restless mind in the library adjacent to Mr. Cloet's parlor.

Captain Machin arrived with an update. He had sent scouts to investigate the earlier gunfire and was awaiting their return, though he did not anticipate word for a few hours more. Until such time, we would have to content ourselves with the reassurance that the fighting had not reached the Iron Works. The general's plans remained secret.

Heavy footfalls exited the parlor to situate themselves in the dining room, an invitation to dine with us having been extended to Machin since he'd arrived right before Éabha announced supper. Not quite ready to abandon the cozy settee I'd claimed by the fire, I continued reading.

"Ah, there you are." Jonathan appeared in the library doorway. "Miss Moore, would… Have you read all of that today?"

With only a few more sentences to go until the end of the page, I held up a finger to stall him. A patient chuckle humored me. My reluctance to relinquish the copy brought a puzzled turn of his head. He examined the cover, cocking an eyebrow at its contents. A woven ribbon was produced from a side table drawer to be placed between the pages, the book laid down with a promise of its waiting there for me. Offering his arm to escort me, he brought a flutter to my chest as he leaned in close, smiling.

Mr. Cloet, on the other hand, was glowering across the dining room table at Machin, who stood opposite him, when we entered. Anna was ignoring the disturbance by conferring with Éabha at the side table. Their heated debate about why the captain determined the final work needed to be done onsite when all could be accomplished at the Iron Works ceased when we joined them.

Supper began with the same formal bowing of heads. At the conclusion of the blessing, Éabha collected bowls two at a time to serve a soup generously stocked with beef, cabbage, and other vegetables. Community loafs of bread lay scattered on the main table, which the diners broke with their hands, serving themselves. A collection of preserves, butter, and honey was also available to slather as we wished, and the hard cider flowed.

A safer topic was addressed, which promised to avoid the risk of rekindling the earlier tension between host and guest captain, as Jonathan complimented Jacob's improved skill with a sword. The parents relaxed into conversation about their son's dedicated practice with some of the trained workers. Machin admitted to indulging the boy, as well.

Color washed over Jonathan's cheeks as he offered me the bowl of raspberry preserves.

Machin was respectful, if a little guarded, when he answered my questions about his own training. Originally from Staffordshire, he came to America to inspect the copper mines in the Boston region. He had apprenticed in his youth to a canal builder, Mr. James Brindley, for which he was grateful because it gave him the opportunity to study mathematics and mechanics and such. Now, he told us, he was a lieutenant with the artillery, serving in the Highlands of New York.

Mr. Cloet seized on the title. "You are not a captain, then, eh?"

Machin, being taller and broader than petite Anna, was difficult to see around to where she sat on his other side, but from the sounds of it, she reacted to the slight to their guest.

"Has not the commission of captain been approved by the Congress?" Jonathan asked Machin, then directed a chastising look at Mr. Cloet.

"Not as of yet," Machin addressed us with humility, "though the general assures me he has made the application."

"Ever slow to act, if there are but a hundred words to be bandied about on the subject before," Jonathan complained. "Never you mind. His Excellency has made the application and recounts you in his report as a proper captain. You may assume the rank with honor."

"Very kind of you. I hope none do think ill of me for wearing the cockade and epaulette the general has bestowed upon me. I should not like to insult his Excellency by failing to don his offering."

"Indeed. Nor should you neglect to give him such thanks," Jonathan replied. "How fares your shoulder?"

Machin chuckled. "I can say at least this, I know when it should rain because my shoulder is good enough to report such news before the first cloud is sighted."

Jonathan, being an excellent storyteller, provided a passionate retelling of Machin's role in the defense of Fort Montgomery that was riveting. Praise for his fellow captain's service to the Cause was often repeated, for he had suffered a British musket ball to pass through his chest.

Machin's voice dropped with embarrassment as he answered, "It is but my duty to see the fighting done and carry on once more with all the general requires."

Anna suggested we retire to the sitting room. Compliments were given to Éabha for the delicious meal as everyone rose with satisfied expressions, a patted belly here and there, and approval of the prospect of a peaceful glass of wine by the parlor fire.

Jonathan circled the table to offer his arm, contentment brightening his smile, and after seeing me seated into the same wingback as the night before, he opted for its partner by my side. Machin declined the place of honor by the hearth, as it rightfully belonged to Mr. Cloet.

Anna excused herself once the refreshments were served to check on the children and assist Éabha with the clearing away of supper. The men rose to standing, as custom required. I offered to help, but she waved me back to my spot, exclaiming, "Of course you should stay to hear the report."

Encouraged by her declaration, I stayed, my not-so-secret joy apparent to the whole world, I'm sure. Jonathan's fingers traced the curve of my face while the others turned to reseat themselves.

Their conversation about the status of the Chain picked up right where they left off before supper and carried on at length. Around the second or third or maybe fifth time Mr. Cloet caught me stifling yet another yawn, he interrupted, saying, "Do accept our sincerest apologies, Miss Moore. You have much been left to the company of men. We are poor company indeed for a woman. Our heads, you see, are stuffed with business and glory. We have not room left during these times of war for genteel companionship and the polite society your sex does deserve. Though, have a care, for when arms are laid down and peace declared once more, the lads shall be hungry as dogs. Then, it shall be the women who will no longer know peace when they are laid down in arms."

Mr. Cloet was rewarded for his speech. The two captains flushed, with the addition of Jonathan sputtering his wine. Our host wasn't alone in his laughter, amused as I was by his crass apology. "I'm managing just fine. It was nice to be able to read for a few hours. It's rare for me to get such a long stretch for myself."

Machin jumped in, saying, "You read, Miss Moore?"

"Indeed," Jonathan answered. "She was near finished with Paine's pamphlet when I did fetch her to supper."

"How remarkable."

"I don't know about remarkable," I said. "But yeah. *Common Sense*."

"Would that we all had common sense," Mr. Cloet mused.

I chuckled along with him. "I always meant to read it, but never found the time before. It was nice to have the opportunity." Not to mention the opportunity to hold an original publication in my hands.

"Always?" Jonathan asked.

My heart skipped a beat. "Well, my dad tried to get me to read it. Called it one of the most influential writings of the free world…"

Oh hell.

I wasn't making my time snafu any better.

Jonathan leaned in to ask gently, "When did your father die?"

The idea of my father dying hurt, especially since I was determined to see him again. "Why do you ask?" It came out in a whisper.

"The pamphlet was published little more than two years ago. To have always meant to…" It wasn't accusatory, the way he said it. Rather, he paused and studied the ground before filling in the silence, saying, "…you must still have been at home less than two years prior."

I squirmed in my seat. Machin saved me. "Had you a governess, Miss Moore?"

"No." I sighed, relieved. "I attended public school, college, then law school."

"Law school?" He was astounded.

"How many years were you?" Mr. Cloet spoke over Machin.

Jonathan nodded to the captain, though I could practically hear the wheels in his head turning. The men sat forward in their respective chairs. Even Éabha, who'd been circling the room, refreshing the supply of wine, was curious, as well, as I described in general terms the public-school system and its extra-curricular activities.

"Did *you* participate in debate?" Machin was intrigued by its mention.

"I did, and I prized several times." Despite wishing the attention to my world would cease, I couldn't help bragging a little. Debate Team had been an escape from my mother. Every debate was the battle I could never win at home. Every trophy, validation.

"Most impressive," Mr. Cloet said.

"I dare say," Machin agreed, and for once, the two men left a comment without dispute.

"Miss Moore is a rare specimen of woman." Jonathan toasted me with his wine.

With the distance of centuries between us and homesickness rearing its ugly head as it was, I wondered if maybe I'd been unfair to my mother. Had I ever listened to her side?

Mr. Cloet was kind enough to change the subject when he

noticed my delayed response in thanking the men. "Jonathan, is not your uncle a man of the law? Over there in the Virginia Commonwealth." He winked at me when no one else was looking.

"A distant cousin," Jonathan answered.

"He had a man there with him. Oh heavens, what is the fellow's name? Member of the Congress, is he not? The both of them. It is said, he wrote the grievances against the king. Not that the king has paid any mind." Mr. Cloet kept feeding Jonathan clues, but neither of them could figure out the man's name.

"Do you mean Thomas Jefferson?" I asked. "Who wrote the *Declaration of Independence*?" The idea Jonathan might hold a connection to the future president percolated all sorts of possibilities. One cup of coffee with the man couldn't hurt…

"*Ja*, that is the man." Mr. Cloet was thrilled to have found the answer at last. "It is said, he denounced the enslavement of Africans—and he a Virginian!—but the Congress made him remove the complaint. Are you acquainted with him, Miss Moore?"

"Just read about him," I said. Jonathan's brows were knitted when I looked in his direction to ask, "Do you know him?"

"How is it you know of my kinsman's student?" he asked in return.

"Well, like I said, I've read about him." The suspicious look didn't lessen at my explanation, though an excuse was good enough to present itself. "Jonathan, everything you do here is monumental. The whole world is watching. Do you really think people outside the Colonies aren't paying attention?"

"Outside these United States, if I may," Machin corrected me.

I apologized and repeated the correction. It was hard to marry in my mind what I thought of as the colonial period with its blossoming status as my home country.

"True enough, Miss Moore," Mr. Cloet agreed. "True enough. Eh, Jonathan?"

"What *we* do here," he pointed out. "You are a party to the rebellion yourself now, Miss Moore."

"Yeah. I am." The truth—one I'd avoided, pretending I hadn't been sucked in to become an active participant in the Revolution—made my stomach churn. At Jonathan's continued stare, I finished, "And I'd rather die than see the fight for independence fail."

The words sounded good, and I meant them through and through. I'd rather be killed, preferably in an instant by a stray bullet, than have to live with the knowledge I'd caused the downfall of American democracy before it even began. But this new turn in the conversation was more uncomfortable than the one I'd been trying to escape.

"Bravely met." Mr. Cloet slapped his palm against his thigh. "Let us hope, however, our women will not be called to such a sacrifice. Our countrymen are men of valor and honor. We have tamed the wilds of this land, not to mention the French! If we have grown so slovenly by our hearth that we cannot protect our womenfolk, then we are not a people worthy of our homeland."

"Here, here," Machin agreed.

"Indeed. It is rumored," Jonathan said, "that another of British delegates is to be dispatched to the Congress to broker a truce,"

Mr. Cloet snorted. "With terms such as we must lay down arms, kiss the king's *kont*, and continue to quarter his soldiers, I should wager."

Machin lent his opinion, saying, "I think a truce is unlikely. In December, we stood alone and refused. France has now allied herself with the rebellion." He shifted forward to address Mr. Cloet's surprised expression. "The terms were decided earlier this year. They, too, shall be sent to Congress for ratification."

"Such a choice! England or France. It boggles the mind. Having seen the filth of France fall with mine own eyes, by my own sweat and blood—for in my younger days, I too, did raise arms to defend my lands and her people—I shall believe it not until I do witness France's weapons turn to the defense of our nation against those of England's armies."

"I was not aware you had fought in the Seven Years' War, sir. You have my respect." Machin toasted Mr. Cloet.

The toast was returned with praise of the younger men who must take up the arms their elders had hoped to retire, though the men agreed not all, as his Excellency was once more in the fray. A round was raised to our commander-in-chief, General Washington.

I heard the conversation as if from far away. Firelight held me captive while I struggled with the desperate need to go home, which was clashing against the lingering memory of fingers tracing the curve of my shoulder.

Jonathan made a point of topping off my wine with the call for a toast and, having noticed my expression, said, "Miss Moore, there is something that I must tell you. I have only learnt of it this day."

I abandoned my lonely study of the fire to give him my full attention. He looked to Machin for support as he explained, "As you are only partly aware, Captain Machin and myself are assigned to works associated with the construction of fortifications along the river. The captain has informed me that the land there, known as West Point, is owned by a man of means, a Master Stephen Moore." He paused, as if waiting for a response. "Could this be the reason for your arrival in the Americas?"

I swallowed, feeling Fate had just betrayed me. "No. It's not."

"But likely there is a connection."

I set my wineglass down too hard. Red liquid sloshed onto the tea table between us. "I've told you. I'm not from the Colonies." I shook drops from my hand, flustered, looking around for something to clean the mess.

Jonathan produced a white handkerchief from his endless supply and grabbed onto me before I could pull away, pressing the cloth to my skin in a feign of drying the wine spilled there. "Nevertheless, what if you have come to visit this man?"

"No, Jonathan."

"There is more. Several of the Connecticut regiments are currently stationed there. You told me once that you were from Connecticut. What if—"

"A long time ago." I tried to stop him, but he continued talking over me, undeterred by my stalwart denials.

"—you came with your family from Connecticut—"

"I haven't lived in Connecticut since I was, like, two."

"—to meet your family here, in the Americas."

"The answers lie in the woods where we met," I insisted.

Machin appeared alarmed by my reaction to the news. He lifted from his chair, a fraction of an inch, before resuming his seat. His mouthed words were muted by Jonathan's continued speech.

"It may be that you have forgotten, lost in the heat of the fighting as you were. Moore's Folly is not many miles from where we did meet. If you were to see him again, mayhaps it would help you to recall—"

"Jonathan!" I yelled. Everyone froze. "*Moore* is my married name. I would never visit the family, even if I knew them."

"*Zegen mij*," Mr. Cloet breathed.

My protector, the skilled soldier and awkward gentleman who'd just hours earlier captured my heart, released my hand with a jolt, looking like he'd been sucker-punched.

I clutched the edge of my chair with both hands and focused on an indigo tulip blossoming along the floorcloth's border while I faced the raging storm inside. The threat of being pawned off on Justin's ancestors instead of finding my way home was nauseating. I'd never before regretted keeping my married name, the one bit of spite I'd allowed myself, knowing how it galled Justin.

Mr. Cloet ventured first to say, "Please forgive us, Mistress Moore—"

"Don't call me that."

"My dear wife and I would never have encouraged you to dishonor your sacred vows."

"Of course not." My clipped response didn't elicit further apologies, though—were I thinking clearly—I would've realized I owed Mr. Cloet one myself.

"How am I to address you?" Jonathan intoned, his gaze falling to the floor, his expression unreadable.

I hoped my answer would help. "Savannah. Jonathan, I'm—"

"You have said that you do not remember coming here. The answers you seek are like to be found with this man, Moore."

"You promised to take me back to the hillside where we met. The answers lie there."

Instead of responding, he bolted to his feet, searching for something uncertain, then crossed to the window to study the area behind the house.

I rose to follow him. "You do remember, right? How to get there? You'd tell me if you didn't. Right?"

"Aye."

"Promise me you'd tell me. Promise you're being honest with me."

"Understand me. I can deliver you to that portion of the forest. I remember well the place. What stops me is the danger. I have been receiving reports of the area."

"Reports? How? When? We've been together almost the entire time." Zeroing in on Machin, I noticed he looked surprised, too, at the news, but dropped his gaze to avoid being drawn into the confrontation.

"I cannot tell you," Jonathan answered. "I must ask that you trust me."

"Trust you?"

"Aye, trust me. I have given you no cause to doubt me, though the same cannot be said of *you*," he returned viciously.

"Wait a minute."

"My mission here draws to an end. We will travel to Moore's Folly at first light."

"You can't abandon me with a total stranger."

"If he is, in fact, a stranger once you have met, *madam*, then and only then, will I chance traveling into enemy territory for another man's wife." He spat the last few words at me.

"You have no right to— You know nothing about me."

"Of that, we are in perfect agreement!" he shouted.

Tears poured down my face. He'd wounded me more than he

could ever know.

Part of me wanted to explain about Justin. Throw every disgusting bit of our history together in Jonathan's face and douse the anger in his eyes. But how could I explain what our lives held back in the twenty-first century? What difference would it make?

I couldn't face him anymore. I couldn't face any of them.

Behind me, Anna hovered in the doorway, directing Matilda to take the children to bed. Their papa would visit them before long to wish them *goedenacht*. Their footfalls receded into the hallway toward the stairwell.

Machin commented on how the hour had grown late. He was expected at the home of Mr. Brewster. Compliments to Mistress Cloet and Miss Carroll for supper. A handshake was exchanged with his host. Jonathan remained where he was, brooding out the window, which left Machin to mumble a goodnight from where he stood.

I forced a similar response, though foregoing the formality of addressing the captain face-to-face and curtseying or shaking or engaging in whatever social niceties were required, since Jonathan didn't offer any clues as to what was appropriate. What he did condescend to do was bid the Cloets to remain as chaperone. I withered at the request. Éabha escorted Machin to the backdoor in their place with promises of a lantern for the captain's journey.

"We shall need to travel to West Point for another purpose," Jonathan reported. I dried my eyes before meeting his stare. "Major DeForest bade you go to Fort Clinton for news of his location."

"Jonathan…" Mr. Cloet hesitated, the tension having only just dissipated between his guests. "Fort Clinton was destroyed in the autumn and lies further downriver."

"What?" I breathed in shock.

"The regiments may be at West Point, as you say," Mr. Cloet hurried to add.

"Indeed. Major DeForest lied to you," Jonathan told me. "Fort Clinton fell alongside Fort Montgomery. The army encamped at West Point is most like to have news of Major DeForest's relocation."

"It was a test," I realized. "He was testing me, and I failed. No wonder he doesn't trust me. Which means, he must suspect you even more." My stomach sank. I didn't bother to hide the renewed tears. It didn't matter how much Jonathan might hate me. I'd inadvertently damaged his reputation and placed him at greater risk than he already was with the militia. "I'm sorry. I didn't know."

He reached out at my apology, but with the name, "Miss Moore," on his lips, his fist dropped, and he grimaced.

Anna was clutching Mr. Cloet's arm, watching me intently. She shook her head when she caught Jonathan's eye. Mr. Cloet took refuge in the floorcloth's pattern. It was a sad recreation of the previous night. My only avenue of escape was the door to the hallway.

"Jonathan, listen," Anna implored.

"I have not your gift, Anna," he retorted.

"Then speak to listen."

"Don't bother," I told them from the doorway. "I don't think there's anything else to say. Maybe it's best if I keep to myself until we go."

I exited the room for the last time.

Chapter Forty-Nine

Curled up in bed, I clenched the blankets against the knot in my chest, confused about whether it was better to find Jonathan and try to explain, or give it a day or two, or to not say anything and allow what never should've started between us to die. As the hours dragged, I drifted in and out of consciousness, sometimes spellbound by the flickering flames. Sometimes, I saw nothing.

A whisper of satin shifting in the room woke me.

Anna rose from in front of the hearth, the glow of the catching logs contorting the shadows on her face and gown. She gasped. "Savvy?" Her attention darted back toward the fire. Smoke, clean and white, drifted from the grate.

She hurried to my side. Golden curls tumbled over her shoulder, spilling onto my stomach, when she reached to shush me with outstretched fingers.

I clasped her hand before she could brush my own locks from my forehead. "It's not what you think. I could never cheat on someone. I'm not… I didn't mean to hurt him. He… I didn't know what to do. He was so mad. I didn't think he'd listen."

"Sleep," she encouraged me. "Tell him all in the morning."

"Everything?" I sought the key tumbling from my shift onto the mattress.

Could I tell him everything?

"I think, my dear, there will come a time when you must."

The heady scent of lavender unfurled around us, making me drowsy. Even Anna swayed, her eyelids drooping. Whisking her hand away, she dashed into the hall, biddings of *goedenacht* trailing after her.

A draft breezed over me as the door swung shut. The click of the latch sealed me in.

The room was stifling and getting worse. My shift pasted itself to my ribcage as the linen dampened. The air grew thick, oppressive, the fragrance of lavender potent. With it came a sensation of electricity sparking along the contours of my body, penetrating my skin. The voice inside me was being swept into a void, desperate to be heard: Anna was trying to drug me.

I struggled against the undertow drawing me away from myself. Hot. Too hot. I was burning.

Blankets snagged my limbs. I stumbled from the bed, unable to focus on my surroundings. The shock of reaching the floor so quickly shot up through my knees where they struck the wooden boards. I inched forward, pulling myself with my arms. My fingers grazed the coarse iron of the poker where it leaned against the wall.

I stretched out again. It clattered to the floor. Scraping the poker along the brick hearth, I dragged it through the ashes. The weight was near impossible as I fought against the haze darkening my vision to extract the smoldering bundle of lavender.

Somehow, I did it. The radiance of the flowers faded and crumbled, their fragrance souring to the stink of charred weeds. The odor was unbearable. Heat seared my skin unnaturally as the magic wormed inside me. Crawling away from the hearth, I grabbed onto the chair closest to the window to haul myself upright.

I pried the shutters apart. Numbness was seizing my body. It was like trying to move mountains. Metal clicked with each attempt as I fumbled with the latch, unable to make it turn. It released with a sudden flick, and pressing upward with the last of my strength, I forced the window open to let in the night air.

Chapter Fifty

A violent shudder roused me. Peeling my cheek from the window ledge, I found wisps of ice looming around my mouth and nose. I was freezing, but I was so relieved to have escaped the unnatural heat of Anna's influence, I didn't care.

The room was pitch-black. Not even the dim ruddiness of cinders to see by. Except, it wasn't. Passing motes of sapphire light glittered throughout. Darting, skittering, floating—they tingled against my skin as my fingers explored their wake, warming me as I welcomed them inside. I splayed my fingers and willed them to come together. A puff burst above my palm.

I was ravenous. Every muscle alive. Electric. Hungry to move. Hungry to run. Hungry to… Then, the desire began. More than desire—desperation took hold. My gaze went unbidden to the bedroom door. My thoughts kept going. Mr. Cloet hadn't warned me about that.

The wind kicked up, sending the shutters shrieking on their hinges. I bolted to the open window, hoping the fresh air would sweep away the cravings, both frightening and exciting. The bluster stung against my skin, but the desire didn't stop. An emptiness starting like a twinge in my chest grew. I had to get out of the house. Maybe go for a run.

Cloaks billowed against shadowed figures in the yard below me. Peering around the ledge confirmed the upturned face was Anna's. The man she leaned toward scanned the upper level of the house. I ducked behind a shutter. Although the source was unclear, their features were aglow. The light bluer on her than on him. Jonathan. Together, they turned and exited the property through the iron gate, dissolving from sight when they did.

Even in my raw state, not knowing what it all meant, an undying certainty that I had to follow them, invisible or not, gnawed at me. The emptiness inside ached for what they carried with them. The *something* inherent to who they were. It would satiate the desire.

Snatching my clothes from their perch on the chair, I whisked on my pants and exchanged the shift for my shirt. The single choice for footwear was the original pair of brown heels from Anna. I double-knotted them onto my bare feet, grabbed my cloak, and rushed down the back stairs, hoping the complaining from the wooden steps wouldn't be overheard.

Jonathan and Anna must be nearing the pond, I calculated once I reached the stone wall. A shimmer coursed along the dimensions of the iron gate, denying me passage. I pressed my hands into the archway and met with continued resistance. The seemingly empty space bulged against my hand, more solid than air, yet refusing to yield.

"Let me go," I commanded.

Sparks still flickering within the fibers of my muscles flared, and the boundary's power bent to my will. A sapphire glow clung to me as I forced my way through. Once on the other side, it melted off my body, sliding back into place. It rippled within the gate's opening, then faded from sight.

Mesmerized, I sought to explore the surface with my fingers, but remembered Jonathan and Anna had been rounding the bend only moments earlier.

Follow them.

Running my outstretched hand in an arc, I found a pocket of heat from the magic they were using to remain invisible. Lured onto the forest pathway, I ran the entire way to the pond, following in their wake. Leaves caught at me, crumbled beneath my feet, and scattered as I moved.

I wished I had McIntyre's skills of moving silently.

Another flare sparked, though it was weaker than before.

The ducks were slumbering on the far end of the pond, undisturbed by my approach. Even the peepers were keeping their distance. I stumbled when I collided with a fallen branch cowering in the gloom. Regaining my footing, I ignored the sting in my shin and hurried around the bend. My targets would've reached the break in the trees by then. Only when I was approaching Murderer's Creek did it occur to me. The sound of the branch's snap had been silenced.

And I laughed, giddy with excitement about what I could do with magic collected inside me. My abilities had begun to open. I had only to seek magic out.

Empty rock bed greeted me once I dashed into the clearing. It didn't matter. The trail they left was like a cord, knotted around their throats. All I had to do was tug on the rope and follow. Rough logs tapped against my fingertips as I crouched low, scurrying along the dock to survey the ravine. Willing myself invisible, I peered over the edge to search for movement, though I wasn't sure if the magic still worked. Whatever remained, lingering inside me, was faint. I needed more.

The gleam from the lantern they'd brought brightened. Not a lantern. It came from them. They couldn't hide their task from sight. Not with the vast amount of magic at work. I saw everything. Backs turned, arms outstretched, clutching the Great Chain—Anna with Jonathan by her side. The light reflecting off the links intensified, blue and gold and silver waves cascading down length of the Chain in both directions, an earth-bound lighting sluicing along arteries on the metal's surface. Those arteries pulsed and thickened, sprouting fissures that cut through the iron.

Heat like fog rolling off a summer ocean crossed the ravine and engulfed me. I was a moth to its flame, helpless against its beckoning to possess it—the magic they were casting. Muscles tense, my breathing coming faster, I crept backward toward the pathway leading to the Iron Works. Picking my way down the grassy border, I slipped on a rocky patch but regained my balanced.

The magic dimmed. The desire eased with it, giving me time to consider what I was doing.

I had to resist. I couldn't interfere. Not with this. I had to let history take its course.

But what if Jonathan never made it here the first time? What if he was only here, now, because of me?

Except Mr. Cloet knew what his wife was, knew she influenced him with her magic, told me we could resist them. Our people. If Jonathan and Anna were there to help, using their magic to ensure success for the Americans, then Mr. Cloet would've been there with them. He would've helped them, made it possible for them to complete their task without having to sneak off in the middle of the night. Or knowing how close I'd been to seeing my abilities awaken, he would've, at the very least, warned me to let them go.

Their purpose had driven them into the forge. Scanning the ravine, I was alarmed to discover there weren't any soldiers anywhere. The glowing fissures continued to spread along the Chain, fainter but nonetheless violating the metal like rot on a dying tree.

No, they were tampering with that important barrier to the river. The Chain never failed the Americans during the War. Not the first time. Not before I arrived and changed things. I had to stop them.

I dashed to the wooden structure, pressing my back against the outer portion. Firelight from the massive furnace stained the inner walls by the open doorway, glinting off the stone floor in a bloody smattering, swelling and shifting and dying endlessly.

The smell was different. Not the polluted stench of metal filings adrift in the stagnant air. It was more pungent, a deep, earthy fragrance.

Deciding to chance it, I peered into the forge. Sweat beaded on my brow instantly. The heat was crushing. Not just from the inflamed coals—magic blazed within the enclosure.

A soldier in blue slouched on a stool near the entrance, his head heavy. Further in, another was stretched out on the ground, snoring. At the mouth of the furnace were Jonathan and Anna. The workers and soldiers slumbered at their feet, powerless.

Jonathan was extracting a large, metal tooth from the maw of the chimney. The iron shone where it'd been induced by the flame to melt. She held back the sleeve of her cloak while she reached over it, brightness slipping from the confines of a glass bottle as she tipped her hand. It glittered around the metal bar, congealing into a viscous gold leaching into the iron. The growl of the furnace swallowed whatever words she was incanting.

I fell back against the outer wall and drove my fist into my mouth to keep from screaming. The pain, as the famine in my chest demanded I go inside, was unbearable.

A scrape of metal from Jonathan sliding the iron bar into the furnace carried across the distance. They'd completed their task. There was nothing I could do to stop them. They'd contaminated the iron and done something to the Chain itself. They were traitors, and I was the idiot who'd given him the means to reach the Iron Works in time to complete his treacherous mission. I'd saved his life and followed him blindly, never questioning him like Auden or Major DeForest had, even though Jonathan had warned me, himself, how he wasn't to be trusted.

Like a tempest threatening violence, the air thickened with a presence closing in. Deep in my bones, as if we had been cut from the same cloth, I knew it'd sensed the same thing I had, wanted what I wanted. It was racing toward the Iron Works, drawn to the same flame. Only a few miles away, lessening with each slam of my heart against my chest. The voice inside screamed at me to escape while I still could.

I fled from the side of the forge. Rocks shifted as I scrambled up the hill, causing me to slip. The bite of my palm splitting open on a rock sheared through my arm. It didn't matter. I had to get away. I flung myself forward, using my hands to crawl back upright so I could run.

Just as I reached the top of the embankment, a bird swooped into my face, streaks of silver flame trailing after it. It hovered in front of me, refusing to let me by. Anna called my name from the ravine below. The bird darted to where I'd jerked my head around, screeching at me. I couldn't hear what she yelled next.

I tore off into the evergreens, too afraid to look behind me.

A flash of silver lighted overhead.

The trees thinned once I rounded the pond, the house coming into sight. I almost made it. The bird rushed at me, knocking me off-balance. Air whooshed out of my lungs when my back collided with the ground. Ducks scattered from the far end of the pond, their shock echoing around us.

A weight plopped onto my chest. I couldn't see the source. My hair was tugging my head backward, being consumed from underneath me. Coldness crept up the sides of my face, numbing me, but it brought my vision into focus. The little, blue bird was hopping on my chest, pecking and screaming at me.

It fled to a nearby tree as a mantle of pure nothingness seeped through the air above me. It was a void, blotting out the stars, the light, the air, the energy, everything around it. But from within its black heart—hatred, loathing, and a lust for revenge and death slithered outward, tempting the same abhorrence to propagate in me.

Dizziness flooded me as the dream locked away in my mind was freed and I remembered why the Darkness hunted me in my nightmares. *Who* the Darkness truly wanted.

I shuffled backward as fast as I could. Water sloshed against my shoulders and face. I'd fallen into the pond and was retreating further into its freezing depths. Pain shot through my left hand when the gash connected with a decaying branch. Weeds swarming beneath the surface snagged my wrists. Wrenching my hands free from the clutch of grasses, I found water all around, leaving me to flounder. My waterlogged clothes dragged me under.

A spark lighted the pond around me. Somehow, rational thought cut through the panic. I forced myself to stop thrashing, even as my lungs ached. Bubbles. They were going in the same direction. With a focal point, I was able to force my legs downward and connect with solid ground to push off. My head broke the surface. Algae-laced fluid spewed from my mouth as I gasped, frantic.

The blue bird made a dash between me and the Darkness, like a silver comet hurtling across the water. The Darkness lashed out and enveloped the bird, weaving and twisting and writhing around it, squeezing inward. A horrible shriek perished from inside. Jonathan's voice cried out in agony across the distance.

The Darkness spat out the body of the bird. It fell with a sickening thud at the water's edge. Stretching outward again, the pressure in the air shifted, searching.

"No," I screamed and sloshed toward it. Searing heat rose from my chest, stopping me. I tore at my shirt for the source and withdrew the ribbon from its hiding place. The key dangling from its end flared to life, hot against my face. Holding it higher, I yelled, "Leave us alone."

Silver danced in threads, whirling around my hand, before driving into me. Its fire ripped through my veins, blazing along my extended arm to flame into my very soul, waking a consciousness from deep within me.

The Darkness hesitated. Its density shifted; its attention fixated on me. I wasn't who it was seeking. It wanted Jonathan. Still, there was a connection, thrumming, alive in the light surrounding and consuming me, drawing strength from within the hidden recesses of my being to where a piece of Jonathan's soul resided, joined with mine since before I was born. The ghost of a thing that had not yet happened.

And the Darkness was willing to tear into me to get at him.

The force of a hurricane bore down on me as that vengeful, hate-filled void surged toward me. Hesitation and fear never occurred to me. Whatever I'd become, it wasn't going to let the Darkness steal what Jonathan had given to me. His power rushed out of me to meet the hurricane's fury, burning me from the inside outward as our combined voices thundered, "*Ultra non nox erit!*"

Lightning shattered across the empty expanse surrounding me. At the sound of the command echoing through the night, the Darkness fled. The air was sucked away as it shot into the atmosphere to vanish to the South. Tree branches twisted, thrashed, and broke in its wake. Leaves flew upward, then blew apart into thousands of pieces, slicing the air. The pond's contents rushed over me, entombing me within a tunnel of water until it reached its pinnacle, then hurled back to Earth, wrenching me downward with it. Once more, I was under the surface, struggling to find my way free.

Coldness followed, driving through me like frost crackling along my veins, and the part of Jonathan's soul bound to mine spirited away to sleep once more.

Chapter Fifty-One

Ribbon wilted from my fist. Blue, dirty. The dye, blurred. Dangling from the end, an old key.

My mind was fuzzy. Thoughts gone sluggish. The cold threatened to claim me if I didn't get warm and soon. Grasses snagged at my pants as I stumbled toward a break in the water's borders leading to dry land. Fatigue weighed on me too. Everything hurt.

A dark lump clung to the surface of the water. A dead bird, its body captured by lapping waves from the shore. It was the little, blue bird who'd found me at the campsite and wanted the ribbon I wore, who followed us the night we'd traveled to the Cloets' house. The same bird from the Iron Works. He'd tried to warn me. He'd also tried to stop the Darkness from attacking me.

I wound the key around my neck, freeing my hands to scoop the poor thing from the water. Mud smeared his dingy, blue feathers. I stroked his chest, drawing the filth away with my fingertips. He didn't stir.

Cradling the bird close to my mouth, I whispered, "Don't die," wishing on the last embers of magic within me to heal him. My palms tingled at the wish. "Don't die."

Movement. He was alive!

Barely. He was dazed, muscles rigid, unable to move.

That'll be you if you don't hurry.

Staggering back toward the house, relief flooded through me as I neared the gate. "Almost there." I breathed into my hands to warm myself and the bird quaking within. But the gate rejected me. No matter how I pushed, pressed, or rushed at it, the protections wouldn't let me pass.

"Please," I begged, falling to my knees. Exhaustion and pain dug in deep, draining me. "Please."

Light glimmered off the frost underneath me, growing brighter. I raised my head to see Anna standing in front of me, her body engulfed in sapphire flames flowing through and around her. My tears and soaked clothes were met with detached judgment. "What do you want?"

"I want to go home."

Blue waves flashed as she passed through the gate, unhindered, and rushed to within an inch of me. Hands grabbed both sides of my face, clutching me painfully as her fingers dug in. Breath hot on my skin, she stared hard into my eyes. She was terrifying. "Tell me the truth."

"I just want to go home." I tore at her wrist, trying to break free. The skin on my palm was badly burned. I couldn't close my fingers enough to grab hold of her. The jolt of pain shocked me. I cradled the bird against my chest to avoid dropping him.

"What is that?" she demanded, eyeing where a weak chirp escaped through my fingers.

"He's hurt."

"Who is hurt?" She pursed her lips, waiting for an answer. Shivering, I tilted my hand away from my body to show her my charge cradled inside. Anna's eyes flicked to mine, surprised. "You found him." There was relief in her voice, as well.

"He saved my life. From the Darkness. By the pond." Because somehow, he was also bound to Jonathan.

I'd witnessed the silver flame of his power trailing in his wake at the water's edge. With the bird nestled into me, I could *feel* the connection between them. It was hesitant to make itself known at first, like spring sunlight peeking out from behind stormy clouds. It flowed more freely between us as I welcomed it in, this sense of serenity, reassurance, as if he was right there beside me, embracing my hand with his.

I hoped she would take pity on me because of it.

Her brows knit. "*He* saved you?" She asked, pointing at the bird.

"He tried to stop the Darkness. It… it hurt him."

"Tell me. What did *you* do?"

"I don't know. It went… It left. I made—"

Tremors wracked my body. Magic had used me, and now the last of it fizzled out and was gone. Iciness consumed my insides in its absence. Even my tears were freezing. I panicked as I felt myself slipping away.

Anna shushed me, trying to calm me. The fire around her

dimmed, though never completely extinguished. Instead of brushing my cheek with her raised hand, like I expected, she snagged the pale ribbon around my neck and lifted the key to where she could see it better. The metal was tarnished. "You have drained it."

She grasped me by the chin to draw me in with her eyes. I couldn't look away. "Swear on all you hold dear: you shall never harm me or my family."

"I swear, Anna. I just want to go home."

Her power coursed through me like a gale smashing a boat against a craggy shore, locking the promise in place. The sensation of it ripping out of me, the force of it, winded me.

Strong arms underneath mine hauled my failing body to standing. "We must get you both inside before you catch your death." The iron gate loomed in front of us. "Give me the bird." She repeated herself when I stared.

"No," I whispered and held him closer.

"Can you walk?" She dropped her hold without waiting for an answer and crossed toward the protective boundary, leaving me crumpled in a heap while she strode, unhindered, past those metal spears and carved thorns, superfluous to the magic concealed within.

I rolled onto elbows and knees. One knee. Forearm pressed into my bent leg. Hauled myself to standing. The world pitched as I swayed.

Anna waited, watching. Worry made me hesitate.

What will she do to me if obey her?

But I was done, dizzy with pain. There was nowhere else I could go.

She nodded once.

I gave in and offered up a hand.

The gate ensnared me. Blue flames raked through me, searing me. Seized limbs, organs, the air in my lungs, the blood stilling in my veins. Scoured every corner. Roared through my mind. Searched my intensions. I tried to catch it. Take control of it. Make it do what I wanted, like the motes of light in my room, but I was spent, and it overpowered me.

Anna caught me once the gate finished its task and released me, her body bolstering mine as she led me forward. Lingering woodsmoke welcomed us as we side-stepped through the backdoor. Her willful insistence silenced the back stairs' groaning.

Jonathan's door was shut tight.

She left me slumped against the edge of the bed and rummaged through the dresser drawers. I gasped awake when her fingers grazed my wrist. Instead of fighting me as I shied away, she offered the washbasin to me and told me to place the bird inside. A folded pillowcase blanketed the porcelain bottom. She promised it would not be harmed. It needed to be cared for.

Reluctantly, I did as I was told.

Speaking comforting words to it, her footsteps slow and light, she was gentle when she carried the wounded bird to the dresser. Clatter from chair legs being set near the lifeless fireplace woke me again. Anna faltered by the singed remains of lavender by the hearth. Gray flecks drizzled off the ruined stems when she lifted them to take a careful sniff.

Brushing the remnants from her hands, she turned her gaze on me. Lips pursed, eyes scrutinizing, she was trying to decide what to do with me. A tilt of her head as she inhaled meant she'd found the answer.

She briskly assembled a collection of wood in the firebox, then disappeared from the room. There was a whine of the door across the hall. She had a candle when she barged back in. Flames roared to life in the grate with its mere touch.

My clothes were stripped. My body wrapped in a blanket from the bed, and then I was deposited in the chair by the hearth. A metal clatter followed the motion of Anna's hand over the dresser. She'd swiped the key from around my neck.

"Where's Jonathan?" I whimpered.

"Wife?" Mr. Cloet pushed into the room.

"My own!" Anna said. "You wake?"

"I felt a curse pass over our home."

"It has gone."

"*Ja.* I felt that, as well. Captain Grey?"

"It would seem. You did not tell me she was one of you," Anna accused. She snatched my hands to study them, pulling my focus away from the door and back to her. Her skin rivaled the fire in the hearth. Its heat flared the pain in my injured palms.

Mr. Cloet sighed. "She was not yet aware herself."

She dropped her hold of me to face him. "She is aware now. Her eyes have opened!"

"Where's Jonathan?" I turned to Mr. Cloet, desperate.

"He has taken ill," she replied.

"Ill?"

"Do you know what he is?"

"I don't care," I rushed to tell her. It shouldn't matter to me what they were. Even the realization they were traitors couldn't stop the inconvenient truth—I needed Jonathan to find my way home.

"The woman is in love with him, Anna," Mr. Cloet said. "She is not a threat to any of us."

She glared at him. "Not all are as willing to put aside the war between our peoples as you, husband."

"If you kill her, Jonathan will never forgive you. You may create enemies where you least expect them. Think on that."

Anna leaned in close, seizing my face. Flames revived around her. "Do you know what *you* are?"

She was scaring me again. Did she mean: did I know I was a threat to them because they were traitors? Or to her because she was a witch? If she was a witch, power alive within her, power I could steal for myself, what were Mr. Cloet and I, if not witches like her?

It was the indignant stiffening of her body as she declared, "I am no witch!" that made me realize she could hear my thoughts. Had heard everything from the day I arrived. A scowl followed my discovery. "We are the Enlightened, Jonathan and I."

Mr. Cloet shook his head. "Wife, this is not necessary."

"I will not chance she would harm us or send more of your kind." She turned back on me, her eyes fierce.

"I have a son, Anna," I begged. "You know I have a son."

"Oh, Savvy. How we misunderstand one another." She brushed a loose strand of hair from my face.

"Just let me go home to my son."

"*Eius obliviscaturque eorum quae ficisti.*"

She drove her palm into my forehead.

An inferno erupted in my skull, fracturing who I was, everything I knew. It crashed against a barrier, confined to my physical body. Ricocheting back on itself, like a tempest trapped within a bottle, the firestorm scorched the threads of my mind. A doorway opened, flung wide in my center. Raging faster, stronger, sucking the fragments of my memories inward—the curse drove all of me inside, into a cavern, deep, dark, and forsaken. The prison door slammed shut.

And the nightmare began.

Acknowledgements

Many thanks to the following people without whom this dream of mine would not have been made real.

Jodi Christensen, my most wonderful editor and life-long friend. Have we really, only *just* met? Thank you for plucking me from the writers' querying trenches (on the same day I was literally trudging through the Battlefields of Yorktown,) sharing your excitement for my story, and all the many, many hours you have given me. I could not have done this without you and the fantastic people at Champagne Book Group, who truly love and take excellent care of their authors.

Miranda and Ron Boers for taking my gobbledygook and magically translating it into actual Dutch. You have spared my ancestors the chore of rolling over in their graves from embarrassment (I hope!). *Dank u wel!*

Kellen Crest, author, for your wonderful feedback, encouragement, and fantastically silly and passionate dives into history with me. Sending you a big hug across this vast country of ours and wishing you so much success in your own writing.

Ben deGonzague for serving as my self-defense consultant. Thank you for your willingness to read random passages for accuracy and explain Jiu Jitsu technique over the phone. The only silver lining of quarantine was that you couldn't actually demonstrate on me in person!

A.J. Enos for inspiring me to start writing again for myself.

Stephen Gottlieb, professor and author, for starting me on my exploration of the people of the Revolutionary War. It is a joy whenever our families get together, which is never often enough.

Robert Heverly, professor, for the great kindness of your time and counsel.

Shira Love for tearing my early drafts to pieces and helping me find the perfect replacements to glue it all back together again even stronger. Your countless hours reading multiple versions and bouncing ideas around have been invaluable.

Olivia Marine for serving as my nautical consultant as well as thought counselor. I cannot wait for our next passionate exchange about history and so much more over tea and sandwiches.

Glen T. Marshall, Town Historian, New Windsor, NY for the amazing period maps of Orange County, medical documents, and discussion.

Valerie Martin for all the free medical consultations for this book and the privilege of your friendship. Girls' night is coming! I can feel it in our future.

Steve Sheinkin, author, for the advice, inspiration, and nerding-out with a fellow history lover. Coffee anytime!

Titania, my furry co-author, whom I promised the #WritingCommunity I would include when that magical day of publication arrived. Where would I be without her taking up my entire footstool while I write?

Keith Willis, author, for the emotional support, industry advice, and just generally being super awesome. May all your dragons be well-wrangled and take you to fantastic places.

Elizabeth V. Woodruff, Media Relations from the U.S. Military Academy at West Point, for her good humor and dedication to trekking along the rocky coast of the Hudson River with me in the rain. Those were truly awe-inspiring hours.

To all my friends and family here unnamed—your love and encouragement are the fuel that keeps this writing flame going. Eternal gratitude to you all.

About the Author

Kiersten hails from New England. Growing up, the battlefields of Saratoga were her backyard, tourist sites like Fort Ticonderoga were an easy day trip, and Kiersten couldn't have cared less back then. It wasn't until journeying into adulthood that she grew to love books, and even then, not until she became a museum educator that she discovered the fascinating world of history.

A walking contradiction, she has a fondness for coffee by day, tea after dinner, doesn't watch television often but late-night comedians on their YouTube channels every evening, adores cats but not their claws, the idea of dogs unless it comes to owning one, and hates the outdoors unless it involves Revolutionary War sites or kayaking.

Kiersten currently lives in Upstate New York with her family: The Husband, Useful Son, and Subsequent Son, as they are affectionately known on social media, along with her two furry children, her co-author and research assistant.

Kiersten loves to hear from her readers. You can find and connect with her at the links below.

Website/Blog: https://www.kierstenmarcil.com
Facebook: https://www.facebook.com/kiersten.marcil.9
Instagram: https://www.instagram.com/kierstenmarcil
Twitter: https://twitter.com/KierstenMarcil

Visit her website to learn more about the stories, beliefs, and world of the men and women who lived through the American Revolutionary War. Plus, you will discover extras such as a map of the Highlands of New York and a glossary of the eighteenth-century slang and the Dutch and Scottish phrases used in this book.

Thank you for taking the time to read *Witness to the Revolution*. If you enjoyed the story, please tell your friends and leave a review at your favorite site. Reviews support authors and ensure they continue to bring readers books to love.

Now turn the page for a peek inside *Sophie's Key*, book one of a time travel romance that sweeps the reader from the present to the Old West by Jodi Jensen.

Two doors. One key. The choice of a lifetime.

After inheriting a long-abandoned farm, Sophie Sanders trades her empty existence for a fresh start in Utah. Moments into her new life, she uncovers a wooden screen door that sends her spiraling into 1901 where she meets Texas Ranger and widower, Jacob Warren. When an injury leaves Sophie reliant on Jacob and his hospitality, she resolves to keep her time-traveling secret. Before long, she finds herself falling for the rugged Texas Ranger despite her modern sensibilities constantly being at odds with his old-fashioned values.

When the only thing that keeps her anchored in the past, a silver skeleton key given to her by a Romani woman, is taken during an attack, Sophie must depend on Jacob to help her get it back. The strength of their newly formed bond is tested as they race to discover who's behind a string of accidents and recover Sophie's key before time runs out.

Excerpt

Chapter One

Mt. Pleasant, Utah

Sophie glanced at the scrap of paper in her hand, then back out the windshield and chuckled at the thoroughly country directions from the gas station clerk.

Turn left at the blackened tree stump.

Sure enough, the charred remains of a tree marked the entrance to a narrow dirt road. Washboard ridges crossed from one side of the hard-packed dirt to the other, and her old Jeep rattled as she bumped along.

Turn right at the crossroads, go half a mile,
then right again after crossing Warren's Bridge.

She took the second turn, then followed the road until she came to the bridge. A broken green sign that read *Sanpitch River* stood propped against the guardrail. She parked, approached the bank, and shook her head as a snort escaped her. She'd expected something more, something bigger, something like… a river. Instead, she found a burbling creek about ten feet across.

A gentle breeze stirred and blew strands of long, red hair across her face. She lifted her chin and basked in the sun's warm caress for a moment, then scanned the fields around her. She paused, her gaze lingering on an old roof partially obscured by the low branches of a nearby tree. Based on the information she received from the probate lawyer, that had to be the old, abandoned farm she inherited from her mom. Between her dead-end job as a bank teller, and a recent break-up, her mother's death had been the final straw. After the funeral, she'd said goodbye to her friends and packed her things. It was time for a fresh start.

She returned to her Jeep and picked up the scrap of paper on the seat beside her.

Take the next left you come to (another
half mile or so) and there you are.

"Alrighty." Scrunching the paper, she tossed it over her shoulder, then crossed the bridge.

Moments later, she turned on the tree-lined driveway, charmed by the white clapboard farmhouse and big, faded red barn the instant they came into view. True, the overgrown yard gave the place a distinct aura of desertion, but with the rugged Utah Mountains in the distance and the acres of fields surrounding the remote farm, she was giddy with delight.

As she slowed to a stop in front of the house, her heart swelled and excitement coursed through her. She didn't understand her sudden surge of happiness, but she didn't care. She had the overwhelming feeling she'd come home.

~ * ~

The next day, Jeep unpacked and house explored, Sophie went to the barn. She yanked the double doors open with a screech of protest from the rusty hinges. Sunlight streamed through the weathered slats and lit the scattered strands of hay to a deep golden hue.

A variety of decrepit farm tools hung on the wall opposite a tack room in the front of the barn, while rows of stalls lined both walls farther back. She walked the length of the building and peeked into each one. Most were filled with old furniture or boxes, while the final stall held an assortment of antique wood-framed windows.

She doubled back to the ladder that led to the loft. At the top, she discovered a massive stack of cardboard boxes covered in a thick layer of grime.

She blew the dust off the closest one, then opened it to reveal a collection of paperback books. She set the carton aside and reached for the next box, this one filled with dishes. Yet another box contained an array of ladies' things: perfume bottles, jewelry, handkerchiefs, and hair clips, which she dug through, setting aside the bits that appealed to her.

When she finished with that carton, she sat cross-legged on the floor. She picked up a white jeweler's box the size of her hand and opened it. The inside was lined with white satin and emblazoned with *Tiffany & Co.* on the inner top. A silver and yellow butterfly brooch lay cradled in the white satin. She removed the pin, held it up to the light, and turned it over as she smiled at the sparkling yellow stones in the wings. Etched on the back in tiny letters were the words *Tiffany & Co.* The brooch reminded her of her mother, and she pinned it on her shirt.

She set the jewelry box aside and relaxed. Her gaze drifted around the rest of the loft until it landed on a large burlap-covered object wedged between two ancient wooden posts on the far wall.

Curious, she scrambled to her feet and crossed the room. She planted her palm against one of the posts for balance as she stood on her tiptoes and fumbled around for a loose edge on the rough fabric.

Unable to reach, she turned and dragged the box of books over, then stood on it and peeled back the wrapping to expose the corner of a wooden door.

She wriggled the door until she got it free, then stood it against the wall. As she removed the rest of the burlap, she realized it was a wood-framed screen-door, and in perfect condition. She moved back to get a better look and marveled at the exquisite workmanship.

A row of carved spindles spread across the middle with quarter sections of wagon wheels in the top and bottom corners. The wood had been stained a rich dark brown and was adorned with a silver handle and keyhole. The door was beautiful, and she had just the right spot for it.

She maneuvered the screen-door to the edge of the loft and slid it down the ladder ahead of her, careful to hang onto the top corners until the bottom settled on the dirt floor. Next, she walked the door in front of her, left side, left foot, right side, right foot, through the barn, across the yard and onto her front porch. Once there, she retrieved her new drill and a handful of screws.

It was almost as if the door had been made for this house, the way the hinges lined up and fit snug into the door frame. She tightened the screws and backed up to admire her work.

When she closed her hand around the silver handle, a wave of lightheadedness washed over her.

As she stepped over the threshold of her new home, the edges of her vision darkened and silver specks danced before her eyes. The air around her grew thick and heavy as the silver specks shot in all directions. Rocking back on her heels, she blinked, over and over, trying to clear the dizzying, whirling spots as they twisted around her.

She fumbled for the doorjamb, but her hand moved through the wood like it wasn't even there. Her legs tingled and skin crawled with stabbing prickles and stings. Body twitching, she tried to step away, but when her foot came down, it never touched the floor.

Falling through the air, jolts of piercing spasms racked her body. The silver specks flashed into brilliant streaks of light that followed her on her downward spiral.

She opened her mouth to scream, but drew an abrupt breath of clean, fresh air. Confused, she blinked a few more times, then her vision went black as her head hit the ground.

Chapter Two

"Papa!"

Sophie woke to the sound of a child's voice, faint and far away. Her head spun as her muddled mind strove to make sense of the noise.

A tiny weight settled on her shoulder, and for a moment, she was anchored. She cracked an eyelid and glimpsed a small anxious face. Her eyes flew open as a young girl cast a brief look through the open doorway.

"Papa! Papa!"

Who is this child?

She struggled to sit as lightning bolts of stings shot down her arms and paralyzed her fingertips. Her hand slid across the floor, and she banged her elbow on the hardwood—

Wait…

Hardwood floor?

Her mouth went dry, and her heart pounded. She blinked at the now empty doorway, then stared into the darkened room.

Where'd the screen door go?

The questions swirled through her mind like leaves on a windy day. She frowned as she searched her memory.

She'd hung the door, that much she was sure of. Then she'd fainted. Or had she fallen?

Confused by the whirl of unanswered questions, she shook her head.

Her gaze shot to the little girl with the dark brown braids, freckles, and huge blue eyes. "Who *are* you?"

The child jumped up and took off. "Papa!" she yelled.

Sophie labored to her feet but stopped short as her head swam. She grabbed the doorframe for support, then took a deep breath and willed herself not to fall. A couple deeper breaths while she stared at the tips of her pink cowboy boots, and at last things came back into focus.

What the—?

The floorboards on the porch were different. Newer, rougher.

"Can I help you?"

She whipped her head up and turned, startled by the rich masculine voice at the other end of the long porch.

Deep blue eyes met hers from beneath a dusty cowboy hat, and her heart gave an involuntary start as a thrilling buzz of awareness jolted her. Their eyes held, and for a single, mind-boggling moment, everything else melted away.

A movement behind him caught her attention, and she tore her gaze from his as the girl peeked out from behind his long lean legs.

Her heart slammed against her ribs at the sight of the man's hand as it rested on a pistol at his hip.

She froze, eyes fixed on the gun, and tried to remember to breathe.

His hand relaxed, and he took a cautious step toward her. "You okay, ma'am?"

A crash erupted from inside the dim recesses of the house. She jerked her head and, out of the corner of her eye, caught a dark and bulky shape as it streaked across the room.

"Bear!" the man bellowed in outrage.

The little girl shrieked.

Sophie turned, careened down the front steps, and fled.

"Wait—"

But she kept going, down the dirt driveway, then turned and sprinted for the bridge.

She ran until her forehead beaded with sweat, and her lungs burned.

Wait—where's the bridge?

She darted a glance over her shoulder.

The only things behind her were sagebrush and fields. The house was nowhere to be seen.

She slowed to a brisk walk as her skin prickled with unease. While the mountains in the distance were familiar, her immediate surroundings were not.

She stopped short and turned in a circle, startling a couple of large black birds who pecked at a dirty white heap on the ground. At her intrusion, one bird flapped its wings and glared while the other one let out a tremendous *squawk.* A soft breeze carried a stench unlike anything she'd ever encountered.

Oh, God—a dead sheep.

She pressed a hand to her lips, stumbled back, and gagged. As the birds returned to their vulgar feast, her stomach lurched. She whirled around and raced for a grove of nearby scrub oak. Once sheltered by the bushy leaves and tangled branches, she bent over and retched.

After a moment, she stood back and wiped her sleeve across her face. Her chest heaved, and she gulped air until a burst of noise in the distance startled her. She clamped her mouth shut and tilted her head. There it was again—a distinct bark. With clammy hands, she tucked her hair behind her ears, then crept to the edge of the grove.

There, on the other side of the field, was the man from the porch. He had a rifle laid across his arm as he sat atop a horse. A large white dog barked and paced by the horse's feet.

Her belly knotted as he scanned the area, but her heart gave a funny little stutter. Part of her wanted to spring from the bushes and wave at him, attract his attention. The other part, the part that witnessed his hand on the gun back at the house, screamed at her to stay hidden.

Her breath caught in her throat and stuck when he reached into his vest and pulled out a hand-held telescope. He pointed it at the grove, and her stomach gave an ugly turn. She dropped to a crouch behind the thicket, hoping to hide her telltale red plaid shirt.

What does he want? And why the gun?

Seized by an instinct as old as time, she bolted—through the grove and out the other side into a newly plowed field. Frantic, she searched for somewhere to hide, and the instant she spotted a dry canal, she made a break for it.

As soon as she leapt into the waist deep ditch, she popped her head up to find the dog bounding in her direction with the man on horseback right behind.

She ducked down in the ditch and crawled crab-like as fast as she could go.

The dog's ferocious bark drew closer.

Panting, she scrambled faster. Her fingers snagged on roots, but she pushed on.

The horse was so close she heard its hooves as they hit the ground.

At the sharp snap of a branch behind her, she pushed herself off the ground and ran, her only goal to put as much distance as possible between herself and the vicious dog.

The man yelled, but she couldn't hear him over the dog's endless growling bark. She knew they were close but didn't dare slow down.

Suddenly, her foot came down hard and sank deep into a hole. Her momentum propelled her forward, and she banged her shin against the solid rim of the burrow. A white-hot flash of pain darted straight up her leg. She stumbled and fell flat onto her face in the ditch, crippled by her injury.

She turned her head to the side and let her breath come in sobbing gasps, certain at any second now the dog would leap into the ditch and attack her as she lay helpless.

What a stupid way to die.

Her heart hammered as four powerful horse legs thundered to a halt at the top edge of the ditch. From where she lay, she had a perfect view of the brown underside of the horse's heaving belly as well as the man's pant legs and boots.

The dog snarled, and she cringed.

The horse reared.

"Duck!" the man growled.

She jumped, then whimpered in pain as the movement joggled her leg.

The dog stopped in its tracks. Her eyes widened when the horse settled too.

The man leaned over and looked down at her. "If I were you, I'd try not to move."

Chapter Three

Sophie stared at the man as he dismounted. Her entire body trembled, and she was pretty sure her mouth hung open wide enough to catch a fly or two. With a concentrated effort, she snapped her mouth shut, and followed his every move as he stowed his rifle in its scabbard.

The man shot a glance at the midday sun, then gestured to the saddlebag and showed her both of his empty hands. "I'm going to get you some water."

As nervous and jittery as she was, that deep, rich voice sent a delicious chill right down her spine, and all she could do was nod.

His eyes flickered in acknowledgement and a hint of a smile played on his lips. He'd noticed.

Her cheeks flushed with embarrassed heat. What on earth was wrong with her?

The man turned his back and rummaged through the saddlebag, muscles moving and bunching beneath his tan shirt and vest. The horse fidgeted, and he spoke to it in a low murmur as he patted it on the rump.

Unable to tear her fascinated gaze away, she licked her dry lips. The gritty grains of dirt on her tongue jarred her back to her senses. She propped herself up on one elbow, almost grateful for the bolt of pain in her leg and the distraction it provided. Serve her right if he kidnapped her, what with her gawking at him like this.

"I told you not to move." He turned, and hopped into the ditch with her, carrying a faded blue bandana and a metal canteen. "That leg might be broken."

She stared at the boots in front of her face and bit back an angry retort at his bossy tone. Though it only took a few seconds for him to unscrew the lid on the canteen, it seemed much longer as he towered over her.

When he crouched beside her and offered the damp cloth, she snatched it from his fingers with a shaky hand and wiped the dirt from her face. "Are you a doctor?" She risked a peek at him, and her pulse quickened.

"Are you?" A flash of amusement twinkled in his eyes.

"Hardly!" She snorted.

Chuckling, he offered his canteen but instead of handing it over, he held the cool metal to her mouth and tilted it so she could drink. Drops of water dribbled from her lips, and his fingers grazed the soft spot under her chin, sending a shiver through her as he wiped the water away.

He took the bandana from her and poured a bit more water over it. "What's your name?"

"Sophie." An involuntary sigh slipped from her lips, and she swore the blood pulsed a bit faster through her veins when he swept her hair aside and draped the cool cloth over the back of her neck. The thoughtful gesture brought a few seconds of relief to her overheated skin.

The man pressed the canteen to her lips again. "Sophie who?"

A hefty whiff of his masculine scent drifted up her nose as she drank, and she had to turn her head away, unable to think with him this close. She swiped the back of her hand across her mouth, then cleared her throat. "Sanders, and you are?"

"Jacob Warren. I'm a Texas Ranger." He screwed the lid back on the canteen, then motioned to the huge white dog. "The mutt over there's called Duck, we're—"

The second the dog heard its name, he leapt into the ditch with them and a shower of dirt and pebbles flew as his entire body wagged in delight.

An involuntary *eek!* burst from her lips, and she cringed as the dog bumbled around and jostled her injured leg.

"Duck, stop it. Go on now, get out. Go!" Jumping up, he shooed the dog away. "Are you okay?"

She rested her cheek on her forearm as her thoughts churned a mile a minute. Her leg throbbed in time with the heavy thump of her heart. *Texas Ranger?* Wasn't that like a cop? She spotted a large sagebrush and turned her focus there. With deliberate slow, deep breaths, she inhaled the fragrant aroma of sage until she calmed her mind, and the pain lessened.

Him being a Texas Ranger might explain the guns, but not why he chased her. She turned toward him, the question poised on the tip of her tongue, but at the last second, she hesitated.

"Sophie?" Suspicion grew in his eyes as her name hung in the air between them.

Her stomach gave a queasy flutter, and she took a couple more careful, deep breaths. "I'm okay now."

"I was about to say we're going to get you out of here until the dog went stupid." He gave the animal in question a scowl, then crouched beside her once more.

Duck curled up on the top edge of the ditch, lifted a hind leg, and licked himself.

She let out an amused huff. "Dogs, huh?"

Shrugging, he gave her an awkward pat on the back and nodded at her injury. "You ready?"

"Maybe you'd better call someone," she suggested, loathe to jar her leg again.

His face went so blank it was almost comical. "What?"

"Call someone," she repeated. "You know, for help."

His boots stirred up dust as he stood, turned in a complete circle, then frowned. "There's no one out here, 'cept us."

She tilted her head back and squinted at him. What was he playing at? "Don't you have a cellphone?"

"A what?"

"A cellphone?"

Pushing his hat up, he narrowed his eyes and studied her for a moment. "Did you hit your head when you fell?"

She closed her eyes and counted to ten. When she opened them, she found him still staring at her.

His forehead creased in confusion, and an annoyed flicker danced in his deep blue eyes.

She changed tactics.

"Well, did you at least kill the bear?" she demanded.

"Bear?" His eyebrows lifted and disappeared under the brim of his hat. "What bear?"

"Oh, for hell's sake," she muttered. This was quite possibly the most aggravating conversation she'd ever had in her life.

"At least that answers that." His demeanor changed at once, and all traces of confusion vanished. He climbed out of the ditch, every inch of him full of purpose and determination.

She glared after him. "Answers what?"

"You're not one of those religious types over there in Mt. Pleasant." He yanked the rifle off his horse. "Now, what's this about a bear?"

"Wait—religious types? What?" What the hell was that supposed to mean?

He stalked all the way around the horse, scanning the empty fields as he went, then sank to one knee at the top edge of the ditch. "Yeah, you're not one of those Mormons. They don't cuss," he said, by way of explanation. He drove the butt of the rifle into the dirt and gave her a pointed look. "Now—bear?"

"I'm not the one who said there was a bear." She flapped a hand at him. "You are."

His jaw dropped open.

"Well, you are." Her voice rose, along with her temper. "Earlier, you shouted *'bear!'*"

They stared each other down. Blue flames blazed in his eyes as realization dawned. "So—that's why you ran?"

"Of course," she snapped as she planted her palms flat on the ground, clenched her teeth, and pushed herself up to her hands and knees. Pain tore through her like a bolt of lightning and she faltered, when suddenly a strong arm caught her around the middle and helped ease her foot out of the hole.

"Do you ever do as you're told?" He scowled as he got her turned over and laid her leg out with extreme care.

She sunk her teeth into her bottom lip and wiped a drop of sweat from the side of her face. "I can't stay here all day."

He frowned at her jean-covered leg and boot-clad foot. "Blast it, woman, what if it's broken? Do you want to make it worse?"

"It's not." She winced and spoke around the tightness in her chest. "It's not," she repeated. "It can't be broken."

He reached into his vest and pulled out a flask. "Since you're not one of those religious types, you better have some of this." He thrust it into her hand. "Whiskey." Without another word, he turned, picked up his discarded rifle, then went to tend to his horse.

She sniffed the flask, grimaced at the potent fumes, then took the tiniest possible sip. The liquid heat scorched a trail down her throat and made her eyes water.

He took a brief look over his shoulder. "Go on then, you're going to need it."

The next sip was better. The one after that, even better, and soon she was calmer. A small warm glow built in her belly and soothing tendrils worked their way through her as she sat contemplating him. He was tall and lean, with broad shoulders, exactly how she liked. And that hair! Thick, wavy, and long enough to brush the collar of his shirt. Her fingers curled at the sight, and she itched to wind them through the dark mass. Men shouldn't have hair like that. It wasn't fair, she decided as she stroked a strand of her own straight red locks.

She took another sip from the flask and pretended not to look at him while she fiddled with the lid. Her surreptitious gaze drank in every detail of the man in front of her, from the strong line of a stubborn jaw to the faint shadow of a scar below his left ear that disappeared into his dark hairline.

Wonder how he got that?

She unscrewed the lid and had yet another sip, aware it was rude to stare, but unable to stop herself.

She'd never seen anyone dressed like him before, from his dark brown trousers tucked into his tall plain boots, to his vest and tan button-down shirt. All of it seemed different, like the material was wrong somehow, though she couldn't quite put her finger on how.

Her leg hardly hurt now, and the rest of her body radiated a warm buzz.

"Hey, Texas Ranger," she called out. "What're you doing in Utah, anyway?"

He didn't answer, but his shoulders stiffened.

Undaunted, she had one more sip and grumbled, "You never told me if you got the bear or not."

"Let's take a gander at that leg," he said, his voice tight. He turned from the horse, large knife in hand.

Her heart sped up, and she tensed at the sight of the blade.

Kneeling by her feet, he took hold of the hem of her jeans. "I'm not going to hurt you."

The movement bumped her leg. "Ouch," she mumbled under her breath as she shot him a dirty look.

His brows furrowed together as he fingered the material for a moment. When he positioned the knife to cut the denim, she hurried to take another hasty sip from the flask. She braced herself as he ripped her favorite pair of jeans to the knee.

At his sharp intake of breath, she angled forward to see the tip of his knife pointed at the sparkly pink stitched shaft of her designer boot and a question in his eyes.

Warmth flooded her face. "They were a gift."

He paused and checked her boot from a couple of different angles. "I'll have to cut it, there's no other way."

"From an old boyfriend, no biggie." She tossed back another swig from the flask, then added, "I was cleaning out the barn in them."

His eyes widened at her statement, but he didn't speak, only bent to his work.

Her body clenched, and she sucked in her breath as he made a careful cut down the side. It wasn't until he slipped the boot off her foot that she let the air out of her lungs with a relieved, whiskey-scented *whoosh!*

He gave her a once-over, and though his expression was serious, there was a definite spark of amusement in his eyes.

"I thought it was going to hurt." She shrugged.

The sight of her rainbow striped sock brought a puzzled frown to his face, but he removed it without a word and tossed it on top of the ruined boot.

She strained to get a better view as he ran his fingers down both sides of her leg, probing as he went. She yelped when he touched the area around the ugly purple knot forming on her shin.

Aside from the promise of an impressive bruise and swollen foot, it didn't look as bad as she'd feared.

"I don't think anything's broken," he told her at last. The lines of concentration and worry on his face while he examined her leg had vanished. "But I don't think you'll be walking on it for a few days."

"Probably not," she agreed. What the hell was she supposed to do now?

"Where are your people?" He sheathed his knife, then looked at her, his eyes alight with speculation. "I can take you to them so they can tend to you."

"People? I don't have any people," she said, taken aback. *What's he talking about—people?*

He paused a moment. His gaze met hers, searching, and filled with questions. "You have no people? No family?"

"No, I'm alone," she admitted.

"You ran away twice." His voice was smooth as silk, but underneath there was a hint of an edge. "Why'd you run the second time?"

"You had a gun." She wanted to tell him how scared she'd been when he chased after her with his gun, but the idea seemed laughable now.

He tucked a finger under her chin and inched closer. His breath on her face was as warm and soft as a summer breeze, his voice low and seductive. "Can I trust you around my daughter?"

"Yes," she said, without hesitation. She stared into his deep blue eyes and a tickle of awareness rippled through her. Somewhere inside of herself, something stirred. A longing that hadn't been there a few moments ago.

For an instant, there was a flash of that same yearning in his eyes, then he bent and scooped her into his arms. His touch set her nerve endings shimmering like hundreds of little heat waves skimming over the surface of her skin.

"Let's get you out of here."

Chapter Four

Sophie leaned back against Jacob, feeling like her heart would jump right out of her chest. She'd never been on a horse before, and now here she was, perched atop one, half-drunk on whiskey, and cuddled up to a virtual stranger, albeit a handsome one.

The man was handsome, not the horse, she amended as she stifled a giggle. *What on earth would my mother have said?* She gave a mild snort at the thought.

Jacob's hand appeared with the flask. "Drink."

"What? Oh, no, I'm okay." She pushed his hand away.

"You're not going to be if it wears off." He brought the flask to her mouth again. "Now, drink."

She sighed and took two long swallows. It was either that or end up with it spilled down the front of her. "How old is your little girl?"

The flask disappeared. "Six."

His arm tightened around her middle as the horse plucked its way down an embankment.

"Oh, that's nice." She relaxed against him as they splashed through a bubbly creek and drops of cool water hit her bare foot. "I was six once, you know."

"You don't say." He clicked his tongue at his horse, then pressed tight against her while the animal scrambled up a hill on the other side.

She twisted in the saddle and gazed up at him. "Yeah, and I bet you were, too."

"I was." He cracked a crooked smile. "Now, turn around."

She turned and melted against him. Her eyes were heavy, her limbs weightless. She concentrated on raising her arm, then draped it across the one of his that was wrapped around her.

At once anchored, she let her eyes close. "I liked being six," she murmured as she drifted off.

~ * ~

Sophie woke sometime later to the strange sensation of tiny sharp combs picking at her hair accompanied by a loud humming vibration near her ear. Opening her eyes, she found a ball of gray and black striped fur purring right in front of her. She jerked her head away and startled the cat, who hissed at her.

Panicked, she batted at the animal, whose paw had become tangled in her hair. The terrified cat meowed as it yanked its paw in earnest. She covered her face with her hands to hide from the sharp claws. "Are you kidding me?"

"Hold still," a stern voice commanded.

She froze and peeked from between her fingers as Jacob plucked the animal from the bed and dropped it on the floor.

"That's Bear." His eyes glittered with humor. "My daughter named him."

Sophie eyed the cat, whose tail was puffed out and sticking straight into the air. The tip flicked back and forth in a casual, but haughty manner as it stalked away. "Bear, huh?" She lifted an eyebrow at him. "Figures." The thing was huge, larger than any house cat she'd ever seen. Close to the size of her childhood cocker spaniel, if she had to guess, and just as fat and fluffy.

His lips twitched, and he gave her a small shrug.

She pleated the quilt with her fingers. He'd brought her back to his place, but since she hit her head this morning, she didn't know *where* that was. "So, listen, I appreciate your help and all, but I need to find my house."

Silence filled the air, and she peered up from the bunched section of blanket in her hand.

Folding his arms, he leaned against the bedpost, blue eyes ablaze.

Her heart fluttered, then settled into a faster rhythm. Breathless, she lifted her chin and waited.

"Thought you said you were alone," he drawled at last.

"I am—"

"Then you'll stay here." He raised a hand to forestall her protest. "For a day or two, until you can get around. Then we'll talk."

"But—"

"I insist." He narrowed his eyes as if he dared her to argue, then gave a short nod. Apparently, that settled it.

She sighed and let it go in favor of a more urgent matter. She cleared her throat and focused on the quilt again as she traced one of the star-patterned blocks with her finger. "Okay, um, would you mind if I used your, uh, bathroom? Please?"

"Bathroom?"

The confusion in his voice made her look up.

Right then the door burst open, and the child from earlier skipped inside, a basket over one arm. "Seven eggs, Papa!" She set the basket on the table, then ran to hug him. "There was eight, but I dropped one."

His face lit as he picked up his daughter and hugged her back. "Meri, this is Sophie. She's hurt her leg and needs our help until it mends."

"Hi Sophie! I'm sorry Bear scairt you. Papa says he's a bad kitty sometimes, but I like him fine." Her father set her on the floor, and she smoothed her blue calico dress, then climbed on the bed. "My whole name is Meredith Lily Warren," she said as she carefully pronounced every single syllable, "but everyone calls me Meri."

Sophie smiled. "Meri, I like that." With rosy red cheeks and light blue eyes that sparkled, she was the very definition of merry, and she smelled like sunshine, grass, and outdoors.

The little girl ran a small finger down the bridge of Sophie's nose. "You have freckles, just like me."

Her heart squeezed, charmed by this precocious child, and she tapped the end of Meri's nose. "I sure do, but yours are cuter."

"Meri, get down, Sophie needs to…uh…" He paused, his gaze flickering around the room.

Meri bounced on the edge of the mattress. "Needs t'what?"

He gave Sophie a blank look and shrugged.

She gritted her teeth as the bed jostled and her leg stiffened against the flash of pain.

Snatching Meri up under her arms, he deposited her on the floor, but she turned right back to Sophie, "Do ya need the outhouse? I always do when I wake up!"

"Outhouse?" Sophie gawked at Jacob. "You don't have a regular bathroom?"

His confusion mirrored hers, but right now the press of her full bladder demanded attention. She threw back the quilt and slid her injured leg over the edge. She had to get out of this bed and use the bathroom—er, outhouse—whatever!

He grabbed a rough wooden crutch from against the footboard and thrust it at her. "Here, use this."

She took hold of the hand brace in the middle and prayed the single leg of wood would support her. Shoving the padded curve of leather under her arm, she eased her weight onto the crutch as she stood.

So far, so good.

Meri hopped and clapped while her braids flopped around. "Yer doin' it!"

Her excitement was infectious, and Sophie laughed as she leaned with her weight on the crutch. Slowly, carefully, she limped across the wood planked floor, tucking her hair behind her ear as she went.

She made it to the porch with only some minor throbbing in her leg and paused as her eyes adjusted to the bright sunlight.

"C'mon." Meri leapt down all three of the stairs and landed in the dirt.

Sophie froze, overcome with such a strong sense of déjà vu she was helpless to do anything but stand there and look around as her mind raced.

A long, narrow porch with three wide steps—the same as this morning—

Then there was the barn. A big one, right across the yard from the house.

Exactly like—

"It's right over there!" Meri drew her attention to a lone little structure on the far side of the clearing.

The outhouse.

She blinked and shook her head as the world shifted back into focus.

"C'mon," Meri climbed the stairs and tugged at Sophie's hand.

"Leave her be. You're going to make her fall if you keep pulling on her like that." Jacob took her elbow. "You all right? Need some help?"

"I'm okay." She shrugged his hand off. "Let me do this myself." She took a careful step followed by a couple more, then gave him a hasty thumbs-up, in too big of a hurry to worry about his frown when she did so. Once she reached the outhouse door, she turned and waved. "Umm, I've got it from here, thanks!"

"Okay, we're going to do the afternoon chores." He took his daughter by the hand. "Holler if you need anything."

~ * ~

In retrospect, Sophie thought as she closed and latched the door behind her, the outhouse was neither as bad as she feared nor as pleasant as she could've hoped, but that was about all that could be said for the experience.

"Sophie?"

She jumped, dropped the crutch, and banged her head against the outhouse door with a dull thud. "Oh! Ow, son-of-a-gunner!" She rubbed her head and bent to retrieve the crutch.

"I'm so sorry." A young woman in a blouse with billowy sleeves rushed forward. "Are you okay? Sophie?" The woman hesitated, "You *are* Sophie?"

"Yeah. Who're you?"

The young woman patted the dusky purple scarf tied around her head and tried to smooth her unruly, long, dark hair, then moved closer and lowered her voice. "I must speak with you alone."

Sophie glanced around at the empty farmyard and fields, then back at the woman. "This is about as alone as it gets, here, by the outhouse. Now, who are you?"

The woman took a deep breath. Her fingers grazed a pendant that hung on a silver chain around her neck before digging into the pocket of her long flowing skirt. "My name is Selina. Selina Loversedge. I'm Romani, and a matchmaker, and you're a traveler."

"Right…" Sophie tried to take a step back but couldn't because the outhouse door was behind her. She shifted the crutch and put the padded leather under her arm, intending to go around the woman.

"Listen, Sophie—"

She stopped short. "How do you know my name?"

Selina took her hand from her pocket. "Take it, it belongs to you."

"What is it?" Sophie reached for the large silver skeleton key in Selina's outstretched palm.

"Look close, what do you see?"

Sophie held up the key, stunned to see her name engraved on one side, while the numbers one, nine, zero, and one were etched on the other side. "What? Where did you get this?"

The woman touched her pendant again, a miniature hourglass. "This may not be the safest time and place to talk, so listen, I'll make this quick." Her dark eyes grew anxious. "You're not in your own time. This morning you went through a door. A very special door that brought you here, to this time. To 1901."

"Oh, be serious!" But the rough wood of the outhouse was at Sophie's back. *I'd never use such a thing in my own time!* She shook her head. *Impossible!*

"You don't have to believe me, Sophie. Look around you," Selina said, with a nod at the same empty farmyard and fields. "I know you have questions. I'll come back soon, when I can stay longer. Until then, you must keep the key safe. Do you understand? You can't get back to your own time without it."

"But…but, why?" She shook her head again. This made no sense. *Time travel isn't possible, and even if it is, why me? Why now?*

Selina shrugged and gave her a small, knowing smile. "Our destinies are intertwined, yours and mine. Yours brought you to the right place. Mine brought you to the right time. Make the most of it."

Sophie leaned her head back against the outhouse and closed her eyes. This morning she *had* found a door. A beautiful wooden screen-door. She'd hung it, walked through it, then fainted, or fell, or something…

Something strange had happened, that much she was sure of.

She gripped the key hard enough in her hand to leave an imprint and opened her eyes. "So, you expect me to believe…"

The woman was gone.

Out Now!

What's next on your reading list?

Champagne Book Group promises to bring to readers fiction at its finest.

Discover your next
fine read!
http://www.champagnebooks.com/

We are delighted to invite you to receive exclusive rewards. Join our Facebook group for VIP savings, bonus content, early access to new ideas we've cooked up, learn about special events for our readers, and sneak peeks at our fabulous titles.

Join now.
https://www.facebook.com/groups/ChampagneBookClub/

Made in the USA
Middletown, DE
07 April 2023